PREACHER'S STRIKE

Look for these exciting Western series
from bestselling authors
William W. Johnstone and J.A. Johnstone

The Mountain Man
Luke Jensen: Bounty Hunter
Brannigan's Land
The Jensen Brand
Smoke Jensen: The Early Years
Preacher and MacCallister
Fort Misery
The Fighting O'Neils
Perley Gates
MacCoole and Boone
Guns of the Vigilantes
Shotgun Johnny
The Chuckwagon Trail
The Jackals
The Slash and Pecos Westerns
The Texas Moonshiners
Stoneface Finnegan Westerns
Ben Savage: Saloon Ranger
The Buck Trammel Westerns
The Death and Texas Westerns
The Hunter Buchanon Westerns
Will Tanner, U.S. Deputy Marshal
Old Cowboys Never Die
Go West, Young Man

Published by Kensington Publishing Corp.

THE FIRST MOUNTAIN MAN
PREACHER'S STRIKE

WILLIAM W. JOHNSTONE

AND J.A. JOHNSTONE

PINNACLE BOOKS
Kensington Publishing Corp.
kensingtonbooks.com

PINNACLE BOOKS are published by

Kensington Publishing Corp.
900 Third Avenue
New York, NY 10022

PUBLISHER'S NOTE: Following the death of William W. Johnstone, the Johnstone family is working with a carefully selected writer to organize and complete Mr. Johnstone's outlines and many unfinished manuscripts to create additional novels in all of his series like The Last Gunfighter, Mountain Man, and Eagles, among others. This novel was inspired by Mr. Johnstone's superb storytelling.

First Printing: January 2025
ISBN-13: 978-0-7860-5176-2
ISBN-13: 978-0-7860-5177-9 (eBook)

10 9 8 7 6 5 4 3 2 1

Printed in the United States of America

Chapter 1

"No, sir," Preacher said a few minutes before the trouble started. "No, sir, I won't do it. No way, no how."

He picked up a mug of beer from the bar in Red Mike's Tavern and downed half the suds in a healthy swallow.

He set the mug down and dragged the back of his other hand across his mouth, wiping away the foam clinging to his drooping salt-and-pepper mustache.

Then he continued, "Every time I get mixed up with Englishers or any other European folks, all hell breaks loose and I wind up fightin' with swords or some such loco ruckus."

The man who had come up to him at the bar said, "But, Mr. Preacher, if you would just hear me out—"

"No 'mister,' just Preacher. And I done told you, whatever the job is, I ain't interested."

"But it may well be a matter of life and death, sir, and the life of which I speak is that of a young woman. A young, innocent woman."

Preacher frowned into his beer and told himself to stand firm.

"I ain't sure I ever met an innocent woman," he said.

"They're people, and people ain't innocent. They all got secrets and faults. I got way more than my own share of flaws."

"That's true of all of us, I suppose," the man beside him replied. "However, in this case, the young lady in question actually is deserving of our sympathy, as well as our assistance, if we can provide it. Assuming, of course, that it's even possible to locate her."

Preacher grunted. "If she's west o' the Mississippi, I can find her if anybody can."

"That's what the fellow at the hotel told me," the man said with a hopeful smile. "'Find Preacher,' he said. 'If anyone can locate your cousin, it's Preacher.' He's the one who suggested that I inquire at, ah, Red Mike's." The man glanced around the tavern with its smoke-filled air, rough furnishings, and boisterous clientele. "Evidently, this is your, ah, home away from home when you're in St. Louis."

That was true enough, Preacher supposed. To most people, Red Mike's was just a squalid riverfront dive, but anytime he found himself in St. Louis, this was where he came for a mug of beer and companionship. Mike himself, the big, rugged, redheaded Irishman who ran the place, was a longtime friend.

Mike drifted along the bar now and said, "This fella botherin' you, Preacher?"

"Naw," the mountain man said. "We're just palaverin' a mite, that's all."

Mike nodded. "Well, ye let me know if ye need me to toss him out on his ear."

"Reckon I can handle that myself if it needs doin'."

The stranger laughed and said, "I might take offense at such a discussion, gentlemen, if I didn't know that you were being humorous."

"Yeah, ye just go ahead and tell yerself that, mister," Mike said with a dark, unfriendly gaze. "I know a darned Englishman when I hear one."

"Oh, but I'm not from England, despite my accent," the man said. "I'm from—"

Before he could continue, one of the tavern's other patrons bumped heavily against his shoulder, staggering him and forcing him to catch himself against the bar.

"I say!" the stranger exclaimed. "Please, watch where you're going, sir."

The man who had collided with him swung around sharply and said, "What the hell! Are you talkin' to me, you damn popinjay?"

It was true that the stranger was well-dressed, making the comparison to a bird's gaudy plumage an apt one. He wore a tight-legged brown tweed suit over a tweed vest, a white shirt, and a silk cravat. The tweed cap he wore came to a sharp point in front and sported a green feather in the band. Such dandies were seldom seen in Red Mike's.

On the other hand, the man who had run into him was exactly the sort of customer usually found in the tavern. He was a riverman, dressed in canvas trousers, a homespun shirt, heavy work shoes, and a felt hat with a broad, floppy brim. The muscles of his arms, chest, and shoulders stretched the shirt's fabric. His face was scarred and craggy with plenty of souvenirs from bare-knuckle brawls in the past.

Two men of the same type stood behind him, grinning as if they knew what was about to happen.

Preacher had a pretty good idea his own self.

The foreign stranger said, "I'd merely request that you pay a bit more attention to where you're going, my friend. You almost knocked me down. If I'd had a drink in my hand, I most certainly would have spilled it."

The riverman poked a long, blunt finger against the stranger's chest with enough force to make him take a step back. "You're the one who damn well needs to watch where he's goin'. This is a place where men come to drink."

"I assure you, sir, I am indeed a man."

The riverman let out a contemptuous snort.

"Couldn't prove it by me," he said. "Dressed so fancy and lookin' so purty, I think you're really a gal."

The stranger's jaw tightened. "I'll thank you not to impugn my masculinity, sir."

The riverman poked him in the chest again and said, "I'll impugn whatever the hell I want to." He glanced at his friends and added, "What the hell does 'impugn' mean?"

Neither of them appeared to have a clue.

Preacher had been watching this byplay with only mild interest as he sipped the rest of his beer. He might have stepped in before now, because he didn't much cotton to rivermen. Too many of them were bullies, and this fella seemed to fit that mold.

But he didn't owe the foreigner anything and hadn't invited the fella to talk to him. The gent was on his own.

Although Preacher did sort of have to admire the way

he was standing up to a varmint who was half a head taller and probably sixty pounds heavier. No fear showed in the stranger's pale blue eyes.

Red Mike took a hand, leaning on the bar and saying to the riverman, "I don't want no trouble in here, Kennedy."

"Then you hadn't ought to let pesky little gadflies like this come in here," Kennedy shot back. "And don't go tellin' me you don't want trouble. There's a brawl in this tavern two or three times a week."

"Maybe so, but that don't mean I have to like it!"

The stranger turned back to Preacher and said, "Perhaps we could adjourn to one of the tables and I could explain more about the proposition I'd like for you to consider."

"Done told you already, I ain't takin' the job," Preacher said.

With a scowl twisting his face, Kennedy clamped a hand on the stranger's shoulder and said, "Don't turn your back on me when I'm talkin' to you, you little—"

Clearly, he was about to add some obscenities that would have turned the air in the tavern blue, but he didn't get the chance to spew that venom.

The stranger turned swiftly, said, "Take your hands off me, sir!", and punched him in the nose.

Chapter 2

Kennedy's head rocked back slightly. His eyes widened. He looked more surprised than hurt, even though a little blood leaked from his left nostril.

He recovered quickly from the shock of being struck and said, "Why, you—"

He didn't finish that curse, either, because he was too busy swinging a big, knobby-knuckled fist at the stranger.

The man ducked the blow with apparent ease. Kennedy wasn't very fast. As the stranger came back up, he peppered two more punches, a left and a right, to the riverman's nose.

Blood actually spurted this time.

Kennedy howled, whether from anger or pain or both, Preacher couldn't tell.

The riverman lunged at the stranger, evidently intending to grab him in a bear hug and crush him until his ribs cracked. The stranger twisted out of the way, snatched Kennedy's hat off his head, and whipped it across his face a couple of times.

Being swatted like that wouldn't hurt Kennedy, but

it disoriented him. He groped for the stranger but missed. The man danced to the side and gave Kennedy an open-handed slap on the left ear.

"Ow! Blast it, that hurt!"

The stranger slid back out of reach.

"We can shake hands and call the conflict at an end, if you'd prefer," he said.

Unfortunately for him, that move brought him within reach of one of Kennedy's friends, who grabbed him from behind and crowed, "I got him! I got him, Lafe!"

"Hang on to him, Remi!" Kennedy cried. "We'll teach the varmint a lesson!"

Preacher looked into his mug in disgust. Not only was it empty but now he was going to have to do something that went against the grain for him.

He was going to get involved in somebody else's trouble.

But he couldn't abide an unfair fight. Never had, never would.

"Hey!" he said as he turned.

Kennedy had been about to crowd up against the stranger and thrash him, but he paused to look angrily at Preacher.

"What?"

The mountain man crashed the empty mug against Kennedy's forehead, where his lank dark hair had receded a considerable distance.

The heavy glass vessel didn't shatter, but the blow had enough force to drive Kennedy to his knees. The third man yelled a curse and charged Preacher, who tossed the empty mug to Mike behind the bar. The tavern keeper recovered from his surprise enough to catch it, although he fumbled it slightly.

Preacher leaned aside from the fist his attacker threw at him. His right hooked into the man's belly, stopping him short and making him bend forward.

That put him in perfect position for the left cross that Preacher threw. The man's head snapped to the side from the force of the blow. His knees buckled and he went down, landing in a heap on the sawdust-littered puncheons.

While Preacher was dealing with those two, the stranger had managed to work one arm loose from the grip of the man holding him. His hand darted across his body to the man's other hand and grasped the middle finger. A sharp twist and jerk snapped the bone with a distinctive crack like a stick breaking. The man howled in pain and let go completely.

The stranger whirled around, lowered his head, and butted his opponent in the face.

At the same time, he lifted a knee into the man's groin.

Those two swift, efficient, and downright vicious strikes were enough to knock all the fight out of the man, who doubled over, groaned, and collapsed to huddle on the floor in a tight ball.

Preacher saw that and was surprised the fancy-dressed foreigner could fight like that. He must have more experience than he looked like he ought to.

Preacher stepped toward him and was about to say something when the stranger looked at him and reached under his tweed coat with a move almost too fast for the eye to follow. He plucked something from a vest pocket. Preacher barely had time to recognize it as a gun before the weapon came up and flame and powder smoke gouted from the barrel.

CHAPTER 3

The gun was a pepperbox, but Preacher was only vaguely aware of that, what with the muzzle flash and the sound of it going off almost right in his face.

He knew instantly that he wasn't hit. Either the stranger wasn't a very good shot, to miss at such close range, or else he hadn't been shooting at the mountain man after all.

The latter turned out to be the case. Preacher heard a groan and a clatter and looked over his shoulder to see the riverman called Kennedy sagging against the bar.

The bloodstain on the right shoulder of Kennedy's shirt told Preacher that was where the pistol ball had struck him. A barstool lay on the floor on its side near Kennedy's feet. That was plenty to tell Preacher what had happened.

Kennedy had gotten up, grabbed the barstool, and been about to smash it over Preacher's head when the stranger shot him.

A blow like that would have busted Preacher's head clean open. Might've even killed him.

The mountain man knew that. He looked at the

stranger again, jerked his head in a nod, and said, "I'm obliged to you, mister. I thought you was tryin' to kill me, but it looks like you may have saved my life."

"You wouldn't have been in danger had you not come to my assistance. It was the least I could do when I saw that fellow on the verge of striking you down treacherously from behind." The stranger slipped the pepperbox back in his vest pocket. "As a gentleman, I consider it a matter of honor, and, of course, I would never dream of trying to capitalize on any such obligation to convince you to at least listen to my proposal."

Preacher sighed. "If all that jabberin' means you still want to talk to me but don't figure it's right to ask, don't worry about it. Mike, draw us a couple of beers, will you?"

"Sure," the big Irishman said. "Just let me tend to a little housekeepin' first."

He pointed to some regular patrons and told them to drag Kennedy and his friends out of the tavern and leave them in the street.

"Kennedy's shot," one of the men protested. "He needs a doctor."

"Ye can fetch one for him if ye want," Mike said. He was drawing the beers for Preacher and the stranger now. "But I'm not payin' for it. Mayhap ye could see if he has enough coin for a sawbones in his pockets."

Or maybe they would just rob Kennedy and his friends and leave them in the alley beside the tavern, Preacher thought. Such things happened all the time in the rough frontier town of St. Louis. It was none of his business.

He dropped a coin on the bar to pay for the beers, picked them up, and carried them to an empty table in a corner. The stranger followed him.

When they were seated, Preacher pushed one of the beers across to the stranger.

"This don't exactly make us even," he said, "but I reckon it's a start."

"It's more than enough," the man said. He picked up the mug and went on, "My name is Geoffrey Fitzwarren. Here's to newfound friends."

Preacher thought calling himself and Fitzwarren friends might be stretching things a mite, but he grunted and nodded and clinked his mug against the other man's. They drank, and as he lowered his mug, he said, "It's good to meet you, Geoff. That don't mean I've changed my mind about takin' the job you want me to do."

"To find my cousin Charlotte, you mean."

Preacher's lips tightened under his mustache. The missing girl had a name now. Knowing what it was didn't make it any easier for him to be stubborn.

He changed the subject by saying, "Did I hear you right? You claim you ain't from England?"

"That's correct, yes. As far as it does."

"What does that mean?"

"Have you ever heard of Alpenstone?" Fitzwarren asked.

Preacher frowned and shook his head. "Is that some kind of a rock?"

The question brought a chuckle from Fitzwarren. "I speak, dear boy, of the Grand Duchy of Alpenstone, my beloved homeland. It's a small but beautiful sovereign state in the mountains where France, Switzerland, and the German Confederation come together."

Preacher suppressed the urge to warn Fitzwarren never to call him "dear boy" again.

"Never heard of it," he said.

"Few people have, especially in this country."

The mountain man frowned and leaned forward. "You look and sound like you came here straight from London. How'd you wind up in this Alpenstone place?"

"Well, you see, the Grand Duchy was part of the Habsburg Empire, and my family is connected to the Habsburgs through old King George, don't you know. There came a point some years ago when the next in line of succession as the Grand Duke of Alpenstone was a Fitzwarren, and that's how it all came to pass, you know."

Preacher turned that information over in his mind and tried to make it form a coherent picture. After a moment, he said, "You folks are from England, but you live in this little Alpenstone place and sort of run things?"

"Exactly."

"That makes you the king?"

Fitzwarren laughed again. "Hardly! I'm related to the royal family, but it's a sort of distant relation, you know. I'm a minor functionary at court, the sort who's sent on missions no one else particularly wants, such as locating my cousin Charlotte."

"She's royalty, too?"

Fitzwarren shrugged and said, "If you want to be precise about it, yes, that's true. She's thirteenth in the line of succession, but a great deal would have to happen before she would ever be declared Grand Duchess."

"How far down the line are you?" Preacher asked, curious.

"Much, much farther, I assure you."

Preacher rasped his fingertips over his beard-stubbled jaw as he thought some more and then said, "I reckon it wouldn't hurt anything for me to hear more about whatever it is you got in mind."

A smile broke out across Geoffrey Fitzwarren's face. "That's excellent," he said. "Just excellent. You see, several years ago, dear cousin Charlotte left Alpenstone. Ran away, I should say. Stole off during the night without a word to any of her family and disappeared. It was reported that she was seen in Paris, but after that, she dropped out of sight."

"Why would she run off like that?" Preacher thought about pictures of places in Europe he had seen in books. "Didn't she like livin' in a castle?"

Fitzwarren hesitated before answering. He wore an embarrassed expression as he said, "She didn't leave Alpenstone alone. There was a man involved."

Preacher leaned back in his chair and took another swallow of beer.

"She ran off with some fella," he said, nodding in understanding.

"That's right. An American who was visiting the Grand Duchy. His name was Barrett Treadway."

Preacher perked up again. That name was vaguely familiar to him, but he couldn't have said why. He tried to remember where he'd heard it before but had no luck.

"Charlotte was only seventeen when she disappeared," Fitzwarren continued. "Just the right age for her heart and mind to be consumed with romantic notions. I'm sure she believed that she was in love with this man Treadway and that he loved her and they would be happy together forever."

"Maybe that's what happened," Preacher suggested.

Fitzwarren made a face. "Please. We're both old enough to know that, save for very rare instances, love such as that simply doesn't exist. A relationship that's beneficial for both parties is hardly the same thing as birdsongs and rose petals."

Preacher let that go and asked, "How come you think your cousin's somewhere out here on the frontier? I ain't never been to Paris, but I know it's a hell of a long way from St. Louis."

"When I was charged with locating poor Charlotte, I started by picking up the trail in Paris. I was able to follow it to England. To Liverpool, to be precise."

Preacher nodded. He knew about following a trail, even though most of the other stuff Fitzwarren was spouting meant about as much to him as the other side of the moon.

"In Liverpool, I discovered that Charlotte and Treadway had booked passage on a ship bound for Boston. I did the same, and upon arrival in Boston, further inquiries led me to Philadelphia."

"You ain't sparin' no expense, are you?"

"The family very much wants Charlotte to return home. We wish to put her little misadventure behind her and reunite her with her loved ones in Alpenstone."

Preacher wasn't the sort to tiptoe around anything. He asked, "Do you know if she and this Treadway varmint ever got hitched?"

Fitzwarren winced again. "I'm afraid that bit of information remains unknown."

"Then there's a good chance she's been livin' what high-toned folks would call a scandalous life for the past few years."

"Perhaps. But nevertheless, my mission remains the same. I traced Barrett Treadway to St. Louis."

"Hold on a second. You followed Treadway here, but not your cousin?"

Fitzwarren's voice was heavy with solemn gloom as he replied, "Somewhere between Philadelphia and here, my poor cousin Charlotte disappeared again. From what I've been able to ascertain, when Treadway showed up here, she was no longer traveling with him."

For a moment, Preacher didn't say anything. Then: "That ain't good."

"No. Indeed, it is not. But no matter where Charlotte is or what has happened to her, it's up to me to discover the truth. And that's where you come in. If anyone has the answers I need, it's Barrett Treadway. I'm told that he purchased supplies and outfitted himself for a fur trapping expedition into the mountains."

"He went off to become a mountain man!" Preacher slapped a hand on the table. "I knew that name was sorta familiar for some reason. Reckon I must've heard talk somewhere about a trapper called Treadway."

"You're not acquainted with him?" Fitzwarren asked with a faint note of hope in his voice.

Preacher shook his head. "Nope. Never laid eyes on the man. I never heard much about him, but I want to say that what I did hear makes me think he might've headed out to the Beartooth Mountains."

"You're acquainted with these mountains?"

"I know most places west of the Mississipp', north o' the Rio Grande, and south of the Canadian line. Yeah, I been to the Beartooths. Been a while, but I reckon I could find my way around all right if I needed to." Preacher's voice didn't contain any false modesty as he added matter-of-factly, "Once I've traveled over a trail, I generally don't forget it."

"And that's exactly why I want to hire you. You're my best chance of finding Barrett Treadway, and Treadway is my best chance of discovering what happened to Charlotte."

Preacher drew in a breath. "You know there's a chance she ain't alive no more."

"I know that," Fitzwarren said, "and yet as long as breath remains in my body, as long as the faintest chance exists that I can locate her and return her to the bosom of her family, I will never give up, Preacher. Never."

The mountain man looked across the table at this strange visitor from a foreign land. Preacher had dealt with European nobility on several occasions in the past, and as he had told Fitzwarren, those arrangements had never worked out well for him. He had always found himself up to his neck in trouble and had barely survived some of those dustups.

But Fitzwarren looked and sounded so blasted sincere,

so concerned about his cousin's fate, that Preacher felt a pang of sympathy for the man.

"Well, hell," he muttered. "I was plannin' on headin' in that direction anyway . . ."

"Does that mean you'll do it?" Fitzwarren asked quickly, hope leaping into his voice again. "You'll help me find Treadway, and, I pray, my cousin as well?"

"I can't guarantee nothin'," Preacher said, "but I reckon I can give it a shot." He paused, then added, "You folks from Alpenstone don't do a bunch of sword-fightin', do you?"

"As it happens, I'm an excellent fencer, old boy!"

Preacher rolled his eyes and tried not to sigh.

Chapter 4

Preacher hadn't been back in St. Louis very long when Geoffrey Fitzwarren approached him in Red Mike's. He had mentioned Canada to Fitzwarren but hadn't explained that he had only recently returned from a perilous journey to those northern climes.

That trip had been long and dangerous. Preacher had been accompanied by his good friend Bjorn Gunnarson, the half-Crow, half-Norwegian warrior known to his mother's people as Tall Dog, as well as his mountain man friends Audie and Nighthawk. With them beside him, he had had valiant allies in the frequent battles the group had encountered.

When the adventure was done and things had been put right in the settlement of Skarkavik, where the friends and relatives of Tall Dog's father tried to live as much like their Viking ancestors as they could, Tall Dog had chosen to remain there for a time among his father's people. He, too, wanted to live as a Viking and explore that part of his heritage.

Preacher couldn't blame him for that. But he couldn't stay in Canada, either. He was an American, blast it, and his home was in the high country, the Rocky Mountains where he had spent most of his life after leaving his family's farm as a very young man to go and see the world, at least that part of it west of the Mississippi River.

He and Audie and Nighthawk had headed south again. His friends had branched off along the way, eager to explore a secluded valley they had heard about where the trapping was supposed to be excellent, while Preacher had proceeded on alone to St. Louis.

His plan was to take it easy for a spell, then outfit himself and head west again with his longtime trail partners, the rangy gray stallion called Horse and the big, shaggy, wolflike cur known only as Dog.

Maybe to a certain extent he was just unsociable at heart. He needed those periods of solitude in his life to give his brain and his spirit a chance to rest and cool off from being around people.

Why in blazes had he agreed to take some blasted foreigner out to the Beartooth Mountains?

He asked himself that question the next morning as he climbed the steps to the porch of the Hotel Lamont, where Geoffrey Fitzwarren was staying. He didn't have an answer, except that maybe Fitzwarren's story about his lost cousin had moved him somehow.

Preacher would have denied it up one way and down the other, but he knew he had a bit of a romantic streak in his own nature. It was a narrow one, mind, and he kept it corralled most of the time, but every now and then it slipped out and landed him in some trouble.

He hoped this wouldn't be one of those occasions.

He and Fitzwarren had agreed to meet at the hotel this morning and discuss preparations for the journey. As Preacher entered the lobby, he heard his name called from the dining room that was through an arched entrance to the left.

Geoffrey Fitzwarren had gotten to his feet at one of the tables and waved for Preacher to join him. The mountain man did so, telling a waitress he passed along the way, "Bring me a pot o' coffee, a big ol' pile o' flapjacks, some eggs, and a steak." He nodded toward Fitzwarren and added, "That fella yonder'll be payin' for it."

Fitzwarren was bareheaded this morning, revealing his crisp, fair hair. He wore a different tweed suit and vest but looked as impeccable as the night before. He gestured toward the empty chair at the table and said, "Good morning, old boy. I trust you slept well."

Preacher had spent the night in the loft at Patterson's Livery Stable, where he always left Horse and Dog when he was staying in St. Louis. If he had to have a roof over his head, he figured it was better to be surrounded by animals rather than people. Critters were more trustworthy.

"Slept just fine, mighty fine," he said as he sat down.

Fitzwarren swept back the tails of his coat and resumed his seat. "I saw you speak to the serving woman. I assume you told her to bring you some breakfast."

"That I did."

"I'll take care of that for you, of course."

Preacher chuckled. "Told her that, too."

"From this point forward, I'll be paying for all of your expenses until we return to St. Louis, successful in our mission, I hope. In addition, I intend to pay you a fee of two hundred American dollars no matter what the outcome of our efforts. I know we didn't discuss financial details last night—"

"Two hundred dollars is fine," Preacher assured him. "That's a heap of money. You must really want to find this cousin of yours."

"More than anything else in the world, I assure you."

Something about Fitzwarren's tone of voice struck Preacher as odd. He studied the man for a moment, seeing the concern in Fitzwarren's eyes. European folks, he recalled, especially the ones in those so-called noble families, had a habit of marrying their cousins.

He wondered if this was more than just a job the grand duke had given Fitzwarren. Maybe he had personal reasons for wanting to find the missing Charlotte.

That was none of Preacher's business and didn't matter to him one way or the other. He said, "We'll find that Treadway varmint if he's out there to be found, and with any luck, that'll lead us to Miss Charlotte. Just because she wasn't with him when he got to St. Louis don't mean they didn't meet up again somewhere else later."

"At this point, that is my profound hope and, indeed, our best chance of locating her, I'd say."

The waitress arrived with Preacher's coffee and told him his food would be ready shortly. As the mountain man took an appreciative sip of the strong black brew, Fitzwarren asked, "How many men will we be hiring to accompany us to the, ah, Beartooths? Bearteeth?"

Preacher frowned. "I figured it'd be just the two of us.

I'd get a couple of saddle mounts for you, a spare horse for me, and a pair of pack animals for our supplies, and that's all we'd need."

Fitzwarren shook his head and said, "Such a Spartan arrangement isn't necessary or even desirous. I can easily afford to pay for a larger party, and it would be safer to travel with several seasoned, well-armed companions, would it not?"

"Thieves are less likely to attack a bigger bunch, and so are Injuns," Preacher agreed with a shrug. "But it's slower goin' that way, too. Two men can make better time."

"I'd prefer to increase our chances of arriving at our destination alive and whole. There's another consideration, as well. I want to take a wagon along, because if we're successful in our mission and find Charlotte, we can't expect her to ride horseback all the way from the mountains back to St. Louis."

What Fitzwarren was saying made sense, Preacher supposed. Taking along more men and a wagon would slow them down considerably, but it would be safer and make for an easier return trip if they located Charlotte. She had run away from Alpenstone several years ago. Time wasn't of the essence now.

"All right, I reckon we can play it your way."

"Excellent!" A worried expression suddenly appeared on Fitzwarren's face. "Although I certainly don't want you to think that I'm unwilling to take your advice. You're the expert on these matters, after all."

"You're footin' the bill," Preacher pointed out. "You get to have a say in how things are done." His voice took on a firm tone as he went on, "But once we're out there on the frontier, I'm in charge. If I tell you to do somethin', there's a good reason for it, and you'd durned well better do it without a whole bunch of arguin'."

Fitzwarren smiled and held up his right hand. "I give you my solemn word that I'll comply, Preacher. You're in charge, and I'll follow your commands as if you were the Grand Marshal of the Royal Army of Alpenstone."

"Reckon I can't ask for any more than that."

The waitress brought two large platters loaded with food and set them on the table in front of the mountain man. Preacher had a hearty appetite and dug in with enthusiasm. Fitzwarren cleaned up the rest of the food on his plate, which obviously had been a much smaller amount to start with.

Preacher washed down his food with healthy swallows of coffee. One of the times when he was doing that, Fitzwarren asked, "Will you be able find competent men we can hire to come along with us?"

Preacher nodded. "Yeah, that shouldn't be a problem. This time of year, there are quite a few men who have brought in a season's worth o' pelts, sold them, and are still at loose ends before headin' back to the high country."

"How many do you think we need?"

Preacher considered for a moment and said, "Five ought to be enough. That'll make half a dozen, countin' me, and most anybody who'd consider jumpin' us will think twice about takin' on that many fightin' men."

"We'll be seven fighting men, counting myself," Fitzwarren pointed out. "I'm an excellent shot."

"Yeah, you proved that last night at Red Mike's, I reckon. That little pepperbox won't do you a heap of good out in the tall and uncut, though."

"I can handle a regular pistol or a rifle or a shotgun with equal skill, I assure you."

"Where we're goin', you may get to demonstrate that," Preacher said.

While he had finished the meal and polished off another cup of coffee, they continued discussing preparations for the journey. Patterson ran a wagonyard as well as the livery stable, and Preacher knew he could get a sturdy vehicle there, along with a team of good draft horses. He would also go back to Red Mike's and put the word out that he was looking to hire a handful of experienced men for a trip to the Beartooth Mountains and possibly beyond.

As he stood up to leave, he said, "I'll go to the general store and give 'em a list of the supplies we'll need to take. They can be puttin' the order together today. If I can find some good men, ain't no reason we can't pick up the goods first thing in the mornin' and head on out."

"That sounds superb," Fitzwarren said as he got to his feet, too. He used his napkin to dab at his lips and dropped it on his empty plate. "I'll walk you out. You can find me here anytime today. I'm sure you'll need to secure more funds as we go along, but in the meantime, let me give you this for expenses."

He took a drawstring purse from inside his coat,

opened it, and handed Preacher five ten-dollar gold pieces.

"That'll do for a start, all right," the mountain man said as he hefted the Liberty gold eagles. He stowed them away in a pouch attached to his broad leather belt.

That belt also supported a pair of holstered Colt Patersons that had been presented to Preacher by a company of Rangers down in Texas after he'd helped them out with a little ruckus a year or two earlier. He had a sheathed bowie knife attached to the belt as well. Usually he carried a tomahawk tucked behind it, too, but here in town he had left the 'hawk with the rest of his gear at the livery stable.

Preacher and Fitzwarren left the dining room and walked through the lobby to the hotel's front entrance. They stepped out onto the porch, and Preacher began, "I reckon I'll see you later—"

That was as far as he got before a man's harsh voice shouted, "There they are! Get 'em!"

A split second later, the roar of gun-thunder filled the warm morning air.

Chapter 5

Instinct made Preacher whirl swiftly toward the source of the shots. At the same time, he threw his right arm across Geoffrey Fitzwarren's chest and shoved the man back through the open double doors, out of the line of fire.

As a rifle ball hummed past Preacher's head, he spotted the attackers and recognized them as Kennedy and the other two rivermen who had clashed with him and Fitzwarren at Red Mike's the previous night.

Kennedy's right arm was in a sling, but he had a revolver in his left hand and thrust it toward Preacher as he pulled the trigger. One of the other men had a Colt, too, and the third had just fired the narrowly missing rifle shot at the mountain man.

The three assailants stood at the corner of the building, just beyond the end of the porch. As Preacher crouched, his hands dropped with blinding speed to the butts of the Patersons on his hips. He had discovered that he had a natural talent for shucking those irons and getting them into play quickly.

Pistol balls chewed splinters from the porch post

beside him and sprayed them in the air. He felt one of them sting his cheek as his thumbs looped around the Colts' hammers and eared them back. The triggers, which had no guard, dropped into firing position as he cocked the weapons.

The man with the rifle was trying to reload and fumbling in his nervousness as he did so. Preacher aimed at Kennedy and the other man since they were the more immediate threats. In this day and age of modern repeating weapons, it took a special kind of fool to bring a single-shot rifle to an ambush, the mountain man thought fleetingly. He fired as the Colts came level.

The guns roared and bucked in his fists. The heavy lead ball from the left-hand gun found its target, plowing into the chest of Kennedy's companion and knocking him backward as if he'd been punched by a giant fist.

Kennedy threw himself to the side, causing the shot from Preacher's right-hand gun to miss. Taking cover at the corner of the building, Kennedy leaned around it and continued blasting. Preacher had to dive forward onto the porch to avoid the barrage. Pistol balls sizzled through the space where he had been a split second earlier.

The hammer of Kennedy's gun clicked on an empty chamber. He ripped out a curse and ducked back around the corner, probably intending on reloading, although that would be awkward with one arm in a sling.

He hadn't pulled back quite far enough. Part of one leg, little more than an inch of it, stuck out past the corner. Preacher drew a quick bead and fired again.

Through the smoke that came from the Colt's muzzle, he saw blood fly.

Howling in pain, Kennedy reeled out from behind the building. He clapped a hand to his thigh where the ball from Preacher's gun had torn away a chunk of flesh.

Then, evidently realizing he was out in the open again, he jerked his head toward Preacher, just in time for another carefully aimed shot to strike him in the center of the forehead. The ball bored all the way through his brain and exploded out the back of his skull, leaving a fist-sized hole leaking blood and gray matter.

Kennedy flopped to the ground, dead before he landed.

Another shot roared, this time behind Preacher and to his right. He twisted and rolled and brought the Colts around, but he held his fire when he spotted Geoffrey Fitzwarren standing in the hotel's entrance, a smoking flintlock pistol in his hand.

Preacher looked the other way and saw the third ambusher, the one with the rifle, toppling like a tree. The man landed on his face and the rifle skidded away in the street.

"I reckon he must've got that rifle reloaded after so long a time," Preacher commented as he lowered the Colts.

"Yes, and he had a perfect shot at you," Fitzwarren said. "Fortunately, I was armed and was able to get my shot off first."

"Lucky for me," Preacher said. "Not much for him."

He got to his feet with a lithe ease that belied the fact he was approaching middle age. Holding the Colts ready in case he needed them, he stalked along the porch until he was close enough to get a good look at all three attackers.

Kennedy was dead—no doubt about that with his brains blown out. The other two men appeared to have crossed the divide, as well. Preacher stepped down off the porch and toed their bodies to make sure.

Satisfied that none of the rivermen represented a threat anymore, he pouched the Colts.

"That was a good shot," he said to Fitzwarren when he rejoined the man on the porch. "Especially with a gun that looks like it dates from the Revolutionary War."

"You mean the Colonial Rebellion?" Fitzwarren laughed. "Never mind, I'm just having a bit of sport with you, old fellow. This pistol isn't quite that ancient, but it's well-made and very dependable. The range was a bit much for my pepperbox, you know. But a gentleman is prepared for any eventuality."

He looked past Preacher at the three corpses. Townspeople were gathering around the bodies now, satisfying their morbid curiosity.

"It appears those louts were holding a grudge from last night and intended to settle the score."

Preacher grunted. "Their mistake."

"One they won't make again." Fitzwarren frowned. "Is the constabulary going to take a dim view of this affair?"

"You mean, will the law care that we killed those varmints? Not likely. There were plenty of folks around who can testify that they started the shootin', if it comes to that, but I reckon it probably won't. Folks generally stomp their own snakes out here and mind their own business when it comes to somebody else's stompin'."

"An admirable attitude indeed," Fitzwarren said. "Shall we resume our preparations?"

"Might as well," Preacher said. "The day ain't gettin' any younger."

A block away, a young man leaned against the wall of a building, next to the door of a hardware store, and heaved a sigh of relief.

He had thrown himself into the alcove where the door was located when the gunfire started, instinctively taking cover, but it was obvious by now the shots hadn't been aimed at him after all.

Instead, some sort of gunfight had taken place up the street. The violent fracas had nothing to do with him.

That was a welcome change, thought Bellamy Buckland.

He was in his early twenties. As far as he was concerned, that age was the prime of life, and he looked it, being a bit taller than average, broad-shouldered, and muscularly built under the buckskin shirt and the brown whipcord trousers he wore. The trousers were tucked into the tops of tall black boots that had once been polished to a high sheen.

Now the boots were spotted with mud and other things Bellamy Buckland didn't want to think about. It was impossible to keep anything clean out here on the frontier.

As if prompted by that thought, he took off his black

hat and brushed dust from it, then put it back on, settling it on hair as black as a raven's wing. The narrow mustache that adorned his upper lip was the same shade. He had to shave frequently to keep dark stubble from blurring the strong lines of his jaw.

He dropped his hands to the butts of the two flintlock pistols he carried tucked behind the dark red sash tied around his waist. It was reassuring to feel the smooth wood of their grips and know that he could defend himself if trouble sought him out.

He had no reason to believe it would do so while he was here in St. Louis, but he had made many enemies over the course of his young life. That was only natural when a man was as handsome and reckless and driven by hearty appetites as was Bellamy Buckland.

Trouble dogged his trail, and it had for quite some time now.

Chapter 6

St. Ruthven's College, Albemarle, New Hampshire— One Year Earlier

Bellamy Buckland jerked his head up from the pillow as the woman in bed beside him let out a soft cry of alarm. A second earlier, a door had slammed somewhere downstairs, jolting both of them out of a light, satisfied doze.

Bellamy threw the sheet aside and bolted out of bed.

"Saints preserve us!" the woman hissed. "It's him. He wasn't supposed to be back for another hour. Get out of here, quickly!"

"That is entirely my intent, dear Edith," Bellamy said as he grabbed for the clothes he had discarded hastily earlier in the evening.

He stuffed his stocking-clad feet through the legs of his trousers and pulled the garment up around his waist. Holding his boots, shirt, and coat, he leaped to the window and thrust up the sash.

He knew that a sturdy limb of an elm tree extended close enough to the window that he could reach it.

Experience had taught him to always be aware of potential escape routes, especially when he was indulging himself with a married woman.

The heavily stomping footsteps of this lady's husband were ascending the stairs now. Bellamy could hear them plainly. He leaned out the open window, dropped his clothes and boots to the ground, and threw a leg over the sill.

"Bellamy, darling, wait!" The soft cry came from the bed, where the lady had sat up and was clutching the covers in front of her more than ample bosom. "When will I see you again?"

"Some questions we're not meant to know the answers to, my dear," he told her. "Whenever sweet Providence allows, I suppose."

"But—"

Bellamy heard no more. With a lithe, athletic grace, he swung himself out the window, hung by his hands from the sill for a moment, and then dropped the six feet to the ground. He landed gracefully, going to one knee for only an instant before he sprang up again.

He snatched his boots, shirt, and coat from the ground and retreated into some nearby shrubbery. The branches clawed at his bare torso, but he paid them little heed.

Getting what one wanted in this world always came with a price.

A few minutes later, now fully dressed, Bellamy emerged from the concealing bushes and strode along one of the flagstone paths that crisscrossed the grounds of St. Ruthven's College. As he passed one of the stately redbrick buildings, he glanced at a particular window and smiled in the darkness.

Tomorrow, he would be sitting in the lecture hall on the other side of that glass, listening to Professor Elihu Stockard ramble on endlessly about the natural sciences.

Professor Stockard would have no idea that twelve hours earlier, the handsome young man in the second row had been in bed with his wife Edith, transporting her to places where the good professor could never take her.

At that thought, Bellamy began to whistle a merry tune, expressing the pure, simple joy he felt at being young, healthy, and alive.

He had almost reached the boardinghouse at the edge of campus where he lived when he spotted several figures on the steps of the house. The men looked as if they were waiting for someone, and Bellamy felt a sudden stirring of alarm that it might be him they sought.

He stopped short and then began to back away in the shadows of the elms that lined the path, hoping none of the men had noticed his approach. He could always retreat to one of the taverns in Albemarle and spend the night there if need be. Several of the local tavern keepers appreciated his patronage and would be willing to lend him a hand.

He was about to turn and hurry away into the darkness when one of those waiting at the boardinghouse said, "I think I see something over there! Is that him?"

"It is him!" said one of the others. "Get him!"

Bellamy whirled around and broke into a run as the men leaped down from the steps and charged after him, shouting as they ran. The cries were a mixture of sulfurous curses and angry demands that he halt.

Bellamy ignored all of them and ran like the wind.

He remained on the path. The trees and shrubs on the college's grounds would just slow him down right now. He wanted to put some distance between himself and his pursuers. If he could do that then maybe he would go to ground and try to hide. He knew every inch of St. Ruthven's and was confident that he could give them the slip.

Bellamy was a fast runner. The shouts and the rapid footsteps slapping on the path fell farther behind him. He was tempted to slow down, look back over his shoulder, and laugh at them, just to infuriate them that much more. But that wouldn't be a smart thing to do, he knew. He continued speeding through the shadows, arms pumping and legs flashing.

His heart pounded in his chest, but it was an excited rhythm. His blood sang in his veins. Certainly, his pursuers represented a threat to his well-being, but danger made him feel more alive. It always had, ever since he was a boy.

With all that exuberant emotion flooding through him, it was no wonder he completely forgot about how the extreme cold of the previous winter had caused one of the stones in the path to tilt upward a bit. It wasn't sitting at much of an angle. It stuck up only an inch from the surrounding stones.

That inch was enough.

The toe of Bellamy's left boot struck the edge of the tilted stone at full speed. That leg went out from under him and he pitched forward, momentum robbing him of any chance to maintain his balance. He crashed to the flagstones with a terrific force that knocked every bit of breath out of his body.

Bellamy lay there stunned, his head swimming, unable even to drag air back into his lungs. Dimly, he heard the pounding of approaching footsteps. A man's voice seemingly far away shouted, "There he is! Grab the rotten scoundrel before he can get away again!"

Strong hands clamped around his arms and hauled him roughly to his feet. His captors didn't loosen their grips once they had picked him up. Instead, they jerked him back and forth between them, causing his head to loll loosely on his shoulders.

At least he could breathe again now that he was upright. He gasped. The world seemed to be spinning the wrong way around him. A ball of sickness churned in his belly.

A brutal openhanded blow across his face shocked him back into coherence. The madly whirling scenery around him settled down and once again became the pastoral, shadow-dappled landscape of the St. Ruthven's College campus.

Two men held his arms, their grasps painfully tight. Another man stood directly in front of him, with several more figures gathered behind him.

The man confronting him said, "You thought you could get away with it, did you, Buckland?"

"Hit the rascal again, Melville!" urged one of the man's companions.

"Teach him a lesson!" added another with a tone of vicious eagerness in his voice.

They were all fellow students at St. Ruthven's, Bellamy knew. The ringleader was Melville Atherton, the son of a banker from Boston. Bellamy could have put names on the others if forced to, but it seemed rather meaningless at the moment. They were all cronies of Melville's. Most of them had been at the card game the previous night during which Bellamy had taken more than a hundred dollars out of Melville's pockets.

"I'll teach him a lesson, all right," Melville said. Enough light penetrated the trees for Bellamy to make out the sneer on the fleshy face of the other young man. "I'll teach him not to think he can get away with cheating his betters."

Despite the way his captors' fingers were digging cruelly into his arms, Bellamy laughed.

"Two things are wrong with that statement, Melville," he said. "I never cheated you. I didn't have to. You're just a terrible card player. And you're hardly my better. None of you lads are."

"That's right," one of the men holding him said. "Why, Buckland here is nobility, don't you know? If you don't believe me, just ask him. He'll tell you!" A harsh laugh, followed by, "Isn't that right, Duke?"

"Tell us, Duke!" jeered another of the mob. "Tell us how rich and important you are."

"I'll tell you nothing, son," Bellamy drawled. "It would be a waste of my time and breath, because none of you are intelligent enough to comprehend what I might say."

"I've heard enough from him," Melville said. "Hang on tight, boys."

He braced his feet squarely, drew back his right arm, and drove that fist into Bellamy's midsection. The blow was powerful enough to sink wrist-deep.

The sickness had receded a bit, but it came roaring back with that punch in the stomach. Even with the two men holding him, Bellamy jackknifed forward. The supper he'd had earlier before sneaking into Edith Stockard's bed came bursting out of him, along with the wine he'd drunk to wash it down. Melville Atherton had to leap back to avoid being splattered.

Melville might have fallen, but his friends were right there to catch him and hold him up. They laughed and whooped, thoroughly enjoying this experience.

The two holding Bellamy jerked him upright again. Melville stepped over the puddle of vomit and smashed his right fist against Bellamy's jaw.

He followed that blow with a left and then another right. Bellamy's head jerked violently back and forth. Something warm leaking down over his lips told him his nose was bleeding. He tasted blood inside his mouth, too. One of his teeth must have cut the inside of his cheek.

A part of his brain stood apart from the beating, coolly assessing the damage being done to him. He'd always had that ability to retreat from trouble, to continue thinking calmly and logically no matter what the circumstances. That detachment came in handy—and sometimes even allowed him to figure out a way to escape whatever travails were plaguing him.

Tonight, however, it told him that there would be no escape. There were too many of his enemies, and they were too angry to listen to anything he might have to say. He couldn't fight his way out of this dilemma, and he couldn't talk his way out of it, either.

Realizing that, his brain determined on the only reasonable course of action.

He would make Melville Atherton pay a high price for whatever pleasure he got from his revenge.

Throwing his weight suddenly on the two men who held him, Bellamy lifted his right leg and drove the heel of his boot into Melville's groin.

Melville screamed like a little girl as he clapped both hands to the injured region, bent over, and staggered backward. The agonized sound warmed Bellamy's heart.

A second later, he was treated to the ludicrous sight of Melville's feet slipping in the vomit and throwing both legs out from under him. Melville fell straight down, his buttocks crashing onto the flagstones. The impact must have made the pain in his groin even worse, if that was possible. His scream rose to an even higher level.

"Melville!" one of his friends cried as Melville toppled over onto his side and curled up around the pain.

Bellamy threw back his head and laughed.

They closed in around him then, swarming like a pack of starving wolves. Fist after fist crashed against his head and body. After a while, the young men holding him lowered him to the path, but the punishment didn't end there. Once he was on the ground, it was easy for his tormentors to kick and stomp him.

That detached part of his brain retreated, unable to withstand what was happening to him. Bellamy rocked back and forth, only vaguely aware now of the beating he was receiving. His consciousness receded more and more until finally it was gone completely.

Except for one tiny, amusing memory of the way Melville Atherton had screamed like a girl, and then that winked out of existence, too.

Chapter 7

Bellamy ignored the stares from his fellow students as he trudged into Thackery Hall the next morning.

He knew he looked terrible. Both eyes were blackened and swollen almost shut. He could see where he was going, but only barely. Bruises darkened his cheeks, his nose was nearly twice its normal size, and his lips were suffused with blood, too.

For all of that, his face looked better than his body did. When he'd studied it in the looking glass in his room before struggling into clothes, he'd seen that it was one enormous yellowish-purple bruise.

Based on the twinges of pain he felt when he took more than the shallowest breath, he was convinced he had a cracked rib or two, as well.

But he was up and moving around, and his brain was working.

He was already starting to think about how he was going to settle the score with Melville Atherton and his cronies.

He shuffled into the lecture hall and glanced toward the lectern, where Professor Stockard stood looking through his notes for that day's lecture. The professor's stooped posture, buzzard-like face, wild gray hair, and bushy side whiskers provided a sharp contrast to his wife Edith, who, thirty years younger than him, was still glowing with youth and health and whose gently rounded body deserved much more attention than the aging academic could provide.

Bellamy didn't feel any guilt over furnishing Edith with what she needed. Not one damned bit.

He was making his way toward the bench where he normally sat when he felt eyes on him, and he sensed that this regard was more intense than the surprise and curiosity his battered appearance provoked in his fellow students. He looked toward the lectern again and saw that Professor Stockard was watching him now.

The professor's gaze was coldly furious. On more than one occasion in the past, Bellamy had seen someone looking at him as if they wanted to murder him.

That was the way Stockard was glaring at him.

Oh, for heaven's sake, Bellamy thought. For some unfathomable reason, Edith must have informed her husband of what had happened.

He expected Stockard to rage at him and order him to get out of the lecture hall, but the professor didn't say anything as Bellamy limped to his seat.

Melville Atherton usually sat on the same bench as Bellamy, several places farther along. Today there was no sign of him, but several of his friends were in attendance. They had been part of the wolf pack the night before, and they looked at Bellamy this morning with smug, self-satisfied smiles.

Since the lecture had not yet begun, Bellamy moved closer to the group and asked in a quiet voice, "Where's Melville this morning?"

The smirks disappeared. Glares replaced them.

"He's too badly injured to go anywhere," the nearest of the young men answered. "You nearly killed him."

"Unless you've gone blind, you can see that I'm not in very good shape myself, but I'm here."

The scowl on the face of the young man he was talking to deepened. "You don't understand. The doctor from Albemarle has sent word to Melville's father in Boston strongly urging that he come and get Melville and take him to a hospital there." The man looked at Bellamy as if he were something to be scraped off a boot. "Poor Melville may never be the same again."

"If you're looking for sympathy," Bellamy responded coldly, "you won't find it here. You and the rest of your gang could have killed me, you know."

"We didn't. We stopped short of injuring you seriously. You can't deny that."

"Was it intentional that you left me alive, or simply an accident?"

"I won't dignify that with an answer."

A shadow fell over Bellamy. He looked up to see Professor Stockard standing there just in front of the curving benches, hands clasped behind his back.

Stockard cleared his throat and said, "Some misfortune seems to have befallen you, Mr. Buckland."

Bellamy summoned up a smile, even though it hurt

his lips. "I'm fine, Professor, but thank you for your concern."

"I was merely stating a fact, not expressing concern. You look as if you should be receiving medical attention, not attending this lecture."

"I didn't want to miss out on any of your fascinating insights, Professor."

"Yes, well." Stockard cleared his throat again. "That is your decision."

He turned and went back to the lectern, where he fiddled with his notes for a few more moments and then gripped the stand on either side as he stared out at the benches full of students.

"We have been speaking of Mammalia in recent sessions," he began. "Today I wish to concentrate on one creature in particular, rather than the various classes. Weasels are of the genus *Mustela* of the family *Mustelidae*. They are nocturnal creatures and natural predators, sneaking in where they do not belong at night and stealing those things that are not theirs, despoiling everything they touch with their filthy paws."

With every word he spoke, Stockard's hostile stare homed in more and more on Bellamy. By the time he paused, he was looking directly at the young man, and it was obvious to everyone in the lecture hall that he was speaking directly to Bellamy, as well.

Maybe Edith had revealed the truth about their affair to her husband, Bellamy thought. He felt bad enough that he couldn't bring himself to care that much.

"Weasels are disgusting beasts that serve no purpose,"

the professor continued. "They should be wiped out, eradicated from the face of the earth, by any means necessary."

One of the students spoke up, asking, "Um, Professor, will this material be covered on the next examination?"

Stockard didn't seem to hear. His hands were clutching the sides of the lectern tightly enough now that all the blood had been forced from his fingers. The muscles of his arms trembled from the effort he was exerting to control himself.

Bellamy recognized those signs. They weren't good. Stockard might be working himself up to something.

"Do you have any comment on the subject of weasels, Mr. Buckland?" demanded Stockard.

"Me?" Bellamy said, determined to brazen his way through this unexpected confrontation if he could. "Why, no, I don't, Professor. Weasels are found primarily on farms, aren't they? I've never lived on a farm. To be honest, I don't believe I've ever laid eyes on a weasel."

"I have," Stockard grated. He let go of the lectern and moved out from behind it. Lurching forward in an unsteady step toward the benches, he continued, "I am looking at a dirty, disgusting weasel right now."

This had gone far enough, Bellamy decided. All the other young men were staring at him now, their gazes going back and forth between him and Stockard. They might not be aware of what, exactly, was going on, but they would have to be blind not to realize that something was transpiring.

"Perhaps I should leave," Bellamy said as he began to rise to his feet. He found it hard to believe that Stockard would attack him physically, but anything was possible when discussing the wounded pride of a cuckolded husband.

He was confident that if it came down to an altercation, he could hold his own against the older man, even in his battered state, but he didn't want to be forced to do that. He'd prefer to salvage his academic career, if possible, and he couldn't do that if he thrashed an elderly professor.

"Stay where you are!" Stockard bellowed before Bellamy could stand up. He reached under his long black coat and produced a pistol, which he pointed at Bellamy. Startled cries came from the other students as they scrambled to their feet and hurried to get as far out of the line of fire as they could.

Bellamy sat still, not wanting to spook Stockard into pulling the trigger.

"Professor, what are you doing?" he asked. "You shouldn't have a gun in a lecture hall. Please, put it away before someone gets hurt."

"Someone has already been hurt," Stockard declared. "When I returned home yesterday evening, I found my poor wife in a distraught state. She was crying, almost hysterical. She told me that you came to my house and asked to see me on some flimsy excuse, and when she informed you that I wasn't there, you attacked her! How dare you, sir! How dare you!"

The little minx had lied to her husband. Bellamy tried not to groan in dismay. Why hadn't she just not said anything? The old fool was so oblivious, he probably never would have suspected a thing.

Edith's nerves must have gotten to her, he thought. Either that or she had deliberately implicated him because she wasn't satisfied with his answer when she had asked him when she would see him again. It was impossible to tell what a woman would do or what her motives for her unpredictable actions might be.

"Professor, I give you my solemn oath that I never attacked your wife."

That was true; it had been more like the other way around, Edith grabbing him as soon as he came in the door and practically ripping his clothes off him.

"I swear it on my honor—" Bellamy continued.

"Honor!" Stockard interrupted him. He thrust the pistol toward Bellamy. Its barrel shook, but at this range, the professor couldn't miss. "Weasels have no honor! They're filthy vermin, and I'm going to give you exactly what vermin deserve!"

He pulled the trigger.

Chapter 8

Nothing happened, which didn't surprise Bellamy, because he had noticed a second earlier that the professor's pistol wasn't cocked. Stockard could squeeze that trigger all day and the gun wasn't going to go off.

Not unless he realized that and pulled back the hammer, that is.

That possibility definitely existed. Bellamy jumped to his feet and leaned over the bench in front of him to reach for the gun. He wanted to snatch it out of Stockard's hand before the man realized what the problem with it was.

Stockard backed off with surprising agility for a man of his age and physical condition. He let out an incoherent yell of frustration and jerked the trigger again, still with no results.

Then his eyes widened and Bellamy knew the professor had just figured out what was going on. Stockard took hold of the gun with his other hand as well and struggled to pull the hammer back with both thumbs.

Bellamy stepped up onto the front bench and leaped to the floor. He grabbed the pistol and forced Stockard's arms up as he barreled into the older man. Bellamy's stiff, aching muscles protested at this sudden burst of action, but he ignored the pain and wrenched the pistol out of Stockard's grasp.

Stockard fell back more. He caught his balance, hesitated for a heartbeat, and then came at Bellamy, flailing his arms wildly as he tried to punch the younger man.

Without looking, Bellamy tossed the pistol into the benches behind him. He didn't want Stockard to have a chance to grab it again. He threw up his arms to block the professor's blows.

"Professor, stop it!" Bellamy said. "I don't want to hurt you! Stop fighting!"

Stockard just screeched curses, spewing words and phrases Bellamy wouldn't have thought a distinguished middle-aged academic would even know, let alone use.

By now the other students had congregated on the far side of the room to watch the confrontation in stunned amazement. Other students and instructors who'd been passing by out in the hall must have heard Stockard's ranting and raving. The door into the lecture hall was open now, and more than a dozen faces peered curiously into the large room.

Bellamy continued trying to ward off Stockard's frenzied attack, but he couldn't block all the blows. One of them got through, and Stockard's bony right fist rapped hard into Bellamy's already puffed-up lips.

The pain when that punch landed made Bellamy strike back instinctively. He didn't hit Stockard, but he thrust both hands against the professor's chest and shoved hard.

Stockard flew backward, arms and legs flapping like a scarecrow, and crashed into the front of the lectern. He bounced off and fell forward on his face.

"He's going to hurt the professor!" yelled one of the students on the other side of the room. "Get him!"

Bellamy had heard too many shouts of "Get him!" in the past twelve hours. He knew this exhortation came from one of Melville Atherton's cronies. After what had happened to Melville, his friends would seize any opportunity to mete out even more punishment to Bellamy.

Well aware of the danger he was in, Bellamy turned and scrambled over the front bench. Why hadn't he hung on to that pistol? he asked himself.

He searched desperately for the gun. He hadn't been looking when he tossed it up into the seating area and didn't know exactly where it had landed.

From the corner of his eye, he saw half a dozen of the other students rushing toward him.

His frantic gaze finally fell on the pistol. He lunged over another bench, tripping and falling. He reached out and closed his hand over the gun butt just as the closest member of the mob was about to grab his coat from behind.

Bellamy twisted and brought the pistol around. He eared back the hammer and thrust it in his would-be attacker's face. The young man suddenly found himself staring down the gun's barrel from a distance of only a few inches. He stopped short and looked stricken, as if he were about to faint.

The rest of them halted their charge, too. One of

them said, "That's only a single-shot pistol. He can't shoot all of us."

"Shut up, Hannigan!" cried the young man who was staring down the barrel of the gun. "It's not you he's going to shoot, now is it?"

Bellamy pushed himself upright. The gun didn't waver as he did so. He said, "I don't want to shoot anybody, but I'm not going to just suffer a beating again. That's never going to happen." He paused. "Some of you help the professor up. Make sure he's all right."

A couple of the students took hold of Stockard and lifted him gently to his feet. He moaned and shook his head.

"It looks like he's not really hurt, just shaken up," one of the men helping him reported. "No thanks to you, Buckland."

"I was just defending myself," Bellamy said, his voice cold and hard. He commanded the man he was covering with the pistol, "Back off."

The man did so. Carefully, keeping the gun pointing in the general direction of all of them, Bellamy climbed over the benches and reached the floor in front of the lectern again. He began edging toward the door.

Stockard straightened, recovering now from the shock of being knocked down. A crazed anger still lurked in his eyes as he looked at Bellamy and cried, "Get out of here, you scoundrel! Get out of my class!"

"All right, Professor. I'm going."

"And keep going! You're through here at St. Ruthven's,

Buckland. I'll see to it that you're expelled. I want you out of here, out of this town, or I'll have you arrested!"

"I don't think you can do that."

"Just try me," Stockard said. "Try to defy me and see what happens." The professor's lips drew back from his teeth in a snarl that made him look like a feral animal. "I'll destroy you, you little weasel. I'll destroy you. See if I don't!"

Bellamy knew that Stockard meant what he said. Whether the old man was capable of following through on that threat, Bellamy couldn't say. He didn't particularly want to find out.

He had no friends here at St. Ruthven's. No real friends in the town, either, other than tavern keepers and harlots, and none of them were going to stand up on his behalf. Not that it would do any good if they did.

Sad to say, it looked as if his academic career might well be drawing to a close. Bellamy had enjoyed it in many ways. He had a sharp, active mind and truly enjoyed learning.

Plus there were always fellow students who had higher opinions of their gambling skills than their talent warranted. He had told Melville Atherton the truth: he didn't cheat, although he was perfectly capable of it. He didn't need to.

He would have other opportunities somewhere else, he told himself. He would go back to the boardinghouse, pack the few possessions he had, and shake the dust of this provincial backwater off his boots.

"Let me pass," he told the people clogging the doorway.

If they were determined to get him, he couldn't stop them. He knew that. There were too many of them, just as the fellow had said. They could overwhelm him with ease.

And to tell the truth, he probably wouldn't even fire the one round in the pistol. He didn't want to kill anyone. That would just get him hanged. Even here in peaceful New Hampshire, they would string up a murderer.

Perhaps the men blocking his path weren't aware they were in no real danger. They backed off and scattered, leaving a broad aisle for Bellamy to pass through. He backed through the door, turned rapidly, and swung the pistol from side to side in a threatening manner in case anyone was waiting outside in the corridor to jump him. When that didn't happen, he headed for Thackery Hall's main door.

No one tried to stop him.

As soon as he was outside, he threw the pistol into the bushes and broke into a run toward his boardinghouse.

He got a lot of strange looks along the way, but that was all. He had just reached the boardinghouse and started up the steps to the porch when the front door opened and a woman stepped out.

She stopped and cried, "Bellamy!" as she lifted a hand to her mouth.

"Edith!" he said. "What the devil are you doing here? Haven't you caused me enough trouble already?"

"I came to warn you. To tell you not to attend my husband's lecture this morning."

"A bit late for you to be telling me that. I just came from there."

"Oh, no! He forced me to confess to him what happened last night, darling. He's always been suspicious of me. He worries about the difference in our ages—"

"So you lied to him and told him I attacked you."

"No! Well, not exactly. I simply couldn't tell him the entire truth—"

"That it was your idea to go to bed with me?"

She gave him a cold, angry stare.

"There's no reason to try to make things worse," she said. "What are you going to do?"

He shrugged and said, "I'm leaving. Your husband threatened to have me expelled. I don't know if he can do it—"

"He can. Elihu and the president of the college are old friends. The man will do anything Elihu asks of him."

"I thought as much. I suppose I'll move on. Perhaps try to attend a different school or find something else to do with my life."

She surprised him by suddenly gripping his left arm with both hands.

"Take me with you," she begged.

Bellamy could only stare at her in amazement and disbelief.

"Have you lost your mind?" he finally demanded when he found his voice again. "After what you've done?"

"Don't doom me to this stifling existence, please,

darling! If I have to stay here and pretend to be happily married to Elihu, I truly will go mad!"

Bellamy shook his head. "That's no concern of mine. You should have thought of that before you married him."

"Bellamy, I beg you—"

She stopped short and looked over his shoulder, clearly surprised by what she saw. Bellamy heard the clopping of hoofbeats and the rattle of wheels and turned to see a fancy coach pulling up in front of the boardinghouse, a vision of highly polished hardwood and gleaming gilt trim. The four black horses in the team hitched to it were magnificent animals, prime examples of horseflesh.

The coach's driver wrapped the lines around the brake lever, vaulted down from the box, and stepped quickly to the door. When he opened it, a short, stocky, well-dressed man wearing a beaver hat climbed out.

Three more men followed him out of the coach. They were well-dressed, too, but taller and heavier, powerfully built with close-cropped dark beards on rugged faces.

"Oh, no," Edith breathed behind Bellamy. "That's Linus Atherton."

Bellamy swallowed. "Melville's father?"

"That's right. I've seen him at college functions. And those men with him . . ."

Bellamy didn't need her to go on. He knew perfectly well who Linus Atherton's companions were.

They were the men the banker from Boston had hired to beat him within an inch of his life, if not closer.

Chapter 9

Linus Atherton stalked toward the porch with a scowl on his bulldog face.

"Are you Bellamy Buckland?" he demanded. "I was told I could find you here."

For a second, Bellamy considered lying, but then he discarded the idea. In all probability, Atherton would have been told what he looked like. The banker had to be confident already that he had found the man he was looking for.

"I'm Buckland," Bellamy admitted. Behind him, he heard Edith edging away. Whatever was about to happen, she wouldn't want to have anything to do with it.

"Do you know who I am?" Atherton asked heavily.

None of the men who had followed him up the walk had spoken a word yet. Bellamy had a hunch they didn't talk much.

They would have other talents.

"I don't believe we've ever met," Bellamy said, keeping his tone casual, although it took some effort. "I've been informed, however, that you're Linus Atherton."

The man grunted. "That's right. You know my son."

"Indeed I do."

Atherton gestured vaguely at Bellamy and said, "He's responsible for the condition you're in."

The statement took Bellamy a little by surprise. He would have supposed that Atherton believed his son was a perfect little angel who could do no wrong. Most rich men were blind to their children's imperfections. Bellamy had seen plenty of evidence of that in his own life.

"I had some trouble with Melville, yes," he allowed cautiously. So far, this conversation wasn't going exactly the way he'd expected it to.

"He claims you cheated him at cards."

"You've spoken to him?"

"That's right. I received word in the middle of the night that he'd been injured. The college sent a fast rider with the news. I left Boston before first light this morning. A short time ago, I was able to visit briefly with him in the college's infirmary. He was rather groggy from the sedative he'd been given, but he was able to tell me what happened last night."

"For what it's worth," Bellamy said, "your son was mistaken in his accusation. I never cheated him at cards or anything else. I'm simply a superior player."

Atherton waved a hand and said, "Oh, I don't doubt that for a minute. The boy's an idiot. A fathead so full of himself that it's a wonder he doesn't burst."

Now Bellamy really was shocked. Evidently, Linus Atherton had a fairly clear-eyed and accurate opinion of his son.

"But that doesn't change anything," Atherton went

on, bursting Bellamy's fleeting bubble of hope that the banker would be reasonable. "He's still my son, and he's been badly injured. I'll be transporting him to Boston shortly, where he can receive better medical care, but I'm confident the physician here is correct in his diagnosis: Melville will never father any children or, perhaps, even function properly as a man again."

"Believe me, Mr. Atherton, I'm sorry about that," Bellamy said. He wasn't lying; he was sorry things had gone as far as they had, although he felt no actual sympathy for Melville. "You have to understand the situation I was facing. Your son and his friends were about to unjustly inflict a great deal of pain and suffering on me."

Arching a bushy eyebrow, Atherton said dryly, "I can see by your physical condition that they were successful in their effort."

"Well, yes. I was outnumbered six to one. There wasn't much I could do to stop them."

"They didn't give you that beating until after you'd ruined Melville for life, though."

"I was trying to fight back any way I could," Bellamy said with a note of desperation in his voice. "I tried to convince Melville that I hadn't cheated him, but he wouldn't listen."

Atherton shook his head. "No, the boy never does."

"I lashed out at him, I admit that. I was trying to break free and escape—"

"You were trying to punish Melville as much as he and his friends were about to punish you," the banker broke in. "Do you know how I know that?"

Bellamy didn't answer, assuming the question was a rhetorical one.

It was. Atherton went on, "I know that because I would have done the same thing, Mr. Buckland. You don't get anywhere in this world by giving up hope and admitting defeat." He clenched a fist. "You fight, even though in the end you may be vanquished anyway. You fight because sometimes, you win. It may be rare, but sometimes you win."

Bellamy took a deep breath and nodded. "I'm in agreement with you there, sir."

"I'm not surprised. I can sense that you and I have some things in common, young man. Perhaps more than my own son and I do." Atherton shrugged. "Which makes me regret this even more, but I have no choice. If I don't do something about what's happened, the lad's mother will never have anything to do with me again." He shook his head. "In some ways, that's a not unpleasant prospect, but when she gets her dander up, she can make my life a living hell."

He turned his head and nodded to the three black-suited men with him.

"Don't kill him, boys, but as close as you can come to that prohibition without breaking it, go ahead."

Once again, Bellamy devoutly wished that he had hung on to that pistol.

CHAPTER 10

St. Louis

A barrel full of what appeared to be flour toppled off a wagon passing by and crashed into the street, raising a cloud of white dust.

That noise jolted Bellamy out of the memories that had played in vivid detail inside his head during the past few minutes.

He was just as glad that he'd returned to the present. He had no desire to relive the beating he'd endured at the hands of Linus Atherton's hired ruffians.

He'd had no place to run. When he had whirled around and made a dive for the rooming house's front door, he found it locked. Edith Stockard had retreated into the house, and he didn't doubt that she was the one who had locked it, the traitorous witch. She'd been angry with him over his refusal to run away with her, he supposed, and she had taken out that anger by making it impossible for him to flee Atherton's men.

Not that it was likely he would have gotten away. They were on him in an instant, demonstrating amazing speed for such large, bulky individuals. They had dragged him down off the porch and into the small yard in front of the boardinghouse.

Surprisingly, this thrashing hadn't hurt as much as the one the night before. Maybe he was growing accustomed to being in agony, Bellamy had thought at the time.

After they had gotten through punching and kicking him, the men had climbed back into the coach with Linus Atherton, and off they went to collect Melville and take him back to Boston.

Bellamy had crawled over to one of the trees in the yard, used a feeble grip on the rough bark to help pull himself up, and then sat with his back propped against it.

At some point, he'd heard the boardinghouse's front door open and had lifted his head to see Mrs. Courlander, his landlady, set his valise out on the porch.

When she realized he was looking at her, she just shook her head sadly and solemnly, and Bellamy knew he was done here. He wouldn't be permitted to so much as set foot in the house again.He was expecting nothing less. He had been exiled from St. Ruthven's College and the town of Albemarle.

After an unknowable time, he had struggled to his feet, limped over to the porch, picked up his valise, and walked away without looking back.

For the most part, the months since then were a blur. Since he didn't have a horse, he had begged a ride from a farmer bound for Manchester with a wagonload of produce.

The taciturn New Englander hadn't asked a bunch of

questions about how he'd come to be so bloody and bruised, and Bellamy had been grateful for that.

Once in the city, he had gotten a job scrubbing mugs and glasses and sweeping out at a pub. His injuries healed, and one night he had asked if he could play in a poker game going on at the pub.

The other players had laughed at him as he stood there still wearing the canvas apron from his job. They had called him a scullery maid, but they'd waved him into a chair.

That proved to be a mistake for them. Before the night was over, he had a modest stake.

Since they weren't nearly as good as they thought they were, he could have won even more without much effort, but he had learned his lesson. Cleaning up at a poker table drew attention, and attention drew anger, and anger caused punches and kicks to rain down on him.

Even though it went against his normally extravagant nature and rankled him quite a bit, it was safer to win little by little and build up that stake gradually, which was what he did over the next few weeks.

When he had enough money to afford it, he moved on to Boston and repeated the process. From there it was New York, and then Philadelphia. At each step, he was better dressed and had acquired more in the way of clothes and other belongings.

For some reason, without him ever thinking about it at length, his steps tended westward. He had no destination, only an unsettled feeling that never allowed him to stay too long in any one place.

Perhaps he was destined for the life of a wanderer.

Along the way, there were card games and women—sometimes married but always beautiful—and a few scrapes from which he'd been forced to beat a hasty retreat. He never let himself be cornered again, because he had realized one undeniable truth:

If he was ever surrounded by enemies again, he would fight to the death. He would make them kill him rather than submit to another merciless beating.

He had learned that lesson from Linus Atherton: even facing almost certain defeat, always *fight*.

With that sentiment echoing dimly in his head, he now found himself wandering into a riverfront tavern called the Green Duck. It was a pretty squalid place, but Bellamy staked himself out a position at a table in a rear corner and told a serving wench to bring him a beer, and to keep them coming.

He took a deck of cards out of the possibles pouch at his waist and began toying with them.

Within half an hour, he had a game going.

The day passed pleasantly as the other players came and went and the cards flew back and forth on the table. Bellamy won some, lost some, and slowly built up a nice pile of coins in front of him. He flirted quite a bit with the serving wench who brought drinks and food to the table. She was a buxom redhead who looked like she would make an agreeable companion for the night, once he was done playing.

As evening came on, another man joined the game.

He sat down across the table from Bellamy and gave him a curt nod.

"Howdy. All right to get in this game?"

"All are welcome, my friend, as long as they have the wherewithal to pursue the end they desire."

The stranger frowned. "You mean I can play as long as I got the money to ante up?"

"Exactly."

"Then why the hell don't you say so?" The man slapped a gold piece on the table in front of him. "That oughta keep me goin' for a while."

"Indeed it will," Bellamy agreed. The deal was his at the moment. He began passing out the cards.

The stranger had come in with several other men, but while he had looked around, spotted the game going on, and come directly to the table in the back, his companions had ambled over to the bar. They ordered drinks and engaged in boisterous laughter and conversation. They were all bearded and dressed in rough frontier fashion.

That same description applied to the man who had joined the card game, except that he didn't sport a beard. His only facial hair was a dark mustache that drooped over thin lips below a prominent, hawklike nose. His unshaven chin receded a bit.

Bellamy had found that many men possessed of that particular physical trait weren't overly bright, but he judged that wasn't the case here. The stranger's weak chin didn't denote a lack of mental acuity. On the contrary, a sharp, penetrating intelligence was visible in the man's dark eyes.

Bellamy saw something else in the man's gaze, too. Cruelty, perhaps. Ruthlessness, to be sure. He was not a man it would be wise to cross.

The two revolving pistols he wore tucked behind a leather belt were further evidence of that. The wooden grips of the weapons showed signs of considerable use.

The stranger folded fairly early the first couple of hands he played. After throwing in his cards the second time, he said, "Reckon if I'm gonna play cards with you boys, I ought to introduce myself. Name's Knox. Zadicus Knox."

Bellamy had never heard the name Zadicus before, but it seemed to fit the man. He nodded and said, "It's a pleasure to meet you, Mr. Knox. My name is Bellamy Buckland."

Knox grinned. "That's a mouthful, ain't it? Got any other handle I can call you by, friend?"

That question made some bitter memories resurface—memories of being taunted by Melville Atherton and his friends simply because he had mentioned his background.

No point in clinging to that bitterness, Bellamy told himself. Those days were long months and thousands of miles away. Why not embrace what they had intended as an insult?

"Some people call me Duke," he told Zadicus Knox.

"Duke," Knox repeated. "Duke Buckland. I like that. Sounds like a proper man's name." He nodded. "From now on, you're Duke."

Bellamy thought it was unlikely he would ever see Knox again after tonight, but if the man wanted to call him Duke, what could it hurt?

He nodded and said, "That's fine."

The other four players at the table introduced themselves. A couple of them were rivermen, and the other two struck Bellamy as being either clerks or none-too-successful businessmen. He didn't care about their names.

Play continued. Zadicus Knox won a few small hands, but that was enough to eat into the pile of coins in front of Bellamy. He told himself to start paying more attention to the game. Knox was a smart, worthy opponent, as Bellamy had sensed instinctively from the first.

As the evening wore on, the other players at the table had less and less luck. The game evolved into a competition primarily between Bellamy and Knox.

That was often the way these things developed, Bellamy knew, but he wasn't particularly happy about it. Rivalries built up that way, and so did hurt feelings. Someone with enough competitiveness in their makeup could easily get angry if they lost in the end.

That anger could lead to violence, as it had with Melville Atherton and on other occasions Bellamy had witnessed.

He didn't want that with a man like Zadicus Knox, who looked like he would gut an enemy without blinking an eye. Judging by the scowl on his face as the game progressed, Knox might be building up to do just that.

It bothered him, but Bellamy began losing a few hands he should have won. In that way, he fed enough money back to Knox that the man's scowl turned back into an arrogant, self-satisfied grin.

Bellamy still won enough to do a little better than

break even for the day, though. He could be satisfied with that for now.

A more suitable victim would come along later. They always did.

"You got plans, Duke?" Knox asked a while later. One of the other players had the deal and was shuffling, and the question sounded like an idle one.

"I try not to make too many plans," Bellamy answered just as casually. "I've found that life has a way of following its own path, no matter how much we try to guide it."

"That's sure enough true." Knox picked up the mug of beer beside his pile of winnings and guzzled down what was left in it before setting it back on the table with a thump. He used a big, bony hand to wipe away the flecks of foam that clung to his mustache.

"I've found that short-term plans are the ones with the best chance of succeeding," Bellamy went on. He smiled. "For example, I plan to win this next hand."

Knox laughed. "Oh, you do, do you? I reckon the rest of us might have somethin' to say about that!"

"Of course. But there's more chance of that immediate goal coming about than there is of me making an elaborate plan for tomorrow and having it all come true."

"True enough, I suppose," Knox said with a slow nod. "But if you don't never give any thought to the future, you wind up just bein' carried along like a twig a-bobbin' on a river. You might get throwed around and turned any whichaway."

This was a surprisingly profound discussion to be having with an unlettered ruffian in a sordid riverfront tavern, Bellamy thought. He said, "You know what you're going to be doing in the future, Zadicus?"

He figured they were on good enough terms now for him to use the other man's given name.

Knox lifted a hand and tapped his forefinger against his temple where his hat was pushed back.

"You're damned right I have. I got a plan. Mind you, it may not work out. That's hard to say. But I know what I'm goin' after and how I'm gonna do it." He paused and gave Bellamy a shrewd look. "You want in on it?"

That was what he'd been angling for in this conversation, Bellamy thought.

"I appreciate that invitation, I truly do. But I believe I'll have to decline your kind offer."

"You sure about that?"

"I am. I'm content, for the time being, and look forward to where life will see fit to transport me next."

Knox's forehead creased. "Where you from, anyway? You don't talk like a born and raised American."

"That's because I'm not," Bellamy said. "I'm actually from a place called—"

The crash of the door being thrown open interrupted him. Several men charged into the tavern. The one in the lead yelled, "Zadicus Knox!"

He leveled the pistol in his hand at Knox's back.

Chapter 11

Knox reacted instantly to the threat. He threw himself out of the chair and dived to the floor.

The man with the gun pulled the trigger. The weapon boomed, the report deafening in the close confines of the tavern, as it spewed thick gray smoke.

The heavy lead ball passed through the space where Knox had been a split second earlier and slammed into the table, scattering cards and coins as it sprayed splinters in the air.

Traveling at a downward angle, the ball punched through the table and narrowly missed Bellamy's hip before striking the floor behind him. Without pausing to think about what he was doing, he allowed his reflexes to take over. His right hand dipped quickly to the sash at his waist and drew out the flintlock pistol tucked away there.

He cocked the pistol as he leveled it and squeezed the trigger. The roar of the shot and the echoes from it added to the sudden chaos in the room as men shouted curses and questions and scrambled for cover.

Through the haze of powder smoke in the air, Bellamy

saw the man who'd tried to kill Zadicus Knox knocked backward by the ball that struck him in the right shoulder. He half turned and stumbled as he cried out in pain, dropped his pistol, and clapped his other hand to the wound, which was already welling blood.

He fell clumsily to the floor, but the other men with him crowded forward around him, equally bent on reaching Knox. Some of them were brandishing pistols, too.

They must not have noticed Knox's friends standing at the bar, or else hadn't been aware that Knox was accompanied by anyone. With angry cries, Knox's allies plowed into the newcomers from the side.

As Bellamy shoved himself to his feet, he saw lantern light reflect from knife blades. Men screamed as cold steel drove into their flesh.

This brawl was going to get very bloody, very quickly, Bellamy knew. Even though he had gotten himself involved by firing that shot, he wanted no more part of whatever violence was going on. He just wanted to get out of here.

He shoved the empty pistol behind his sash and reached down to scoop a handful of coins from the table. He figured he wouldn't get the exact amount of his winnings, but a little less, a little more, it didn't matter.

It was more important to put the Green Duck behind him as quickly as possible.

When he had first come in, he had taken note of a door at the end of the bar. He made a habit of studying his surroundings wherever he was, just in case he needed an escape route on short notice. That caution had saved his hide and perhaps even his life several times.

Now he dashed toward the door, not knowing where it led but certain that he couldn't reach the tavern's front door through the melee going on. With any luck, there would be a back exit somewhere he could use.

Someone ran into him from the side. The collision staggered him for a moment, but a strong hand clamped on his arm and kept him from falling.

"Sorry," Zadicus Knox said as he kept his grip on Bellamy's arm and tugged him along. "Looks like you and me got the same idea, Duke."

The redheaded serving wench Bellamy had flirted with earlier ran to the door at the end of the bar and threw it open.

"Through the storeroom!" she told them. "There's a door into the alley!"

That was welcome news. Bellamy and Knox couldn't go through the door at the same time. When Knox released his arm, Bellamy hung back a step to let the other man go first.

He knew that otherwise Knox would run into him again and they might get jammed up there. Bellamy didn't want that.

More gunshots crashed behind them as Bellamy charged through the door after Knox. The battle was really getting serious now.

They found themselves in an unlit storeroom. Crates were stacked around. Enough light spilled through the open doorway from the main room for Bellamy to see where he was going, but the shadows were thick.

Knox paused at a door on the other side of the room. A heavy wooden beam sat in brackets barring the door on the inside. Knox fumbled with the beam, finally lifted it free of the brackets, and heaved it aside. He grabbed the latch and jerked the door open.

Knox disappeared into the darkness of the alley with Bellamy right behind him. He heard Knox's hurried footsteps slapping the hard-packed dirt to his left and headed in the same direction.

If any obstacles were lurking in the darkness, maybe Knox would trip over them first and warn him, Bellamy thought.

He heard more footsteps pattering closely behind him and glanced over his shoulder, but he couldn't see anything in this stygian gloom.

All he could do was keep moving and hope whoever was following him wouldn't shoot him or sink a knife in his back.

Light appeared ahead, a faint glow that told Bellamy they were nearing the end of the alley. A silhouette loomed against the light. That would be Zadicus Knox. He stopped just before the shadows ended and stood there dragging in deep breaths. Bellamy caught up to him.

"That you, Duke?" The low-voiced question came from Knox. "Who the hell—"

Bellamy came to a stop, and so did whoever was following him. He turned and gripped the butt of the pistol that was still loaded.

"Who's there?" he asked in a whisper.

"Don't worry, it's just me." A throaty laugh followed the declaration. "Amelia."

The redhead who had helped them escape! Bellamy was surprised, but he couldn't say he was disappointed she had come with them.

"What are you doin' here, gal?" Knox asked. "You hadn't ought to be runnin' around with a couple of desperate characters like Duke and me."

"I wanted to make sure you got away," she said. "I don't have any use for Constable Macklin." A hurt anger crept into her voice. "He uses his position to bully the tavern keepers and take advantage of the girls who work for them."

Bellamy caught his breath at her words, almost as if he'd been punched.

"Wait a minute," he said as his eyes widened in shock and dread. "One of those men was a constable?"

"That's right," the girl called Amelia said. "The one you shot, in fact. And the other men who came in with him all work for Macklin."

"I, I, you mean to say that I—"

Zadicus Knox laughed and said, "That's right, Duke, you done plugged a lawman—and I reckon that makes you just as big an outlaw as me and my partners!"

Chapter 12

Bellamy's mind reeled. He had done a number of things in the past that could have gotten him in trouble with the law. Linus Atherton certainly could have pressed charges against him for assaulting Melville.

But he had never done anything as serious as shooting an officer of the law. Judging by what Amelia had said, this Constable Macklin was rather corrupt, but that likely wouldn't matter to the authorities.

Bellamy had shot the man, and for that, he could go to prison. No doubt he *would* go to prison if he were arrested and brought to trial.

Amelia pointed and said, "You boys go along the street here and turn left just past that buggy shop. Take the next alley on the right, and it'll bring you to the river. With any luck, you can find some skiff along that stretch and row across to Illinois. Once you're there, Missouri law can't touch you."

"We're obliged to you, gal," Knox said. "Reckon you could do one more thing for us?"

"What's that?"

"You saw the fellas who came into the Green Duck with me this evenin'?"

"Sure. They've been with you before."

"Any of 'em who come through that fracas with whole skins, you tell 'em to meet me an' Duke on the other side of the river tomorrow. We got a reg'lar meeting place over there. They'll know where."

"I can do that," Amelia said.

Bellamy had followed the hurried, hushed conversation between the other two only vaguely, but Knox's last comment had caught his attention.

"Wait a minute," he said. "I'm fleeing to Illinois with you?"

"Only if you don't want to wind up behind bars." Knox shook his head but sounded more amused than rueful as he added, "Shootin' a lawman, that'll get you in a whole heap of trouble, Duke."

Bellamy bit back a frustrated curse. All he'd wanted to do was play cards, build up his stake a little more, and drift along to whatever life had in store for him next.

Instead, fate had played one of its usual tricks and made him a fugitive. He might have done more than just wound that constable. The man might have bled to death from the injury.

In which case, the gallows would be waiting for Bellamy if he was caught.

"All right, let's get out of here," he said. He didn't see that he had any other choice. "Thank you for your help, Amelia."

"Come back and see me the next time you're in St. Louis," she urged.

"I'm not sure I'll ever be coming back here."

"Oh, this little stink will blow over," she assured him. "Nobody really likes Macklin, not even the men who work for him."

Bellamy had a feeling that wouldn't make much difference in the long run, but he didn't argue with her. His eyes had adjusted to the darkness in the alley enough that he could make out the shape of her. He leaned in, kissed her on the cheek, and said, "Thank you again."

"Oh, go on with you!" she said. He could tell by the sound of her voice that she was blushing, which was probably uncommon for a young woman who worked as a serving wench in a tavern. She wouldn't receive much kind or thoughtful attention in those circumstances. When she did, she couldn't help but respond to it.

"Come on," Knox growled. "You can kiss her some other time, if there is another time."

"Goodbye," Bellamy said. He slipped out of the alley and trotted along the street behind the tall, rangy figure of Zadicus Knox.

They followed Amelia's directions and reached the river with no trouble. It was early enough in the evening that people were still moving around on the streets, but no one tried to stop them.

The moon hadn't risen yet, but the stars were out and provided enough light for Bellamy and Knox to see the small wharves that lined this section of the Mississippi. The steamboats were tied up about a quarter of a mile to their right. Up here were the smaller skiffs Amelia had mentioned, as well as keelboats that transported cargo up and down the river.

"This one will do," Knox said as he stepped into one of the boats. It was about fifteen feet long, with three benches and a couple of sets of oars. "Come on, Duke."

Bellamy supposed that stealing a boat wouldn't get him in much more trouble than he was already in. He was about to step aboard when a man yelled, "Hey! What the hell are you doing?"

He looked around to see a shadowy figure running toward them. It might be the boat's owner, or maybe just someone who thought they looked suspicious.

Bellamy heard a noise from behind him, and the man hurrying toward them suddenly stopped, staggered, and collapsed.

"Get my knife," Knox said.

Bellamy realized that what he'd heard had been Knox throwing a knife at the man accosting them. The man was lying on the ground now, twitching and jerking his legs.

"Get my knife, I said," Knox repeated.

Bellamy wanted to groan in despair, but instead he hurried over to the man and bent to feel around for the knife. His fingers brushed the hilt. The man let out a rattling breath and then was still.

Bellamy felt sick but swallowed that, too. He wrapped his fingers around the knife's bone handle and tugged. The blade came free of the dead man's flesh with a sucking sound.

"Come on, come on," Knox urged. He sounded impatient but not the least bit bothered that he had just killed a man.

Not that he had any right to feel superior, Bellamy reminded himself. He had, at the very least, badly wounded a man earlier this evening, and a representative of the law, at that. There was a good chance he had killed the constable.

It occurred to him to wonder why Macklin had burst into the Green Duck with several deputies, obviously intending to take Knox into custody, but Macklin hadn't hesitated to shoot, either.

Knox had referred to himself as an outlaw, and clearly, he was.

Bellamy couldn't afford to worry about such things right now. He hurried back to the boat, stepped aboard, and held out the knife to Knox.

"Use it to cut the rope," Knox ordered.

Bellamy did as he was told. From the looks of things, for better or worse, he was now a member of Zadicus Knox's gang.

What was the old saying?

Might as well be hung for a sheep as a lamb.

It seemed like he might be about to find out if that was true or not, he thought as he sat down, took hold of the second set of oars, and joined Knox in rowing out onto the smooth, dark surface of the Mississippi River.

Chapter 13

The next morning, Bellamy and Knox were well hidden in a grove of trees on the eastern side of the great river, about a mile upstream from Illinoistown, the village across the Mississippi from St. Louis.

Knox assured Bellamy that they would be safe here. He pointed out the remains of a fire and explained that he and his friends had camped here before.

"Missouri law can't do a damn thing on this side of the river, Duke," he said as he sat leaning against a tree trunk and smoking a pipe. "Also, I reckon that little red-headed gal was right. Nobody over there is gonna break his back lookin' for you just 'cause you shot Macklin."

He puffed on the pipe a couple of times and then took it out of his mouth to point the stem at Bellamy.

"Now, don't get me wrong, if you was to show up in St. Louis right now and they could grab you without havin' to go to too much trouble, they'd sure do it. Some judge'd be happy to throw you in jail or sentence you to hang, dependin' on what kind of mood he's in and whether or not you killed ol' Macklin. Some folks have got it in their heads that law an' order is a good thing, even though that notion seems plumb loco to me."

Bellamy was leaning against another tree, exhausted, thirsty, hungry, and utterly depressed.

"You're saying I can't ever go there again."

"I'm sayin' I wouldn't, if I was you, just to be safe."

"Amelia said the trouble would blow over."

"Would you want to take that chance, knowin' it's your freedom—or your neck—that's at stake?"

"Well, no, I probably wouldn't," Bellamy answered honestly.

Knox grinned. "Lucky for you, you don't have to."

"What do you think I should do instead?"

"Why, you oughta throw in with me and my bunch, of course! We can always use another good man, especially with this deal we got comin' up. Also, I don't know how many of my boys might've got theirselves killed in that ruckus last night, or tossed behind bars when it was over. We might be shorthanded, and I'd just as soon not be, considerin' what I've got in mind."

He might as well indulge his curiosity, Bellamy decided. What else did he have to do right now, with everything that had gone wrong?

"What is this great plan you have in mind?" he asked.

Knox puffed on the pipe for a few moments so that a cloud of gray smoke wreathed his head.

Then he said, "Have you ever heard tell of a fella named Preacher?"

Bellamy frowned. "What sort of preacher? What denomination?"

"Not *a* preacher. That's his name. That's what ever'-body calls him. Just Preacher."

"No, I've never heard of the gentleman," Bellamy said, shaking his head. "Are you saying he's not a minister?"

That brought another laugh from Knox. "Not hardly! He's a mountain man. A fur trapper. And accordin' to the stories, he can outshoot and outfight any man on the frontier." Knox paused. "Except me, o' course. Preacher's been lucky until now. He's never run up against Zadicus Knox."

The man was certainly full of himself, as well as being a walking contradiction where Bellamy was concerned. The trouble in the Green Duck wouldn't have broken out if Knox hadn't been there, and Bellamy never would have shot Constable Macklin.

On the other hand, he wouldn't be here in Illinois, safe from the law for the moment, if not for Knox. Bellamy couldn't bring himself to feel grateful to the outlaw, but he was willing to keep an open mind.

He was also interested in what Knox was saying. He commented, "It seems rather odd to call the man Preacher if he's a fur trapper."

"The whole thing goes back to when he was captured by a bunch o' Blackfoot warriors," Knox said. He leaned forward as if warming to his subject. "Preacher and them Blackfeet hated each other, you see. A mighty powerful hatred. I don't rightly know how it got started, but accordin' to the stories I've heard, they been at war for a long time. It ain't no surprise that when they got their filthy redskin hands on him, they figured on burnin' him at the stake. They planned on dancin' around and enjoyin' theirselves while he roasted to a crisp."

"He must have escaped, if he's still around."

"Yeah, they had him tied to a stake and was gonna light the fire come sunup. But along durin' the night, Preacher had hisself an idea. He started preachin' at them Injuns, you know, yellin' and exhortin' and callin' down hellfire an' brimstone on 'em. They must've thought that was plumb amusin' at first, but he didn't stop. The sun come up, and he just kept a-goin'."

"They didn't set him on fire because he was preaching at them?" Bellamy asked, getting caught up in the story in spite of himself.

Knox shook his head. "That's right. Because, you see, Injuns are scared right outta their skin by crazy folks. They believe that a fella who's lost his mind has been touched by the spirits, and they don't want to anger those spirits. By mornin', they were startin' to worry that maybe Preacher was crazy, and when he kept it up all day and on into the night, they was sure of it. After so long a time, they just gave up and let him go."

Knox shook his head and added, "They probably wished they hadn't, 'cause he killed a whole heap of 'em after that and still does whenever he comes across any of 'em."

"And that's why he's called Preacher?"

"Yep. The story got around, and the name stuck. I don't have no earthly idea what his name was before that. I'm sure he had one, but I don't recollect ever hearin' it."

"It's a good story," Bellamy admitted. "Whether it's true or not."

Knox scowled at him and demanded, "Are you callin' me a liar?"

"Not at all," Bellamy answered quickly. "I'm sure that's the way you've heard the story. It's just that tales like that sometimes get exaggerated."

"Not when it comes to Preacher. If anything, the yarns folks spin don't do him justice." Knox puffed on the pipe again. "But like I said, he ain't ever run up against me. Things are gonna change after he does."

"You mean this plan of yours has something to do with Preacher?"

"He's in St. Louis," Knox said. "I heard talk yesterday that he was lookin' to recruit men to go along on a trip out to the Beartooth Mountains. Accordin' to the rumors, Preacher's been hired by some European fella to take him out there and look for somethin'."

That statement immediately sharpened Bellamy's interest. He sat up straighter.

"Do you happen to know where in Europe this fellow hails from?"

"Nope," Knox replied. "Nobody I talked to said a thing about that. But there's one thing I do know. The varmint's got to be rich. Ever'body in Europe is."

"I don't know that you can go so far as to say that," Bellamy responded.

"Maybe not, but this fella, whoever he is, has enough money to hire Preacher, and a fella who puts as much stock in bein' a lone wolf as Preacher's supposed to don't come cheap. Not only that, but if he can afford to hire half a dozen more good men to come along, plus furnish all the horses and the supplies it'll take for a trip like that, he's got to have plenty of money. There just ain't no gettin' around it."

Bellamy nodded and said, "You're thinking about seeing if he'll hire you and your friends?"

"Hire us?" Knox tipped his head back and let out a braying laugh. "Hire us, hell! We're gonna follow that bunch and let 'em get a good ways away from St. Louis. When the time's right, we'll kill Preacher and ever'-body else, grab that rich fella, and hold him for ransom! If his family ain't willin' to pay to get him back whole, hell, we'll just send him back one piece at a time."

That shocking pronouncement made Bellamy stare at his companion. He couldn't find any words to say.

Knox didn't have that problem. He went on, "You throw in with us and you'll get a share of the payoff, too, Duke. You never know, you might wind up bein' as rich as one o' them real dukes before this is over."

He raised his head abruptly, peered through the trees, and got to his feet, brushing off the seat of his trousers as he did so.

"Here come the rest o' the boys. You got to make up your mind, Duke. Are you one of us or not?"

Bellamy wasn't sure, but he thought he sensed a threat behind the question. Now that Zadicus Knox had revealed what he was planning to do, if Bellamy refused to join the gang Knox might decide to kill him just to make sure he didn't tell anyone about it. Bellamy wouldn't put such ruthless behavior past the outlaw leader at all.

Going along with Knox would put him even farther beyond the reach of the law, Bellamy reasoned. And just because he agreed to join Knox's gang now, that didn't mean he would have to continue the association in the future. He wouldn't have to take part in the mass murder and kidnapping Knox planned to carry out. When he got a chance, he could slip off and go his own way again.

Of course, that would leave this so-called Preacher and his companions at the mercy of a ruthless outlaw and his equally bloodthirsty followers, but Bellamy didn't know Preacher or any of the others. He couldn't be expected to look after everybody else in the world, especially when his own hide was at stake.

"Well, what's it gonna be?" Knox prodded as Bellamy heard hoofbeats approaching along the river.

He managed to smile as he said, "I can't tell you how much I appreciate that kind offer, Zadicus. I'll be happy and honored to join you and your merry band."

That got him an odd look.

"I ain't quite sure what you mean by that," Knox said, "but it don't matter." He came over and slapped Bellamy on the back. "You're one of us now, Duke!"

Chapter 14

Preacher had spent the day before visiting Red Mike's and other taverns where he was well known, putting out the word that he was looking to hire good, trustworthy men for a trip west.

He didn't provide any more details than that. He was hoping he'd be acquainted with all the men he recruited and his name would be enough to prompt the right sort to seek him out.

He could share where they were going and what they'd be looking for once the deal was set up.

By that evening, he had talked to more than a dozen men and settled on five of them. He told them to meet him at the Hotel Lamont, where he planned to introduce them to Geoffrey Fitzwarren.

Fitzwarren arranged to have dinner with the group in a private dining room. It wasn't overly fancy, Fitzwarren told Preacher, but when the mountain man walked in and looked around, he saw a polished floor, burgundy curtains on the windows, a snowy white cloth on the table, and four wall sconces holding oil lamps that cast a warm light over the room and reflected off the silver and china on the table.

The place looked downright luxurious to him. Of course, he wasn't used to living in castles like Fitzwarren was.

The two of them were waiting there when the first of the recruits arrived. He was a big man in buckskins, taller even than Preacher but lanky and rawboned, with a rugged face topped by a thatch of rumpled, reddish-brown hair.

"This here's Dennis Burke," Preacher said to Fitzwarren. "We've knowed each other a few years. Dennis, meet Geoffrey Fitzwarren. He's the fella we're gonna be workin' for."

Burke took off his hat and held it in his left hand while he used his right to shake with Fitzwarren.

"Pleased to meet you, Mr. Fitzwarren," he said. "Preacher says you're all right, and any fella Preacher vouches for is mighty fine with me."

Fitzwarren smiled and said, "I certainly hope to live up to that endorsement."

Burke had barely arrived before two more men showed up. Fitzwarren's eyebrows rose in surprise as he saw that they were twins, medium-sized men with close-cropped dark beards and bushy eyebrows.

"Meet Lee and Horace Thorpe," Preacher told Fitzwarren. "We trapped one of the high valleys in the Tetons together four years ago. Boys, this here is Mr. Geoffrey Fitzwarren." Something occurred to him and he glanced over at Fitzwarren. "'Mister's' all right, ain't it? I hadn't ought to be callin' you 'Earl' or 'Baron' or some such?"

Fitzwarren laughed. "Not at all. Mister is fine. Although I'm not one to stand on ceremony, gentlemen." He shook hands with the Thorpe brothers. "After we all get to know each other, I'd be pleased to have you call me Geoffrey."

"Good to meet you," one of the brothers responded.

"Likewise," the other added.

The next man to arrive was one whom Preacher hadn't met before today, but he had picked the hombre over some others he was acquainted with. Instead of sporting buckskins, he wore tight brown trousers with gold embroidery down the sides, a red silk shirt, and a short, tight black jacket. He took off a flat-crowned black hat as he entered the private dining room.

"Salvador Perez," Preacher said, "meet Geoffrey Fitzwarren."

"A Spaniard?" Fitzwarren said.

"I am from Mexico, señor," Perez said.

"I wasn't aware that there were Mexicans living in this region."

Preacher saw Perez stiffen slightly and said, "There are plenty of folks from Mexico livin' on this side of the border. Most of 'em are further south, but you can find 'em almost anywhere. I recollect one time when I was with a bunch trappin' up along the Canadian border, there was a fella from Sonora who didn't savvy nothin' but Mex and another fella who'd come down from Canada and didn't speak nothin' but French. They got along just fine, and become good friends, in fact."

"Would you prefer that I do not join your party, Señor Fitzwarren?" asked Perez.

"Good heavens, I have no objection to you joining us, sir," Fitzwarren answered without hesitation. "I was a bit surprised, that's all." He extended his hand. "If Preacher believes you'll be a good addition to our group, I'm all in favor of the idea, I assure you."

Perez didn't respond immediately, but before the moment could turn awkward, he clasped Fitzwarren's hand and said, "Gracias, señor."

Preacher put in, "The fella who runs the livery stable tells me Señor Perez is a mighty fine hand with horses. I figured we could use somebody like that."

"Indeed," Fitzwarren said with a firm nod. "Welcome to the group, sir."

That just left one man who hadn't shown up, and he rolled in a few minutes later.

That was a good description of his arrival, because he seemed almost as wide as he was tall, with a large belly under his homespun shirt and thighs like the trunks of young trees in wool trousers. A big grin wreathed his moonlike face.

"Howdy, Preacher!" he greeted the mountain man in a deep, booming voice.

"Howdy, Eugene," Preacher said. He waved a hand toward the newcomer and told Fitzwarren, "This is Eugene Kelleher, the best camp cook you're likely to find west of the Mississippi."

"And I got plenty o' evidence to back that up!" Kelleher said with a laugh as he thumped the flat of his hand against his protruding belly.

"Don't let his looks fool you, though," Preacher added. "He can fight like a cornered badger when he has to."

"Perhaps we'll be fortunate and you won't have to do battle with anyone," Fitzwarren said as he extended his hand to Kelleher.

The man gripped it with fingers as thick as sausages and said, "You don't mean that, do you, boss?"

Fitzwarren looked puzzled.

"Why, I thought I did," he said. "Is there something wrong with hoping for a peaceful journey with no trouble?"

"Nothin' wrong with hopin'," Kelleher said, "but the chances of it happenin' are slim to none. We're gonna be travelin' with Preacher! That ugly galoot attracts more trouble than a barrel o' molasses draws flies!"

"Dadgummit, who you callin' ugly?" Preacher demanded.

Fitzwarren gave him a look, lifted one eyebrow, and said, "I notice you're not denying Mr. Kelleher's claim that trouble follows you."

"I don't deny nothin'. But I'm still here, and that ought to say somethin'."

"Indeed it does, and I hope it bodes well for all of us." Fitzwarren faced the group and went on, "Sit down, gentlemen. We'll have a fine meal, and then Preacher and I will tell you what this journey is all about."

The meal was a good one, with plenty of fried chicken, thick slices of ham, greens, biscuits, gravy, and apple pie, all washed down with several gallons of strong black coffee.

"Not bad," Eugene Kelleher allowed, "but once we're out on the trail, you boys'll see that I can do better."

"Don't want to see it," Horace Thorpe said.

"Yeah, food don't help anybody if all you do is look at it," his brother Lee added.

"You'll eat it," Kelleher predicted. "Better stock up good on provisions, Preacher, because these fellas are gonna be puttin' away a heap of grub."

Dennis Burke drawled, "Where we're goin', there'll be plenty of game, too. Just make sure there's enough coffee in our packs. You can't go out of a mornin' and shoot a bag of coffee beans."

"And how do you know where we're goin'?" Horace asked. "Preacher ain't said yet."

Burke shrugged. "He said we'd be headin' west. Ain't no place out there where the game ain't plentiful."

"Ah, but you are wrong about that, amigo," Salvador Perez said. "Go far enough west and there is a great desert where nothing lives except snakes and lizards. I have seen it. It is a valley of death."

"I've seen it, too," Preacher said, "and that ain't where we're headed." He glanced at Fitzwarren and went on, "We're goin' to the Beartooth Mountains. Any of you been there before?"

"I have," Burke said. "But it's been a while."

As it turned out, he and Preacher were the only ones who had done any trapping in the Beartooths. None of the others had ever laid eyes on those mountains.

"How come they call 'em the Beartooths?" Horace wanted to know.

"You ever seen a bear's teeth?" Preacher asked.

"Well, not close up, I reckon. And I'm almighty thankful for that."

"I have seen 'em, a lot closer than I'd like, and a couple of the peaks in the Beartooths stick up so sharp-like that they look like teeth."

"Occam's razor," Fitzwarren said.

The others turned their heads to look at him in complete bafflement—except for Preacher.

The mountain man nodded and said, "That's right. You're talkin' about the idea that the simplest answer to any question stands the best chance of bein' true."

It was Fitzwarren's turn to look confused.

"No offense, Preacher, but I wouldn't expect you to be familiar with the concepts of a fourteenth-century philosopher."

"Ol' William of Ockham." Preacher nodded solemnly. "Yep. Smart fella." He maintained that casual pose for another moment before he had to laugh. "I've spent a heap of time up in the high country with a fella named Audie who used to be a college professor before he gave up that life to become a mountain man. He can sit by a campfire and recite Shakespeare and Marlowe and all them old English scribblers for hours, and he talked a mite about them philosophizers, too. That's how come I know about Occam's razor. I might not have ever had much schoolin', but bein' around Audie is an education in its own self."

"This fellow sounds quite interesting. Is he, perchance, in St. Louis?"

"Nope, he and his pard, a Crow warrior called Nighthawk, are up north of here a good ways, doin' some trappin'. If they were in these parts, I would've asked 'em to come along with us. You can bet that little hat with the feather on that."

Dennis Burke spoke up, saying, "So we're goin' to the Beartooths. Now how about tellin' us why."

The others nodded in agreement.

"We're lookin' for a man named Barrett Treadway," Preacher said. "Any of you happen to know him, or at least heard tell of him?"

"I have not been in St. Louis very long," Perez said. "I'm afraid I knew very few people here."

Dennis Burke and the Thorpe brothers shook their heads, but Eugene Kelleher said, "I remember the fella. Came through here, what, a little more'n a year ago?"

Preacher looked at Fitzwarren, who nodded and said, "That agrees with what I've been able to find out, yes."

"Do you recall anything else about him, Eugene?" asked Preacher. "Was he travelin' with anybody?"

Kelleher frowned in thought as he pondered that and searched his memory. He shook his head and said, "I don't think so. I don't remember him spendin' time with anybody in particular."

"Did you speak with him?" Fitzwarren asked.

Kelleher shrugged. "Passed the time o' day with him once in a tavern. Drank a couple o' beers whilst we were talkin'. That's all." The man's round face lit up suddenly. He pointed a finger at Preacher and went on,

"You're right, he said he'd heard about a valley out in the Beartooths where the trappin' was supposed to be good. He talked like he was plannin' to head that direction and check it out."

"That's good," Preacher said. "We know we're on the right track, anyway."

"What is it about Treadway that's so important?" Lee Thorpe wanted to know.

Fitzwarren cleared his throat. "At one point he was traveling with a cousin of mine. I'd very much like to know what happened and where my cousin is now."

Preacher noticed that Fitzwarren didn't say anything about his cousin being a young woman. If he wanted to be cautious and play his cards close to the vest, that was his business, Preacher supposed. He would respect Fitzwarren's discretion, at least for now.

"Like I said, he was by himself when I saw him," Kelleher went on with a shrug. "But he could've been plannin' to meet somebody. There's no way I would've known unless he said somethin' about it."

"I understand," Fitzwarren said with a nod. "I appreciate you sharing what you do know, Mr. Kelleher."

Burke said, "So we're lookin' for Treadway, but the one we're really after is your cousin, right, Mr. Fitzwarren?"

"That is correct."

"The fella must be important to you."

"Well, there are few things in this world more important than family."

Mutters of agreement came from around the table.

Fitzwarren got to his feet and picked up his coffee cup.

"This isn't fine whiskey or wine, gentlemen, but I'd like to propose a toast anyway." He held out the cup. "To the success of our quest!"

The other men rose and echoed the toast. "To success!"

"And to comin' back with whole skins," Eugene Kelleher added.

"I'll drink to that," Preacher said.

Chapter 15

Preacher had made all the arrangements for their departure, so when the men rendezvoused at Patterson's Livery before sunup the next morning, they found a wagon fully loaded with supplies waiting for them.

A team of four sturdy draft horses was hitched to the wagon. In addition to their saddle mounts, the men were taking along eight extra horses and a couple of pack mules in case they had to abandon the wagon at some point. The horses from the team could be used as pack animals, too, if need be, or ridden if circumstances warranted.

Preacher asked Salvador Perez to handle the wagon. The Mexican nodded and said, "Of course, señor." He tied his horse to the back of the wagon, then climbed agilely on the box and took up the reins.

The others were all mounted, including Geoffrey Fitzwarren. Preacher had suggested that he could ride on the wagon, too, but Fitzwarren had insisted that he preferred to be on horseback.

"I was riding after the foxes at an early age, you know," he commented.

Preacher nodded. "Yeah, I've heard about them fox hunts. No offense, but they never seemed quite sportin' to me."

"I suppose from the point of view of the fox, they're not."

Now, as Preacher looked around at the men in the gray predawn light, he asked, "Everybody ready to go?"

He got nods and declarations of agreement all around. Turning Horse so that he was in the lead, he called out, "Let's roll!" The group left the livery stable and moved along the street with Dog bounding out ahead.

Leaving this early, they didn't draw much attention, which was just the way Preacher wanted it. While he had told Geoffrey Fitzwarren that outlaws and Indians would be less likely to attack a well-armed party of this size, that didn't entirely rule out the possibility. There were plenty of ruffians in St. Louis who might be greedy enough to follow them and try to steal their supplies and horses.

They would be in enough danger once they reached the mountains. He didn't want to tempt fate on the first part of their journey.

Later that morning, an hour after sunrise, Bellamy Buckland stood on the eastern side of the river and watched nervously as half a dozen men on horseback approached him and Zadicus Knox.

"Damn it," Knox said. "I don't see Jim Collins or

Ed Stuart. They must've got theirselves killed or else thrown in jail over that fracas at the Green Duck."

The riders reined in and swung down from their saddles. Bellamy had never seen a rougher, more dangerous-looking bunch in his life. A couple of them cast suspicious glances at him and looked like they would be happy to cut his throat just on general principle.

"Howdy, boys," Knox greeted them. He jerked his head toward Bellamy and added, "Meet Duke Buckland. He's ridin' with us now."

One of the men who appeared the most hostile toward Bellamy said, "Wait a minute. Ain't he the one who plugged Macklin and caused all hell to break loose?"

"He didn't shoot Macklin until Macklin tried to kill me," Knox snapped. "I don't know about you, Hanley, but when a fella sticks up for me, I stick up for him."

The outlaw called Hanley shrugged. "Hell, I don't care, Zadicus. I was just curious, that's all."

"Where are Jim and Ed?"

"Ed wasn't fast enough when the rest of us made our break outta there," Hanley replied. "The law grabbed him. Last I saw, they were puttin' the boots to him. There's a good chance they stomped him to death. As for Jim, he's dead for sure. He wound up bein' cut bad in the fight, and he was leakin' blood so bad, it looked like he'd already lost half of what he had in him."

Knox shook his head and heaved a sigh. "I sure hate to hear that. They were good boys. Fit to ride the river with, that's for sure. How about the rest of you? Anybody hurt bad?"

"Scrapes and bruises, that's all."

Mutters of agreement with Hanley's statement came from the other men.

"I reckon that redheaded trollop told you fellas to meet me over here like I asked her to?" Knox asked.

"Yeah, but we would've rendezvoused here anyway. We knew you'd want to get across the river and away from Missouri law."

One of the other men asked, "What are we gonna do now, Zadicus?"

"Same as we talked about yesterday," Knox declared without hesitation. "Nothin's changed except we lost a couple o' men, and we got one back in Duke here. We're still goin' after Preacher and that rich fella who hired him."

"Speakin' of Preacher," Hanley said, "I figured you might want somebody keepin' an eye on him, so early this mornin', a couple of us went down to that livery stable where he was talkin' to the owner yesterday. We were watchin' from an alley across the street when Preacher showed up with a bunch of other men. The liveryman had a wagon loaded with supplies and some extra horses and pack mules waitin' for 'em."

Knox smacked his right fist into his left palm and said, "I knew it! I knew they were gettin' ready for a trip o' some sort and would be outfitted proper-like. Preacher ain't the kind to do anything halfway."

"The whole bunch pulled out before dawn, headin' upriver," Hanley reported.

"How many of 'em?"

"Seven altogether. Preacher, that fancy-dressed fella he's workin' for, and five more men."

"You know any of 'em?"

Hanley shook his head. "No, I didn't, but they looked plenty tough. Just the sort of hombres you'd expect to throw in with Preacher."

"We're pretty damned tough, too," Knox said, "and there's eight of us. We've got 'em outnumbered!"

"Only by one," Hanley pointed out. He gave Bellamy a meaningful, unfriendly stare. "And we don't know if we can count on that one."

The man's attitude was starting to grate on Bellamy despite his own uncertainty about joining up with this group of brigands. He said in a sharp tone, "You can count on me, and if you have your doubts, sir, you can feel free to try me out and see if I can take care of myself."

"Hold on here," Knox said quickly. "We don't want trouble amongst our own selves. We're all on the same side."

"I ain't convinced of that," Hanley said as his eyes narrowed in anger. "All I've seen of this fella so far is a hothead who gunned down a lawman. We don't know if he can handle trouble, let alone back any play the rest of us make."

"As I said," Bellamy told him coolly, "feel free to determine that for yourself."

One part of his brain was yelling furious imprecations at the other part. It was true that life in this country had toughened him up considerably, and he certainly found himself in more than one physical altercation since coming to the United States.

He had survived all those scrapes. In fact, he had emerged victorious in them except for the two occasions when he had been either vastly outnumbered or in too battered a condition to defend himself properly.

Now he was healthy and in good shape, and although Knox's gang was far superior in numbers, he had a hunch that Hanley would tackle him alone if it came to blows. The man seemed far too proud to enlist the aid of his fellows.

A snarl twisted Hanley's lips as he glanced at Knox and asked, "What about it, Zadicus? You're the one who's adopted this cub. You want me to just ignore the disrespectful way he's talkin' to me?"

Knox sighed. "No, I reckon you can't do that. I wouldn't want you to. If you did, you wouldn't be the sort o' fella I want ridin' with me." He paused. "But the same's true of Duke here. He's stickin' up for hisself, and I can't complain about that."

Hanley nodded and said, "Well, then—"

He didn't get any farther than that, because he launched himself at Bellamy without any warning, clearly intending to strike first in this battle and try to end it with one blow.

Chapter 16

Unfortunately for the outlaw, Bellamy halfway expected such a treacherous move and was ready for it. He twisted to the side and swayed back out of the way of the sledgehammer blow Hanley tried to bring down on the top of his head.

Missing so badly threw Hanley off-balance and caused him to stumble forward a couple of steps. Bellamy grabbed the man's left arm, stuck his foot between Hanley's calves, and heaved.

Momentum, along with Bellamy's assistance, made Hanley plow face-first into the ground.

He was wide open and helpless, and for a second, Bellamy considered kicking him in the side. He might break a rib or two and end this fight.

But that wouldn't be an honorable thing to do, and he didn't want to incapacitate one of the gang members. He wasn't sure how well Zadicus Knox would react to that.

He moved back instead, fists clenched, bouncing lightly on his feet as he waited for Hanley to get up.

That didn't take long. Sputtering and spitting because

of the dirt and grass in his mouth, Hanley pushed himself onto his hands and knees and then surged all the way up to his feet, turning with an incoherent roar to charge at Bellamy again.

Bellamy danced out of reach of the groping arms, knowing that if he allowed Hanley to get hold of him, the outlaw might crush the life out of him. He brought both fists up in the classic fisticuffs stance and darted in to pepper a swift combination to Hanley's face. The punches landed solidly and rocked the outlaw's head back.

At that moment, Bellamy could have kicked Hanley in the groin, as he had kicked Melville Atherton months earlier. But that hadn't worked out too well for him then, and he sensed it might not now. Hanley's friends might not consider that a fair move and decide to involve themselves in this fight.

He backed off again and waited to see what Hanley would do next.

Blood was leaking from Hanley's nose. He dragged the back of his right hand across it and winced at the pain. He growled as he looked at the crimson smear on his hand.

"That fancy fightin' won't get you anything out on the frontier where we're goin'," he said.

"I don't know about that, Hanley," called another outlaw. "So far it's got you a bloody nose!"

Several men joined in the laughter at that gibe. Hanley's face turned brick red with rage. He came at Bellamy again like a maddened bull.

For the first time, though, Hanley showed signs of fighting more intelligently. His apparently out-of-control charge was a feint, Bellamy discovered when he tried to duck out of the way again.

This time he ran right into a fist that Hanley brought around in a looping blow. It caught Bellamy on the jaw, and before he knew what was happening, he was sailing backward, feet in the air, to come crashing down on his back.

His head spun and the hard landing knocked the breath out of him, but his senses still worked well enough to realize that Hanley was barreling at him again, and this time the outlaw wasn't going to turn aside.

He was going to trample Bellamy like a runaway horse.

Bellamy forced his muscles to work. He jerked both knees up and bent his legs. When he straightened them, the heels of both boots sank into Hanley's midsection.

Once again, Hanley's momentum worked against him. With a massive effort, Bellamy brought his legs up and back and levered Hanley right over him. Hanley yelled in alarm as he flew through the air, his arms and legs flailing wildly but uselessly.

Bellamy heard a heavy thump as he rolled onto his side and struggled to get some air back into his lungs. Throwing Hanley over him like that had taken every bit of strength he had left. The next time Hanley came at him, he wouldn't be able to stop the man from doing whatever he wanted to.

Fortunately, that wasn't going to happen. Bellamy lifted his head when he realized the other outlaws, who had been hooting and hollering and shouting encouragement to their friend, had suddenly gone silent.

Bellamy saw Hanley sprawled motionless on the ground near a thick-trunked tree. Had he struck his head against that tree and knocked himself out? Or worse?

Hanley groaned. Bellamy closed his eyes for a second, grateful the man wasn't dead, anyway.

Zadicus Knox slapped a hand against his thigh and let out another of those donkey brays of laughter.

"Don't worry, boys," he told the other men. "Ol' Hanley managed to hit the hardest part of him against that durned tree—his head!"

Knox came to Bellamy's side, reached down to grasp his arm, and lifted him to his feet. He slammed an open hand against Bellamy's back between the shoulder blades, almost knocking him down again.

"That was one hell of a fight!" Knox went on. "You sure proved what you said, Duke. Nobody's gonna doubt now that you can take care o' yourself."

Bellamy had recovered enough of his breath to say, "I would really prefer . . . not to have to fight . . . my friends."

"Don't worry about that. Nobody's gonna bother you now." Knox looked at the others. "Ain't that right, boys?"

One of the outlaws loosed a whoop of agreement that was soon echoed by the others. Most of them were grinning now. Bellamy sensed that his defeat of Hanley meant the rest of the gang would accept him now as one of them.

He was a member of a bloodthirsty outlaw band about to set out on the trail of a legendary mountain man, intent on a spree of robbery, murder, and kidnapping.

He forced himself to return the grins as he tried to tell himself that things could be worse.

Chapter 17

Preacher, Geoffrey Fitzwarren, and their companions rode north along the Mississippi River until they came to the place where the Missouri River flowed into the Father of Waters from the west.

From there, they would follow the Missouri as it turned northward, but when they reached the area where Preacher could spot some familiar landmarks, they would leave the river and head almost directly westward.

At that point, they would be some five to six weeks away from their destination, but only if nothing happened to delay them, such as bad weather, Indian attacks, or other hazards.

Preacher knew better than to expect that they would make it all the way to the Beartooth Mountains without running into any trouble, but as he glanced over his shoulder at the wagon and the riders strung out behind him, he had a hunch they would be able to handle most of the problems they might encounter.

Having the wagon along meant that they couldn't travel quite as fast as they would have without it, but Salvador Perez proved to be a skillful teamster and kept the horses moving at a good pace. He was also considerate of the animals and made sure his team got enough rest along the way. In the long run, that caution would save them time and trouble, Preacher knew.

The first few days of the journey, they covered upward of fifteen miles per day. Preacher was quite satisfied with that rate of progress.

After they had made camp the third evening out from St. Louis, he walked over to Geoffrey Fitzwarren and asked, "How are you holdin' up?"

He had noticed earlier when they all dismounted that Fitzwarren seemed to be walking around a bit gingerly.

With a rueful smile, Fitzwarren said, "I'm discovering beyond a doubt that spending an hour or so in the saddle for a fox hunt is a great deal different from riding for hours on end and covering dozens of miles in a day. I seem to be hurting in muscles I didn't even know I had."

"We ain't goin' dozens of miles in a day," Preacher pointed out. "We've been coverin' more than a dozen, but not all that much more."

"Really?" Fitzwarren's eyebrows rose in amazement. "I must say, the distances out here have seemed endless and the hours interminable." He chuckled. "Or even the other way around."

He grew more serious, stood straighter, and squared his shoulders.

"But no matter. I'm fine. Don't worry about me, Preacher. I won't slow us down or fall behind. I give you my word on that. And if we're successful in finding dear Charlotte, then all the aching muscles will be well worth it, won't they?"

"That's for you to determine, not me. But I admire a man with grit, Geoff, and you seem to have it."

"Thank you, Preacher," Fitzwarren said. "Coming from you, I appreciate that sentiment. I truly do."

They had been on the trail two more days when they sighted the first Indians they'd encountered. They had seen a few white pilgrims so far—fur trappers on the way west, more than likely—but they hadn't spoken to anyone except each other.

The men had been taking turns riding ahead of the main group to act as scouts. Today Dennis Burke was filling that role, and it was early afternoon when he came riding back to join the others in a hurry.

Preacher saw Burke coming when the man was still several hundred yards away. Burke topped one of the rolling hills that stretched alongside the river and vanished down the near slope almost instantly, which told Preacher that he was moving fast. Preacher reined Horse to a stop and held up a hand in a signal for the others to halt, as well.

Fitzwarren nudged his mount alongside Preacher's before stopping. He asked, "Is something wrong?"

"Burke's foggin' back our way, ridin' hellbent-for-leather."

"I assume that colorful phrase means that he's moving quickly?"

"He ain't wastin' any time, that's for durned sure. Out here on the frontier, when a man's movin' that fast it's usually because there's somethin'—or somebody—after him."

Fitzwarren's eyes widened. "Indians, do you think? Or outlaws?"

"Could be either one," Preacher said. "I been keepin' an eye on his back trail and I ain't seen anybody followin' him yet. But that don't mean they ain't there. The fact that they ain't callin' a heap of attention to theirselves makes me think it's more likely to be Injuns."

Burke appeared about five minutes later, finally slowing his lathered horse to a walk when he was about fifty yards from the halted group. He came on to join them and lifted a hand in greeting. Preacher thought his expression looked concerned but not panic-stricken.

"Find somethin' interestin' up there, Dennis?" the mountain man asked.

Burke nodded. "I spotted about a couple dozen Indians headed this way, movin' along the bluffs beside the river."

"That's big enough for a good-sized war party," Preacher said. "But they could just as easily be a huntin' party. Were you close enough to see if their faces were painted?"

"Couldn't tell for sure, but I don't think so."

"Likely they ain't lookin' for trouble, then."

"What are we going to do, Preacher?" Fitzwarren asked.

Preacher tugged on his right earlobe for a moment and then scraped his thumbnail along his jawline, rasping it over the thick beard stubble—habitual gestures he often displayed when he was deep in thought.

After several heartbeats had gone by, he declared, "They're between us and where we're goin'. Probably wouldn't do any good to try and skirt around 'em. We'll keep movin' and see what happens."

To Burke, he added, "Tell the others to keep their eyes open and their powder dry."

"You don't want me to go back to scoutin'?" asked Burke.

"No, we'll run into 'em soon enough if we're goin' to, and this country is open enough that we ought to see 'em comin' in plenty of time."

Burke nodded and rode back to join the rest of the group. Preacher turned to Fitzwarren and went on, "I want you to ride beside the wagon, Geoff. If there's trouble, you can take cover under it. Listen to Perez and do what he tells you."

"What are you going to do?" Fitzwarren wanted to know.

"I'll be up here in front, where if there's any trouble, I can meet it head on."

"Mightn't it be better if we all formed a tighter, more cohesive group?"

"Bunch up so that we make a smaller target?" Preacher shook his head. "Not a good idea."

"We might appear more impressive that way."

"Trust me, they probably know already how many of us there are."

Fitzwarren looked sharply at him and asked, "How would they know that unless they're already watching us?"

"I reckon you just answered your own question," Preacher drawled.

That made Fitzwarren look uneasy, but he dropped

back to ride alongside the wagon as Preacher had told him to do.

Preacher was a mite annoyed at Fitzwarren for questioning his orders and suggesting some other course of action when the mountain man had made it clear that he would be in complete command out here. He would have a discreet talk with Fitzwarren about that later on, Preacher decided.

That is, if that wasn't a war party looking for blood and scalps they were about to run into and they survived this day.

Chapter 18

Preacher felt eyes watching him from a distance just a couple of minutes later, but a good twenty minutes went by before he saw the Indians approaching.

They weren't getting in any hurry.

Even before they were close enough for him to see how they wore their hair and decorated their buckskins, Preacher could tell by how tall and straight they sat on their ponies that they were Osage.

The Osage towered over most of the other tribes out here and were fierce fighters, but they had gotten along reasonably well with the whites in recent years and Preacher was confident they wouldn't attack his party without good reason.

He had already called Dog back to pace alongside Horse. The big cur had spotted the Osage, too, and growled deep in his throat as the hair on the back of his neck rose.

"Take it easy, Dog," Preacher told him quietly. "They may be friendly. We're gonna give 'em the chance to show us one way or the other."

Both Dog and Horse had an almost supernatural ability to comprehend what Preacher said to them. Dog growled again, just to get the last word, so to speak, but the threatening sound was quieter and his hair eased down some.

Preacher kept riding until he had drawn within fifty yards of the Indians leading the approaching group. They hadn't shown any threatening signs so far. He reined in there to wait for them and made a signal to Perez to bring the wagon to a halt. The other men would follow suit.

Three of the Osage warriors moved ahead of the others, then one of that trio pressed even farther into the lead. The other two hung back a bit on his flanks.

Preacher figured that was the chief approaching him. He sat straight in the saddle, his gaze level and non-committal as he waited. He had his long-barreled flint-lock rifle resting horizontally in front of him where he could bring it into play quickly if he needed to.

The chief stopped twenty feet from Preacher, his two companions five feet farther back on either side. He was a tall, well-built man with his hair shaved to a prominent tuft on the top and back of his head. Buffalo grease kept it standing up, and natural dyes had turned it orange. An eagle feather was bound in it.

He wore buckskin leggings, but instead of a shirt, he had a blanket draped around his shoulders, leaving his broad chest bare. A war ax was tucked through a loop at his waist and he carried a lance in his left hand.

The other warriors in the party were armed with lances, axes, bows, and arrows. Preacher didn't spot any rifles among them. Many of the tribes had some firearms they had picked up through trade or conquest, but most preferred to use their traditional weapons as much as possible.

Preacher wasn't as fluent in the Osage tongue as he was in some of the other Indian languages, but he knew enough to get along and make himself understood. He lifted an open right hand in the universal symbol for peaceful intentions and said, "Greetings to the Osage, whose land this is."

"Greetings," the chief returned. "I am Falling Rock. Who are you, and what are you doing here?"

"I am called Preacher."

The mountain man spoke his name in English. Fitzwarren and the others would know he had just introduced himself.

He thought he saw a flicker of recognition in Falling Rock's dark eyes.

"Preacher is a name known to many," the Osage chief said. "But this is not the land where the man of that name is usually found."

"That's true," Preacher allowed. "My hunting grounds lie farther west and north of here. Yet I go where my destiny takes me, and today I am here."

"Do you mean to stay? Do you lead these men here to settle? To cut down trees to build lodges and rip up the ground to plant seeds?"

Preacher shook his head. "We wish only to travel through the land of the Osage, Chief Falling Rock. We are friendly and will cause no harm to your people or the land."

Falling Rock considered this and said, "Then there is

no reason why the Osage should be unhappy that you are here."

"None at all," Preacher agreed. "We would like to leave this land knowing that you and all the Osage are our friends."

The conversation was formal and respectful on both sides. Preacher knew that attitude stood the best chance of getting them through without any trouble.

"Wait," Falling Rock told him.

Preacher nodded. The chief turned his horse and held a low-voiced discussion with the two men who had accompanied him out here. They would be some of his senior warriors. Preacher couldn't make out any of the words, but he could tell that none of the men seemed excited or angry about anything.

After a few minutes, Falling Rock swung his pony back around and said to Preacher, "You are welcome in the land of the Osage. You and your friends may go peacefully on your way."

"Thank you, Chief." Since the Osage were inclined to be friendly, Preacher ventured a question. "We're looking for a white man named Barrett Treadway. He would have come through here about twelve moons ago, perhaps traveling by himself or perhaps with a young woman."

"Many white men travel through our land on the way to the mountains to trap beaver," Falling Rock answered. "Some are friendly and some are not."

"I don't think this man Treadway would have been looking for trouble." Preacher had gotten a description of Barrett Treadway from Fitzwarren, so he went on,

"He is a man a little shorter than me with fair hair and very blue eyes. And he has a depression in his chin, here."

Preacher laid a fingertip on his own chin where Fitzwarren had told him that Barrett Treadway had a distinctive dimple.

Falling Rock thought about it long and hard, taking his time and deliberating, as Indians were prone to do, before he finally nodded.

"I have seen a white man who looks like that," he said.

Preacher felt a surge of excitement. It would be quite a stroke of luck if they found a lead on Treadway's whereabouts so quickly, but such a thing certainly wasn't beyond the realm of possibility. For all its vast size, sometimes the frontier could seem like a small place.

"And was this about twelve moons ago?"

"It was," Falling Rock answered.

"Was he alone, or was the young woman with him?"

"He was not alone—"

Again Preacher felt his interest quicken.

"—but he was not with a young woman," Falling Rock continued. "There was another man with him."

Preacher's spirits fell slightly, but he asked, "Do you know the other man's name?"

"I do not know either man's name," Falling Rock replied. He was starting to sound a bit impatient. "All I know is that a man who looked like the one you asked about rode through the land of the Osage. He was dressed and equipped like a fur trapper, as was his companion. We watched them, but they did not stop and went on their way. That is all I know and all I can tell you."

"We're much obliged to you for your help," Preacher said with a nod, "and for your friendly welcome."

"Do you intend to follow this man all the way to the mountains?"

"If we have to. We have an idea where he was going."

"Good fortune to you and your companions."

Falling Rock lifted the rawhide reins attached to the crude hackamore on his pony's head. Preacher turned and waved for his companions to pull aside. Perez guided the wagon closer to the river, and the others followed.

The large party of Osage warriors rode past, regarding the white men with curious stares but not displaying any signs of hostility. Preacher didn't know where they were coming from or where they were going, and he hadn't asked. It would have been rude to do so.

Fitzwarren nudged his mount up beside Preacher and asked with an eager expression on his face, "Did you find out anything? I heard you mention Barrett Treadway's name."

"Falling Rock—that's the Osage chief I was talkin' to—says that a white man who looked like the description o' Treadway you gave me came through these parts about a year ago."

"Really? That's splendid! What about Charlotte?"

Preacher shook his head. "Treadway had a travelin' companion, but it wasn't a gal. He had some other fur trapper ridin' with him. More than likely some fella he met in St. Louis, I'd say, and they decided to throw in together."

"But no sign of my cousin?" Fitzwarren looked and sounded disappointed as he posed the question.

"I'm afraid not."

Fitzwarren thought about it for a moment and then said, "I suppose we can't even be sure that it was Tread-way the chief saw. It could have been just some fellow who resembled him. Unless he introduced himself?"

Preacher dashed that hope. "Nope. The chief didn't talk to him and didn't know anything about him except the way he looked."

The Osage were dwindling in the distance to the south now. Fitzwarren gazed after them and said, "I suppose it's better than nothing."

"They decided to be friendly and let us go on through their land in peace," Preacher pointed out. "I'd say that's a whole heap better than nothin'."

He didn't mention it to Fitzwarren, but he had a very strong hunch that not every encounter they had with Indians out here would turn out that way.

Chapter 19

Zadicus Knox's gang started to complain only a few days after leaving St. Louis.

Bellamy had learned from conversations with Knox and some of the other men that despite looking like hardened frontiersmen, they actually hadn't spent much time out here. They were from Ohio, Kentucky, and Tennessee and had started running together as a gang in the mountains of Tennessee, where Knox had been born and grew up.

With the law making things hot for them because of crimes they had committed, the men had drifted west, and during that journey, Knox had solidified his command of the group.

When they reached Memphis, they pulled off several robberies, but again with the law on their trail, they had been faced with the decision of going downriver to Natchez and eventually New Orleans or upriver to St. Louis.

They had gone north and continued their lawless ways around St. Louis and in the western reaches of

Illinois across the river, holding up travelers and raiding isolated settlements.

Bellamy had a feeling that they had killed several people while committing those crimes, but he didn't press them for details. He didn't want to know too much about his companions, since he still intended to leave the gang as soon as he got a good chance—though that determination had faded somewhat when he realized just how vast and untamed this land was. Staying with them might be a lot safer than setting out on his own, at least for now.

Knox was the restless sort and was always ready to move on and try for bigger payoffs. He was convinced that kidnapping and ransoming the man who had hired Preacher would provide just such a payoff.

The rest of the group appeared to support that idea, too, but they were anxious to get on with it, and the farther they got from civilization, the more their impatience grew.

"How long are we gonna follow these fellas, Zadicus?" Jennings asked as they rode beside the Missouri River a week after leaving St. Louis. "Don't you reckon we're far enough from town now to go ahead and jump them?"

"We're gettin' there," Knox said. He and Jennings were riding side by side at the head of the group. Bellamy was a few yards back, riding next to a massive, red-bearded man known only as Bull, no doubt because of his size. Hanley and the other men were scattered to both sides of them.

Knox went on, "As long as we can follow their tracks,

it doesn't matter how long we stay on their trail. We can make our move when the time's right."

"Yeah, but we're startin' to wonder if that time's ever gonna get here."

Bellamy saw the look Knox cast over at Jennings and thought that he wouldn't want to be in the man's boots right now. Knox didn't like having his authority challenged.

Bellamy was a little surprised Knox didn't reach over and knock Jennings out of the saddle. Instead, Knox glared and said, "We'll jump those fellas when I'm damned good and ready. What does it matter to you when we do it?"

They were talking loudly enough that the rest of the group could hear what they were saying. Hanley nudged his horse forward and said, "I'll tell you why it matters, Zadicus. The longer we stay out here and the farther from St. Louis we get, the bigger the chance some damn redskins will come along and jump us."

Knox snorted. "Have you seen any redskins?"

"No, but that don't mean they ain't out there, watchin' us and waitin' for a chance to lift our hair," Hanley said, obviously unwilling to back down.

Knox turned in his saddle to glower at Hanley and then called, "Bull, come up here!"

The red-bearded giant kneed his mount forward. Because of his size, the horse he rode had to be large and sturdy. He glanced over his shoulder and rumbled, "Come with me, Duke."

Bull had sort of adopted Bellamy during the time they'd been out here. Bellamy had no idea why the big man felt that way. They had absolutely nothing in common.

However, Bellamy figured that it wouldn't do any harm to have a large, powerful friend, and it might even be advantageous at times. He had smiled and listened to Bull's rambling stories about growing up in Tennessee. Evidently, he and Knox had known each other since childhood, although they hadn't been close friends.

Bull and Bellamy rode ahead to join Knox, who said, "Bull, you're the best tracker in the bunch. Have you come across any Indian sign?"

Knox's assessment of the big man's ability was correct. Despite Bull's hulking size and dull-witted personality, he had eyes like the proverbial hawk. He'd had no trouble following the tracks left by Preacher and the others, even though that group still had a considerable lead on them.

Bull shook his shaggy head in response to Knox's question and said, "Nope, Zadicus, I sure haven't. O' course, you got to remember I ain't ever been in these parts before. The Injuns they got around here could be a whole heap different than the ones we growed up around, back yonder in Tennessee. They was mostly Cherokee and Chickasaw, and they ain't all that different from white men."

Bellamy wondered if that statement was true. He didn't know all that much about the native people of this country. He hadn't had the opportunity to learn about their habits and way of life.

He might get that chance during this journey, he told

himself, but if he did, that wouldn't necessarily be a good thing.

"Injun sign is Injun sign," Knox snapped. "They don't shoe their horses, right?"

"Not usually, as far as I know."

"Well, have you seen any unshod horse tracks?"

"Nope," Bull said. "Nary a one."

"There you go," Knox said with a triumphant sneer aimed at Hanley. "There ain't no redskins in these parts, so you can stop worryin'."

That seemed like a pretty big conclusion to jump to, especially since it was based on nothing but what Bull had just said. You couldn't prove a negative, Bellamy remembered reading somewhere. The lack of unshod hoofprints didn't actually mean anything except that they hadn't seen any Indian sign yet. It didn't mean no Indians were around.

He knew that pointing this out to Knox would do absolutely no good and would just irritate the gang leader. That knowledge prompted him to keep his mouth shut instead.

Some of the men continued to grumble, but they were leery of getting on Knox's bad side and didn't openly challenge him. The gang moved ahead, still on the trail of their quarry.

The next trouble came a few days later, and surprisingly, Hanley wasn't the source of it.

The group had camped and spent the night in a clearing on a shallow bluff that overlooked the Missouri

River. A couple of hundred yards away, a trail led down to the river, so plenty of water was available, if not exactly handy.

While most of the men lingered over coffee after breakfast the next morning, a couple of them took the horses to the river to let them drink and also to fill the canteens. The conversation around the fire was desultory until an outlaw named Roscoe—Bellamy had no idea what his last name was, or if that was his last name—stood up, threw the dregs from his tin cup into the fire, and announced, "I'm goin' back to St. Louis."

"The hell with that," Knox responded as he looked up at Roscoe. "We didn't come all this way just to turn around and go back empty-handed."

"I didn't say any of y'all had to come with me. But I'm sick and tired of ridin' through mile after mile of empty country for no good reason."

Knox set his own cup aside and came to his feet.

"The ransom we'll get for that rich fella is plenty of good reason to be out here," he insisted.

"What ransom?" Roscoe shot back at him. "What rich fella? I ain't seen hide nor hair of either of those things." He gave a disgusted snort. "All we're really doin' is chasin' some pipe dream of yours, Knox."

Bellamy knew Knox couldn't allow this affront to pass, but even armed with that knowledge, he was surprised by Knox's sudden reaction.

The other men let out startled yells, too, when Knox dived across the fire, tackled Roscoe around the waist, and brought him crashing to the ground.

If Bellamy had been forced to guess, he might have

said that Knox would whip out a pistol and gun down Roscoe where he stood as punishment for defying him.

Knox must not have wanted to lose a man, even for such a grievous sin. But he didn't mind dealing out a beating to Roscoe. He brought his knee up into Roscoe's groin, causing the man to howl in pain.

That howl was cut short as Knox hammered a fist into Roscoe's mouth. Knox pushed himself up, straddled Roscoe's midsection, and punched him again and again, left and right, jerking Roscoe's head back and forth. Bellamy had to swallow a feeling of sick revulsion as he saw how bloody and swollen the man's face was becoming under the terrible punishment Knox was dealing out.

Knox had struck too swiftly, too savagely, for his victim to even attempt to defend himself. Roscoe was too stunned to do anything except lie there on the ground and take it.

After a dozen or more brutal blows, Knox paused in his assault. He reached to his waist and drew his hunting knife from its sheath. Grabbing Roscoe's right ear, he put the razor-sharp blade against the top of it.

Then, with a gleeful grin on his face, he turned his head to look at the rest of the gang and demanded, "Well, boys, what do you think? Reckon I ought to slice ol' Roscoe's ear clean off so he'll remember never to talk to me like that again?"

Stunned silence hung over the camp. None of the outlaws wanted to take a stand one way or the other.

Knox looked back at his victim.

"Hear that, Roscoe? The fellas ain't speakin' up for

you. I guess that means they want me to cut your ear off—"

"Wait," Bellamy said in a choked voice.

The others all stared at him. He could have assured them that he had been just as surprised by the word coming out of his mouth as they were.

"What's that, Duke? You got somethin' to say?"

Bellamy swallowed again. "We have only a one-man advantage over Preacher's group. I believe it would be wise not to throw away that advantage, slender though it may be."

"I didn't say I was gonna kill him. I just said I might cut his ear off."

"And then he might bleed to death. Even if he doesn't, such a major wound could easily become infected. He could get blood poisoning and die from that."

Knox cocked his head a little to the side. "You reckon?"

"It's possible. I think we should be prudent." Bellamy shrugged. "Besides, you've already beaten the hell out of him. I don't think he's likely to forget that anytime soon."

Knox laughed and said, "No, probably not. All right, Duke, what you say makes sense." He glared briefly at the others. "And you wasn't afraid to speak your mind, which I like in a fella."

That contention was patently untrue, as Roscoe's current condition testified, but Bellamy didn't point that out.

Knox took the knife away and let go of Roscoe's ear. He stood up and slid the blade back in its sheath.

"A couple of you fellas give him a hand," he said as

he gestured vaguely at the man he had just beaten so badly. "You can give him a little bit of whiskey, but no more'n half a cup."

They had brought along several jugs of whiskey, but one of Knox's strict rules was that the liquor was for medicinal purposes only. There would be time enough for celebrating after they had rounded up some more loot, he had declared.

To Bellamy's surprise, the men had gone along with that edict. Maybe they were just afraid to cross Knox, or maybe they realized it was actually a reasonable rule.

Hanley and Bull lifted Roscoe to his feet. He was conscious, but his legs wouldn't obey his brain's commands and flopped uselessly when he tried to walk. The two men had to half carry him to keep him upright. They led him over to the fire and lowered him into a sitting position near the flames, which were beginning to die down and soon would be just embers. Bull knelt beside him and kept one hand on a shoulder to make sure Roscoe didn't pitch forward into the fire.

Hanley said, "I'll get that whiskey for him as soon as Phillips and Earnshaw get back with the horses."

The jugs were in the packs, which were already loaded on the horses because the group would be breaking camp soon and getting back on the trail.

Knox hitched up his trousers, looked satisfied with himself for disposing of another challenge to his authority, and then studied his knuckles, which were scraped and bruised from battering Roscoe that way. He flexed his fingers.

Bellamy was sure Knox considered a little discomfort

a small price to pay for teaching not just Roscoe but the entire group a lesson.

After emptying the dregs from his own cup into the fire, Bellamy began gathering up his gear. He didn't have much and it didn't take long. He straightened from the task, his possibles bag slung over his shoulder, his rifle in one hand, and looked along the river toward the trail where Phillips and Earnshaw had taken the horses. He had heard something that caught his attention. It sounded like a man running.

Earnshaw burst into sight at the top of the trail and charged along the bluff toward the others, shouting a word that instantly made all of them jerk around toward him.

"Indians! Indians!"

Chapter 20

Any man who wasn't already holding a gun immediately grabbed one, except for Roscoe, who was still too muddled and in too much pain to be fully aware of what was going on.

The others, led by Zadicus Knox, ran to meet Earnshaw.

Knox stopped the panicky outlaw by grabbing his shoulders and jerking him to a halt.

"What the hell!" Knox said. "What are you yellin' about, Earnshaw?"

It seemed pretty obvious to Bellamy what had put Earnshaw in such a state. The man had been telling them all at the top of his lungs only a moment earlier.

"Indians!" Earnshaw said. "Phillips and me s-seen 'em just now, up the river!"

"How close are they?"

"I dunno." Earnshaw gulped and made a visible effort to bring his rampaging emotions under control. "They were still a ways off."

"Did they see the two of you and the horses?"

"I don't think so. As soon as we spotted 'em, we got

the horses back in some brush where it'd be harder to see 'em. Then Phillips stayed there to look after them whilst I come a-runnin' to fetch you boys."

Knox clamped his hands tighter on Earnshaw's shoulders and said, "Listen to me, damn it. How many of the redskins are there?"

Earnshaw was a small man with a round face, watery eyes, and gray beard stubble. He always reminded Bellamy of a rabbit. He swallowed hard again now and said, "There were two, I think. Yeah, two of the red varmints."

Knox stared at him for a couple of heartbeats and then said, "Two? All this fuss over two blasted Injuns?"

"But where there's two of 'em, there could be a whole bunch more, Zadicus," Earnshaw whined. "You know that."

"He's right," Hanley said. "They're like cockroaches."

Knox looked at him. "What do you do with cockroaches?"

Hanley seemed confused by the question, but he ventured, "Stomp them?"

"Damn right that's what you do. Stomp 'em. And that's what we're gonna do to those Injuns. Come on."

"Wait a minute. You mean to kill them?"

"They can't go back to their filthy little village and tell anybody about the bad ol' white men if they're dead, now can they?"

Bellamy wondered if he looked as shocked as he felt. Knox was talking about cold-blooded murder.

But he had already steeled himself to the likelihood

that all his companions were killers, so there was no reason for him to be surprised, he told himself.

However, the other members of the gang also looked hesitant following Knox's callous statement, and Bellamy hadn't expected that.

Knox must have seen the same unease on their faces as he looked around at his men. He said, "What the hell is the matter with you boys? You want a whole big war party comin' down on us?"

"But if we kill those redskins," Hanley said, "won't that just make the rest of their tribe come lookin' for us? And they'll want revenge, Zadicus."

"If those fellas disappear, then the rest of the varmints won't know what happened to 'em. They won't have any reason to suspect us."

"You're sayin' we need to kill 'em and then hide the bodies."

Knox rolled his eyes in exaggerated disgust. "Finally! Somebody who uses his head for somethin' else besides a place to hang his hat."

He looked around at the others and went on, "Hanley, Bull, Jennings, Duke, you boys come with me. Earnshaw, you stay here in camp and look after Roscoe."

"What's wrong with Roscoe?" asked Earnshaw.

That question put a grin back on Knox's face. "He's feelin' a mite under the weather right now. Don't you worry about it, just stay here like I told you. The rest of us will take care o' them Injuns."

Bellamy bit back a groan of dismay. He didn't want to be involved in this. He wished Knox hadn't picked him to come along.

But there was nothing he could do about it now without earning a reprisal of his own from the gang leader, and he didn't want to risk that.

He might have to go along with Knox and the others, but that didn't mean he had to kill anyone, he told himself. If any shooting took place, he could make sure he missed.

Leaving Earnshaw behind, Knox hustled the other men to the trail leading down to the river. Bellamy hung back, bringing up the rear. Someone had to be last in line, he reasoned, so it might as well be him.

The trail slanted down the face of the bluff overlooking the Missouri. It was wide enough for several men or a couple of horses, and the slope was an easy one. The outlaws reached the narrow bank alongside the river in a matter of moments.

Twenty yards upstream, the bank widened to about fifty feet. Brush and several cottonwood trees grew there, providing cover for Phillips and the gang's horses. Bellamy spotted the animals hidden in that concealment, but not until he and Knox and the others had drawn closer.

They made their way into the brush. Phillips greeted them by saying, "I'm sure glad to see you fellas. I was afraid those redskins might find me while I was down here by myself."

"Where are all these bloodthirsty Injuns that got you and Earnshaw so terrified?" asked Knox.

"Blast it, Zadicus, you'd be a mite worried, too, if you were afraid a war party was about to swoop down on you!"

"Earnshaw said there were only two of 'em."

Phillips made a face and then looked embarrassed.

"There's no tellin' how many more of them might be lurkin' around somewhere close by," he insisted.

"You still didn't tell me where they are," Knox said.

Phillips pointed upstream. "See that place where the bank bulges out some? They were up past that, maybe three hundred yards away. They were coming this direction, and after a while, I couldn't see 'em anymore because of the way the bank sticks out. But they were headed this way, that's for sure."

"Must not have been in a hurry," Knox said, "or else they would've been here by now."

"They were just sort of moseying along," Phillips allowed.

Bull said, "It's a huntin' party, more than likely, Zadicus. Maybe they'll turn around before they ever get here and head back where they came from. They might be doin' that already."

"Or they might not be. Lay low, boys. We'll wait a spell and see what happens. If those Injuns don't show up, we'll count ourselves lucky and be on about our business."

Knox didn't say anything about what would happen if the Indians didn't turn back, Bellamy noted, but he didn't want to think too much about that.

Knox, Bellamy, Hanley, and Bull crouched to kneel in the brush to watch the riverbank through gaps between the branches. Phillips and Jennings were with the horses farther back in the trees, doing their best to keep the animals quiet.

From time to time throughout the journey since they

had left St. Louis Bellamy had caught Hanley casting unfriendly glances in his direction. The man didn't try to start any trouble, but Bellamy knew Hanley probably held a grudge against him because of their previous clash.

He needed to have eyes in the back of his head, he warned himself, because if shooting broke out and Hanley got the chance to plant a bullet in Bellamy's back, Bellamy wouldn't put it past him. Not for a second.

They didn't have long to wait. Two figures appeared on the bank, walking leisurely beside the river. They had ruffs of hair sticking up at the backs of their heads and wore buckskin leggings and shirts. Quivers of arrows were slung on their backs, and each man carried a bow.

"They're just out huntin' like I figured," Bull whispered to Knox, keeping his voice down as much as he could. The words still came out of his powerful chest as a rumble. "And they ain't much more'n kids."

Bull was correct about that, Bellamy saw as the two Indians came closer. He doubted if either had reached the age of twenty yet. Of course, in their tribe, it was likely they were considered full-grown warriors, but actually, they weren't much younger than he was.

"If we stay where we are," Bellamy whispered to Knox, "perhaps they won't see us and they'll go on their way without noticing anything out of the ordinary."

Knox nodded slowly and replied, "Yeah, we could play it that way, all right."

The two young men were laughing and talking as

they ambled along the river. They were close enough now Bellamy could see that one of them had a couple of rabbit carcasses slung across his shoulder with their front legs tied together. They were out hunting, as Bull had said.

"Or we could do this," Zadicus Knox said.

He stood up without warning, revealing himself in the brush, and brought his rifle to his shoulder as the two young Indians exclaimed in surprise at the sight of him.

The next instant, before either of the Indians could move, Knox's rifle boomed. One of the warriors jerked back and fell, a fist-sized chunk of his head blown away by the ball from Knox's weapon.

Chapter 21

Even though Knox had made it clear earlier what he intended to do about the Indians, Bellamy was still shocked and horrified enough by the sudden violence that he couldn't do anything except kneel there in the brush and gape at the bloody scene along the river.

The second Indian was frozen in his tracks, too. He stood there staring down at the body of his friend for what seemed like seconds but in reality was only an eyeblink of time.

Knox was standing there in the open, ten yards away, with an unloaded rifle, and so far he had made no move to reload. The Indian could have drawn an arrow, nocked it on his bow, and sent the shaft flying at Knox.

Instead, when the young man finally snapped out of his shock, he turned and ran, bolting back along the riverbank the way he had come.

"Get him!" Knox ordered.

Hanley and Bull sprang to their feet. Bellamy was right behind them, but he hesitated to take action.

The other two men didn't. They brought their rifles to their shoulders and fired almost at the same time. The shots came so closely together that the roars of their reports blended into one.

Both rifle balls slammed into the fleeing Indian's back, throwing him forward in a wild, stumbling run. He veered toward the river, lost his balance, and pitched headlong into the water, landing with his moccasin-shod feet still resting on the muddy edge.

Bellamy saw the faintly pink tinge in the ripples flowing around the young man's body and knew the color came from blood.

Hanley and Bull lowered their rifles. "We got him!" Bull said.

"You sure did," Knox said. "That was good shootin', boys." He looked at Bellamy. "But you didn't even get a shot off, Duke."

Bellamy forced a smile onto his face and waved a hand at the other two men.

"I never got a chance to," he said. "These fellows were just too swift in their reaction and too accurate in their fire."

Hanley looked pleased with himself as he nodded and said, "Yeah, that was some pretty good shootin', wasn't it?"

"Before you get too full o' yourself, you'd best go make sure that Injun's good an' dead," Knox said.

"I'll do that," Bull offered.

He handed his rifle to Hanley, left the brush with a crackle of branches, and walked over to the river, pulling a pistol from the waistband of his trousers as he went. He reached down with his other hand, grasped the right ankle of the Indian lying in the water, and dragged him out onto the bank.

The man didn't move. From the way he'd been lying facedown at the edge of the river, with his head under the water, it was pretty obvious he was dead.

That didn't stop Bull from aiming the pistol at the back of the man's head and firing it. The heavy lead ball shattered the Indian's skull like a broken clay pot. Bull looked around at the others with a proud grin and asked, "Never hurts to be sure, does it, Zadicus?"

"It sure doesn't, Bull," Knox replied. "Drag both of those carcasses over here. We're gonna have to figure out a good spot to cache them and make sure the other redskins don't find 'em."

In the end, it was Bellamy who came up with a suitable resting place for the two dead Indians. While searching along the base of the bluff, he found a depression that had been hollowed out by previous floods. It was deep and long enough for Bull to stuff both corpses into it.

Bellamy didn't like the callous way the big man handled the bodies, but the Indians were beyond caring, he told himself. What mattered now was making sure their deaths didn't come back to haunt Knox's group and put them in danger.

All the men used their knives to hack at the bluff above the hiding place until a miniature avalanche took place. Rocks and dirt cascaded down, completely covering the hollow and its grisly contents.

"That ought to do it," Knox said as he took a step back and brushed his hands together. "It looks like the bluff just collapsed there from rain washin' it out. One of you boys fetch a broken branch and use it to wipe our tracks out."

By the time they were ready to leave, there was little sign of their ever having been here.

"The only thing I'm worried about," said Hanley, "is that some other redskins may have heard those shots and come to see what happened."

"If they do, they won't find those bodies."

"They might if they look hard enough."

Knox snorted. "And it might start rainin' buffalo, too. Damn, Hanley, you worry too much. If you're that spooked, maybe we'd best get on outta these parts."

"That's all right with me," Hanley said. "The sooner we put this business behind us, the better."

Bellamy couldn't argue with that statement. He wanted to put some distance between them and the dead Indians, too.

By now, Phillips and Jennings had taken the horses back up onto the bluff. The other men returned to the camp and found the animals ready to ride.

Earnshaw had given Roscoe some whiskey—apparently more than the cup that Knox had decreed. Roscoe was conscious and able to stand up but very unsteady on his feet as he tried to walk to his horse. Bull helped him get mounted.

Once he was on the horse's back, Roscoe clung to the saddle and leaned over to vomit. Knox frowned in apparent disgust but didn't say anything.

The group started north along the river with Bellamy bringing up the rear as usual. Roscoe hadn't said anything else about leaving the gang and going back to St. Louis. After what had happened to him, Bellamy didn't expect that subject to come up again.

No one said anything about the dead Indians, either.

Since he was the last one in the group, he saw the nervous glances the others threw over their shoulders. Even Knox was keeping an eye on their back trail just in case there was any pursuit. If more Indians were coming after them, they wanted to know about it as soon as possible.

They might not be talking about what they had done, but they hadn't forgotten about it.

Bellamy knew it was going to be a long time before he could put the incident out of his mind. The images of the two young men's deaths were still painfully vivid.

Nothing unusual happened that day. They made camp that night more than ten miles upriver from where the killings had taken place.

Bellamy supposed the guards posted around the camp were more alert than usual—he knew for sure that he was—but by morning, an air of relaxation had settled back over the group. Roscoe seemed more like himself, although he was very quiet and kept his eyes downcast most of the time.

Knox strutted around with a grin on his face and said, "I told you boys there was nothin' to worry about. We done the right thing by gettin' rid of those red heathens. The world won't never miss a couple o' worthless varmints like that."

No one argued with him. Bellamy kept his eyes on the campfire as he sipped the last of the coffee in his cup.

They broke camp and rode out. Knox and Bull were in the lead, with Bull keeping an eye on the tracks left by Preacher's group to make sure they didn't lose the trail.

The rest of the gang strung out behind, with Bellamy last in line. The others didn't seem as worried today and didn't spend as much time looking back, but Bellamy couldn't shake the uneasy feeling he had. He checked over his shoulder fairly often, and because of that, he was the first one to notice dust rising in the distance behind them.

Hanley was riding closest to him. Bellamy called to the man, "Hey, take a look back there."

With an annoyed expression on his face, Hanley swung his horse around.

"What the hell is it?" he asked.

Before Bellamy could answer, Hanley abruptly sat up straighter in the saddle as his eyes widened. Without saying anything else to Bellamy, he jerked his horse around to the front again and jabbed his boot heels into the animal's flanks. The horse's hooves pounded the ground as Hanley rode ahead quickly to join Knox and Bull.

"Zadicus!" Bellamy heard him exclaim. "Riders comin' up behind us!"

Knox reined in. They all did. Almost as if they'd practiced doing it at the same time, the men simultaneously turned their horses to peer back in the direction they had come from.

Bellamy had discovered it was difficult for him to judge distances out here, but he estimated that the grayish-brown dust cloud was a couple of miles behind them.

"Must be a lot of horses to be kickin' up that much dust," Bull said.

Knox grimaced and said, "Yeah, you're right. That's a good-sized bunch."

"And they're comin' this way," Hanley said. "Damn it, I'll bet it's a bunch of Injuns! They found the two we killed, and now they're comin' after us!"

"Settle down," snapped Knox. "We don't know nothin' of the sort. Hell, that could be anybody."

"Oh? Who else have we seen out here, Zadicus?"

Bellamy halfway expected Knox to react suddenly and violently to Hanley's insubordinate tone, but it appeared the situation might be too dire for that. Knox's jaw clenched in anger, but he controlled it.

"We better get out of here," Earnshaw whined.

"We're goin'," Knox said. "Come on."

He turned his horse north again and heeled the animal into a fast lope. The rest of the men followed.

It seemed unlikely to Bellamy that they would be able to outrun the pursuit. Indian ponies were said to be quite swift. It might be smarter for them to look for someplace they could fortify and fight off the Indians if it came to that.

He didn't know how well Knox would take to such a suggestion, but Bellamy decided he wasn't going to worry. His skin was at stake here, too, after all. He nudged his horse ahead a little faster to try to catch up to the gang's leader.

Before Bellamy could pull even with Knox, Bull yelled, "Look up yonder!"

The big man leveled an arm and pointed ahead of them. All the men reined their mounts to sliding stops at what they saw.

More dust was rising in front of them. The cloud wasn't as big as the one raised by the pursuers, but it was substantial enough to represent another good-sized force.

"Well, it looks like they got us caught between a rock and a hard place," Knox drawled. He was trying to sound casual, Bellamy thought, but the strain was evident in his voice anyway.

"More Indians?" Hanley said. "How the hell did they get in front of us?"

"I don't know, but we'd best not go chargin' straight into their faces." Knox stood up in his stirrups and looked left toward the open prairie and then right toward the Missouri River. "We might be able to make it across the river, but from what I've heard about the Missouri, the mud out there is mighty bad. We'd be liable to bog down and maybe even drown." He nodded. "I reckon we'd better head west."

"There's nothing that way to stop them from chasin' us," Hanley said.

"They're gonna chase us no matter which way we go. But when they catch us, we'll sure give those red devils a hot welcome!"

Chapter 22

The men rode hard, not sparing their horses now that they were trying to escape from the jaws of the deadly trap closing on them.

Bellamy wasn't sure how the group of Indians behind them had communicated with the ones coming down from the north, but they must have in order to catch the white men between them like this. He had heard talk about Indians using smoke signals and thought it must have been something like that.

Not that it mattered one little bit, he told himself. The only important thing was getting away from the savages who wanted to kill them.

He didn't accept for one second Knox's desperate suggestion that someone other than Indians was responsible for the dust clouds. Bellamy knew the truth in his gut, and so did the rest of the men.

The terrain here consisted of grassy, low-rolling plains with a few ranges of hills visible in the distance. The landscape looked flat but actually wasn't—it sloped up to shallow ridges and then dropped down into broad depressions. Clusters of low-lying brush sprouted here and there.

None of that provided any cover. They would have to reach the hills before their pursuers caught up to them if they were going to have any chance to fight off the Indians. Judging by the size of those dust clouds, once the two groups combined, the Indians were going to outnumber them by three or four to one, at the very least.

That merger was taking place behind them now, Bellamy saw as he looked over his shoulder. The two dust clouds came together as one, and that one moved toward them, gradually growing larger as the pursuers cut down on the lead Bellamy and his companions had.

"Zadicus, they're gonna catch up to us!" Earnshaw said. His eyes practically bulged out of their sockets with fear.

"Just keep ridin', damn it!" Knox replied. "When we get in them hills, we'll find a place to fort up. Once those savages get a taste o' hot lead, they'll turn tail and run, you can count on that!"

Bellamy didn't share that confidence. Knox might not mean it, either. His words had the distinct sound of a child whistling on his way past a graveyard.

Knox led the way toward the nearest hills. When it became obvious that the pack animals were slowing them down, he yelled, "Turn loose o' them horses!"

"We'll lose all our supplies!" Hanley protested.

"Better our supplies than our hair, blast it!"

Nobody could argue with them. Phillips and Jennings, who had been leading the pack horses, let go of their reins. The horses continued running after the saddle mounts, unwilling to leave their equine companions, but they were weighted down more and couldn't keep up. They began falling behind.

They might be able to recover some of the supplies later, Bellamy thought. The Indians were bound to be after vengeance and might not care about loot. That was a slim hope, but there was nothing wrong with clinging to it.

Every time he looked over his shoulder, the dust behind them was closer—so he stopped looking over his shoulder and concentrated on his riding instead. He knew good and well that if his horse were to step in a hole and go down, none of the others would stop for him. They would just keep going and leave him for the vengeful Indians.

The nearest hill was only half a mile away now. Bellamy saw the slope ascending in several terrace-like steps. There were no trees or rocks to provide shelter, but the hill itself would give them some cover if they could reach the top of it.

Knox waved them on and shouted, "Come on, come on!" When he got to the bottom of the hill, he put his horse up the slope in a lunging run. The others followed.

Bellamy couldn't resist the urge to look back. The Indians were close enough for him to see them now, which meant there was no longer any doubt about their identity. They sported the same ruffs of hair as the two young hunters had worn.

He turned his attention back to what he was doing. His heart slugged heavily in his chest. He didn't want his horse to fall now, this close to a place where they could make a stand. Knox reached the top of the hill and disappeared. Bull was right behind him, then Hanley, and Bellamy and the others boiled over the crest in a bunch. Bellamy hauled back on the reins to bring his horse to a stop.

Knox was already out of the saddle with his rifle in his hands. Hanley swung down, too, and jerked his rifle to his shoulder. Knox reached over, grabbed the barrel, and pushed it down before Hanley could fire.

"They're still too far off, damn it. You'd just be wastin' powder and shot." Knox raised his voice. "Earnshaw, you and Roscoe hold the horses. The rest of you boys get ready, but hold your fire until I give the word. We got to let 'em get closer 'fore we start the ball."

Bellamy dismounted and handed his horse's reins to Earnshaw. The rabbity little outlaw, along with Roscoe, gathered the horses and led them down the hill's far slope. Bellamy took a look in that direction and saw that the hillside fell away and then climbed again, forming another hill behind them. Some of the Indians could circle around and try to come at them that way, but the ground was rugged and it would be more difficult.

Even so, the possibility existed, and they would need to keep an eye out too.

Phillips dragged the back of his hand across his mouth and asked, "Do you reckon we can hold 'em off?"

The question seemed to be directed at everyone, not any of the gang in particular. But it was Knox who answered, "We got to. We don't have any choice if we want to keep our hair."

He let out a laugh, causing the others to glance at him in surprise.

"Hell, it's gonna be a good scrap," he went on. "Might as well enjoy it, fellas. It ain't every day you get to do somethin' like this."

"I'd just as soon not ever do anything like it," Hanley muttered.

The others clearly felt the same way, but no one else said anything. They swallowed hard, checked their rifles, and waited as the Indians charged ever closer. The seconds whizzed by, and the war party seemed to cover the ground with blinding speed.

"Hanley, Duke, Jennings," Knox called. "You boys get down on one knee. You'll shoot first. Bull and Phillips and me will wait and give the varmints a second volley whilst you're reloadin'. We'll go back and forth like that so's we can keep up a steady fire. Aim for the ones in front. Every one o' the heathens we put down will just get in the way of the others. That'll break up their charge."

That seemed like a reasonably intelligent strategy to Bellamy. Back home, he had studied warfare and tactics, although he was far from an expert on the subject. It still appeared that they had no chance against such overwhelming odds, but at least they could make the Indians pay a hefty price for their revenge.

Bellamy knelt between Hanley and Jennings. As they watched the Indians approach and tense nerves drew even tighter, Hanley said quietly, "No hard feelin's about that fight between us, Duke. You've turned out to be all right, I reckon."

Hanley believed they were going to die, and he wanted to get that off his chest before they did, Bellamy thought. Even though he wasn't completely sincere about it, even now, he replied, "No hard feelings, Hanley."

With a chuckle, Hanley added, "My head pounded for damn near a week after wallopin' it on that tree trunk, but you whipped me fair and square, even if you did get a mite lucky. I can't hold that against a man."

"I was fortunate, indeed." Bellamy gave him that much. "I wouldn't want to tangle with you again."

He started to add *my friend* but decided that would be carrying things too far, even under these dire circumstances. None of these outlaws was his friend, and they never would be.

There was no more time for talk. The leading edge of the war party was less than a hundred yards away now. Bellamy pressed his rifle's butt against his shoulder and laid his cheek against the smooth wood of its stock. He drew back the weapon's hammer, then sighted over the barrel and aimed at one of the warriors in the front rank.

"Get ready now," Zadicus Knox said in a low voice. Bellamy barely heard him over the pounding of the ponies' hooves. The sound rose up the terraced slope like a roll of thunder.

Knox cut through that with a shout of "Fire!"

Bellamy squeezed the trigger.

He was ready for the hard kick against his shoulder and the loud boom that assaulted his ears. The sound of the other two rifles going off added to that roar. He peered through the gray smoke that spewed from the muzzle for a second before realizing that he couldn't tell if he'd hit his target or not.

No time to waste worrying about that. He reached for his powder horn and began reloading.

On either side of him, Hanley and Jennings were carrying out the same task. Bellamy looked down at what he was doing. He had used the rifle enough that he was capable of reloading without watching what his hands did, but he couldn't afford a fumble or a misfire. Better to make sure he did everything right.

A volley of shots crashed out from the men above and behind them. This time when Bellamy glanced up, he didn't have a cloud of powder smoke obscuring his vision. He saw two of the Indians tumble off their ponies. The mounts, suddenly riderless, veered and bumped into the animals racing closely alongside them. Flashing legs tangled and a horse went down, then another and another.

Bellamy's rifle was ready. He snapped it back to his shoulder, vaguely aware that Hanley and Jennings were doing the same thing on either side of him. He drew a bead on one of the Indians and pulled the trigger.

If the seconds had been so fleeting before the attack started, the minutes that came after dragged out into seeming hours. Bellamy loaded and fired, loaded and fired, all while trying to ignore the fear that gripped him. His mind was numbed, so he became a purely physical creature of muscle and bone, his movements automatic. The constant roar of gunshots deafened him; the acrid tang of gun smoke made his eyes and nose water, but he paid no attention to that. He existed only to fight. He fought only to kill. After a while, it no longer mattered whether he lived or died as long as he got another shot off before his destiny befell him.

Then, gradually, he became aware of someone yelling. After a moment, he realized the voice belonged to Zadicus Knox. Knox was shouting, "Hold your fire! Hold your fire!"

Bellamy lowered his rifle. Reaction hit him and he began to shake. He had to lower a hand and rest it on the ground to brace himself—if he hadn't, he might have collapsed.

"They're pullin' out!" Hanley said. "We beat 'em!"

Bellamy looked over at him and then at Jennings. Both men appeared to be unhurt. He checked himself. No blood on his clothes, no unusual pain. He wasn't wounded.

Twisting his head around, he looked at Knox, Bull, and Phillips. They were all right, too. It bordered on miraculous, but it seemed that they had all come through the battle unscathed.

Hanley straightened to his feet. "What about Roscoe and Earnshaw and the horses?"

"They're fine," Knox said. "None of those damn heathens even tried to flank us." He laughed. "They figured we'd keep runnin' and they'd just catch up and overwhelm us. They didn't count on us stoppin' and puttin' up a damned good fight!"

From the looks of things, he was right. The Indians were retreating, once again raising a cloud of dust, but this one was going away from the outlaws, back toward the Missouri River.

Bellamy rested his rifle's butt on the ground to brace himself as he pushed to a standing position.

"Perhaps they're just regrouping and plan to attack us again," he suggested.

"The way they took off, they don't look like they're gonna stop until they get to the river," Knox said. "They don't appear to be slowin' down none, either."

That was true. As difficult as it was to believe, they had repelled the attack and perhaps even caused the Indians to give up their thirst for revenge.

"I'll bet we killed the damn chief," Knox went on. "That took the heart right out of 'em."

That seemed like as plausible an explanation as any.

The Indians had taken their dead and wounded with them, but several dead horses littered the slope near the bottom of the hill. It had been a close thing, Bellamy thought—as close as he ever wanted to come to disaster again.

"Now what do we do?" asked Hanley. "We can't go back to the river. That's the way the Indians went. We'd be likely to run right into 'em again."

"We have to go back to the river to pick up Preacher's trail," Knox said. "But what we'll do is strike north from here and then cut back over to the river after we've gone ten or fifteen miles. That ought to take us around those redskins. Preacher's bunch was stickin' pretty close to the Missouri, so we shouldn't have much trouble findin' their tracks again. Ain't that right, Bull?"

"If the tracks are there, I'll find 'em," the big man said confidently.

They had run the horses hard earlier, during the mad

dash for the hills, so they waited for a while before leaving to give the animals time to rest. Knox posted guards to watch in all four directions while they remained on the hilltop, just to make sure the Indians didn't try to double back or circle around.

The sky stayed clear. No dust rising anywhere in sight. A sense of peace settled back down over the prairie.

It wouldn't last, Bellamy told himself. He was well aware of that. But for now, he would accept the respite gratefully. He had come through this battle, and the experience would harden him, prepare him for the next time he had to fight for his life.

And there *would* be a next time. He had no doubt of that.

For now, though, he felt almost like a frontiersman. It wasn't a bad sensation.

Chapter 23

There came a day when Preacher called a halt and waved Geoffrey Fitzwarren up to join him a short distance ahead of the rest of the group.

Preacher turned Horse and pointed to the west.

"See that high ground stickin' up a mite, way over yonder?" he asked.

Fitzwarren leaned forward in the saddle and squinted. After a moment, he shook his head and said, "I'm not sure. I think perhaps I do."

"You'll have a better look at it later when we go past it," Preacher told him. "That's Eagle Butte. I've seen it several times comin' at it from this way, and I know that's what I'm lookin' at."

"Oh, I believe you, Preacher, never fear. I have complete faith in you. And what does it mean again, that we've come in sight of this Eagle Butte?"

"It means this is where we turn west, away from the river. We'll go on by Eagle Butte and keep headin' in the same direction, and that's how we'll get to the Beartooth Mountains."

"How soon will we reach them?"

"Five or six weeks from now, I'd say, dependin' on what we run into between here and there."

Fitzwarren nodded and said, "Yes, now that I think about it, I believe you mentioned that to me before." He shook his head and looked slightly disappointed. "I keep forgetting how incredibly vast this land is. Where I come from, we could have ridden across several countries in the time since we left St. Louis! I wish there were some quicker way to get there, but there's just not, is there?"

"Nope, afraid not," Preacher said. "You were hopin' we'd catch up to Treadway before now, weren't you?"

"One can't blame a fellow for hoping, can one?"

"I reckon not."

During the journey they had encountered several bands of Indians, all smaller than the group of Osage they had met. The Indians had been peaceful and willing to answer Preacher's questions, but none of them knew anything about Barrett Treadway or would admit to having seen a white man matching his description.

They could have been lying, of course, but Preacher's gut told him they were telling the truth, and he had learned to trust his instincts.

The party remained stopped for a while to allow the men and horses to rest. Then Preacher called out the order to mount up. Heading what Preacher reckoned to be due west, they pulled out and left the Missouri River behind.

Several more days of traveling across the monotonous plains brought them to Eagle Butte. Preacher explained to Fitzwarren that the low mesa had gotten its name from the eagles that frequently flew in circles above it in search of prey.

Beyond that, the terrain was mostly flat again, but at least there were some hills visible to the west now. When Fitzwarren spotted them, he exclaimed, "I say! Are those the Beartooth Mountains?"

Horace Thorpe happened to be riding with Preacher and Fitzwarren. He guffawed and said, "We're a long way from seein' the Beartooths, Mr. Fitzwarren. Those are just little hills that don't even have a name. Out here, a peak's got to be a heap higher than that before we call it a mountain!"

"I'm familiar with mountains, old boy," Fitzwarren said coolly. "I grew up tramping through the Alps, you know."

It was a mild rebuke, but it was enough to make Horace look embarrassed.

"Sorry, boss," he said. "I didn't mean nothin' by it."

"Don't give it another thought, my friend," Fitzwarren assured him. "Naturally, being a native of this land, you believe everything here is bigger and better. And most of the time, I daresay you'd be right. There's nowhere else quite like America, is there?"

"Not that I've ever run across," said Preacher. "Of course, the only other places I've been are Canada and Mexico and one o' them islands down yonder in the Caribbean Sea."

Fitzwarren looked at him in surprise. "Good heavens, man, what were you doing down there?"

"It's a long story," Preacher responded with a wave

of his hand. "Fightin' pirates and such. I'll tell you about it around a campfire sometime, if you want."

"Yes, indeed, very much so. If you don't mind my saying, you're a man full of surprises, Preacher."

"Better than bein' borin', ain't it?" Preacher said with a grin.

Eagle Butte disappeared behind them, but the hills in the distance didn't seem to come any closer—another example of the vast distances of which Fitzwarren had spoken.

Eventually, though, as the days passed the men began to be able to tell they were making some progress. The dark aspect of the hills became green because of the trees that covered their slopes.

"That actually looks quite appealing," Fitzwarren said. "It reminds me a bit of home."

"Once we get into the real mountains, I don't know how the Beartooths will stack up against them Alps of yours," Preacher said. "I've seen pictures of 'em in some of Audie's books, and they seem like pretty impressive mountains. But I reckon you'll feel a lot more at home, anyway."

"I can't wait."

But they had to wait, because the only way to get there was to keep going.

Dog made a habit of ranging far ahead of the rest of the party. One afternoon, as they were approaching a line of trees that marked the course of a small stream, the big cur burst out of those trees and dashed toward Preacher and the others, running hard so that he was stretched out and low to the ground.

Preacher sat up straighter in the saddle as soon as he saw Dog acting that way. He knew it couldn't be anything good causing such a reaction.

Sure enough, just a few seconds later two riders bolted out of the trees, as well, hard on the trail of the big cur. They were mounted on swift ponies and didn't use saddles, only blankets. That and the buckskins they wore, along with the feathers in their hair, told Preacher they were Indians.

The one in the lead guided his pony with his knees as he drew an arrow from the quiver on his back and nocked it to the string on his bow. Seeing that, Preacher muttered a heartfelt "Damn!" and brought his long-barreled rifle to his shoulder.

He aimed high, but not too high, and hoped that would be enough. The rifle's boom rolled across the landscape as he squeezed the trigger.

The sound was enough to make the Indian jerk in surprise as he loosed the arrow. The shaft flew well wide of Dog.

Preacher dug his boot heels into Horse's flanks and the big stallion responded instantly, lunging forward into a gallop. The two Indians slowed their mad chase but kept coming toward the white men. Both had arrows nocked now, and the one in the lead let out a shrill, angry, yipping war cry.

Preacher rapidly cut the distance between himself and the two warriors. He didn't look back to see if any of the others were following him. He figured they might be, but he also figured he could handle two enemies if he needed to.

Until he knew more about the situation, he didn't want to kill anybody unless he had to. He was close enough now to recognize the way these two wore their hair and the decorations on their buckskins. He reined Horse to a stop with his left hand and held up his right with the palm out.

He hoped that gesture would do the trick, but he moved his left hand closer to the butt of the Colt revolver on his hip, just in case.

The Indians stopped short, too, and stared at Preacher. Dog had reached his trail partners and turned to face his pursuers, snarling now as he bared his teeth.

"Hush, Dog," Preacher said quietly.

The two Indians lowered their bows. Both were in their middle twenties, formidable warriors in the prime of their lives.

Preacher said in a tongue he knew they would understand, "Don't you have anything better to do than chase a man's dog?"

"Dog?" the one who had fired the arrow said. "That is a wolf!"

"He's a dog, and I should know, since he's been my friend for years."

A smile broke out on the second Indian's face. "You are Preacher!"

"I am," the mountain man confirmed.

"We have never met, but we have heard much about you. I am Bent Tree, from the band led by Red Rock. This is Tall Grass."

Preacher nodded and said solemnly, "I have heard others speak of Red Rock. He is known to be a wise and courageous chief, and I am sure his warriors are the same."

Tall Grass still frowned and didn't look as happy to meet Preacher as his companion seemed to be.

"We took that beast for a wolf," he said.

"He probably has some wolf blood in him," Preacher allowed, "but his name is Dog and that is what he is."

"We did not know," Bent Tree said. "If we had known he was a friend of Preacher, we would not have bothered him."

"No harm done, I suppose. You can put your arrows away now."

Tall Grass's eyes narrowed in suspicion as he looked past the mountain man. He said, "I will not put my weapons away until I know that I am among friends."

Preacher heard hoofbeats and the creaking of wagon wheels coming up behind him and knew the rest of the group had caught up to him. He glanced over his shoulder and saw them spreading out, guns bristling in their hands, so he couldn't blame Tall Grass for reacting that way.

"Take it easy, fellas," he drawled in English. "These warriors are Absaroka. Sometimes called Crow. Their people have been good friends to me for a heap o' years now. I don't know their chief, but I've heard of him and I'd be willin' to bet we've got some mutual friends."

"You're saying they're trustworthy?" asked Fitzwarren.

"That's right."

Fitzwarren looked around at the others and said,

"You heard Preacher, gentlemen. Let's put away our firearms and be friends."

The men lowered their guns. Tall Grass and Bent Tree slid the arrows back in their quivers. They moved their ponies forward, coming closer to Preacher. Geoffrey Fitzwarren came up alongside the mountain man.

Tall Grass nodded toward Dog and said in the Crow tongue, "He really does look like a wolf."

"I'll give you that," Preacher agreed.

Fitzwarren spoke up, saying, "Preacher, if these men are friendly and you believe them to be trustworthy, perhaps you could inquire of them concerning Barrett Treadway and my, ah, cousin."

"That's just what I was fixin' to do," Preacher said. "Although they may not want to talk to us about that. They might prefer that we go to their village and ask their chief, Red Rock. But we'll give it a try."

He faced the two warriors again and went on in their language, "We're searching for a white man and a white woman traveling together." He described Barrett Treadway and Charlotte Fitzwarren and told the Indians their names.

Both Tall Grass and Bent Tree sat up straighter on their ponies and looked interested. Preacher could tell by their reaction that his words had struck a nerve.

"You know these people?" he asked.

"A white man named Treadway visited among our people," Bent Tree replied.

"Around twelve moons ago?"

"That is right. But there was no white woman with him. No woman of any kind."

"He was alone?"

Tall Grass said, "Another man was with him. A fur trapper like the one called Treadway."

"What was his name?"

The two Indians looked at each other. Bent Tree shrugged and said, "We never heard it. He was not friendly and kept to himself. But Red Rock might know. He talked with both of them."

"These trappers are your friends?" Tall Grass asked.

"That's right," Preacher said. He didn't go into details about their mission, because that didn't matter at this point. "We'd like to find them."

"You will not find the man called Treadway," Tall Grass said, his face and voice serious.

"Why's that?" Preacher asked as a sudden foreboding welled up inside him.

"Because he is dead."

Chapter 24

Fitzwarren must have been able to tell from the way Preacher tensed that something important had just been said. He asked, "What is it, Preacher? What are they saying?"

"They recognized Treadway's name," Preacher replied, his voice curt. "Let me find out more."

"What about Charlotte? Did they say anything about Charlotte?"

"I'm tryin' to find out." Preacher switched back to the Crow tongue and asked the two warriors, "Are you sure Treadway is dead? What happened to him?"

"We cannot be certain—" Bent Tree began.

"But the warrior who told us about it had no reason to lie," Tall Grass broke in. "He was a Lakota who has visited with us before. He had been staying with a band of Teton Sioux in the mountains, and he said that this man Treadway came among them, pretended to be their friend, and then dishonored one of their young women." Tall Grass scowled. "They might have punished him and then allowed him to live, but he fought back against them and they killed him. He deserved his fate."

Preacher wasn't going to debate that justification, one way or the other. He asked, "What about the other man? Was he still with Treadway?"

"I do not know," Tall Grass replied.

"Nothing was said about him," Bent Tree added.

"Preacher, please." Fitzwarren's voice cracked slightly from the strain. "What are they telling you?"

Preacher didn't see any way he could keep the news from Fitzwarren. "They say Treadway's dead."

"No!"

"They claim they heard that he got into a ruckus with some Teton Sioux and they killed him."

"And Charlotte?"

"They don't know anything about Charlotte. They never saw Treadway with a woman, only with that other trapper."

"This other man, do you think we could find him?"

"Might be hard, not knowing anything about him," Preacher said. "But accordin' to Tall Grass and Bent Tree here, their chief talked with both Treadway and the other fella, so maybe he can tell us more."

"These, what did you call them, Teton Sioux? Can you find them?"

"I reckon I probably can." Preacher shrugged. "They might not be too happy to see us, though."

"They don't get along with white men?"

"That's hard to say. That bunch is touchy to start with. If Treadway caused 'em enough trouble that they killed him, they might not be too friendly to any others of his kind."

Preacher thought back on what he knew of the Teton

Sioux, named after the mountain range farther west, although they could be found in other places.

They had never been as hostile to the whites as, say, the Blackfeet. In fact, in the early days of the fur trade, they had been friendly to the mountain men who had ventured into their hunting grounds. Preacher remembered hearing about how some fella who had first come through those parts with Lewis and Clark had started a settlement right in the heart of Teton Sioux country and had married up with one of their women.

That had been a few years before Preacher came west, and by the time he was roaming around the high country, that settlement was gone. That is, if it had ever been there to start with. It might have been just a story.

But there was no doubt that the Teton Sioux had grown more unfriendly and clashed with the white trappers more and more often as the years passed. If Barrett Treadway hadn't been a novice in the mountains, he might have known enough to steer clear of them.

Even so, he might have survived venturing among them if he hadn't caused any trouble. Once Indians decided to be hospitable, they would usually stick to that stance unless provoked.

"What are we going to do now?" Fitzwarren asked.

"Hold on a minute," Preacher told him. He turned back to the two Crow warriors. "Do you think Red Rock would allow us to visit your village and speak with him?"

"Preacher has always been a good friend to our people," Bent Tree said. "I believe he would welcome you and consider you an honored guest."

"Even though you shot at one of his warriors," Tall Grass added with a slight frown.

"I shot only to warn you not to harm my dog," Preacher said. "If I had shot at you, we would not be talking now." Under his breath, he added in English a scornful, "Old son."

Tall Grass glared a little harder. He might not have understood the words, but the tone of Preacher's comment was plain.

He didn't say anything else, though. He just turned his pony and started back the way he and Bent Tree had come from. Bent Tree, with a friendlier look on his face, inclined his head to indicate that Preacher and the others should follow.

Preacher said to the rest of the group, "We're gonna pay a visit to where these folks live. They're friendly, and their chief may be able to help us, so all you boys be on your best behavior. Don't go startin' no trouble."

Eugene Kelleher chuckled and said, "You know us, Preacher. We're just a bunch o' regular little choirboys."

Chapter 25

The Crow village was a good-sized one. Close to fifty teepees were set up along the bank of a creek lined by cottonwood and aspen trees. Quite a few children were running around, but they stopped their playing to stare at the riders approaching the village. Several dogs ran to greet the visitors with snarls and growls, but they backed off as Dog returned their threats.

The women going about their work halted what they were doing, too, and the warriors gathered from their various activities. A middle-aged man took his place in the forefront of the group. Preacher figured he was Red Rock, the chief of this band.

With Tall Grass and Bent Tree riding beside him, Preacher knew the Crow would assume they had come in peace. The two warriors nudged their ponies forward, dropped lithely to the ground, and spoke with Red Rock, their words too quiet for Preacher to overhear what they were saying.

The mountain man reined in, swung down from the saddle, and motioned for his companions to remain mounted and stay where they were. Red Rock strode forward and Preacher went to meet him.

"My warriors tell me that you are the one called Preacher," the chief said as they came to a stop facing each other about ten feet apart.

"I am called Preacher," he confirmed.

"We have heard many stories about you." Red Rock paused. "Your name is known from where the sun rises to where it sets. It is told that you have killed many Blackfeet."

The Crow and the Blackfeet were mortal enemies, so Preacher didn't hesitate in replying, "I have made war on them, and they have made war on me, for more seasons than I can remember. I have sent many of them to the land beyond this one."

The faintest suggestion of a smile played over Red Rock's lips.

"Then you are a friend to the Crow, and you are welcome in our village. The friends of the man called Preacher are welcome as well."

Preacher nodded and said with a solemn expression on his face, "It is our honor to visit your village, Chief Red Rock."

"My warriors also say that you wish to ask me about some other white men who came among us."

"If that is agreeable to you."

"Come to my lodge," Red Rock invited. "We will smoke and talk."

Preacher turned, caught Fitzwarren's eye, and waved him forward. To Red Rock, he said, "I would like to bring one of my friends with me. He is the one who is looking for the other white men."

Red Rock nodded in agreement.

Fitzwarren dismounted, handed his reins to Lee Thorpe, and walked over to Preacher and Red Rock. Preacher said to the chief, "This is Geoffrey Fitzwarren. He comes from a faraway land seeking news of the one called Barrett Treadway."

Preacher saw a flicker of something in Red Rock's eyes. The chief said again, "We will talk in my lodge."

Preacher nodded and then said to Fitzwarren, "This is Red Rock, the chief of this band of Crow."

In English, Fitzwarren said, "It is a great honor to make your acquaintance, Chief Red Rock."

Preacher translated that. Red Rock gave Fitzwarren a curt nod and then turned toward the largest of the Crow teepees. Preacher said to Kelleher, "I'm leavin' you in charge, Eugene. You and the boys can see to waterin' the horses in the creek."

"Don't worry, Preacher." Kelleher glanced at the dozens of stalwart Crow warriors gathered nearby and added, "We ain't likely to start any trouble with this bunch. We've all got more sense than that."

Preacher knew that was true. He nodded to Fitzwarren and they followed Red Rock.

A few minutes later, the two of them were sitting cross-legged on buffalo robes inside Red Rock's lodge, next to the fire that sent its smoke drifting out through the opening at the teepee's top. Red Rock sat on the opposite side of the fire, flanked by two more middle-aged warriors. The chief didn't introduce them, but

Preacher knew they must be Red Rock's lieutenants and counselors.

Under his breath as they walked into the lodge, Preacher had warned Fitzwarren that he would need to be patient. Indians had their own way of doing things, and when they were discussing important matters, they couldn't be rushed. They would have to allow Red Rock to proceed at his own pace.

Preacher was glad he had done that, because he could tell Fitzwarren was anxious to find out what the chief knew about Barrett Treadway.

Fitzwarren kept his nerves under control and sat there with a friendly expression on his face as Red Rock filled and lit a pipe, took a few leisurely, meditative puffs on it, and then passed it to the warrior on his left.

The pipe went on around the circle of men. Preacher and Fitzwarren took their turns, and when the pipe got back to Red Rock, the chief set it aside and said to Preacher, "The men you seek were here. One called Treadway, as you said, and another called Williams."

To Fitzwarren, Preacher reported, "He says Treadway was here with another trapper named Williams. That name mean anything to you?"

"Not a thing in the world," Fitzwarren answered. "He must have been someone Treadway met in St. Louis on his way out here."

"More than likely," Preacher agreed. He turned back to Red Rock and, even though Tall Grass and Bent Tree had said already that there wasn't, he asked in the Crow tongue, "Was there a woman with them?"

Red Rock shook his head solemnly. "No woman, only the two white men."

"Do you recall if either of them mentioned a woman? Her name would be Charlotte."

"It has been twelve moons, but I remember no talk of a woman. The one called Treadway did most of the talking. Williams sat with Treadway and kept his head down, saying little."

"What did Treadway talk about?"

"He asked about the fur trapping in the mountains to the west. I told him it was good but that some of the Teton Sioux now considered the area to be their hunting grounds and might not be friendly if he encountered them."

"How did Treadway take that?"

A disapproving frown creased Red Rock's forehead. "He said that he and his companion would be careful," the chief replied, "but that they wished to make a great deal of money and were willing to take their chances." Red Rock made a disgusted noise. "White men are very foolish in their pursuit of this thing they call money, which seems truly worthless to me. You cannot eat it or build a lodge from it or wear it as clothing. What good is it?"

"That's a fair question, Chief," Preacher said. "I don't have an answer for you."

He could tell that Fitzwarren was getting pretty antsy, so he turned to the man and summarized the conversation with the chief so far.

"So Treadway and Williams left here headed west?" Fitzwarren asked when Preacher was finished.

"Yep. Straight toward the Beartooths, just like we thought."

"And they didn't say anything about Charlotte?"

"Not that the chief remembers. He seems to be a pretty sharp ol' boy, so I reckon I trust what he's tellin' us."

Fitzwarren looked like he wanted to groan in dismay. "Then we have nothing more to go on than we did before we encountered these people."

"Well, we know Treadway's partner was called Williams. That don't really tell us much, though."

Fitzwarren's voice was grim as he said, "Charlotte must have died on the journey between Philadelphia and St. Louis. Either that, or Treadway simply abandoned her somewhere, the despicable lout."

"Does that sound like somethin' he'd do?"

"I was barely acquainted with the man during his visit to Alpenstone. I disliked him on sight, however. I can believe he would do such a thing."

Fitzwarren put a hand to his forehead and closed his eyes for a moment. When he opened them, he went on, "If Charlotte was left on her own, penniless in a strange land, there's no telling what she might have had to do in order to survive. Under such circumstances, after such a long time, it would be virtually impossible to ever find her."

"It don't seem likely," Preacher agreed.

"I swear I'd kill the scoundrel, if he weren't already dead," Fitzwarren declared. "That is, if we're certain that he actually did meet his demise at the hands of those, ah, Sioux."

"Let me ask the chief about that." Preacher turned

back to Red Rock and went on, "Your warriors told me that a visitor to your village later brought word of Treadway's death."

"This is true," said Red Rock. "A Lakota named North Wind who has no real home but wanders the prairie because something is missing in his head."

"He's touched by the spirits?" Preacher asked quickly, thinking that if the fella was loco, the information he'd passed along might not be reliable.

Red Rock dashed that hope with a shake of his head. "North Wind is a medicine man. He claims that he has no need for a home. His spirit is restless but strong. He can be trusted."

"North Wind is the one who told you the Teton Sioux killed Treadway?"

The chief nodded. He repeated the story Tall Grass and Bent Tree had told Preacher earlier.

Something occurred to Preacher. He asked Red Rock, "What about the other man? The trapper called Williams? Did the Sioux kill him as well?"

"North Wind said nothing about that."

Possibilities quickened Preacher's pulse. "So he could still be alive?"

Red Rock spread both hands in a universal gesture of uncertainty and said, "I do not know. Treadway was the one who insulted their honor. If Williams did nothing to anger them, they may have allowed him to live and simply banished him from their hunting grounds. But if he tried to defend his friend, he may have been killed, too. I cannot say."

Preacher translated that exchange for Fitzwarren, who came to the same conclusion as the mountain man.

"This fellow Williams could be alive," he said, "and he might know what happened to Charlotte."

"Seems possible, anyway," Preacher said. "Looks to me like you've got two choices, Geoff. We can go back to St. Louis and you can try to backtrack Treadway from there, or we can push on, try to find out for sure, one way or the other, what happened to Williams, and if he is still alive, we can try to locate him and see if he knows anything."

"Both of those options strike me as having very slim chances for success."

"Yeah, but slim is better than none. I reckon it's a matter of which long shot you'd rather bet on right now."

Fitzwarren considered that question for a moment before reaching a decision. He said, "I won't turn back until every possibility is eliminated. We're going to push on to the mountains and find this fellow Williams if he's still alive."

"Fine with me," Preacher said, not adding that that was a mighty big *if*.

Chapter 26

"I just don't understand it," Bull said as he stood in front of Zadicus Knox. The big man's gaze was directed at the ground, and he looked like he wanted to cry. "I just can't figure out what happened."

"I know what happened," Knox snapped. "I know good and well. You missed the trail, you big lummox! And now there ain't no tellin' how long it'll take us to find it again, if we ever do."

Bull blinked his eyes rapidly and dragged the back of his hand across them. "I'm sorry, Zadicus. I just don't—"

"Damn it, don't say you don't understand it or can't figure it out. I just told you what happened." Knox grimaced. "The question is, what in the hell are we gonna do about it?"

Bull looked so miserable and ashamed of himself that Bellamy almost felt sorry for him. Almost. But he remembered how brutal Bull could be and how quickly and eagerly the big man leaped to carry out Knox's orders, whatever they might be. He couldn't muster up much genuine sympathy.

Following the clash with the Indians, the outlaws had done as Knox ordered, traveling north for a good distance before turning east and going back to the Missouri River. Knox had expected that once they reached the river, Bull would be able to locate the tracks left by Preacher's group and they could take up the trail of their quarry once more.

Instead, Bull had found no sign that Preacher and his companions had come that way. Knox had hectored and badgered the big man cruelly, trying to prod him on to success, but Bull had drawn a blank.

That left only one reasonable explanation.

Preacher and his party had also turned away from the river at some point south of the outlaws' current location. That meant somewhere along the way, Knox and his men had crossed the trail they should have followed—but they had never noticed it.

The only other possibilities were that Preacher's group had turned around and gone back the way they came from, or else crossed the Missouri and headed east. Neither of those things seemed the least bit logical.

Knox stalked back and forth like a feral animal as the men stood around watching him warily. They all knew how unpredictably explosive he was and wanted to be able to get out of the way if he blew up.

Finally, Knox stopped pacing and turned to face the others.

"There's only one thing we can do," he said. "We'll backtrack down the river ourselves. We're bound to come across Preacher's tracks sooner or later, and when we do, we'll be on the right trail again. This has slowed us down a mite, that's all. We're still gonna grab that rich varmint who hired Preacher and make him or his family pay us a bunch o' money."

"They'll have a lot bigger lead on us now," Hanley said.

"They brought along a wagon, so we can move faster than them," Knox argued. "We'll cut down that lead pretty quick-like, I'll bet." He blew out a frustrated breath. "Anyway, we know they're headin' for the Beartooth Mountains, and those are west of here. Hell, if we just keep goin' that way, we're bound to find 'em sooner or later!"

Hanley muttered, "Yeah, and it may take us until we get to the Beartooths, too."

"What was that?"

"Nothin', Zadicus," Hanley replied hastily. "You're right, we'll find that bunch. No doubt about it."

"Damn right, we will."

Despite Hanley's conciliatory words, he shot a glance at Bellamy that conveyed how worried he was. This whole affair was showing signs of turning into a wild goose chase, but all the men knew they would be taking their lives in their hands by pointing that out to Zadicus Knox.

After a few more minutes, the men mounted up and headed south along the Missouri River. Knox and Bull were in the lead. Bellamy was close enough behind them to hear Bull declare, "I'll find them tracks this time, Zadicus. I swear I will."

"You'd better," Knox replied coldly. He didn't say anything else, but the threat behind the words was clear.

Again, Bellamy almost felt sorry for Bull. The big man's eagerness to please his leader was pathetic.

Bellamy no longer knew what to hope for. He didn't want to be part of this any longer, but taking off on his own so far from civilization would be too dangerous.

The best thing, he decided, would be if Knox gave up on this farfetched quest and returned to St. Louis. Bellamy wouldn't have to go into the town itself and risk being arrested for shooting that constable. He could circle around it and follow the Mississippi downriver, perhaps all the way to New Orleans.

He'd heard about New Orleans, with its elegance and culture. A man of his breeding ought to fit right in. He should have gone there to start with, instead of St. Louis, he told himself.

At the time, he had been enthralled with the idea of living a life of adventure, and going off to the wild frontier to be a fur trapper seemed to embody that goal better than anything else he could come up with.

What a foolish notion.

After leaving the Crow village, Preacher, Geoffrey Fitzwarren, and the rest of the party continued heading west. The days and the miles unrolled beneath the hooves of their horses and the wheels of the wagon driven by Salvador Perez.

By now the men had stopped shaving—even Fitzwarren, who seemed pleased by the beard he had grown.

"It makes me look positively piratical, doesn't it?" he

said to Preacher as he stroked the growth on his chin while they rode at the front of the group.

"You forget, Geoff, I've tussled with real pirates. They ain't anywhere as neat and clean as you. You look more like a pirate from a picture book, maybe."

Fitzwarren chuckled. "I suppose I'll have to be satisfied with that."

More days on the trail passed. Preacher didn't know exactly how long it had been since they left St. Louis or even since they had turned west from the Missouri River. Out here, the precise measurement of such things didn't matter. The country was just too big for that.

Fitzwarren still wasn't accustomed to such distances. One day, he exclaimed out of the blue, "We should have reached the Pacific Ocean by now! Are you certain we're not just going around in circles, Preacher?"

The mountain man grinned. "I'm pretty sure we ain't." He raised his right arm and pointed. "In fact, if you want to take a gander up yonder, you might spot somethin' interestin'."

Fitzwarren squinted as he peered ahead of them for a long moment. Then he shook his head and said, "I don't see a bloody thing."

"That dark line on the horizon?"

Fitzwarren concentrated even more. "Well, perhaps."

"Those are the Beartooth Mountains."

Fitzwarren's eyebrows rose now. "Really? At long last? But how much longer will it take us to reach them from here?"

"A few more days," Preacher said. "Another week, at the most, I reckon."

"And once we're there, how long before we find out something about that fellow Williams?" Fitzwarren shook his head and went on, "Never mind. I know you can't answer that question. I'm sorry if I seem to be getting testy, Preacher. I never dreamed it would take me this long to discover what happened to my poor cousin. I realize, as well, that the effort may just be getting started. I may have to return to St. Louis and begin again."

"Might have to go back to Philadelphia and try to pick up the trail there," Preacher said.

Fitzwarren let out a hollow laugh and said, "Let's try to be a bit more optimistic than that, shall we?" He thought for a moment and then added, "Supposing I do have to return to Philadelphia. Would you be willing to come with me and continue assisting with the search?"

"Not hardly," Preacher answered without hesitation. "I've been there. It's too big and crowded a place for me. I ain't used to havin' so many folks around all the time."

Fitzwarren looked from side to side at all the vast emptiness surrounding them and said, "Yes, I can see why that would seem strange to you."

Despite the fact that they still had a lot of ground to cover, being within sight of their destination lifted the spirits of the men. The days seemed to pass a little faster, the miles to be a little shorter. Ahead of them, the Beartooth Mountains steadily grew larger. They weren't just a dark line on the horizon anymore. The men could see that the mountains had some height to them. Eventually, they were able to make out individual peaks.

"I can see what you meant about the name, Preacher," Fitzwarren commented. He pointed. "That mountain there, and that other one, they do look a bit like sharp teeth sticking up, don't they?"

On the other side of Fitzwarren, Horace Thorpe grinned and said, "I reckon you can guess what the Teton Mountains are named for, Mr. Fitzwarren?"

"Well, ah, I suppose so. The name refers to a lady's, ah, bosoms, does it not?"

Preacher chuckled. "I've seen the Tetons many a time, and if that's what the first fella to call 'em that was reminded of, he'd spent too damn long without any gals around!"

On the fifth day after catching sight of the mountains, the men entered the broad mouth of a grassy canyon that curved gently among the peaks. The slopes were covered with pine trees up to a certain height; beyond that, they were gray and rugged rock with swathes of white here and there where snow clung to them, even at this time of year.

After they had gone several miles up the canyon and could no longer see the rolling plains behind them, Preacher called a halt. Up ahead, the canyon widened out into a small valley. A stream emerged from a cleft high on the left-hand side and plunged down in a waterfall that sparkled in the sun. At the base of it was a small but blindingly blue lake mostly surrounded by pines.

"My word, it's beautiful," Geoffrey Fitzwarren said in an awed voice as he stared at the landscape. "I'm not sure they can match the Alps, mind you, but I must say this is the prettiest sight I've seen since I've been in your country."

"You'll see prettier once we get deeper in the mountains," Preacher told him, "but yeah, this is mighty nice. Since we don't know where we'll have to search, we'll camp here by this lake for a spell and use it as our base while we're havin' a look around these parts."

Preacher waved the men on. Dog bounded ahead eagerly, obviously excited by the prospect of having something to chase besides the occasional rabbit or prairie chicken.

By evening, they had made camp beside the lake. The horses were picketed and grazing.

During the journey, Salvador Perez had become Eugene Kelleher's assistant when it came to cooking. Perez built a fire now while Kelleher rummaged among the supplies in the wagon. They still had a little flour—enough to bake some biscuits—some sugar and salt and coffee, and a couple of slabs of salt pork.

Soon, though, they would have to make most of their living off the land. Luckily, there was an abundance of game to be found in these mountains.

Perez had just gotten the fire going well and was still hunkered on his heels beside it when he grunted in pain and jolted forward.

An arrowhead had buried itself in the muscles just below his left shoulder, and the missile's shaft protruded from his back.

Chapter 27

Perez howled in pain as he pitched forward and landed in the fire. Kelleher, who was the closest to him, bellowed, "Preacher!" as he leaped toward Perez.

Moving with surprising speed and agility for a man of his bulk, Kelleher reached down, snagged the back of Perez's shirt, and hauled the screaming man out of the flames.

"Take cover!" Preacher shouted as an arrow whipped past him. He jerked his head from side to side as he looked around for Fitzwarren, who appeared to have wandered off somewhere. Preacher couldn't catch sight of him.

Another cry of pain sounded. Preacher whirled toward it and saw Lee Thorpe staggering toward the wagon.

Lee had dropped his rifle and had both hands wrapped around the shaft of the arrow sticking out of his stomach. He lost his balance and fell. The way he landed drove the arrow even deeper in his body. The bloody flint head burst out his back.

Lee kicked a couple of times and then lay still. Preacher thought fleetingly that the man might be better off that way. He had died quickly rather than lingering in agony as he would have done from a stomach wound like that.

Horace Thorpe yelled, "Lee!" and ran toward his fallen brother. Behind him, an Indian appeared from his hiding place in some brush and drew back the string of the bow in his other hand, readying an arrow to launch at Horace.

A shot boomed and the Indian went over backward. He released the arrow, but it sailed harmlessly into the sky toward the lake.

Geoffrey Fitzwarren ran out of another clump of brush with a smoking rifle in his hands. Preacher knew he had to be the one who'd shot the attacker just in time to save Horace Thorpe.

"Over here, Geoff!" Preacher called as he drew both Colts from their holsters. "Hunt cover, everybody!"

More Indians were emerging from the brush now, yipping their war cries. Preacher bit back a curse, disgusted with himself for allowing the varmints to sneak up on them like that. He backed toward the wagon and opened fire with the Colts as more arrows flew.

The Paterson revolvers boomed and bucked in the mountain man's fists. He recognized the attackers as Teton Sioux, the tribe they'd been warned about.

He didn't know if the Sioux had ever seen repeating handguns before. The way they charged recklessly toward him seemed to indicate they believed his weapons were empty after he fired his first shots.

But after two of the Indians fell, he cocked the Colts again, shifted his aim, and blasted two more of them off their feet. The others, maybe a dozen in all, abruptly broke off their charge and launched more arrows from where they were.

They turned and scrambled for cover as Preacher continued raking them with steady shots from both revolvers. Three more went down, slammed off their feet by the heavy lead balls smashing into their backs.

The Colts' hammers snapped on empty chambers. Preacher carried a couple of fully loaded spare cylinders in the pouch at his waist, but he would need a few seconds to replace the spent cylinders with them.

He had done good work with the guns, killing or badly wounding seven of the attackers in a matter of moments. The man Fitzwarren had downed made eight.

Those were hefty losses for the Sioux war party, especially considering that they had probably expected to wipe out the party of white men by taking them by surprise.

Even so, from what Preacher had seen of them, they still outnumbered him and his companions.

Lee Thorpe was dead. Preacher didn't know how badly hurt Salvador Perez was, but he was out of the fight for now. Eugene Kelleher had dragged Perez over to the wagon and gotten him underneath it, behind one of the big wheels. That would give the wounded man a little cover, anyway.

The others had made it to the wagon, too. Dennis Burke and Horace Thorpe crouched behind it, holding their rifles ready in case they caught sight of a target.

They had positioned themselves on the side of the wagon toward the lake, which was about twenty yards away. The ground was open in that direction, with no concealment for the Sioux to slip up on them.

Geoffrey Fitzwarren was with the other men, coolly reloading his rifle.

Preacher joined them, as well, and got to work switching the cylinders on his Colts.

While he was doing that, he asked, "How's Salvador lookin', Eugene?"

Kelleher had crawled under the wagon with Perez. He said, "I can get the arrow out of him all right. It'll be messy, but I don't think it'll kill him. Looks like it missed all the vitals. He got burned pretty bad when he fell in the fire. Reckon that's what hurt the worst. He's passed out, which is probably good."

"The burns ain't bad enough to kill him, either?"

"Likely not. He won't be doin' any fightin' anytime soon, though, nor drivin' the wagon, neither."

"Take care of him the best you can," Preacher said. He turned to Horace Thorpe. "I'm sorry about your brother."

Horace's face was bleak. "I'll kill ever' one of those filthy redskins to pay 'em back for Lee."

"I reckon Lee would want you to come outta this with a whole skin rather than worryin' about that," Preacher said, but at the same time, he knew how Horace felt. He had gone on the vengeance trail himself more than once in the past.

"You see 'em anymore?" Dennis Burke asked as he straightened a little to peer over the wagon's sideboards.

A second later, he yelped and ducked frantically. An arrow cut through the space where his head had been, coming so close that it knocked the hat off his head. The arrow and the skewered hat landed on the ground behind them.

"I reckon they're still out there," Preacher said dryly.

Burke glared at him. "Dadgum it, Preacher, this ain't no time to be pokin' fun at a fella. That arrow durned near parted my hair. What're we gonna do?"

"There ain't much we can do except try to fight 'em off. I don't figure we could make it to the horses without them cuttin' us down. Anyway, with Perez hurt, we can't make a run for it. That would mean leavin' him behind."

"And leavin' me behind, too," Kelleher added from underneath the wagon. "I'll be damned if I'm gonna abandon this boy."

"That's not happenin'," Preacher assured him.

"That's right," Fitzwarren put in. "They don't seem to have any firearms. This wagon ought to offer us sufficient protection from arrows, spears, and the like as long as we're careful. We still have plenty of ammunition, as well. We're in good shape to withstand a siege."

Preacher wasn't so sure about that. There were plenty of tricks the Indians could try, especially once it got dark.

It wasn't going to do any good to point that out, though. Instead, he said, "Geoff, I don't think it's likely they'll try to get around behind us, but I want you keepin' an eye out in that direction anyway, just in case. You holler if you see anybody movin' around on our flanks."

"Yes, of course," Fitzwarren responded as he turned

to face the lake and dropped to one knee. His head swiveled back and forth as he intently surveyed the terrain.

"Eugene, anything we can do to help you with Salvador?" Preacher asked.

"No, I don't suppose. He's still out cold, so while I've got the chance, I'm gonna push that arrowhead on through and cut it off so I can get the shaft out."

"He's liable to wake up when you do that."

"Yeah, I know, but I, uh, got a flask in my pocket that'll help dull the pain for him if he does."

Preacher chuckled. He knew that Kelleher usually packed some Who-hit-John, but he'd never seen the man drunk, so it didn't bother him for Kelleher to have the stuff.

And Kelleher was right: it sure might come in handy right now.

A minute or so later, Perez let out another howl and Preacher knew the young man had regained consciousness when Kelleher pushed the arrow the rest of the way through his body.

Creating an exit wound like that carried its own risks, but it was the safest method for removing an arrow. Once the arrowhead was out of the body, it could be cut off and then the shaft could be withdrawn. The way the heads were shaped, pulling an arrow out without cutting the head off first did even more damage.

"Whoa!" Kelleher said. "Whoa, there, boy! It ain't gonna help nothin' if you go to jumpin' around. Preacher, I reckon I could use a hand down here after all."

"You boys keep your eyes open," Preacher told Burke

and Horace. He knelt between the wheels and bent down to work his tall frame underneath the wagon.

Kelleher had positioned Perez on his right side so he could reach both the entrance and exit wounds. Preacher grabbed the young Mexican to hold him steady while Kelleher poured whiskey from a flask into the two bloody holes.

Perez yelled some more as his eyes opened wide and seemed about to pop out of their sockets. Preacher's firm grip prevented him from thrashing around in pain.

"Hold on, son," Kelleher told him. "That whiskey'll burn out all the bad stuff in those wounds." He put the flask to Perez's mouth and dribbled some of the liquor between his lips. "And this'll help from the inside out."

Perez's reaction subsided and he lay there breathing heavily with his eyes closed again.

"He's out cold," Kelleher told Preacher. "Thanks for hangin' on to him. I'll get these wounds bandaged up as best I can. He needs to be someplace where I can tend to him proper and he can rest up some."

"I reckon those Sioux out there will have somethin' to say about that," Preacher replied.

And it seemed that they were ready to resume the conversation, because at that moment, Dennis Burke yelled, "Look out! Flamin' arrows!"

Chapter 28

Preacher heard arrows thudding against the wagon as he scrambled out from underneath the vehicle. He surged to his feet and thrust both Colts over the sideboards.

The Sioux had launched a volley of flaming arrows from the brush where they were hidden. The missiles had thick layers of dried grass bound around them that had been set on fire with flint and steel. Three of them had struck the wagon and embedded themselves in the wooden frame.

More of the arrows had fallen around the wagon and were still burning, but the grass where they had landed was too green to catch fire.

Another volley of the blazing brands arced through the air toward the wagon. A couple of them landed inside the wagon bed among the supplies and threatened to set the crates and bags on fire.

"Get those arrows outta there!" Preacher ordered Burke and Horace. "I'll cover you!"

Once again, gun thunder rolled over the landscape as Preacher thumbed off shot after shot from the Colts.

The shots tore through the brush and caused it to shake violently.

After that, the arrows stopped flying.

Burke and Horace pulled themselves up, using wheel spokes to stand on, and rolled over the side of the wagon into the bed. They snatched up the burning arrows and flung them out on the other side, then slapped out the small fires that had been started among the supplies.

Burke crawled to the far side of the wagon bed and leaned out to yank loose one of the arrows that had embedded in the frame. He cried out in pain as he burned his hand doing so, but he hung on to it long enough to throw the arrow on the ground.

He started toward one of the others but hadn't reached it when a regular arrow sailed out of the thicket and struck him in the side, driving deep into his body. He grunted under the impact and collapsed.

Through a gap in the brush, Preacher caught a glimpse of the Sioux who had fired that shaft and triggered his last shot at the warrior.

With a thrashing of branches, the man fell forward into the open and spasmed several times as he died, drilled through the body by the mountain man's deadly accuracy.

But the revolvers were empty now, and it would take time to reload the cylinders. If the Sioux charged them at this moment, the few rounds they had available in their rifles wouldn't be enough to repel the attack.

Thankfully, the Sioux weren't aware of that fact, Preacher realized when they didn't come boiling out of the brush howling for blood. After seeing so many of their number fall to the barrage of lead from Preacher's Colts, they might not want to risk attacking in the open again.

Horace Thorpe had dropped back to the ground behind the wagon after grabbing a couple of the flaming arrows and throwing them out. Panting from exertion and nerves, he said, "What are they waitin' for?"

"I don't know, but I'm hopin' maybe they've decided it ain't worth losin' any more men to keep comin' at us."

"You really think that might be true?"

"It's possible," Preacher said. "There's no predictin' what Injuns'll do. Even after all the time I've spent out here dealin' with 'em, I never know for sure what they're up to."

He got busy reloading the revolvers while he had the chance. Maybe the Sioux were sneaking around and getting ready to try something else, and if they were, he wanted to be able to give them a warm reception.

"Keep your eyes open, Geoff," he told Fitzwarren. "They're liable to try sneakin' around us."

"I haven't seen any sign of them," Fitzwarren replied. "What happened to Dennis? Is he all right?"

Preacher snapped one of the Colts closed and straightened up to steal a glance over the wagon's sideboards.

That was enough for him to see Dennis Burke's motionless body and the small pool of blood around it. Burke's face was turned toward Preacher. His eyes were wide open but sightless.

Preacher crouched again and said in a grim voice,

"Burke's dead. Looks like that arrow probably got him in the heart."

"So we've lost two men, Dennis and Lee," Horace said bitterly. "We're payin' a high price, too."

"I'm sorry, Horace, I truly am," Fitzwarren said. "Your brother was a fine man."

Preacher said, "It ain't no comfort right now, but their losses outnumber ours by more than four to one. An Injun won't keep fightin' if he thinks he can't win."

From under the wagon, Eugene Kelleher put in, "But he won't forget those losses, neither, and he'll come back to avenge those men."

"More than likely," Preacher agreed. "But maybe not today, if we're lucky."

No arrows had been fired at the wagon for several minutes. More time dragged past. Preacher looked around, didn't see Dog anywhere, and whistled.

The big cur came trotting out of the brush where the Teton Sioux had been hidden.

Preacher heaved a sigh of relief. "The Sioux are gone," he told the others.

"How do you know?" Horace asked.

"Because if they weren't, we would've heard a hell of a commotion in that brush just now. Dog would've gone after 'em, and there would've been a heap of snarlin' and yellin'."

"You're willin' to bet your life on a dog?"

"That one I am," Preacher said.

He stood up, kept both Colts leveled in front of him, and stalked toward the brush. He had answered Horace Thorpe honestly: he was willing to bet his life on Dog.

But he didn't see anything wrong in hedging that bet a mite, either.

The warriors who had been gunned down earlier were all dead. Preacher found splashes of blood in the brush that told him some of his shots had found their targets, but no more bodies were in evidence.

Either the men he'd hit were just wounded, or else the other Sioux had taken the corpses with them.

Preacher returned to the wagon and pouched the irons. He leaned over to look underneath the vehicle as he asked, "How's Perez doin'?"

"Still out cold," replied Kelleher. "And I reckon that's a good thing. He don't know how bad he's hurtin' right now."

"Well, it may wake him up to move him, but we're gonna have to. We need to get outta here."

"Why?" Geoffrey Fitzwarren wanted to know. "You said this was a good place for a camp, and the Indians have departed now, correct?"

"The live ones are gone." Preacher nodded toward the bodies sprawled between the wagon and the thicket. "The dead ones are still here, and their pards are gonna want to come back and collect them. An Injun won't leave a fellow warrior's body untended to if there's any way to avoid it. They'll make sure he's laid to rest proper-like. The honorable thing for us to do is to let them gather up those fellas."

"And we don't want to be here when they do it," Kelleher said as he crawled out from under the wagon. "Yeah, I reckon that makes sense, Preacher. But where are we gonna go?"

Preacher motioned to indicate their route and said, "We'll circle around this lake and push deeper into the mountains. This valley narrows back down into a canyon, and it runs quite a ways into the Beartooths, if my memory ain't playin' tricks on me."

"Gimme a hand here," Kelleher said as he went down on one knee and reached under the wagon to grasp Salvador Perez's unconscious form.

"I don't figure those Sioux will be back anytime soon, but keep your eyes open anyway," Preacher told Fitzwarren and Horace.

Then he helped Kelleher ease Perez out. Horace lowered the wagon's tailgate, and Preacher and Kelleher carefully lifted the wounded man into the wagon bed, positioning him on his side again and placing supplies around him to keep him propped up that way.

Preacher checked the crude dressings Kelleher had bound onto the arrow holes and saw that some blood had soaked through the cloth. Not much, though, which was a good sign.

Kelleher folded a blanket and slipped it under Perez's head as a pillow, then spread another blanket over him.

That left Lee Thorpe's body to deal with. Horace insisted on helping Preacher wrestle his brother's corpse into the wagon, where they placed it beside Dennis Burke's.

If they'd had a full load of supplies, there wouldn't have been room in the wagon for the two dead men and the unconscious Perez. As things were, it was a tight fit.

None of them was going to complain, though, Preacher thought grimly.

"You'll have to handle the wagon, Eugene," he told Kelleher, who nodded without hesitation.

"I've done that plenty of times before," he said. "We'll need to move pretty quick."

Preacher and Thorpe hitched up the team while Fitzwarren began saddling their mounts. During his time out here on the frontier, Fitzwarren had become a capable rider and horsemen and could handle that chore.

It wasn't long before they were ready to go. Kelleher settled onto the driver's seat and took up the wagon's reins. The other men swung into their saddles, and Preacher said, "Dog, around the lake, scout!"

The big cur took off at a run. Fitzwarren watched him go, shook his head, and said, "Even though I've seen more than sufficient evidence of it, I'm still amazed at how he seems to understand every word you say, Preacher."

"That's what happens when you ride the trails together for a while," Preacher said. "I've been mighty lucky when it comes to partnerin' up out here."

Preacher rode on one side of the wagon, Geoffrey Fitzwarren on the other. Horace Thorpe brought up the rear with the extra horses. They were all on the alert for trouble as they headed around the end of the lake and started up the valley between the rugged peaks.

Chapter 29

There hadn't been a lot of the day left when they made camp the first time, and fighting off the Sioux had taken up quite a bit of the remaining daylight.

Because of that, the group made it only about a mile up the valley from the site of the battle before it was too dark for them to press on.

"It'll be a cold camp," Preacher told the others. "I reckon those Injuns could find us without much trouble if they wanted to, but there ain't no point in makin' it easier for 'em."

Luckily, they had filled their canteens while they were at the lake, although they hadn't gotten around to filling the water barrel attached to the wagon. That wasn't a worry, because there were plenty of small streams in these mountains, running clear and cold from snowmelt. They had jerky they could gnaw for a sparse supper, too.

"We'll leave Salvador where he is in the wagon," Preacher went on. "Eugene, better take a look at him while you can still see at all."

Kelleher nodded. "I'll clean the wounds again and

change those dressin's. I think if we can keep those holes from festerin', the lad will pull through. He'll likely be laid up for a good spell, though."

They had stopped where a rocky bluff overlooked a small clearing. This wasn't nearly as good a camp site as the other place had been, but circumstances hadn't left them much choice.

Salvador Perez regained consciousness while Kelleher was using a whiskey-soaked cloth to clean the arrow wounds. He yelled and tried to sit up, but Kelleher put a big hand on his shoulder and held him down.

"Take it easy, boy," Kelleher told him. "You're wounded and I know it hurts like blazes, but you're gonna be all right." Kelleher lifted his head. "Geoff, come over here."

Fitzwarren joined them and knelt next to Perez. Following Kelleher's instructions, he held Perez still and spoke soothingly to the young man while Kelleher finished cleaning and rebandaging the wounds.

Since there wasn't a heated battle going on around them this time, he was able to do a better job on the dressings than he had earlier.

"There you go," Kelleher said as he sat back. He gave Perez a drink of water from one of the canteens and then put a piece of jerky in his mouth. "Chew on that for a while. It'll take your mind off the pain and give you some strength, too."

When the others had eaten, Preacher said, "Dog and me are gonna go up on that bluff and spend the night there. Don't want those Sioux sneakin' up on it so they can shoot down at us. If anybody comes skulkin' around, Dog'll smell 'em out and let me know."

Fitzwarren eyed the bluff skeptically. Most of the light had faded from the sky by now, so it was just a steep, dark bulk as it loomed above them.

"I suppose now you're going to claim that Dog can sprout wings and fly up there," he said.

"Nope," Preacher said. "But you recollect how I've said he probably has some wolf blood in him? Well, I reckon he might be part mountain goat, too."

"That's simply not poss—" Fitzwarren stopped short. "Oh, you're joshing with me again, aren't you?"

"Maybe a little," Preacher said with a grin. "He's mighty good at climbin', though. You'll see. Come on, Dog."

Despite the darkness, Preacher climbed the bluff as easily as if it had been broad daylight. His keen eyes and iron muscles made that possible.

And with an agility rivaling that of a mountain goat, Dog scrambled up the slope, as well, jumping from one small outcropping to the next. Within minutes, both man and dog pulled themselves over the edge onto the top of the bluff, thirty feet above the clearing.

From here, Preacher could see across the valley, although now that night had fallen there wasn't a lot to see. Just a sweeping vista of darkness culminating in mountains that threw up their rocky ramparts toward the star-scattered darkness above.

A cool breeze blew, carrying with it the soft songs of nightbirds. Preacher heard some rustling in the brush, too, but knew it was caused by the nocturnal ramblings of various small animals. His instincts would have told him if the sounds were caused by humans, and Dog would have confirmed that with a soft growl.

No, it was a peaceful night, and Preacher hoped it stayed that way. In the morning, they would bury Dennis Burke and Lee Thorpe and then push on.

For now, he wanted to get some sleep, the light, one-eye-open, instantly awake slumber that veteran frontiersmen knew how to achieve. He stretched out on the ground—he'd slept on harder surfaces, many times—placed his rifle beside him, closed his eyes, and dozed off almost immediately.

Earlier that day, in the late afternoon, the group led by Zadicus Knox had been at the edge of the mountains when the sound of distant gunfire came drifting through the air.

Knox reined in and signaled for the others to do likewise. He looked over at Bull and said, "Do you reckon that's them? Preacher's bunch?"

"There just ain't no way of knowin'," the big man replied. "I'm sorry, Zadicus. I wish I could say one way or the other."

Hanley nudged his horse forward and said, "From the sound of all that shootin', whoever it is has themselves a small war goin' on."

"Maybe Preacher and his friends ran into some redskins," Bull speculated.

Under the circumstances, that sounded reasonable to Bellamy. How ironic would it be if they followed their quarry all the way out here, only to find that Preacher's party had been wiped out by savages? The many delays in catching up to the other group could have doomed their plan to failure.

Not that he actually cared one way or the other, he reminded himself. He had never intended to align himself with a gang of outlaws. That alliance had been purely a matter of bad luck and necessity.

"What do we do now?" Hanley asked.

"Same thing we've always done," snapped Knox. "We push on."

They heeled their horses into motion and followed the canyon into the mountains.

Bull had picked up the trail a couple of weeks earlier, after seemingly endless wandering that caused mutinous feelings to run high in the gang again. They were so far behind Preacher's group that it had taken this long to get anywhere near them—and they still hadn't quite done so.

Bull assured them they were close now. The gunfire they had just heard seemed to confirm that. Bellamy sensed the anticipation gripping his companions. They were eager to see if Knox's plan was going to work out.

The shooting stopped within a few minutes. Knox called another halt.

"Whatever that ruckus was, it appears to be over," he said with a frown. "I don't want to ride right into some sort of jackpot."

Knox turned his head to glare at the others.

"Hanley, you and Duke feel up to doin' some scoutin'?"

Bellamy knew that wasn't an actual question. Knox was giving an order.

"What do you mean by that, Zadicus?" Hanley asked with a suspicious frown.

Knox snorted. "Just what I said, damn it. You two ride on ahead and see what you can find."

"You mean you want us to get killed instead of you."

Coldly, Knox said, "In case you've forgotten, I'm the boss of this bunch. I don't want you to get killed, but damn right you're gonna risk your lives to protect the rest of us—includin' me—by findin' out what's ahead of us. If you don't like it, Hanley, then you're welcome to try runnin' things for a while—if you think you can do it."

Bellamy knew what that meant, and so did every other man in the group. Zadicus Knox wouldn't relinquish command of the gang without a fight—and if that came about, it would be a fight to the death.

Hanley didn't want to risk that. He glared impotently for a moment and then finally turned his head to growl at Bellamy, "Come on, Duke. Looks like we're gonna be scouts."

Bellamy nodded and moved forward to join Hanley. With their rifles held ready across the saddles in front of them, they rode slowly up the canyon while the other men waited where they were.

"For what it's worth," Bellamy said quietly, "I don't like this, either."

"Don't reckon we've got any choice. Zadicus'd shoot down any man who gave him too much back talk." Hanley shook his head. "Sometimes I wonder why any of us ride with such a loco son of a gun. But he's led us to quite a bit of loot in the past."

He looked around the canyon and then added, "We'd best spread out some."

"No point in giving the enemy an easy shot at both of us, is there?"

"That's right."

The canyon was several hundred yards wide at this point. Hanley angled his horse toward the left-hand wall. Bellamy veered toward the right. Soon they were riding along with quite a bit of distance between them.

The canyon had enough bends in it that the other men quickly fell out of sight behind the two scouts. Bellamy felt his nerves growing taut as he and Hanley penetrated deeper into the mountains.

They rode around another curve, and what they saw prompted both men to rein in sharply.

Dusk was beginning to settle in, but enough light remained for them to see a small lake ahead of them, formed by a waterfall on the left side of the canyon.

"Beautiful," murmured Bellamy.

Hanley was too far away to hear the soft-voiced comment. The outlaw turned his horse and rode over to join Bellamy.

"That looks like a good spot to camp," Hanley said. "Let's go take a closer look."

As they drew nearer, riding side by side now, Bellamy's first impression that this was a lovely, scenic place began to crumble. Nothing had changed about the trees, the lake, the stream, the mountains, or the fading blue vault of heaven above them.

But something had been added: several odd shapes on the ground. For some reason, they caused a feeling of unease to stir within Bellamy.

Hanley must have experienced the same thing, because he slowed and muttered, "What the hell?"

They were close enough now to make out more details. Bellamy swallowed and said, "They appear to be bodies."

"Preacher and his bunch? Damn it, if they've been wiped out by savages—"

"I don't believe they're white men," Bellamy interrupted. "I think they may be Indians."

Hanley squinted. "You might be right. Come on."

They rode closer still. It was obvious the corpses were dressed in buckskins and had feathers in their dark hair.

Hanley reined in when they were about twenty feet from the bodies. Bellamy did likewise.

"They're Injuns, no doubt about that," Hanley said. "Do you know what tribe they're from?"

"How would I know?" asked Bellamy. "I've never been out here before. This is the first time I've ever laid eyes on this particular type of Indian. I'm not even from your country, you know."

"Yeah, yeah," muttered Hanley. He scratched his angular, beard-stubbled jaw. "These redskins look like they've been shot. They don't have any arrows stickin' in 'em, that's for sure. So it's likely Preacher and his bunch are the ones who shot 'em."

"That appears to be the most likely theory, yes," Bellamy agreed.

"And Preacher won the fight, since these dead savages are here and Preacher and his friends ain't."

"Again, impeccable reasoning."

Hanley shot an annoyed glance at his companion. "Are you makin' fun of me?" he demanded.

"Not at all," Bellamy replied. "I think everything you've said is correct—"

He was looking past Hanley as he spoke, and even though the light was getting bad, Bellamy's eyesight was keen enough for him to notice a flicker of movement in some brush beyond the man.

An arrowhead and the shaft it was attached to poked through a gap in the branches, and Bellamy realized with a shock that it was aimed toward his companion.

Chapter 30

Bellamy yelled, "Look out!" at Hanley and raised his rifle to his shoulder.

Hanley jerked hard enough in surprise that the tug on the reins made his horse jump skittishly to one side. That saved his life as the arrow flew out of the brush and whipped past him, missing Bellamy as well.

The next second, Bellamy pressed his rifle's trigger and the weapon boomed as it kicked against his shoulder.

He aimed at the spot where the arrow had come from. In the fading light, with a cloud of powder smoke in the air, Bellamy couldn't see much.

He heard a screech of pain from the brush, though.

Hanley pulled hard on his mount's reins to bring the animal under control and then hauled the horse around as he yelled, "Injuns! Let's get outta here!"

Bellamy heard something flutter past his ear and knew that an arrow had just missed him by the barest of margins. His horse danced to the side as he rammed the now empty rifle back into its scabbard.

Hanley banged his heels against his horse's flanks. The animal jumped ahead, panic-stricken, but instead of breaking into a gallop, it began lunging back and forth, twisting and dancing, paying no attention to Hanley's desperate shouts or the boot heels digging frantically into its sides.

Another arrow sailed past Bellamy as he drew both pistols from the sash around his waist. He had no idea where this unexpected coolness under fire was coming from, but he didn't want to waste it.

He thumbed back the hammers on his pistols as he leveled them at the brush. When he squeezed the triggers, long tongues of flame licked out from both muzzles, brilliantly vivid in the dusk. The shots blended together into one thunderous roar.

Since it was impossible to know how much damage his shots had done, if any, Bellamy stuffed the right-hand pistol behind his sash again, grabbed the reins, and turned his horse. He saw that a few yards away, Hanley had finally gotten his mount under control again.

Both men leaned forward in their saddles to make themselves smaller targets as they galloped back in the direction they had come from.

They hadn't gone very far when several Indians mounted on swift ponies burst out of some trees to the left and raced toward them, howling ferociously and firing arrows from the backs of their ponies.

Hanley yelled in fear and dismay as an arrow drove deep into his horse's neck and caused the animal to stumble. Its head sagged, and a second later, the horse's front legs buckled underneath it.

As it started to collapse, Hanley kicked his feet free of the stirrups just in time. When the horse went down hard in a welter of flailing limbs, Hanley was thrown forward over its head and narrowly avoided having his own skull crushed by a slashing, steel-shod hoof.

He landed hard and rolled over a couple of times before coming to a stop on his belly.

Bellamy raced past the fallen man before he could stop. Part of him—a large part, in fact—urged him to just keep going, to put as much distance between himself and those hostile Indians as he could. Undoubtedly, some of them would stop to murder Hanley, and that might slow down the pursuit.

That was exactly what Hanley would do if the circumstances were reversed, Bellamy told himself.

Perhaps knowing that was the reason he reined in and turned his horse again.

"Hanley!" he cried as he urged his horse into a run. From the corner of his eye he saw the mounted Indians closing in on them.

Hanley looked up, his eyes wide with terror. Bellamy shoved his other pistol behind the sash and stretched out that hand, extending his arm as far as it would go and leaning to one side in the saddle.

Hanley pushed up onto his hands and knees and then surged higher as Bellamy's horse loomed beside him. He flung his left arm up. Bellamy caught Hanley's wrist and Hanley clasped Bellamy's wrist.

The sudden weight was a painful jerk on Bellamy's arm. For a second, it felt almost as if his shoulder was going to pop out of its socket.

But the socket held, and so did the grip of Bellamy's legs around his horse's body. He lifted Hanley off the ground. The kick Hanley added with his legs helped vault him up behind Bellamy. He scrambled to secure his position of the back of the galloping horse.

Hanley wrapped his arms around Bellamy as he settled himself. The horse slowed. It had no choice but to do so since it was carrying double now.

Bellamy looked over his shoulder as more arrows fell around them. The Indians were close. They wouldn't miss very many more shots.

"Faster!" Hanley urged. "You gotta go faster!"

"We can't!" Bellamy said. "The horse can't do it!"

He looked around, searching desperately for any place they might be able to take cover.

He spotted a few rocks and some trees to their right. That wouldn't provide much cover, but it was better than nothing.

As he angled in that direction, he asked Hanley, "Is your pistol loaded?"

"Yes! I'll get it out—"

"No!" Bellamy said. "You won't hit anything from the back of a running horse. Save it until you can aim."

"They might back off!"

"Not from a wild shot!"

The part of his brain that was standing off to one side, watching calmly as this perilous situation unfolded, wondered what had possessed him to start giving orders like that. He had been in danger a number of times previously, and he had never been this cool and collected.

Maybe the journey out here had hardened something inside him. He knew the long days had toughened him up physically, whittling away any softness in his body until he was whipcord lean, strong, and fast. He hadn't noticed the same being true of his mind and heart, but he couldn't rule it out.

He checked again to see how close the Indians were and then guided the horse through the rocks and into the trees. As he reined to a sliding stop, he told Hanley, "Give me your gun!"

"Hell, no!"

"Then you'll have to make the shot. You've got to bring down one of those Indians. That might cause the others to break off their attack, at least for a few moments."

What Bellamy wanted was a chance to reload his own weapons.

Just as when Melville Atherton and his toadies had surrounded him, he didn't want to give up without a fight.

Of course, that hadn't turned out very well, and this probably wouldn't, either. But the urge inside Bellamy to strike back was too strong to deny.

Bellamy and Hanley hit the ground at the same time. Hanley looked like he had his wits about him a little better now. Panic had loosened its grip a bit. He dropped behind one of the rocks onto one knee and leveled the pistol.

With his back pressed against a tree trunk, Bellamy began reloading his pistols.

Hanley's gun roared. Bellamy glanced in that direction in time to see one of the attackers fling his arms in the air. The Indian swayed to the side and pitched off his running pony. Two of the other warriors had to jerk their mounts to the side to avoid trampling the fallen man.

That broke the charge's momentum, just as Bellamy had hoped it would. The Indians slowed and milled around for a few seconds.

Those seconds were precious, because they allowed Bellamy to finish loading his pistols, and he was able to reach the shelter of a large stone slab without having to dodge arrows.

He knelt like Hanley was doing and aimed both guns as the Indians recovered from the shock of losing a man and pounded toward them again.

Bellamy concentrated on a barrel-chested warrior wearing a more elaborate headdress made of feathers than the other Indians. He hoped that this headgear signified a chief or some other important member of the war party. Lining his right-hand pistol's sights on that broad chest, he squeezed the trigger.

Without waiting to see if his shot found its target, he switched his aim to one of the other warriors in the forefront of the party and triggered the left-hand gun.

This time, he saw the man sway back and then fall forward over his pony's neck and slide to the ground, where he landed in a heap.

A few feet away, the stocky warrior in the feathered headdress was also sprawled motionless, knocked off his pony by Bellamy's first shot.

The other Indians reined in even though they were howling in anger at losing those comrades. They turned their ponies and started to withdraw.

Hanley let out a triumphant whoop and raised up from behind the rock. He had reloaded his pistol and fired it after the retreating Indians. One of the warriors jerked but remained mounted and kept going.

"They're on the run!" Hanley exulted. "We beat the filthy red devils!"

Bellamy had already noticed some movement back in the direction they had come from. He looked closer now and saw Zadicus Knox, Bull, and the rest of the gang galloping toward them. They had heard the shots and were coming to see what was going on, Bellamy knew.

"Those Indians are only retreating because they realized we have reinforcements coming," Bellamy told Hanley. "They probably couldn't tell how many were in the group, so they're playing it safe."

"I don't care why they're doin' it, as long as they're not tryin' to kill us anymore."

"That seems to be the case," Bellamy allowed. The Indians who had been mounted were out of sight now. The others who had been hidden in the brush must have withdrawn, as well. No more arrows came from that direction.

Knox and the others thundered up. "Are you boys all right?" Knox called to Bellamy and Hanley.

"I lost my horse, Zadicus. The dirty sons killed it."

"I'm sorry about that, Hanley," Knox said. "We've got extra mounts, though. Come on, you two. Let's get outta here while the gettin's good."

"What about following Preacher?" Bellamy asked.

"There's Injuns between us and him," Knox answered

impatiently. "Let's give them a chance to settle down first. I ain't forgot about Preacher, though, don't you worry about that. We're gonna get him and that rich fella who hired him, and there ain't no amount of redskins in the world are gonna stop us!"

That seemed awfully optimistic to Bellamy, but right now, he didn't want to argue.

He was more concerned about getting out of here with a whole skin, too.

Chapter 31

The night passed peacefully where Preacher and the others were camped. He was grateful for that; after the harrowing attack by the Sioux, the survivors sorely needed some rest.

The next morning in the gray light of impending dawn, Preacher sent Dog off to scout the area. He climbed down the bluff and joined Eugene Kelleher beside the small fire that Kelleher had just kindled into life.

"How's Perez this mornin'?" Preacher asked.

Kelleher hunkered on his heels and placed a coffeepot at the edge of the flames.

"The boy was a mite restless most of the night," he said, "but he was able to get some sleep. I haven't checked the bandages on his wounds yet. I'm waitin' for it to get a mite lighter before I do that."

Preacher nodded and said, "Mornin', Horace," as the remaining Thorpe brother came up to the fire, yawning and stumbling a little as he tried to shake off slumber's cobwebs.

"Mornin', Preacher, Eugene," Horace said. He took

off his hat and raked his fingers through his dark hair, then yawned again. A solemn expression came over his face as he went on, "You know, when I woke up just now, I thought for a second that Lee was still alive. I even looked around for him when I sat up, just like I always do. But he wasn't there."

Preacher put a hand on Horace's shoulder and squeezed.

"I'm mighty sorry we lost him," he said.

"He wasn't just my brother, he was my best friend, you know. There's somethin' missin' inside me now, like a part of me's been torn out and taken away."

"And I reckon you'll always feel that way," Preacher told him, thinking back on the losses he had suffered in his own life. "The hurt'll get less as time goes by, but it won't never go away completely."

"At least we can lay him to rest proper-like and didn't have to leave him for those damned savages to have their bloody sport with." Horace's voice caught a little as he spoke. "Lee loved it out here in the high country. I can't think of anywhere else he'd rather spend eternity."

"I knew Dennis Burke well enough to say he'd feel the same way."

The three men fell into a sober silence for a moment as they stood around the campfire.

Then Geoffrey Fitzwarren broke that silence by coming to them and saying, "Good morning, lads."

Horace just grunted and didn't return the greeting. He scowled at Fitzwarren, who didn't seem to notice, or at least didn't acknowledge it.

They had come out here because of Fitzwarren, thought Preacher, and it was possible Horace blamed the man at least a little for his brother's death.

But they had all been well aware of the risks, and they had signed on for the journey of their own free will. Horace knew that and would come to realize that what had happened wasn't really Fitzwarren's fault.

After the cold supper the night before, coffee and biscuits and fried salt pork tasted wonderful this morning, well worth the small risk of having a fire. Preacher felt human again by the time he finished breakfast.

As he nursed the last bit of coffee in his cup, he stepped over beside the wagon to ask Kelleher, "How's he doin'?"

Kelleher had climbed into the wagon bed a few minutes earlier to check on Salvador Perez. It was the young man who answered Preacher's question.

"I'm all right, Preacher," Perez said. "Very weak, and I hurt like El Diablo himself is tormenting me, but I will live."

Preacher grinned as he rested one arm on the sideboards.

"I'm mighty glad to hear it," he said. "You agree with that medical opinion, Eugene?"

"Indeed I do," replied Kelleher as he straightened from tying a fresh bandage into place on Perez's chest. "The wounds have stopped bleedin', and while they must be mighty sore—"

"They are," Perez confirmed.

"—they don't show any evidence of festerin',"

Kelleher went on. "With enough rest, this boy will be himself again."

Perez snorted. "The hell with rest. I have to get up and drive the wagon."

"You'll not be gettin' up and doin' anything of the sort," Kelleher declared. "You just rest. I'll fetch you some coffee and somethin' to eat while the rest of us, ah, take care of some other chores."

"Digging graves for Lee and Dennis," Perez said. He looked at Preacher and nodded. "I know that they were killed in the fighting. Eugene told me."

Preacher, Fitzwarren, and Horace Thorpe looked around until they found a suitable place for the grave. They had brought along a pair of shovels with the supplies in case the wagon wheels ever got stuck and had to be dug out. They dug only one grave; the two men would be laid to rest together. There were plenty of rocks scattered around that could be piled up to form a cairn that would mark the spot, at least for a while.

Over time, the elements would claim even that, of course. Nature reclaimed everything, Preacher knew, and one day it would be as if he himself had never been here and walked this earth. A fella had to realize and accept that ultimate fate and hope that it all meant something anyway, despite a lack of evidence to that effect.

They wrapped the bodies in blankets and carried them to the grave. Working in grim silence, they filled in the hole and stacked up the rocks to keep predators away. It was late morning before they were finished with the task.

The effort had been enough to put sweat on the faces of the men. Preacher took off his hat, sleeved the beads from his face, and stood beside the grave for a moment. The others joined him, except for Perez, and removed their hats as well.

"So long to good friends, and a brother to one of us, as well," Preacher said. "Here's hopin' the Good Lord will watch over them and not get too annoyed with 'em if they go to roustin' around Heaven too much. I know that Lee and Dennis weren't the sort to sit still in one place for too long. They were too fiddle-footed for that."

"Farewell to valiant comrades," added Fitzwarren as he held his hat over his heart.

"Save a place by the fire for me, brother," Horace said, his voice choked with emotion.

These were practical men. The hard lives they had lived on the frontier gave them no other option than to be that way. There was nothing else they could do for the men they had just buried. They turned away from the grave and went back to work preparing for the next stage of the journey.

Dog had trotted back into the camp during the morning, evidently untroubled by anything he had encountered while roaming around the area.

That told Preacher the Sioux weren't lurking in the vicinity. If they had been, Dog would have communicated that to him by whining and acting eager to lead Preacher to them.

Eugene Kelleher handled the wagon again today as they followed the valley deeper into the mountains. At times, it narrowed down until it was no more than a canyon with steep walls a couple of hundred yards apart.

In other places, the slopes retreated until the valley was more than a mile wide, a grassy park with plenty of trees and brush and small, rocky knolls.

Preacher rode ahead of the wagon, and Dog ranged farther in front than he did. Fitzwarren and Horace stayed with the wagon. Because of that, Preacher was the first one to become aware of how the mountains were closing in from the sides.

The way ahead was blocked, he realized. That wasn't the path he remembered from his last trip through these parts, but people who talked about how the mountains were unchanging were wrong. The landscape *did* evolve. Avalanches took place and closed passes.

From what Preacher could see, that was what had happened here. He reined in and stared for a long moment at the place where the slopes pinched in from the sides and finally came together in an impassible rocky upthrust.

He whistled for Dog and waited. A few minutes later, the big cur came into sight, loping toward him. Dog still seemed unbothered by anything he had found in his scouting.

Of course Dog wasn't upset, thought Preacher. He hadn't run into any Sioux up there ahead of them.

That was because the Sioux were now *behind* them.

Preacher blew out a disgusted breath. It was easy to understand why the Indians hadn't attacked them again.

The Sioux lived in these mountains. They would be fully aware how the route followed by Preacher and his companions was going to play out. All they had to do was fall back, stay out of sight, and follow the men on whom they wanted vengeance.

They were bottled up in here, good and proper. Trapped like sheep in a pen.

And the Sioux would be coming for them, probably soon.

Chapter 32

With Dog loping alongside him and Horse, Preacher hurried back to rejoin the others. Kelleher brought the wagon team to a stop when he saw the mountain man coming.

Fitzwarren and Horace reined in as well. They all sat waiting for him with a visible air of tension gripping them, as if they knew he was about to deliver bad news.

"We need to find a place to fort up," Preacher said without preamble as he brought Horse to a stop.

"What's wrong?" Kelleher asked from the wagon seat.

"This canyon's a dead end, boys. There used to be a pass up ahead yonder that would have led us farther into the mountains, but it's gone now. Looks like a rock slide closed it up since the last time I've been through these parts."

Horace Thorpe looked around. "There were other canyons branching off, back the way we came from. If we could make it to one of those, we might still get out of here."

He had a point, but Preacher didn't believe it was a workable idea.

"I'll bet a hat those Sioux are less than a mile behind us right now, just bidin' their time," he said. "If we try to backtrack too much, they'll realize we've figured out that we're boxed in, and they'll go ahead and hit us. We'll be out in the open when they do, too."

"So you believe we should locate a place we can defend," Fitzwarren said.

"That's right. I recollect seein' a cleft in the wall a little ways back with some rocks in front of it. If that crack is big enough to get the wagon and the horses in it, we can use the rocks for cover and hold off those Sioux."

"Long enough for them to decide to give up and leave us alone?" asked Kelleher.

"Maybe," Preacher replied.

He wasn't optimistic about the possibility of the Sioux ever giving up, though. They had killed too many of the warriors. The thirst for vengeance would be too strong in the Sioux and would have to be satisfied.

Kelleher turned the wagon around and the group began retracing its route. Preacher saw the cleft he'd been talking about up ahead and pointed it out.

Urging the team to greater speed, Kelleher called over his shoulder to his wounded passenger, "Sorry about bouncin' you around back there, lad. We've got to make good time, though."

"Don't worry about that," Perez told him. "Do what you need to do, Eugene. But when we get where we're going, I want a gun so I can fight, too."

Preacher heard that and grinned. The young Mexican might be hurt, but he still had plenty of grit and spirit. He wouldn't be able to handle a rifle, but he could fire a pistol just fine, Preacher reckoned.

Dog, running ahead of the others, suddenly stopped, whirled around, and barked sharply. Preacher heeded the big cur's warning and looked past Dog, back along the canyon. He spotted the group of mounted warriors riding hard toward them.

The Sioux were still three-quarters of a mile away. Preacher and his companions were closer to the cleft where they sought to take refuge, but with the wagon, they couldn't move as fast as a war party mounted on swift ponies.

All they could do was try, thought Preacher.

Well, there might be something else, he amended. He looked around at Fitzwarren and called, "Geoff, I'm gonna ride on ahead and try to slow down those varmints."

"You can't do that," Fitzwarren protested as he urged his mount alongside Horse. "You'll be killed!"

"That ain't my plan," Preacher assured him. "You're in charge, but pay attention to anything Eugene has to say. He's a smart old bird."

"If you're determined to go, I'm coming with you!"

"No, you ain't. And you promised you'd do what I told you!"

With that, Preacher heeled the big stallion into a faster run and pulled away from Fitzwarren's horse with ease. He didn't look back to make sure Fitzwarren was following orders. He'd done what he could, as far as that went.

Becoming aware of the shaggy gray shape racing along for all he was worth, Preacher turned his head and yelled, "Dog, get back with the others! Go back and guard!"

The big cur continued running, obviously intent on engaging with the Sioux. Preacher had to shout again, "Dog! Go back!" before Dog finally slowed and reluctantly turned around to rejoin the others.

That eased Preacher's mind somewhat. With the speed Horse was making and the way the Sioux were charging toward him, the gap between them was disappearing rapidly.

He had passed the cleft in the canyon wall and the Indians were only a few hundred yards away now. Preacher estimated that the war party numbered between twenty and thirty.

Mighty hefty odds, but he intended to whittle them down a tad.

Not just yet, though. He had to wait until they were closer.

They probably thought he was plumb loco, one man charging a whole war party this way.

Maybe he was crazy, he thought as a grin tugged at the corners of his mouth under the thick mustache. He had always been the type to charge hell with a bucket of water.

But he wasn't throwing his life away mindlessly. He had a plan.

Two hundred yards. A hundred.

Close enough.

Preacher hauled back on the reins and brought Horse

to a sliding stop. “Hold steady, old son!” he said as he dropped both hands to the Colt Paterson revolvers on his hips.

The irons whispered out of leather and came up level. Preacher thumbed back the hammer on the right-hand gun and fired as soon as the trigger dropped down into place. The Colt boomed and bucked and spewed fire and lead.

A split second later, the left-hand gun joined in the chorus of death.

Back and forth, right and left, Preacher fired in one steady, crashing roll of gun-thunder that echoed back from the canyon walls in a crazed symphony. The storm of lead scythed into the war party’s front ranks.

The Sioux were packed so closely together that Preacher didn’t have to be a deadly accurate shot—although he was. Warrior after warrior either pitched to the side or flipped backward off his speeding pony as Preacher’s barrage smashed into them. The attack faltered and then broke as the Sioux who hadn’t been gunned down began milling around wildly.

Preacher looked over his shoulder. Fitzwarren and Horace were just reaching the rocks in front of the cleft. The wagon was about twenty yards away but still moving.

The mountain man had done all he could. The rest was up to his companions. He pouched the empty irons, grabbed Horse’s reins, and whirled the big stallion back around.

Chapter 33

Preacher knew it wouldn't take the Sioux long to recover from the devastating onslaught of lead and resume their attack.

"Give it all you got, Horse," he said as he leaned forward in the saddle and dug his boot heels into the stallion's flanks.

Horse leaped ahead, covering a seemingly impossible chunk of ground in that initial bound. When he came down, his hooves were already flashing. He stretched out, muscles working smoothly under his sleek gray hide, and surged over the landscape at incredible speed.

"Trail, Horse, trail!" Preacher yelled in encouragement, not that the gallant stallion needed it.

Preacher turned his head to glance over his shoulder. The Sioux were coming after him, all right, but those few seconds they had delayed had given him and Horse the chance to open up a better lead.

More importantly, Eugene Kelleher had had time to get the wagon to the cleft in the canyon wall. Preacher still didn't know if the opening was big enough—but the wagon disappeared inside it, so he supposed it was.

Horse had plenty of sand, but the strongest, most valiant mount in the world would play out pretty quickly running flat out like this. Preacher felt Horse's stride began to falter just slightly. Not enough that most riders would even notice it, but so finely attuned were they to each other that Preacher knew his old friend had to slow down or risk bursting his heart.

He put a little pressure on the reins, just enough to let Horse know it was all right. The stallion's pace eased slightly, then a bit more. He was still running faster than most horses would ever be able to match.

But no longer as fast as those Indian ponies behind him. At full speed, he had pulled away from them, widened the lead even more, but now the lead was shrinking, even though only by a small margin.

That was enough to encourage the pursuers. They howled and yipped and banged their heels against their ponies, urging them on.

Geoffrey Fitzwarren and Horace Thorpe ran out of the opening in the canyon wall and took cover behind the boulders in front of it. They thrust rifles over the rocks and took aim.

From Preacher's vantage point, it looked like they were getting ready to shoot him, but he knew they were actually aiming at the Indians behind him.

He didn't hear the reports over the rataplan of Horse's hoofbeats, but he saw powder smoke spurt from the muzzles of both rifles. He didn't look back to see if the shots found their targets but concentrated instead on steering the big stallion toward the boulders.

He was already slowing down when he reached the rocks. Horse darted nimbly between the boulders and ran on into the cleft. Preacher pulled his rifle from its scabbard as he swung down from the saddle, his feet hitting the ground before Horse stopped moving.

He turned and ran to one of the boulders that came chest-high on him. The Sioux were only about fifty yards away now. He slid the rifle over the rock, nestled his cheek against the stock, and drew a bead on one of the Indians in the forefront of the war party.

The rifle's sharp crack was a beautiful sound. The sight of the Sioux warrior throwing his arms in the air and tumbling off his pony was welcome, too.

Fitzwarren and Horace had reloaded by now and lined their rifles again. Horace fired first, followed by Fitzwarren. Preacher heard the shots but didn't know if they scored, because he was busy swapping out the cylinders in his Colts, replacing the spent ones with fully loaded ones.

He snapped the revolvers closed and thrust both of them over the rock. The Sioux were in range for the Colts, close enough that he could see their faces twisted with snarls of hate and rage.

Preacher opened fire, sweeping the war party with another deadly hail of heavy-caliber lead balls.

The sound of a rifle shot made him glance over as the Colts ran dry. Eugene Kelleher had joined the battle. Preacher didn't see Salvador Perez. He supposed the wounded man had remained in the wagon, despite what he'd said earlier about wanting a pistol.

The next moment, Preacher saw that wasn't right. Perez lurched forward, leaned on the rock beside Kelleher, and pointed a pistol at the onrushing Sioux. The weapon boomed. Perez was weak enough that the recoil appeared to jolt him quite a bit, but he stayed on his feet.

The terrible volley from Preacher's Colts had slowed the attack, but the warriors who had survived were too close to be turned away now—and there wasn't time to reload.

Arrows flew at the defenders. Most of them glanced off the boulders or splintered against the rock, but enough got through to be dangerous.

Horace Thorpe reeled back with an arrow in his chest. He caught his balance, grimaced, and clutched at the arrow's shaft with his left hand.

With his right hand, he drew the hunting knife from its sheath at his waist and charged at the Sioux, shouting curses.

He had taken only a couple of steps when three more arrows struck him in the torso. He stumbled, weaved to the side, and collapsed.

The arrows stopped flying because some of the warriors were close enough to the rocks to leap off their ponies and attack on foot. Despite his left arm hanging limp because of the wounds in his shoulder, Perez leaped to meet the first Sioux who rushed between two of the boulders. He had reversed the pistol he held and swung it like a club at the Indian's head.

The blow landed solidly but came too late to stop the warrior's momentum from carrying him into Perez. The knife in the Sioux's hand ripped into Perez's stomach.

Perez screamed as the cold steel sliced into his belly, but he was able to strike again with the pistol butt, cracking the Indian's skull. The collision sent both men to the ground, Perez on the bottom with the dead or dying Sioux on top of him. Perez writhed for a second and then lay still.

Kelleher gripped his rifle by the barrel and swung it back and forth like a flail. The stock shattered against an Indian's skull and knocked the man to the ground. Kelleher kept swinging and downed another of the Indians.

He rammed the broken stock into the belly of a third Indian and caused him to double over. Kelleher brought the rifle around in a looping, overhand swing and crushed the back of the man's skull.

Then one of the Sioux leaped on him from behind and began slashing at him with a knife.

Behind another boulder, Geoffrey Fitzwarren coolly drew a pistol and blew the brains out of a warrior who had a tomahawk poised to split his brain open. He ducked a swiping blow from a knife and rammed his shoulder into the chest of the warrior who wielded the blade. Fitzwarren slammed the empty pistol into the middle of the man's face and knocked him out.

Preacher has his knife in one hand and an empty pistol in the other. As Sioux warriors crowded around him, he laid waste to them, slashing throats and crushing skulls with every swing of his arm.

The Indians' own numbers worked against them in this instance; they couldn't get at Preacher without running into each other. But the mountain man was surrounded by enemies and could lash out in any direction and be assured of hitting one of them.

He clipped one of the attackers on the head, causing the warrior's knees to buckle. Preacher knew he had hit the man hard enough to knock him out but hadn't done any serious damage.

A second later, a screeching face was thrust right in front of him and he had to twist aside quickly as the screaming warrior tried to ram a knife into his belly. The blade scraped along his side and ripped his shirt but didn't break the skin.

Preacher didn't miss with his knife. He drove the blade into the side of the warrior's neck so hard that it went all the way through and came out the other side.

Unfortunately for Preacher, the knife grated on bone and got stuck in the Sioux's spinal column. He tried to pull it free, but it wouldn't come loose. He had no choice but to let go of the knife and shove the dead man aside.

Bending quickly, Preacher scooped up the tomahawk dropped by the warrior Fitzwarren had shot in the head. With the 'hawk in his hand, he was transformed into a whirlwind of death, spinning through the enemy and splitting skulls. Blood sprayed in the air like crimson rain. Gore coated Preacher's arm to the elbow.

But for every Sioux who fell, two more savage killers were there to take his place. Fitzwarren and Kelleher were still on their feet and fighting. Horace Thorpe and Salvador Perez were dead, killed in the fierce battle. Preacher, Fitzwarren, and Kelleher shifted until they were back to back to back.

They would sell their lives dearly in hand-to-hand combat until the Sioux overwhelmed them and dragged them down to death.

Chapter 34

A moment later, Preacher reckoned he was hearing things. The gunshots and the yelling couldn't be real.

Then a rifle ball blasted through a Sioux warrior's head and splattered the mountain man with blood and gray matter, and a strident voice howled in English, "Get 'em, boys! Kill the dirty redskins!"

Shots continued to roar, and more of the Indians fell. Men on horseback crowded among the rocks and fired pistols at almost point-blank range.

The Indians who hadn't been gunned down broke off their attack and tried to retreat. A couple of them were blasted into oblivion from behind, but the rest scrambled back to their ponies and fled, screeching in frustrated rage.

"Let 'em go!" yelled the man who seemed to be in charge of the rescue party as he waved an arm at his companions.

He was a big, rawboned man with a dark mustache and a hawk nose protruding above it. He had a hard, dangerous look about him, and so did the rest of his group.

Right now, though, they all looked mighty good to Preacher.

He turned to Fitzwarren, who stood beside him, and asked, "How bad are you hurt, Geoff?"

A trickle of blood ran down the right side of Fitzwarren's face from a cut on his forehead. He wiped some of it away, leaving a red smear behind on his cheek, and said, "I appear to have come through relatively unscathed. I think this minor injury is all I suffered."

Then he stared at Preacher and looked appalled.

"Good heavens, man, you're covered with blood! How are you still standing?"

A grim smile tugged at Preacher's mouth.

"Most of it ain't mine," he told Fitzwarren. "A few bumps and scratches, that's all."

He turned to Kelleher in sudden concern.

"Damn it, Eugene, the varmints damned near carved you to pieces!"

Kelleher had bloodstains on his clothes and several nasty-looking slashes on his face and arms. He insisted, "I'll be fine, Preacher. I've cut myself worse'n this shavin'—"

He didn't get any farther than that because his eyes rolled up in their sockets, his knees buckled, and he collapsed.

Preacher sprang to his side and knelt to grasp Kelleher's shoulders and roll him onto his back.

"Eugene! Blast it, you loco old varmint! Don't you die on us now."

"Injuns got him with their knives, did they?" a voice asked from behind the mountain man.

Preacher turned his head to look. The leader of the rescuers had dismounted and walked over to bend down and peer at Kelleher.

"Yeah, I can't tell how bad he's hurt. I don't reckon you've got a sawbones with you, have you?"

"Afraid not," the stranger said.

Preacher grunted and turned his attention back to Kelleher. "I ain't a doctor, but I've patched up a heap of knife wounds. I'll see what I can do for him. Geoff, check on Horace and Salvador just to make sure there's nothin' we can do for them."

Not surprisingly, a moment later Fitzwarren reported, "I'm afraid not, Preacher. They're both gone."

Preacher had opened Kelleher's coat to expose three knife wounds. As he examined them, he let out a bleak chuckle and said, "Eugene's lucky to weigh so much. That extra fat around his middle kept the knives from penetratin' too far. Those wounds are messy, but I reckon he's got a pretty good chance of survivin' 'em."

Preacher tore off a piece of Kelleher's shirt and began wiping away the blood.

While the mountain man was doing that, Fitzwarren turned to the leader of the rescuers and said, "I don't know who you fellows are, but I'm as happy to see you as anyone I've ever met. We were very close to being overrun by those savages, and I don't believe they would have shown us any mercy if that had happened."

"Yeah, you're mighty lucky we came along when we

did," the man said. "What's the old sayin'? We got here just in the nick o' time."

"You most assuredly did," Fitzwarren agreed with a smile. He extended his hand. "Geoffrey Fitzwarren here, sir, at your service."

The stranger clasped Fitzwarren's hand and introduced himself. "Zadicus Knox is my name."

"How did you and your friends happen to come to our timely aid?"

"We heard all the shootin' and figured somebody was in bad trouble. We decided to take a look, and as soon as we saw it was white men bein' attacked by redskins, we had to take a hand in the game."

"We're obliged to you," Preacher put in without looking up from what he was doing. He continued cleaning Kelleher's wounds and added, "You'd better post a guard just in case them Sioux decide to come back."

"That's the kind of Injun they were, huh? Sioux?"

"Teton Sioux."

"Plumb unfriendly, ain't they?"

"Sometimes yes, sometimes no," Preacher replied. "It depends on a lot of things. But now that we've had a few scraps with 'em and killed quite a few of their warriors, they ain't ever gonna be friendly to us again. I reckon by helpin' us, you've made enemies outta them, too, Knox."

"Don't reckon I care," Knox responded with a shrug. "We had to pitch in and help you boys."

Preacher paused long enough to glance up at Knox. "This your first time out here on the frontier?"

"As a matter of fact, it is. How'd you know that?"

"Oh, just a feelin' I got," Preacher said. It was based partially on the fact that Knox hadn't recognized the attackers as Sioux and partially on gut instinct. The men had the look of Easterners to him. Hardcase Easterners, at that.

A slight feeling of wariness stirred inside Preacher.

But he had to finish patching up Kelleher right now. He would worry about potential problems later.

The other members of Knox's group were still mounted. He said to two of them, "Hanley, Duke, you boys been workin' well together considerin' that you tried to beat the hell outta each other a while back. The two o' you spread out a mite and keep watch. Don't let them redskins sneak up on us."

To Preacher, he added, "You reckon it's likely they'll come back? There weren't more than a dozen of 'em who got away. Seems like they'd want to steer clear of us from here on out."

"Just because there were only a dozen left out of this bunch, that don't mean there ain't more warriors back where they came from."

"Yeah, I suppose that makes sense. I've got men watchin' out for 'em. We'll be ready if they go get help and come back."

Preacher hoped that was true. He also wondered what Fitzwarren would want to do now. With only three members left from their party, would it be possible to continue their search for the man called Williams who had been Barrett Treadway's partner?

Or was it time to abandon that mission and concentrate instead on getting back to civilization alive?

That might depend, Preacher realized, on just what Zadicus Knox and his friends were doing out here.

"What the hell is Zadicus waitin' for?" muttered Hanley as he and Bellamy rode out of the rocks where Preacher and his companions had made what was almost their last stand. "We finally caught up. Why don't he go ahead and kill Preacher and that fat fella while he's got the chance? Then we can take that Englishman prisoner and get the hell outta here."

"I can't really speak for Zadicus," Bellamy said, "but I imagine he wants to keep Preacher around for the moment in case those Indians come back and we have to battle them again. You could see for yourself what a fierce fighter the man must be! The bodies of the Indians he killed were literally heaped around him."

Bellamy hesitated before adding, "And that fellow Fitzwarren isn't an Englishman."

Hanley glanced at him in surprise. "He ain't? He sure sounds like one. Sounds just like you, in fact, Duke."

"People can have a British accent without actually being a native of England. There are subtle differences, but not enough that an untrained ear can distinguish them."

"Really?" Hanley shook his head. "Reckon I'll take your word for it. You both sound like furriners to me. Come to think of it, you never did really say where you're from—"

"We'd better spread out like Zadicus said," Bellamy

interrupted. He didn't want to go into the details of his background with this American outlaw.

Hanley frowned but didn't argue. He turned his horse away from Bellamy's and trotted toward the other side of the canyon. Bellamy blew out a sigh of relief as he headed the other way.

Once Preacher had swabbed the wounds with whiskey dribbled from the flask he found in Kelleher's coat pocket, he had Fitzwarren fetch one of the spare blankets from the wagon.

He cut some of it into strips and used them to tie in place the makeshift bandages he fashioned from other pieces of blanket. That was all he could do for Kelleher right now. More than likely, Kelleher had passed out from loss of blood and needed to rest while he was regaining some strength.

Preacher straightened from that task and sighed as he looked at the bodies of Horace Thorpe and Salvador Perez. Horace had been reunited with his brother Lee sooner than Preacher had expected. Perez would never return to the warmth of his homeland below the border. Both had been good men, and it was a shame to lose them.

He realized he hadn't seen Dog for a while. The big cur had been in the thick of the battle, and for a second, Preacher worried that he had been killed. But when he looked around the area between the rocks and the cleft in the canyon wall, he didn't see Dog's body.

It would have been just like Dog, Preacher reflected,

to chase after the Sioux when they beat a retreat, just to make sure they didn't double back. He almost whistled and called for his trail partner, but a sudden cautious urge stopped him from doing that.

Might be better to let Dog roam around without Knox and the other men knowing he was nearby, Preacher decided.

He turned to study Zadicus Knox and the other men. One of them was enormous, bigger even than Preacher's Crow friend Nighthawk. The others were typical hard-bitten sorts, including one who bore a marked resemblance to a rabbit but managed to look dangerous despite that.

On the frontier, it was considered impolite to ask a man where he came from, but you could inquire as to where he was bound without ruffling any feathers.

"Where were you fellas headed when you decided to pitch in and help us?" Preacher asked Knox.

Before Knox could answer, a groan came from somewhere nearby. The men all looked toward the sound and were shocked by the sight of one of the Sioux warriors thought to be dead pushing himself up from the ground.

His nose was broken and blood covered the lower half of his face, but he was definitely alive and had some fight left in him. He propped himself on his left hand and fumbled with his right for the sheathed knife at his waist.

One of Knox's men swung his rifle toward the Indian and pulled the trigger. Preacher might have stopped him from firing if there had been time, but the man's reaction was quick and there were several other men between him and Preacher.

The rifle ball slammed into the warrior's chest and caused him to rear even higher as his death throes gripped him. He toppled onto his back and kicked his legs a couple of times before lying still again. This time, the sightless, staring eyes left no doubt as to whether he was alive or dead.

"Damn!" Knox said into the silence that followed the shot. "I figured all these redskins were dead. That was mighty foolish of me. Somebody needs to check the others and make sure of it."

"I'll do it, Zadicus," the rabbity little man offered. He drew his knife. "I wouldn't mind cuttin' some redskin throats."

"Especially when they're wounded too bad to fight back, right, Earnshaw?" Knox waved a hand. "But go to it."

Fitzwarren stepped forward. "I say, that isn't exactly sporting, is it? Killing a man in battle is one thing, but cutting his throat when he can't defend himself verges on cold-blooded murder."

Knox frowned and looked like he didn't care for what Fitzwarren had said. The other men looked much the same way.

As for Preacher, he could see both sides of the question. He had dispatched wounded enemies in the past to put them out of their misery when it was clear they couldn't survive. Generally, he didn't lose any sleep over such actions.

Nor would he hesitate to kill bitter enemies such as

the Blackfeet, no matter what the situation. With them, it was always kill or be killed.

Despite the battles he had fought against them, he held no such animosity for the Teton Sioux. But if not for Zadicus Knox and the others, he and Fitzwarren and Kelleher would be dead by now. He didn't want to interfere with them unless it was absolutely necessary.

"Hold on, Geoff," he said quietly. "Knox is probably right."

Fitzwarren looked surprised. "You think so? It seems to me—"

How things seemed to Fitzwarren was doomed to go unspoken, because at that moment, the man called Earnshaw let out a startled, frightened yell as he straightened from the Sioux warrior he'd been about to kill and jumped back desperately to avoid the knife that the Indian swung at his throat.

Chapter 35

This time, Preacher had a clear lane between himself and the unexpectedly revived Sioux. Earlier, he had retrieved his knife from where it had gotten stuck in the neck of a dead warrior. Now he yanked the knife from its sheath and threw it with the same blinding speed that he displayed with his Colts.

He didn't throw it blade first, however. An idea had occurred to him. He threw the knife so that the brass ball at the end of the handle struck first, thudding into the Indian's forehead with stunning force.

The warrior reeled back, dropped his knife, and fell against one of the boulders. The rabbity little man, Earnshaw, piped, "I'll get him!" and was about to lunge with his own knife when Preacher grabbed his collar from behind.

The mountain man thrust Earnshaw back with ease and got between the others and the groggy Sioux. Preacher had seen that the warrior was young, little more than a boy.

His age was why Preacher had moved swiftly to save

his life, but not because it made the mountain man more sympathetic toward him. A warrior that young might be the son of a chief or one of the other tribal elders. Having a prisoner like that could come in handy.

Before the Indian could recover, Preacher swung a hard fist and walloped him in the jaw. The young man's head jerked to the side. He slid down the boulder to the ground and toppled over on his side, out cold.

"What the hell did you do that for?" Zadicus Knox demanded. "I thought you were all right with us killin' any of these redskins who survived the fight."

"I figured I was, too," Preacher said, "but then I realized we might be able to get some use out of this one."

The light of understanding dawned on Knox's face. "Oh, like as a hostage, you mean."

"That's right. I saw this fella was kind of young. Might be the chief's son. The rest of the tribe might want him back bad enough to let us go if they come after us again."

"That's mighty smart thinkin'," Knox said as he nodded slowly. "You don't mind if we get rid of the rest of this vermin, do you?"

Preacher shrugged.

At a curt nod from Knox, Earnshaw went back to checking the bodies. He was even more nervous now and said, "You boys keep me covered in case any more o' these redskins still got some life in 'em."

As it turned out, that wasn't the case. All of the remaining Sioux were dead, and Earnshaw didn't get to cut any throats after all. Once he finished checking them, he looked a little disappointed by the results.

Preacher got his hands under the unconscious warrior's arms, hefted the youngster, then draped the Sioux belly-down over his shoulders.

He stood there for a second, frowning, before he carried the warrior into the cleft and dumped the unconscious form beside the wagon. He got some rope from their supplies and bound the Sioux's wrists together behind the back, followed by securing his ankles with rope as well.

Zadicus Knox had followed Preacher into the cleft and watched what the mountain man was doing with mild interest. When Preacher straightened from the task, Knox said, "You wanted to know where me and my friends were headed. I reckon I could ask the same of you."

Knox hadn't actually answered that question, either, thought Preacher, but he didn't point that out right now.

Instead, he said, "We're lookin' for somebody. Or rather, my friend Geoff is. He hired the rest of us to come along with him and give him a hand."

"Who's he lookin' for?"

"Reckon you'd best ask him that," Preacher replied with a hint of coolness in his voice. Knox was coming close to poking into things that weren't his business, and Preacher would give him only so much leeway even though Knox and the others had saved them from the Sioux.

"Sure," Knox said. He nodded toward the tied-up

Sioux warrior. "You plan on takin' this varmint along with you when you leave?"

"For a spell, anyway."

Knox rubbed his chin, which was a bit on the weak side. "You know that might just act as a lure for more trouble?"

"I know it," Preacher said. "But I'm playin' a hunch that this captive might do us some good in the long run."

"That's up to you, I reckon."

Knox wandered back toward the others, seemingly losing interest in both Preacher and the prisoner.

Preacher checked the Sioux one more time. Still unconscious and tied up securely enough not to be able to cause any trouble. He followed Knox into the open area between the boulders and the cleft in the canyon wall.

Knox's companions had all dismounted by now and were rummaging among the bodies of the Sioux warriors, doubtless looking for anything of value. Preacher didn't figure they would find much, but their scavenger-like actions confirmed the low opinion he had of them.

There was nothing wrong with claiming goods from a defeated enemy if those things were of any use, he reminded himself. He had done the same thing in the past.

The way they talked among themselves and cackled with laughter reminded him of buzzards feasting on a carcass, though.

Fitzwarren was standing next to Eugene Kelleher, who was still stretched out on the ground unconscious.

"Should we put Eugene in the wagon, Preacher?" Fitzwarren asked.

"Eventually," the mountain man replied. "We'll let him rest for a spell longer before we disturb him."

Knox hooked his thumbs in the waistband of his trousers and said to Fitzwarren, "Preacher tells me you're lookin' for somebody."

"That's right. Do you happen to be acquainted with a man named Barrett Treadway?"

"Can't say as I am. You do know this is the first time my boys and me have been this far west, though, don't you?"

"Then you wouldn't know a fellow named Williams." Despite not phrasing it as a question, Fitzwarren's voice held a slightly hopeful note. "He's supposed to be a fur trapper and was traveling with Treadway."

"Never heard of the fella. Sorry."

Fitzwarren shook his head and sighed. "I didn't actually think you'd know either of those gentlemen, but I had to ask."

"What's so important about those two?"

"It's a matter of, ah, family business."

"Back where you come from, eh?"

"That's right."

"Wish I could be of help."

"Considering the fact that you and your friends saved our lives, I'd say you already have been," Fitzwarren replied. He turned to Preacher. "What do you think we should do now?"

"I reckon the first thing is to get outta this canyon we're boxed up in."

"Wait a minute," Knox said with a sudden worried look on his face. "There ain't no way out of here?"

"Not the way we've been goin'," Preacher said. He nodded toward the far end of the canyon. "There used to be a pass that went through up yonder, deeper into the Beartooths, but an avalanche has closed it up."

Knox cast a worried glance back the way they had come from. "Then the Injuns are between us and the back door, so to speak?"

"That's right. That's why we can't afford to waste too much time makin' up our minds what we're gonna do."

"We sure as hell can't." Knox turned to his men. "Get ready to mount up, fellas. We'll be pullin' out pretty quick-like."

They had all heard what Preacher said and looked just as worried as Knox. The big man said, "I'll tell Hanley and Duke."

"No need," said Knox. "We'll pick 'em up on our way outta here."

Fitzwarren said to Preacher, "We need to put Horace and Salvador's bodies in the wagon so we can give them a proper burial later. Do you think it would be possible to lay Horace to rest next to his brother?"

"I don't know if we can take the time," Preacher said, "but we'll see." He turned to Knox. "Reckon you could give us a hand gettin' our friends in the wagon?"

"Sure," Knox replied without hesitation. "It'll take several of us to lift that big fella!"

He was right; four men were required to lift Eugene Kelleher and place him in the wagon bed. Preacher and Fitzwarren helped with that, then laid Salvador Perez in the wagon while two of Knox's men loaded Horace Thorpe's body.

"Can you handle a wagon team, or do I need to do that?" Preacher asked Fitzwarren.

Knox spoke up, saying, "My friend Jennings used to be a teamster before we came west. Why don't you let him drive that wagon?"

Preacher turned to the stocky, sandy-haired Jennings and asked, "Is that right? You've got experience handlin' wagon teams?"

"Plenty, mister," Jennings said. "It'd be my pleasure."

"We'll be much obliged to you for your help."

"Indeed," added Fitzwarren. "To be quite candid, I can drive a buggy, but I've never handled a four-horse team like that or such a large vehicle."

Knox pointed to the tied-up Sioux warrior and asked, "What about him?"

Preacher walked over to the captive and hunkered on his heels to study the young warrior, who appeared not to have regained consciousness. Preacher frowned, thinking that he hadn't punched the prisoner that hard. The captive might be pretending to be out cold but wasn't in any shape to cause trouble, trussed up like that.

The young warrior was slightly built. Preacher didn't have a problem picking him up and throwing the limp form over his shoulder.

"Want a hand with him?" asked the big man, whom Knox had called Bull. It was a fitting name, thought Preacher.

"Naw, he don't weigh that much," the mountain man said. He lowered the prisoner into the wagon bed with Kelleher and the bodies of Perez and Horace.

Everyone was getting ready to mount up. Preacher and Fitzwarren found themselves in relative privacy inside the cleft. Jennings was talking to Knox and hadn't climbed onto the wagon seat yet.

Keeping his voice low, Fitzwarren asked Preacher, "Do you think we can trust these men?"

"I don't reckon we've got a whole lot of choice but to trust 'em right now. They saved our bacon, and throwin' in with them is our best chance of gettin' outta here with whole skins."

"I'm aware of that, but something about them worries me. I think it's just the look of them."

"They seem like a bunch with plenty of bark left on 'em," Preacher agreed. "But all we can do is keep our eyes open and hope for the best."

Fitzwarren nodded. He glanced around and asked, "What happened to Dog? I haven't seen him since that battle with the Sioux started."

"I'm sure he's around," Preacher said vaguely. "He'll turn up sooner or later."

By now, Preacher strongly suspected that Dog was staying away for a reason. The big cur had sharp instincts and was an excellent judge of character. He might have been observing from a distance and was as suspicious of their new companions as Preacher and Fitzwarren were.

If that was the case, Dog would follow along but remain out of sight. He would show up when he was needed, but not before.

Jennings took his place on the wagon. Preacher could tell from the way Jennings backed and turned the team that he was experienced at such a task, just as he'd claimed.

Knox and his men took the lead as the group started back down the canyon. Preacher and Fitzwarren pushed the extra horses along behind the wagon. Preacher saw the sentries, Hanley and Duke, rejoin the others.

They were still a formidable group, ten strong now, and all well-armed. The survivors from the Sioux war party probably would leave them alone, not wanting to risk another attack after the disastrous outcomes of the first two.

But as Preacher had warned, there could be more warriors in the vicinity, and the Sioux who had fled earlier might be racing to fetch reinforcements at this very minute.

If that turned out to be the case, it would be a race to get out of this trap before the jaws were able close once more.

CHAPTER 36

By the time the group reached the spot where Lee Thorpe and Dennis Burke were buried, they hadn't seen any signs of the Sioux. Geoffrey Fitzwarren said, "Preacher, I'd really like to stop and lay Horace and Salvador to rest here."

"Can't do it," Zadicus Knox said with a stubborn shake of his head. "Too big a risk. We need to keep movin'."

"Sorry, Geoff, but Knox is right," Preacher said. He was riding on the left side of the wagon team now, Fitzwarren on the right. A couple of Knox's men had dropped back to keep the pack horses and spare saddle mounts moving.

In the absence of an order from Knox to stop, Jennings hadn't slowed the wagon team.

Eugene Kelleher had regained consciousness and was sitting up in the back of the vehicle, propped against a crate.

"I hate it, too, Geoff," he said to Fitzwarren. "I'd like to see those boys laid to rest proper with words said over 'em. But we need to put all the distance we can behind us, just in case those Sioux varmints come back."

Fitzwarren heaved a sigh. "I know you're right, all of you. This predicament in which we find ourselves is no place for sentimentality. Very well, we'll move on, as you say."

As they continued pushing toward the edge of the mountains and the rolling plains beyond, Preacher looked into the wagon bed. The Sioux captive still lay motionless with eyes closed.

"You seen any signs of life outta that one, Eugene?" Preacher asked with a nod toward the prisoner.

"No, but he's breathin', I think."

"Yeah," Preacher agreed. "Should've come around by now, though."

"I reckon I had already passed out at the time you had your run-in with him. What did you do?"

"A clout on the head with the handle o' my knife, then a good solid right fist."

Kelleher nodded. "That'd knock most fellers out, I reckon."

"But not keep 'em out for several hours. Not unless they had a cracked skull, and I don't think this one does."

"Oh," said Kelleher. "You believe the little varmint's playin' possum."

"I don't know what to believe," Preacher said, "but keep an eye on that prisoner, Eugene, and holler if you see anything that looks alarmin'."

"I'll sure do it." Kelleher paused then added, "By

the way, Preacher, thanks for patchin' me up the way you did."

"How are you feelin'?"

"So weak I reckon a kitten could knock me off a fence post, but as long as I don't have to get up and run around too much, I figure I'll be all right."

Preacher grinned. "You never did cotton all that much to runnin' around anyway, did you?"

"Not exactly," Kelleher said as he returned the grin and patted his more than ample belly.

They stopped in midafternoon to allow the horses to rest. While they were halted, Preacher went over to the wagon, lowered the tailgate, and reached into the bed to grasp the ankle of the Sioux prisoner. He gave it a hard shake and said, "You might as well stop pretendin'. I know you're awake by now, since you ain't dead."

The captive flinched and jerked that ankle loose from Preacher's grasp. The young warrior squirmed away. A hate-filled glare was directed at Preacher..

"Take it easy," the mountain man said quietly. "I don't aim on hurtin' you any more than I already have."

A stream of spat-out Sioux words lashed at Preacher. Kelleher chuckled and said, "The young fella's really tellin' you what he thinks, Preacher."

"That's all right. I don't mind bein' fussed at." To the captive, Preacher said, "You just lay there, don't cause no trouble, and you'll be all right."

Zadicus Knox walked up in time to hear what Preacher said to the prisoner.

"Why don't you go ahead and ask him who he is?"

Knox suggested. "Find out while you can if his pa is a heap big chief."

"I don't reckon I'd get any civilized answers right now. We can do some more talkin' later, once we're outta these mountains and don't have to worry about bein' jumped by a war party any minute."

"That's assumin' we get out all right."

"That's what I'm gonna plan on until I find out different," Preacher said.

Knox shrugged. "I hope you're right." He turned away and called, "Duke, Hanley, you boys have been ridin' out in front and scoutin' for us all day. Why don't you stay back here with the wagon for a spell while Bull and me take the point?"

"Sure, Zadicus," the man called Hanley said. Duke just nodded.

When the group pulled out a short time later, Earnshaw and Roscoe continued to drive the extra horses and bring up the rear. Neither of them struck Preacher as being all that competent, but they could handle that chore all right. Knox and Bull took the lead while Phillips, Hanley, and Duke rode near the wagon, which Jennings was still driving.

Preacher and Fitzwarren rode side by side now, hanging back a bit from the vehicle.

In a low voice, Fitzwarren said, "I haven't seen anything today that makes me trust these gentlemen any more than I did earlier. They never actually explained who they are or what they're doing out here, did they?"

"Nope. I asked Knox flat-out, but he sort of sidestepped the question."

"Do they strike you as fur trappers?"

Preacher grunted. "If they are, they're the worst-outfitted bunch I ever saw. Naw, they didn't come out here after furs, I'd bet a hat on that."

"Then what else could they be doing?"

Preacher said, "A man who don't show up plannin' to work usually figures on takin' somethin' away from the fellas who do."

"They're outlaws, in other words."

"Could be," allowed Preacher.

"Do you think they'll turn on us? Try to steal our wagon and horses and what's left of our supplies?"

"That might be what they've got in mind. I don't reckon I'd put it past 'em." Preacher squinted at the three men riding up ahead. "I ain't seen much of that young fella they call Duke, but he strikes me as bein' not quite as much of a hard case as the others. Of course, maybe he just ain't been ridin' with 'em as long and it ain't rubbed off on him quite yet. With some fellas, it's hard to say what they'll do until the time comes."

"I don't believe he's spoken a word," Fitzwarren mused.

"Not where I could hear him."

The question of whether Duke was as dangerous as his companions would have to be answered later, as would the one concerning what Zadicus Knox planned to do. The more immediate threat of the Sioux had to be dealt with first.

A short time later, Kelleher caught Preacher's eye and waved for the mountain man to come up alongside the wagon. Preacher urged Horse next to the vehicle. Kelleher frowned and asked, "Are you gettin' the same feelin' I am, Preacher?"

"That we're bein' watched? Yeah, the hairs on the back o' my neck started standin' up a few minutes ago."

On the driver's seat, Jennings couldn't help but overhear what they were saying. He turned his head to interject over his shoulder, "I seem to feel like I'm bein' watched, too. Do you reckon the Sioux are back?"

The canyon had widened out into a valley flanked by hills, not mountains. They weren't far from the edge of the Beartooths, which was both good and bad.

Good because they had a chance to get back out onto the plains, where they would have more room to move around in case of an attack.

Bad because if the Indians actually were going to attack them again, it would probably be soon, while a war party would have more cover in the hills and trees.

Preacher eyed the hills and said, "Yeah, they could be lurkin' up there, all right." He looked into the wagon bed at the prisoner, who glared back at him. "You'd better hope your friends don't jump us again. If a bunch of arrows start to flyin' around, one of 'em could hit you just as easy as one of us."

"You reckon he understands English, Preacher?" asked Kelleher.

"I wouldn't be surprised," the mountain man drawled. To the captive, he added, "Maybe you'd better start yellin' your head off and tellin' your pards to stay away, else you might get hurt."

The prisoner just spat at him. It fell short.

"Suit yourself," Preacher said. "You can't claim I never tried to help you."

Over the next few minutes, the uneasy feeling just grew stronger. The thickly wooded hills seemed to be creeping in from the sides, which meant the hiding places for potential ambushers were coming closer and closer.

"Stay close to the wagon," Preacher told Fitzwarren.

"What are you going to do?"

"I thought I'd ride up ahead and make sure Knox is keepin' his eyes open."

Fitzwarren nodded.

Preacher heeled Horse into a faster pace. As he passed between the wagon and Knox's three men, Hanley looked over and snapped, "Where the hell are you goin'?"

Preacher slowed. Normally, he would have ignored the question and the man who asked it, but he figured right now likely wasn't a good time to stir up unnecessary trouble.

"I thought I'd go talk to your boss for a minute."

Hanley sneered. "Why says he's my boss?"

It was obvious to anybody paying the least bit of attention that Zadicus Knox gave the orders in this bunch, but Preacher just said, "Whatever you want to call him. That ain't none o' my business. But he's got the lead right now, and he needs to know to watch out."

"Don't you worry about Zadicus. He knows how to take care of himself, and of us, too. He ain't steered us wrong yet."

"Let's hope things keep on like that."

Preacher nudged Horse again and pulled ahead. He ignored Hanley's shout of "Hey!" behind him. He was done trying to be polite to the man.

Knox and Bull were about a hundred and fifty yards ahead of the wagon. They weren't pushing their mounts hard, but they were moving along at a pretty good clip.

Even so, Horse had no trouble catching up. The big stallion steadily cut down the gap, and after a few minutes Knox must have heard the hoofbeats coming up behind him and Bull. He kept riding but hipped around in his saddle to look back.

Preacher lifted a hand, not in a signal to stop but simply an acknowledgment that he was joining them. Knox waved in return and said something to Bull. Both men slowed their mounts slightly.

Preacher drew alongside them and pulled Horse back to the same sort of ground-eating lope as the other horses.

"Something wrong?" asked Knox.

"My gut tells me that somebody's watchin' us," Preacher said, "and I reckon right here and now there's only one bunch that's likely to be."

Knox's expression turned grim. "The Sioux."

"That's the feelin' I've got. So does Kelleher, and I trust his instincts about as much as I do my own."

Knox snorted and said, "That big tub o' lard?"

"That 'tub of lard,' as you call him, has been knockin' around the frontier for a whole heap of years, and he's got himself outta plenty of dangerous spots. Most fellas who figured he was too soft and too slow to be any kind of threat are long gone on the other side of the divide."

Knox nodded. "All right. So you think the Sioux are fixin' to ambush us?"

"I wouldn't be a bit surprised."

"What should we do?"

"Keep movin'," Preacher said. "Ain't nothin' else we can do at this point. Besides, there's a chance I might be wrong. A mighty slim one, but still a chance."

"All right, fine. We'll—"

That chance Preacher had spoken of, the one holding that his instincts might be wrong, was dashed a second later, before Knox could finish whatever he'd been about to say.

With whoops of pure hatred and rage, a group of mounted Sioux warriors burst out of some trees to the left and galloped toward the white men. Preacher wasn't the least bit surprised, but as he wheeled Horse toward the threat, he saw that it was worse than he'd expected.

The Indians were behind him, Knox, and Bull, racing to cut them off from the wagon and the rest of the party.

Chapter 37

Bellamy heard both anger and fear in the curses that erupted from Hanley's mouth as the man rode beside him. Hanley jerked his rifle to his shoulder and pointed it at the Indians rushing from the hills.

"Wait!" Bellamy said as he reined in. "The range is too far. Better to wait until they get closer."

"Damn it! Let those savages get too close and they'll overrun us!"

Bellamy ignored that and barked, "Stop the wagon," at Jennings. The man hauled back on the reins and brought the team to a halt.

From the wagon bed, Eugene Kelleher called, "One of you boys give me a gun!"

Bellamy pulled one of the pistols from his sash and tossed it to Kelleher.

"You'll only have one shot," he warned. "Make it count!"

Kelleher grinned at him. "I've got powder and shot. I can reload."

Bellamy gave the man a quick grin in return. He was frightened now that they were under attack again, no doubt about that, but the unexpected coolness of nerve he had experienced earlier had returned as well.

From the corner of his eye, he saw Geoffrey Fitzwarren flash past at a hard gallop, heading toward the Indians.

"Come back here, you fool!" Bellamy shouted after him. He thought Fitzwarren must be trying to join Preacher, Zadicus Knox, and Bull, but the man would never make it. The Sioux war party, which numbered more than two dozen, had already split Knox's group.

Fitzwarren must have realized that, too. He reined in sharply, whirled his mount, and started back toward the wagon. The Sioux were close enough that some of them sent arrows arcing after him, but the shafts fell short.

Roscoe and Earnshaw pushed the spare horses closer to the wagon. There was nothing else they could do, no place they could put the animals that would be safe. Like the men, the horses would just have to take their chances for the next few minutes.

Bellamy swung down from his saddle, led his horse around to the other side of the wagon away from the Sioux, and tied the reins to a wheel. Hanley and Phillips followed his lead and did the same with their mounts.

Bellamy slid his rifle from its sheath and laid it over the sideboards.

"Get as low in the bed as you can," he told Kelleher, "and stay out of the line of fire."

The fat man rolled onto his belly, grimacing from the pain of his wounds as he did so. He shifted closer to the other side of the wagon, looked over his shoulder to see where Hanley, Jennings, and Phillips were positioning themselves, and picked a place where they wouldn't accidentally shoot him when he raised up enough to fire Bellamy's pistol at the onrushing Indians.

The other two men flanked Bellamy and readied their rifles. Bellamy looked at the prisoner and saw the young warrior glaring at him but not making any move to interfere with them defending themselves.

The war party split in two, one group veering toward Preacher, Knox, and Bull while the other warriors continued charging toward the wagon.

More arrows began to fly, although the Indians still hadn't gotten in range. Once they did, Bellamy, Hanley, Jennings, and Phillips would have some degree of protection from the vehicle, but Kelleher and the captive would be at the mercy of the falling shafts in the wagon bed. Bellamy wished there had been time to get them underneath it.

Maybe he could get the prisoner under there, anyway, he decided. He left his rifle with the stock resting on the sideboard and the barrel propped on a crate inside the wagon, then ran to the tailgate.

"What the hell are you doin'?" Hanley demanded in a loud voice tinged with panic.

"I won't allow this youngster to be killed if there's anything I can do about it," Bellamy replied as he reached into the wagon to grasp the prisoner's ankles.

The captive began to thrash around and screech what had to be Sioux curses. Bellamy ignored the reaction and pulled the slender, buckskin-clad form to the back of the wagon. He got his arms around the prisoner's waist and lifted, then staggered back a step as the captive's weight sagged against him.

The furious, snarling face was right next to his. Hot breath was in his ear, as well as those shrill imprecations. Bellamy caught his balance and gritted his teeth.

"Let me give you a hand," offered Geoffrey Fitzwarren, who had returned to the wagon and hurriedly dismounted.

"I've got it," Bellamy said. He bent to practically fling the prisoner underneath the wagon, where the arrows weren't likely to penetrate.

The young warrior could try to squirm away, thought Bellamy, but that ought to prove very difficult with arms and legs bound like that.

He hurried back to where he'd left his rifle, snatched it up, and said, "Sorry we don't have time to get you under there, too, Mr. Kelleher."

"I'm fine," Kelleher assured him. "Or I will be as soon as I get a chance to take a shot at those painted devils."

It was crowded behind the wagon now with six of Knox's men using it for cover, as well as Geoffrey Fitzwarren. Phillips was at the back end, and Jennings crouched beside the driver's box, where he had dropped from the wagon after setting the brake. The others, including Roscoe and Earnshaw, were packed in between them.

The horses in the team, spooked by the loud cries from the war party, pulled against the brake lever. That restraint might not hold for long, Bellamy knew.

If the team bolted and took the wagon with them, the

men would be left out in the open, except for Eugene Kelleher.

Arrows thudded into the wagon's body and embedded themselves. The defenders couldn't afford to wait any longer. Bellamy settled his rifle's butt against his shoulder, drew a bead on one of the charging warriors, and shouted, "Fire!"

Preacher wasn't surprised when the war party split up. The larger group continued the charge toward the wagon while eight warriors raced toward Preacher, Knox, and Bull.

Even with the danger galloping toward them, Knox had an eager grin on his face.

"Looks like they forgot about those repeatin' hoglegs of yours!" he said.

"Maybe not," Preacher replied as the eight attackers spread out even more. They weren't a bunched-up target anymore.

The mountain man lifted his rifle and went on, "Let's try to whittle 'em down."

Without even seeming to aim, he fired, and one of the riders twisted under the ball's impact before sliding back and falling off his pony.

Knox's rifle blasted, followed a second later by Bull's. One of the ponies fell, throwing its rider.

The warrior appeared to be unhurt as he scrambled up onto one knee. He had managed to hang on to his bow and began using it to send arrows whistling toward the three white men.

Preacher rammed his empty rifle back in its sheath and pulled the Colts from their holsters.

"No point in waitin' around for trouble," he said. "I'd rather charge it head on!"

With that, he urged Horse into a gallop that had both of them flashing toward the onrushing Sioux. He began firing, powder smoke gushing from the revolvers' muzzles as he alternated left and right, back and forth. Gun-thunder echoed from the hills on both sides as Preacher carried the battle to the enemy.

The volley of rifle shots that erupted from the men behind the wagon was ragged but effective. Several of the attacking Indians toppled off their ponies. With the thick haze of dust and powder smoke floating in the air, Bellamy couldn't tell exactly how many had fallen.

But at least four of the ponies were riderless now, he saw as the air began to clear. The defenders had dealt the attackers a potent blow—but not enough to make the Sioux break off their attack. They were still coming.

While the other men were reloading, Eugene Kelleher grasped the sideboard with his left hand while his right gripped the pistol Bellamy had given him. He pulled himself higher and thrust the gun toward the Indians.

"Come on, you devils!" he yelled. "Just a little closer and I've got somethin' for you!"

Phillips finished reloading first and stepped out a little from the back of the wagon to line up his shot and fire. His rifle cracked, but an instant later he dropped the weapon and reeled back, pawing ineffectually at the arrow in his throat. The arrowhead had driven all the way through and stuck out the back of his neck. He collapsed.

"Tom!" Roscoe yelled. Instead of firing at the Sioux, he darted out from cover to go to Phillips's aid, even though it was obviously much too late for that.

It was a foolish move that cost Roscoe his life. Two arrows struck him, one in the side and the other in the thigh. He broke stride and pitched forward on his face, and as he landed, two more arrows arced down into his back.

The other men fired a second volley, and this time, having hastily reloaded, Kelleher joined in, the heavy boom of the pistol blending with the sharper cracks of the long guns.

Three more warriors fell. The others veered off and turned away.

"They're runnin'!" Earnshaw yelled. "They've had enough!"

That appeared to be the case.

But up ahead, the fight continued between the rest of the war party and Preacher, Knox, and Bull.

Chapter 38

There were six Sioux warriors left in the group charging toward Preacher. One of them threw his arms in the air and pitched off his pony as the shots rolled out from the mountain man's Colts. The fallen man rolled and ended up in a lifeless sprawl.

Another rocked back and then fell forward over his pony's neck. He managed to remain mounted, but the pony veered off wildly to one side, clearly no longer being controlled by its badly wounded rider.

The odds were still four to one against the mountain man, and he was running low on shots. Each pistol contained only two rounds now. He fired another one and saw a warrior jerk and clap a hand to the side of his head.

Even with forty yards between them, Preacher saw the bright red blood on the Indian's face.

The Sioux turned away but didn't fall off his pony. From the way he kept the mount moving, Preacher had a hunch the wound was a messy one, but not necessarily fatal. More than likely he'd just shot the varmint's ear off.

That cut the odds to three to one, but when the

hammers of both Colts snapped on empty chambers a moment later, those three were still coming. Preacher slowed Horse, pouched his irons, and reached for his knife and tomahawk. He'd take the warriors on hand to hand if he had to.

With a ringing cry of "Wahoooo!", Zadicus Knox charged past Preacher. The pistol in his hand roared and spouted fire, and the face of one attacker turned into a crimson smear as the ball smashed into it.

Bull was right behind Knox. He was so big it seemed impossible that the arrows fired at him could miss, but somehow the shafts flew harmlessly past him. Having somebody of that size charging fearlessly at them must have spooked the Sioux just enough to throw off their aim.

Bull closed in swiftly on one of the remaining Indians. The man was trying to nock another arrow when Bull left the saddle in a diving tackle that carried him into the warrior. The smashing impact drove the Sioux off his pony's back and sent him crashing to the ground with Bull on top of him.

As if that weren't enough to fracture the warrior's ribs and quite possibly crush the life out of him, Bull made sure of it by grabbing the man's head in his huge hands and twisting with all the power of his massive arms and shoulders.

Preacher was too far away to hear the resulting snap, but he saw what Bull did and was confident that the Sioux's neck had broken like a branch.

That left just one of the warriors, and he was drawing a bead on Knox with the arrow he had pulled back.

Preacher's arm went back and flashed forward. The tomahawk he threw spun in the air and struck perfectly, its keen edge cleaving the forehead of the final warrior and embedding itself in his brain.

The Indian loosed the arrow as he was falling off his pony and dying, but it didn't come anywhere close to Zadicus Knox.

Bull stood up, lifted the man he had tackled, and held him by the shoulders as he shook him like a petulant child shaking a rag doll. The warrior's head was turned almost all the way around and flopped loosely, showing that it wasn't connected to his backbone anymore.

Knox looked around at Preacher and nodded.

"Much obliged to you," he said. "That was one hell of a throw you just made."

"I've had plenty of practice," Preacher said.

"I'll just bet you have." Knox turned to Bull and went on, "Bull, put that fella down, dadgum it. He's dead. Ain't no point in you shakin' him like that."

Bull tossed the body aside, again looking like a child with a toy. He said, "I know, Zadicus. I just get worked up when somebody tries to hurt you."

"I know. You done good."

Bull grinned hugely, obviously pleased by the praise. His doglike devotion to Knox made him even more dangerous than he might have been otherwise, mused Preacher. Bull would do anything Knox told him to do and never even hesitate.

Preacher rode over to the man he had struck down with the tomahawk, dismounted, and pulled the 'hawk free from the warrior's split skull. He wiped it clean of gore and brains on the dead man's buckskin shirt.

When he turned to look toward the wagon, he saw the last of the fleeing warriors disappearing into the trees on the wooded slope to the north. Fitzwarren and the other defenders had beaten back the attack.

But at what cost, Preacher didn't know yet.

Knox rode over to him. Bull had mounted up again, as well, and followed Knox.

"Looks like the boys came through that little tussle all right. Most of 'em, anyway. I think I see a couple o' bodies on the ground."

Preacher swung up on Horse's back and said with a grim note in his voice, "We'd better go see who we lost."

By the time they got there, Preacher had looked over the figures still on their feet and knew that it was two of Knox's men who were lying on the ground near the back of the wagon.

Geoffrey Fitzwarren appeared to be unharmed, and Eugene Kelleher was sitting up enough to look out from the wagon bed. As he rode up, Preacher didn't see any fresh bloodstains on Kelleher's clothes.

The young Sioux captive lay underneath the wagon, presumably placed there for protection from falling arrows. Preacher didn't know which of the men had gone to that much trouble in the midst of danger, but he was glad somebody had been looking out for the prisoner.

"Damn it!" Knox said when he saw the bodies with

multiple arrows protruding from them. "Phillips and Roscoe both! Are they dead?"

"I'm afraid so, Zadicus," Hanley said.

Knox dismounted and stood over the corpses for a moment, then stepped back to his horse and pulled his rifle from its scabbard. He swung the weapon toward the buckskin-clad figure under the wagon.

"Two for one ain't hardly fair, but it's a start, anyway," he declared with a snarl of hate on his face.

One of his men stepped forward quickly, putting himself between Knox and the prisoner.

"There's no need for that, Zadicus," the young man said. He was the one called Duke, Preacher recalled. "We killed more than a dozen of them, and that's not even counting the ones who died in that battle earlier today. I'm sorry about Phillips and Roscoe, but I'd say the scales are actually balanced pretty heavily in our favor at this point."

Knox glared at him. "You don't want to go challengin' me like this, Duke. You'd best step out of the way."

Since reining in, Preacher had been switching out the spent cylinders in his Colt for fresh ones. The left-hand gun was fully loaded again and resting in its holster. He snapped the right-hand gun closed as he said, "The fella's right, Knox. Killin' that kid ain't gonna change a thing in the world."

Knox turned his scowl toward the mountain man, who stood there holding the revolver in an apparently casual stance.

"With the things I've heard about you, Preacher, you're the last fella I'd think would turn Injun lover.

Hell, you've probably killed more redskins than anybody else west o' the Mississippi!"

"Only the ones that needed killin', and then only when I didn't have much choice. Sure, there are plenty of bad Injuns, and I've dealt with 'em harshly sometimes. But I've fought side by side with a bunch of good ones, too."

"This ain't a good one," Knox shot back with a shake of his head. "He was right in the thick o' that fight earlier, doin' his damnedest to kill us."

"I can't argue with that," Preacher allowed, "but that don't justify cold-blooded murder, especially when havin' a prisoner could help us in the long run."

Knox gave a contemptuous snort. "Yeah, I know what you said about usin' him as a hostage, but I ain't sure things are gonna play out like that."

"The best way to find out is to wait and see."

The two big men stood there for a long moment with their cold gazes locked. Then Zadicus Knox gave an abrupt shrug and said, "The hell with it. Keep your little pet for now. But when we get outta here and he ain't no use to us anymore, we may get some payback for the men we lost."

Preacher didn't respond to that. He just slid the Colt he was still holding back into leather and turned to Geoffrey Fitzwarren.

"Are you all right, Geoff?"

"Yes, I came through again without a scratch," replied Fitzwarren. He smiled faintly. "I seem to have a guardian angel watching over me."

"I'm fine, too, Preacher," Eugene Kelleher said from

the wagon bed. "At least, as fine as I was before that latest fracas got started."

Preacher looked around and saw that the extra horses had scattered during the ruckus, but they had stopped, bunched up, and now were grazing peacefully a few hundred yards away. He said to Knox, "It'd probably be a good idea if a couple of your fellas went and rounded up that bunch."

Knox looked like he was considering arguing on general principles because of the brief clash he and Preacher had had a few minutes earlier. But he must have recognized the logic in the mountain man's suggestion, because he nodded.

"Hanley, Earnshaw, you two go and do that," he ordered. "Bring them back here." He turned back to Preacher. "You reckon we've got time to bury these boys, or do we just add 'em to the corpse wagon?"

"We've probably got time right now," Preacher replied. "It ain't been long since those Sioux took off for the tall and uncut. Let's get all the buryin' done while we've got the chance."

After Preacher put the prisoner back in the wagon, the group had to move over closer to the trees since the ground in the middle of the valley was too hard for easy digging. Kelleher couldn't help with that, but he took on the job of keeping watch on the trees to make sure the Sioux didn't come back. He sat propped up in the wagon bed with a rifle.

Earnshaw joined Kelleher in that task, since he was too small and not strong enough to be very effective at digging.

Within an hour, they had two holes scraped out. Horace Thorpe and Salvador Perez went in one, Phillips and Roscoe in the other. Preacher said to Fitzwarren, "You're the one who's got the most book learnin', Geoff. Reckon you could say a few words over them?"

"I'm not sure I know anything suitable for such an occasion, but I suppose I can try."

Fitzwarren removed his hat and stood by the graves, which were now mounded with dirt. The other men followed suit, even Kelleher in the nearby wagon. Fitzwarren cleared his throat and spoke.

"The poet—and I'm sorry to say I don't recall exactly which one—said, 'For everything exists and not one sigh nor smile nor tear, one hair nor particle of dust, not one can pass away.' I think this means, if you choose to believe it does, that our friends are still with us although we can no longer see or hear them, but whatever it was that made them who they were allows them to watch over us and comfort us with their presence." Fitzwarren took a breath, and even though what he'd just said wasn't exactly a prayer, he concluded with "Amen."

"Amen," echoed Kelleher and the young man called Duke, evidently the only ones among the group spiritual enough to be moved to do so.

Knox was starting to look impatient. He clapped his hat back on his head and snapped, "We'd best get outta here."

Preacher agreed, but he was curious about something and hadn't had a chance to ask about it until now. While the rest of the men were getting ready to ride, he went over to Fitzwarren and said quietly, "It was you who got that prisoner outta the wagon and stashed underneath, wasn't it?"

To the mountain man's surprise, Fitzwarren shook his head.

"No, it was that young fellow Duke who did that," he replied. "I had just gotten back to the wagon as quickly as I could once I realized I couldn't reach you and Knox and Bull before the Indians attacked. When I rode up, I saw Duke dragging the lad out of the wagon. I understood immediately what he was trying to do and offered to assist him." Fitzwarren smiled. "He practically snapped my head off refusing."

"He did, did he?" Preacher asked as a curious frown creased his forehead slightly.

"Well, perhaps I've overstated his reaction a bit. The moment was a rather hectic one, of course. He may have simply been hurrying to accomplish his goal."

"More than likely," Preacher said.

"And speaking of the devil," murmured Fitzwarren.

Preacher looked over his shoulder and saw that Duke had come up behind him. The young man nodded to Preacher and then said to Fitzwarren, "William Blake."

"I beg your pardon?" Fitzwarren responded with a puzzled frown of his own.

"That line you quoted, it's from a poem by William Blake. I'm afraid I don't remember which one, but I'm certain that it's Blake."

Fitzwarren smiled and nodded. "You know, I believe you're right. That's very astute of you, Mister . . . ?"

Duke nodded toward Knox and the others and said, "They call me Duke. That's as good as any."

"I'm acquainted with some actual dukes, you know. I must say, something about you reminds me of them."

That put a smile on the young man's face. "I'm about as far from nobility as you can get, Mr. Fitzwarren."

"Perhaps, but I appreciate your comment."

Duke nodded and turned back toward his horse without saying anything else.

"That's an odd young man," Fitzwarren mused. "The more I see of him, the less he seems to fit in with his, ah, companions." He lowered his voice. "They're a rather motley group."

"Yeah, they are," Preacher agreed. "And I reckon you're right about that young fella. I wonder how he came to be ridin' with a bunch of hard cases like that."

"Perhaps we can ask him if we all get out of this predicament alive."

Preacher nodded, then took hold of Horse's reins. The big stallion had been standing by, waiting patiently for whatever Preacher wanted him to do next. Preacher swung up and settled himself in the saddle.

Jennings climbed onto the wagon seat again and took up the reins. Hanley and Earnshaw moved in behind the group of spare horses. Knox and Bull took the lead. As Jennings flicked the reins against the rumps of the wheelers and the wagon lurched into motion, Fitzwarren nudged his horse ahead to ride alongside the vehicle.

Duke was behind the wagon, several yards back between it and the group of riderless horses. Preacher held Horse in and fell back some himself, easing in behind the wagon and letting Duke catch up to him.

The young man regarded him through eyes narrowed with suspicion.

"Did you want something, Preacher?" he asked.

"Reckon I do," the mountain man drawled, keeping his voice low enough that none of the others could hear what he was saying. "I want to know how come you ain't said anything to the rest of your bunch about that Sioux prisoner of ours bein' a woman."

CHAPTER 39

Damn, damn, damn. How could he have been so foolish? Bellamy knew he never should have gotten that close to Geoffrey Fitzwarren, close enough to look him in the eye and risk being recognized, let alone spoken to the man.

It had been so long since he'd been around anyone who had even heard of William Blake, let alone read any of the man's poems, that he had given in to an idiotic impulse.

But if Bellamy had been upset about his unwise actions of a few minutes earlier, the shockingly unexpected question from the mountain man had just made things immensely worse.

"A—a woman?" Bellamy stammered. "I don't know what you mean."

"Oh, I reckon you do," Preacher said calmly. "When you were puttin' her under the wagon, you didn't want Fitzwarren helpin' you because you figured he might tumble to the fact that she's a gal. For some reason, you want to keep that to yourself."

He had kept his eyes forward as he spoke, but he cast

a sidewise glance at Bellamy as he added, "That is when you figured it out, ain't it? When you picked her up and felt what's under that buckskin shirt? She's got her bosom bound so it ain't noticeable by lookin' at her, but you can still tell it's there when she's pressed up against you."

"There's no need to be crude about it," snapped Bellamy, unable to restrain the chivalrous impulses that welled up inside him.

Preacher chuckled. "I ain't tryin' to be crude, just puttin' things plain so we understand each other. Our prisoner's a gal, and the others are bound to find that out sooner or later. Since we're the only ones who know right now, maybe we can figure out what we need to do about it."

Bellamy sighed and said, "I don't see that there's anything we can do about it. I suppose we could let her go, but if we did, Knox would probably try to kill both of us."

"He might find that a pretty big chore. I don't reckon lettin' her loose would do us much good, though."

"She might be able to escape."

Preacher shook his head. "The way she's been actin', more than likely if she was free, she'd grab a gun or a knife and try to kill at least one of us. She don't want to escape. She wants our blood."

"Is that even possible? I mean, an Indian warrior who's a woman?"

"A while back, I met up with a Blackfoot woman who was as fierce a warrior as any I ever tangled with.

Pure meanness, she was, and she could fight like a wildcat. I'd just as soon never run into her again."

Preacher nodded toward the back of the wagon where the tied-up prisoner was lying and went on, "This one don't seem to be quite as much of a battler, but that's probably because she's younger and don't have as much experience yet."

"I never would have believed such a thing."

"Injuns are pretty tolerant among themselves. Most of the tribes don't mind if somebody wants to act contrary to what normal folks expect of 'em, especially if they don't try to cause no trouble."

Bellamy sighed and said, "I have a great deal to learn about Indians, it seems. As well as everything else out here on the frontier."

"You do seem a mite out of place," allowed Preacher. "This is the most we've talked. You remind me of Geoff."

"Fitzwarren?" Bellamy's mouth tightened. He couldn't stop the reaction or suppress the distaste that crept into his voice as he said, "I'm nothing like Fitzwarren."

He was aware that the mountain man glanced at him curiously when he said that, but he didn't elaborate. His background was his own business, and he wanted to keep it that way as much as possible.

To change the subject, he went on, "I'm not going to allow anything to happen to that young woman. I don't care if she is a Sioux and wants to kill us."

"Your boss seems to be dead set on killin' her to avenge those fellas we buried back there."

"I don't care," Bellamy said with a shake of his head. "And Knox isn't my boss. I may be riding with his group, but that doesn't mean I'm going to take orders from him."

"If you don't, he's liable to kill you. He don't strike me as the sort who likes it when folks stand up to him."

Remembering the swift, brutal violence with which Knox had reacted when Roscoe wanted to turn back, Bellamy could only agree with what Preacher said. Zadicus Knox would show no mercy to anyone who defied him.

"He can try to kill me if he likes," Bellamy said stubbornly. "He'll have to step over my dead body to get to that young woman if he intends to harm her."

"Let's hope it don't come to that. You bein' dead don't help any of us." Preacher rubbed his fingertips over his chin. "Tonight when we make camp, I'll see if I can find a chance to talk to her privately."

"You can speak the Sioux language?"

"Well enough to get along. I'll let her know that we know her secret, and that if she wants to get outta this mess with a whole skin, she needs to try not to cause any trouble and let you and me watch out for her."

"Do you trust Mr. Kelleher enough to tell him, too?" Bellamy asked.

Preacher considered that question for a moment and then nodded.

"Yeah, Eugene would never hurt a woman," he said. "It's a good idea for somebody besides the two of us to know what's goin' on."

"Would he be able to do anything to protect her if it came down to that?"

"Don't let Eugene's looks fool you, or the fact that

he's wounded, neither. Even hurt, that old boy is tough as whang leather."

They left it at that. Not wanting anyone to grow suspicious of their lengthy conversation, Preacher nudged Horse forward to ride alongside the wagon with Fitzwarren. Bellamy watched them talking and felt his jaw tighten with dislike.

If Preacher knew what sort of person he was talking to, he might not be so friendly toward Geoffrey Fitzwarren, thought Bellamy.

He might as well be conversing with a snake.

By the time the sun dropped behind the jagged peaks of the Beartooth Mountains, the wagon and its accompanying riders had reached the plains and left the foothills about a mile behind.

With the casual assumption that he was in command, Zadicus Knox called a halt and declared that they would make camp where they had stopped.

That rubbed Preacher the wrong way—he was accustomed to giving the orders—but he, Fitzwarren, and Kelleher were outnumbered two to one now, so it was only logical Knox would consider himself the boss.

Also, Knox's bunch had pulled their fat out of the fire when the Sioux had them trapped, Preacher reminded himself. Even though he didn't trust Knox or any of the others, with the possible exception of that young fella Duke, he and his companions did owe the hard cases for that.

The spot Knox had picked for their camp was a fairly

good one next to a small creek with shallow bluffs on both sides, set back about fifty yards from the stream.

Preacher surveyed the landscape and then said to Knox, "Might be a good idea to post guards on both of those bluffs tonight just to make sure nobody tries to sneak up on us."

"Yeah, I'd already thought of that," Knox replied curtly, although Preacher got the distinct impression that idea had never crossed the man's mind. "You think those Indians might follow us out of the mountains?"

"They're Teton Sioux, called that because they make their home in the mountains, but they're horse Injuns, too, which means they can ride just about anywhere they damn well please. There are other bands of Sioux that roam these plains all the time."

"You're sayin' they'll come after us?"

"I'm sayin' they sure as hell might."

Knox made a disgusted sound and shook his head. "That ain't no help."

"I'm just tellin' you what I know, and what I figure might happen."

"Fine. I'll post those guards. I was gonna do that anyway."

Preacher didn't believe that any more than he had the first time Knox said it. But the important thing was that they not be ambushed and taken by surprise.

The horses were watered, unsaddled, and picketed by the time darkness began to settle down over the landscape. The wagon team had been unhitched and tended to, as well. The rabbity little gent called Earnshaw had built a fire and was boiling coffee and frying up some salt pork.

"It's too bad I'm laid up," Kelleher said from where he was sitting in the wagon bed. "I'd be happy to take over the cookin' chores if I wasn't."

"Ain't nothin' wrong with my cookin'," Earnshaw responded in a surly voice as he hunkered next to the tiny fire.

"I didn't mean to imply there was, friend. That's just sort of my specialty, is all I was sayin'. That's what I bring to the table when I throw in with a bunch."

Grinning, Hanley said, "I'd be happy for you to give it a try when you're feelin' better, mister."

"Hey!" Earnshaw objected. "You got no call to go insultin' my cookin', Hanley."

"If you can call it cookin'. See if you can cook that pork without one end bein' raw and the other burnt to a crisp this time."

Earnshaw glared and muttered but let the subject drop as he carried on with the chore.

Preacher drifted toward the wagon, and as he did, he said, "Gimme a hand for a minute, will you, Duke?"

"Sure," Duke replied. Judging by the look that passed briefly over his face, he had a good idea why Preacher had asked for his help.

He joined the mountain man beside the wagon and said under his breath, "My name is Bellamy, by the way. Bellamy Buckland. But you should go ahead and call me Duke. That way it won't seem like we're friends."

"Sure," Preacher said easily.

Were they friends? he wondered. They shared a secret, sure enough, but while Duke seemed like a more respectable sort than the rest of Knox's bunch, Preacher had never laid eyes on the man until today. He didn't want to get carried away and start trusting the fella too much. Not until he had more evidence of Duke's character.

Preacher lowered the tailgate and said loudly enough for the others to hear, "I'll take his shoulders while you grab hold of his ankles."

"Here now," said Knox as he approached the vehicle. "What're the two of you doin'?"

"I thought we'd take the prisoner out and let him sleep on the ground tonight," Preacher said.

"What's wrong with just leavin' the redskin in the wagon?"

Kelleher spoke up, saying, "I'll be stayin' in the wagon. I've spent all day breathin' redskin stink. I'd just as soon not spend the night doin' that, too."

Preacher looked down at the ground, feeling a little surprised and puzzled and not wanting to show that reaction on his face. He knew that Kelleher got along fine with Indians and normally wouldn't say such a thing. He must have had a reason for his comment, but Preacher couldn't figure out what it might be.

"You're not plannin' on turnin' the little devil loose, are you?" Knox asked.

"And have him cut all our throats while we're sleepin'?" Preacher let out a disgusted grunt. "Not hardly. I might take the bonds off his ankles so he can walk around a mite and limber up, but his hands stay tied."

"You'd better put a guard on him, too," Knox suggested. "I know how you like to have folks standin' watch."

"I can do that," Duke volunteered.

"I'd be glad to, as well," Fitzwarren put in.

Preacher happened to be looking at the Sioux prisoner when Fitzwarren spoke up. Her head jerked up a little, as if she were reacting to his words. She turned it to look toward him, but only for a second before she looked away again.

Now, that was puzzling in several respects, mused Preacher.

But this wasn't the time or place to delve into those mysteries. Instead, he told Fitzwarren, "Thanks, but I reckon Duke can handle the chore. It'll be simpler that way."

Fitzwarren shrugged. "Of course. Just let me know if you need me for anything."

Once again, Preacher hoped he wasn't making a mistake by trusting Duke.

The two of them lifted the prisoner out of the wagon, carried her several yards away, and then lowered her to the ground next to a grassy hummock. They were on the far side of the wagon from the fire, so shifting shadows covered most of the ground over here. The light from the flames was enough for Preacher to see what he was doing as he started untying the bonds around the captive's ankles.

While Duke stood back a few feet, Preacher said in a low voice, "Listen to me. You understand English, don't you? Nod if you do."

The prisoner glared at him as she had been doing all along. Even in this poor light, he could see the hatred in her eyes.

But now something else was there, too. Confusion,

bafflement, maybe even a little curiosity. And a lot of wariness, as well. She didn't trust him. No, sir, not one little bit.

However, after a long moment had passed, her chin jerked slightly in the faintest of nods.

Preacher chuckled as he continued untying her legs. "I'll take that as a yes," he said. "Since you understand what I'm sayin', let me tell you somethin' else. This young fella and me, we know you're a woman."

The prisoner jerked again at this revelation, this time reacting with her entire body. She tried to pull her legs away from Preacher, but he tightened his grip on her ankles.

"Listen to me," he said. "We ain't gonna hurt you. I give you my word on that. And we ain't gonna tell those other men, neither, or let them hurt you. Well, we might tell the big fella who's been ridin' in the wagon with you, since he's an old friend o' mine and I know he would never harm a gal."

Preacher's voice hardened as he added, "That is, we'd never hurt you as long as you ain't tryin' to kill us or one of the others. You need to get it through your head right now that we ain't your enemy, but you'd best not try to shoot us or cut our throats. You understand that?"

Once again, the prisoner hesitated before responding, but then another slight nod of her head showed that she grasped what Preacher was telling her.

He finished untying her ankles and said, "All right, Duke and me are gonna put you on your feet and let you walk a mite. You'll be pretty stiff from being tied up most of the day. Take it easy startin' out."

He gestured for Duke to take hold of the captive's left arm. He grasped the right, and they easily lifted her onto her feet between them.

When they loosened their grips and let her take some of her weight on her legs, her knees buckled immediately. Preacher and Duke straightened her up and held her as she took several tentative steps.

"There, you're gettin' it," the mountain man said. "We'll hang on to you anyway, just in case."

She lifted her head and turned to look at him, and in the flickering light from the fire, Preacher saw her lips draw back in a snarl as she hissed through clenched teeth, "I'm not going to try to run away, damn you."

Chapter 40

Preacher couldn't help but chuckle at the vehemence in her voice.

"You not only understand English, you speak it, too," he said. "That's good. It means you can tell us your name."

For a moment, she stood there in stubborn, sullen silence. He thought she wasn't going to say anything, but finally she muttered, "I am called Red Dawn Woman."

"I'd say I'm pleased to make your acquaintance, Red Dawn Woman, but I reckon neither of us is all that happy to be meetin' under these circumstances."

"You and your friends invaded my people's land. You ruin the hunting and attack my people for no reason!"

"We don't mean any harm to you or your people," Preacher said. "If you've got a grudge against white folks because of things some of 'em have done in the past, that ain't my fault and I ain't gonna stand by and do nothin' while you try to carry out that grudge. You got that?"

"I understand," muttered Red Dawn Woman as they

continued their slow walk back and forth. She seemed much steadier on her feet now than she had been a few minutes earlier. Blood was flowing and feeling seemed to be returning to her lower limbs.

"We'll treat you fair and make sure the others do, too, and when we get far enough away that your people ain't a threat no more, we'll turn you loose. You ought to be able to make your way back home without too much trouble."

"High Cloud will never let you escape," she said. "He will hunt you down and kill you all!"

"High Cloud," repeated Preacher. "I reckon he's the war chief of your bunch."

"Yes. And he will be the death of you."

"If that's true, it probably won't work out too well for you, neither, you know."

"If I die in battle, it will be an honorable death, and that day will be a good day to die."

"You're a member of one of the warrior societies?"

She didn't answer this time, evidently not considering his question worthy of a response.

Preacher and Duke led her back over to the hummock and helped her sit down on it. Duke said, "I hate to bring it up, but she's going to need some privacy to, ah, tend to her personal affairs, and she'll have to have her hands free, as well."

"If Knox sees us turnin' her loose even for a minute or two, he'll pitch a conniption fit."

"I'm not afraid of Knox," Duke insisted.

"Neither am I, but I don't want to cause too much of a ruckus this close to the mountains." Preacher looked down at the prisoner. "If you can wait a spell, when we bring you some food we'll say you need your hands untied in order to eat. Then while you're loose because of that, you can slip back into the shadows a little and do whatever you need to. But one of us will have to stay close by. Real close, in fact. You won't like it."

The young woman looked up at Preacher and said, "You." She jerked her head at Duke. "Not him."

"That's fine by me," Duke said.

Preacher figured she had picked him because he was older. He was all right with that. He knelt in front of her, picked up the length of rope he had untied earlier, and said, "I'm gonna have to tie your ankles again for now. Don't give me any trouble, you hear?"

She just sat there in sullen silence while he bound her ankles again. Then she slid down so that instead of sitting on the hummock, her back was propped against it.

Preacher straightened to his feet.

"We'll be keepin' an eye on you," he told her. "So don't try anything."

With that, he walked toward the wagon. Duke came with him, and before they reached the vehicle, he said, "Wait a minute, Preacher."

The mountain man stopped. "Somethin' on your mind?"

"Did you notice something odd about the way the, ah, prisoner talks?"

Preacher's forehead creased in a frown as he said, "Now that you mention it, she does have sort of a funny accent, doesn't she? Almost like an Englishman, but not quite."

"That's exactly what I thought. It's as if she learned to speak English by listening to someone who wasn't an American."

Preacher frown deepened. Plenty of Europeans had come to America, of course, and a significant number of them had ventured out to the frontier. He had met many of them.

But he and Fitzwarren had come out here to search specifically for someone with a British background who had grown up speaking English—but not in England.

Charlotte.

Possibilities whirled through Preacher's head. After leaving Philadelphia with Charlotte, Barrett Treadway had arrived in St. Louis without her—or had he? He had been traveling with a fur trapper named Williams, according to what Preacher and Fitzwarren had discovered, but so far Williams was a complete enigma. They hadn't been able to find out a single thing about him other than his name.

Could it be that Williams actually was Charlotte, masquerading as a man? That was unlikely on the face of it, but Preacher had heard stories about women who wore male clothing and pretended to be men. On the frontier, that was safer in some respects, and a way to avoid unwanted attention.

Of course, out here even the roughest of men would go out of their way to respect and protect a decent woman, so such a pose might not actually be safer. But as newcomers, there was a good chance Treadway and Charlotte wouldn't have known that. Pretending that she was a man might have seemed like a good idea to them at the time.

It was quite a stretch, Preacher knew, but he couldn't rule it out. The theory led to some other interesting speculation, too. If the Sioux led by High Cloud had murdered Barrett Treadway, they could have kept his companion Williams as a prisoner. And if Williams was actually Charlotte—

All those thoughts flashed through Preacher's brain in an instant, prompted by Duke's comment about Red Dawn Woman's accent. It was possible there was some totally unrelated reason for the way she talked, but Preacher could think of only one way to find out.

He said, "I've got to talk to that gal again."

"Not right now," Duke said with a note of urgency in his low-voiced words. "Knox is watching us."

Preacher nodded and continued on to the wagon, where he leaned on the sideboard next to where Eugene Kelleher was sitting. Duke moved on around the vehicle and went to stand by the fire and talk idly to Earnshaw, who was still preparing supper.

Quietly, Kelleher said, "What's goin' on, Preacher? I can tell something's not right about that Sioux youngster, and you and Duke were back there talkin' to him for quite a while."

Equally discreetly, Preacher replied, "Before I answer that, tell me how come you said that about redskin stink earlier. That ain't the way you normally talk."

Kelleher snorted. "I could tell you wanted to get that boy outta the wagon, so I was just givin' you more of an excuse for doin' it. I didn't want you havin' to argue too much with Knox."

Preacher nodded slowly and said, "I figured it might be somethin' like that. I'm obliged to you for thinkin' so quick, Eugene."

"This head o' mine is good for a little somethin' besides a place to hang my hat on." Kelleher paused for a second, then went on, "I'll tell you somethin' else I've been thinkin'. I ain't so all-fired sure that that Injun boy is actually a boy."

Preacher didn't say anything for a moment, then asked, "What makes you say that?"

"I spent a lot of time next to him in this wagon today, and I didn't see hide nor hair of an Adam's apple in his neck. He's got a mighty pretty face, too, when he ain't growlin' and snarlin' and lookin' like he wants to carve out your gizzard with a dull knife. You don't notice that because he don't let down his guard very often. I suppose you might find a boy with a face that pretty, but I never saw one."

Resting both arms on the sideboard, Preacher leaned closer, his mind made up.

"I was gonna tell you anyway," he said. "Her name is Red Dawn Woman."

"A warrior woman," mused Kelleher. "I've heard of such things, but I never ran into one."

"I've had a run-in with one. She was a heap meaner than the male warriors."

"This one wants to be mean, that's for sure, judgin' by the way she looks at a fella."

"Here's somethin' else odd," Preacher said. "She speaks English."

"Lots of Injuns do. They learn at mission schools or from fur trappers."

"But this one don't speak it like an American would. More like a Britisher."

"Well, there are plenty of Britishers around she could have picked it up from, too—"

"But accordin' to Duke, it ain't exactly an English accent, neither. Which is strange, because I'd say the same thing about him. He ain't American, no doubt about that, but he don't sound exactly like a Britisher. I know he came out here from the east, but it's more than that."

"Now that you mention it, you know who he sounds like?" Kelleher asked.

"Geoffrey Fitzwarren," Preacher replied.

For a long moment, both men were silent as they looked at each other, although Preacher could almost hear the cogs turning in Kelleher's brain the same way they were in his.

Finally, Kelleher said, "This is so confusin' my head's startin' to hurt."

"There's an explanation," Preacher said. "There may come a time when we have to sit all three of 'em down and get some answers from 'em, one way or another. But right now, where everybody came from ain't as important as where we're all goin'—and if the Sioux are gonna let us get there."

Chapter 41

Red Dawn Woman didn't try to get away. She just sat next to the hummock, glared at the ground, and ignored the men as full night settled over the rolling plains.

Preacher had to give her credit for her cooperation and was grateful she hadn't attempted to escape. Judging by everything he had seen and heard from her so far, her hatred for her white captors ran deep.

When Earnshaw finished preparing supper, the men gathered around to eat. In addition to the salt pork, there were biscuits left over from a previous meal. They were a little dried out and hard, but washed down with coffee they weren't bad. It was a simple but filling meal.

Eugene Kelleher had been right, though. He could have done better. Maybe he would before this journey was over.

After the men had eaten, Preacher picked up the tin plate he had set aside with a biscuit and a couple of strips of salt pork on it. He said, "I'm gonna give this to the prisoner. I'll have to untie his hands so he can eat."

"No, you don't," Knox said. "You can feed him. I don't want that redskin loose to get up to mischief."

"He won't get up to any mischief while I'm right there. I'll see to that."

"Forget it," snapped Knox. "Do like I told you. That damn redskin's lucky I'm lettin' him eat at all."

Duke said, "I'll go along and help Preacher guard the prisoner while he eats, Zadicus. With two of us watching him, I don't think the Indian will try anything. He didn't give us any trouble earlier when we took him out of the wagon."

Knox frowned suspiciously. "You two are mighty worried about that varmint's welfare." He shook his head in obvious disapproval but added, "All right, go ahead. Duke, you stay back a mite and keep your rifle on the Injun the whole time. If he so much as looks at you wrong, blow his brains out. You got that?"

"Sure, Zadicus. There won't be any trouble."

"There'd damned well better not be." Knox turned to the other men. "Hanley, you go up on that bluff to the north and stand watch. Jennings, you take the one on the south. Bull and I will relieve you later in the night."

"Wait a minute," Hanley said. "You're sendin' us out of camp by ourselves? One man on sentry duty ain't got a chance against Injuns! They'll sneak up and cut our throats."

"Blast it, there ain't enough of us left to double up on the job. Tell you what, instead of climbin' the bluff, you can find a place to roost at the bottom of it. Not even an Injun can climb down without you hearin' 'em."

Preacher knew better than that, but he didn't correct what Knox had said.

"If you see or hear anything suspicious, fire a shot and then get back here as fast as you can," Knox went on.

Hanley sighed, evidently realizing that Knox wasn't going to back down.

"Good luck, Jennings," he said to the other man assigned to the first shift of guard duty. "I got a hunch both of us'll need it before this night is over."

That could well be true, mused Preacher. All of them might be in need of some good fortune.

As Hanley and Jennings departed for their jobs, Preacher and Duke walked around the wagon and headed toward the prisoner. Duke had put some coffee in a tin cup and carried it, although he didn't know if Red Dawn Woman would drink it.

She looked up at them as they approached. Only a small amount of flickering light from the campfire reached back here, but it was enough for Preacher to make out the expression on the prisoner's face.

To his surprise, she didn't look angry this time. She appeared more confused than anything else.

"We brought you some supper," the mountain man said. "And when you're done, we'll let you go tend to your business, like we told you before. But you've got to promise not to try any tricks, otherwise things are liable to go hard for you. Duke and Eugene and me are the only ones who wouldn't just as soon go ahead and kill you."

"I will not cause trouble," she said quietly. Now that he and Duke had talked about it, Preacher was able to pick up on the odd accent in her voice even better. The words had a faintly guttural quality about them, as he had heard in the voices of those whose native language was German.

He had her turn to the side where he could reach her arms tied behind her. He untied the rope around her wrists but left the bonds on her ankles.

"You can have your legs loose when you've finished eatin'," he told her.

She rolled her shoulders to ease stiff muscles and then rubbed her hands together to hasten the blood flow and get some feeling back in them. Preacher hated putting a woman through such discomfort, but there was nothing he could do about it for the moment.

She took the plate when he handed it to her and stuffed salt pork in her mouth. Hunger made her eat quickly, with no regard for manners. When Duke offered her the cup, she seized it and gulped down some of the hot coffee, then went back to eating.

"Better take it easy," Preacher advised her. "You're gonna make yourself sick."

She ignored him and swiftly polished off the food, washing it down with the coffee remaining in the cup. When she was finished, she dragged the back of one hand across her mouth to wipe away the grease left by the pork.

As she tossed the empty cup to Duke, she said, "I would have had had tea."

"Good Lord!" Duke said, so surprised that he fumbled catching the cup and almost dropped it before he secured his grip. "You're not an Indian!"

She glared up at him. "You lie! I am a Sioux warrior!"

From where Knox stood beside the back of the wagon, he called, "Hey! What's that commotion over there?"

"Nothin' important," Preacher said. "This Injun's just cussin' us out in his lingo."

"Well, finish up what you're doin' and get him tied up again. You can't ever trust one of those damn redskins."

To the prisoner, Duke said in a low voice, "That's just it. You're not an Indian. It would take a civilized person to wish they had tea instead."

"You are a fool," she grated back at him. "Anyone can drink anything." Her lips twisted in a sneer. "Even an Indian."

"That's true," Preacher said, "but this young fella ain't sayin' anything I hadn't already thought of myself. Where'd you learn how to speak English?"

She glowered stubbornly at him and didn't answer.

"You didn't learn English the way a reg'lar Injun would, from a missionary or a fur trapper. No, I reckon you learned it because that's what ever'body around you was talkin'. You grew up speakin' English . . . in a place called Alpenstone."

It would have been hard to say which of them stared at him with more surprise on their face, Red Dawn Woman or Bellamy "Duke" Buckland.

Chapter 42

It was the young woman who broke out of her stunned reaction and recovered her voice first. She gazed up at Preacher and said, "Please don't let him take me back there. Please."

The hatred and rage had disappeared from her face, replaced by a look of what appeared to Preacher to be pure terror. He wished he could make out her features a little better in the poor light.

So quietly that no one back in the camp or around the wagon could overhear, he said, "You're Charlotte Fitzwarren, aren't you? Also known as the fur trapper called Williams?"

Although the words were phrased as questions, his voice held certainty that he was right. Every instinct in his body told him it was so.

She made a face. "Not Fitzwarren. My name is Courtenay. Charlotte Courtenay."

Come to think of it, Fitzwarren never had said what his cousin's last name was, Preacher realized. All the times he'd talked about Charlotte, that was the only name he used. But it made perfect sense that cousins could have different last names.

To confirm that, he said, "But you are Geoffrey Fitzwarren's cousin, the one we came out here to find."

"That's right."

"This is insane!" The statement came out of Duke's mouth in a burst, as if he could no longer contain it. "You're an Indian woman."

"Plenty of white captives have been adopted into the tribes out here," said Preacher, "although it usually happens when they get hold of a youngster, a boy or a girl, not somebody who's already growed up." He looked at the prisoner again. "You were, what was it, seventeen or so when you came out here with Treadway?"

"I was eighteen by the time we reached the mountains," she said. "I suppose I'm nineteen now. Honestly, I'm not sure. I don't know what month it is, let alone the date." She let out a humorless little laugh. "I'm surprised I even remember how to speak English this well. I thought I had lost most of it during my time with High Cloud's people. But it came back to me as I listened to you men talking among yourselves."

"This is unbelievable," muttered Duke. "I mean, look at you. You're a savage. Less than twelve hours ago, you were trying to kill us!"

She looked down and said, "I was acting as the one I have become. I was Red Dawn Woman, a Sioux warrior." Her head came back up and a look of defiance flashed across her face. "I still am."

"Take it easy," Preacher told her. "If you promise to quit actin' like that, I reckon we can turn you loose—"

"You mean turn me over to my cousin so he can drag me back to a life I hate," she broke in.

Preacher frowned and shook his head.

"I'm startin' to feel like there's a whole lot more to this story than I've been told," he said. "We don't have time to hash it all out right now, so let me ask you this: Would you rather stay tied up and keep on pretendin' to be a Sioux warrior until we have a chance to talk some more?"

"I'm not pretending," she snapped. "I am a Sioux warrior. I earned my place in the warrior society."

"Never mind about that now. Just answer the question."

She sighed. "Yes. Continue treating me as a prisoner. That would seem to be the safest course for everyone."

"All right. Let me untie your legs, like I said I was gonna do."

As Preacher knelt in front of her to loosen the bonds around her ankles, he added, "You still believe this High Cloud fella is gonna come after us?"

"He will. He cannot allow our warriors who were slain to roam the spirit realm unavenged. And if he knows that I am your prisoner—"

She stopped short. Preacher finished freeing her and stepped back.

"Are you sayin' you're more important to High Cloud than any of his other warriors?" he asked.

The young woman looked uncomfortable now as she said, "He believes that in time I will no longer wish to be a warrior and will be content to become his wife. That will never happen, but he hopes for it."

"You and him aren't married now?"

She shook her head. "It is what he wants, but I have refused."

He gestured for her to stand up.

"Let's go on a ways farther out. You can tend to whatever needs tendin' to. But I got to go with you." Preacher glanced at Duke. "You stay here. I'll holler if I need you."

"Fine," Duke said, but he didn't sound too happy about it. He mostly sounded—and looked—confused, still thrown for a loop by the revelation that Red Dawn Woman was actually Charlotte Courtenay.

The prisoner got to her feet, turned, and walked about fifty yards farther out from the camp. None of the light from the fire reached this far.

Preacher said, "This'll do."

She stopped and said over her shoulder, "Aren't you even going to turn around?"

"Nope. But I'll turn sideways so I can just see you from the corner of my eye. Won't be able to tell much about what you're doin', but I'll know it right away if you try to run off or anything like that."

"Fine," she said, not sounding pleased about it.

A few minutes later, she was ready to head back. Preacher told her to go ahead of him and followed. All his senses had been on high alert while they were out here, but he hadn't seen, heard, or even smelled anything unusual in the night. If High Cloud and more of the Sioux warriors were sneaking up on the camp, they were being mighty quiet about it.

Actually, as much damage as the white men had

done to the various war parties that had attacked them, Preacher didn't expect the Sioux to strike again immediately. They would need to regroup and lick their wounds for a while. Tomorrow, probably, they would take up the trail again, but it might be a couple of days before they actually jumped the party of white men again.

When Preacher and Charlotte got back to where they had left Duke, the young man wasn't alone. Zadicus Knox waited there, too, along with Bull.

"I want this redskin tied up good and tight and then tied to one of those wagon wheels, too," Knox said. "I ain't gonna give him a chance to work loose and run off. You know good and well he'd find the rest of his filthy bunch and bring 'em right back here to attack us again."

Knowing what he knew now about the prisoner, Preacher hated to go along with Knox's cruel orders, but he didn't see any way of avoiding them short of provoking a showdown. He wasn't ready to do that yet. If High Cloud did jump them again, it would take their full force to fight off the attack.

Since Charlotte Courtenay wanted to live as an Indian, she would just have to endure the discomfort an actual Sioux warrior would be faced with in this situation.

"I reckon we can do that," Preacher said to Knox. He saw the reaction on Duke's face and thought the young man might be about to object. Not wanting the secret to slip out, Preacher gave Duke a hard look. Duke closed his mouth and didn't say anything.

Knox and Bull didn't leave. Preacher figured Knox intended to watch and make sure his orders were carried out. The mountain man grasped Charlotte's upper arm and marched her toward the wagon, not being any too gentle about it.

Duke, Knox, and Bull trailed along behind.

Eugene Kelleher had a worried frown on his moon face as Preacher hustled the prisoner up to the vehicle, but he didn't say anything, either. Preacher took Charlotte around on the side of the wagon toward the fire, which was burning down now, not quite embers yet but getting there.

On the far side of the fire, Geoffrey Fitzwarren and Earnshaw had already turned in for the night. Preacher saw their blanket-wrapped forms in the dim light.

He told Charlotte to sit with her back to the rear wheel on that side. It was the work of only a few minutes to secure her wrists and ankles and then use another piece of rope to tie her to the wheel. Preacher passed it around both arms and then knotted it around one of the spokes. He did a good enough job that he knew she wouldn't be able to get free. She probably wouldn't be able to sleep too well, sitting up in an uncomfortable position like that, but it couldn't be helped.

Knox nodded, evidently satisfied.

"Keep an eye on the little devil," he said. He looked at Preacher, Duke, and Kelleher in turn and went on, "You three are the ones who seem most concerned about the Injun's welfare, so I'm holdin' you responsible for him. If he causes any trouble, you'll be sorry—and he'll be dead."

Knox turned away and motioned for Bull to follow him. "Let's get some shut-eye before we relieve Hanley and Jennings on guard duty," he told the huge man.

Duke moved over beside Preacher and said under his breath, "What are we going to do? We can't continue this charade indefinitely."

"No, I reckon not," Preacher agreed as the two of them moved farther away from the wagon. "But I can't figure out what's the best thing until I've got the whole story." He turned his head to look squarely at the young man beside him. "And that includes the connection between you and that dadblasted Alpenstone place."

Chapter 43

Bellamy had no real reason to conceal the truth from Preacher, he told himself. He had done so at first simply out of habit, because he never told anyone in this country about his background.

Learning that Geoffrey Fitzwarren was from Alpenstone had only reinforced Bellamy's natural tendency to be closemouthed about himself.

When he first laid eyes on Fitzwarren, he had thought that the man seemed vaguely familiar. Hearing his name had made Bellamy recall that he'd seen Fitzwarren a few times in Lornsburgh, the capital.

But Fitzwarren had always been one of the more anonymous members of the royal family, staying well in the background while his more illustrious relatives ran things.

Bellamy had no reason to fear Fitzwarren discovering his true identity, as far as he knew. By now, however, the habit of being careful was ingrained in him.

He looked squarely at Preacher and responded to what the mountain man had just said.

"I don't know what you're talking about," Bellamy

declared. "I've never heard of this place. What did you call it? Alpenstone?"

Preacher shook his head. "Don't bother lyin' to me."

"It's not a lie. I'm from England. A little fishing town in Cornwall, right on the coast—"

"I've knowed some Cornishmen," Preacher interrupted. "They sound different from you, and different from the way Fitzwarren talks, too. And somebody else."

He nodded toward the buckskin-clad figure tied to the wagon wheel.

"All three of you sound like you came from the same place," Preacher went on. "But it ain't England. It's a place where folks speak English, but they're surrounded by other folks who speak German. It's a good bet 'most everybody in Alpenstone speaks both English and German. Probably at least a mite of French, too, since accordin' to what Geoff told me, the grand dutchy borders a little on France, too."

"Duchy," Bellamy corrected him without thinking.

"Duchy." Preacher grinned. "Ain't much use in you denyin' it, is there?"

Bellamy looked down at the ground for a moment and then raised his eyes to meet Preacher's intent gaze again.

"How farfetched is it that I could come all this way from Europe to the American frontier and still run into not one but two of my countrymen—and one of them pretending to be an Indian? It's just bizarre, beyond imagining!"

"As many miles as it takes in, the frontier's a smaller place than you might think. A man might hide for a hundred years out here and never see anybody he knows, or he might run smack dab into an old friend—or an old enemy—as soon as he gets to where he's goin'."

Bellamy shook his head slightly and said, "Neither Mr. Fitzwarren nor Miss Courtenay is my friend, or my enemy, for that matter. Truthfully, I'm not really acquainted with either of them. I know who they are, of course. They're nobility, members of the family that has ruled Alpenstone for many years."

"And you ain't?"

"Me?" Bellamy let out a humorless chuckle. "I'm a nobody, Preacher. True, my family does have a certain amount of wealth and influence, but I'm my father's second son. Do you know what that means?"

"It means you don't inherit a blasted thing or have any money of your own," Preacher said.

"Exactly. My choices in life boiled down to being a lowly clerk, joining the army, or going abroad. I decided to go abroad, further my education, have some adventures, and make my own fortune here in the United States."

The mountain man nodded. "Those are admirable goals, I reckon."

"Perhaps, but I haven't really succeeded in any of them. I attended an academy back East for a while, but my schooling was cut short by some trouble that was, admittedly, mostly of my own making. I have no money, I'm on the run from the law, and I've fallen in with thieves and scoundrels."

"You mean Knox and his bunch?" asked Preacher.

"That's right." Bellamy hesitated. "I realize we haven't

known each other for very long, but I feel like I can trust you, Preacher." He took a deep breath. "Knox followed your party out here—and he has plans for you."

"You mean it wasn't just luck that brought you fellas to our aid when that war party had us pinned down?"

"We've been following you ever since you left St. Louis," Bellamy said. "Well, we got sidetracked for a while and it took quite a bit of time to find your trail again and catch up, but no, it wasn't just luck. Knox would have jumped you and killed everyone except Mr. Fitzwarren a long time before now, if things had worked out the way he planned."

"Geoff? What in blazes does he want Geoff for?"

"He plans to hold him for ransom and force his family to pay a great deal of money to have him released safely. He assumed that anyone who could hire and outfit a group such as yours was wealthy." Bellamy shrugged. "He was right about that, of course. But he has no idea what the Fitzwarrens are actually worth."

Preacher tugged on his earlobe and then raked a thumbnail down his beard-stubbled jaw.

"The way things have worked out," he mused, "Knox must've decided it'd be better to keep me and Eugene alive for the time bein' so we can help fight off the Sioux if it comes down to that again. Once he decides it's safe enough, he'll get rid of both of us."

"That's what he's thinking, yes." Bellamy paused. "Now you know why I'm out here with Knox and the others. Am I safe in also assuming that our prisoner over there is the reason you and your party made this journey?"

Preacher didn't answer immediately. Instead, he looked at Bellamy for a long moment before he said, "I don't reckon either of us has any real reason to trust the other, except for what our guts tell us. But since we're layin' our cards on the table, I might as well admit that you're right. We came lookin' for Geoff's cousin Charlotte. She fell in love with an American named Barrett Treadway and ran off with him. Geoff set out to find her and bring her back."

"But she doesn't want to go."

"She claims not to," Preacher said.

"What happened to this fellow Treadway?"

"The Sioux killed him. He was travelin' with another trapper named Williams—or that's what they told folks, anyway. Williams was really Charlotte."

"Yes, I heard you say that earlier, and now it makes a bit more sense. When the Indians killed Treadway, they took Charlotte prisoner and made her a member of the tribe?"

"That appears to be the case," said Preacher. "And she's done a mighty fine job of fittin' in, too. Good enough that they let her join one o' their warrior societies."

Bellamy laughed, and the sound held some genuine amusement this time.

"There was always a certain amount of gossip about Lady Charlotte," he said. "When she was young, she was rumored to be quite the tomboy. Always wanting to go riding and shooting with her great-uncle, the grand duke. She was supposed to be highly gifted in those areas, as well." Bellamy spread his hands. "Or so I've heard, anyway. My family didn't move in the same circles as hers."

"I reckon there must've been some truth to the rumors if she could pick up on the Sioux ways well enough to be adopted as a warrior. Most female captives wind up as slaves or the second or third wife of some warrior."

"I'm glad she wasn't doomed to that fate, even if I don't really know her," murmured Bellamy. "I'm still amazed at the way fortune brought the three of us together. I mean, what are the odds that three people from a tiny grand duchy in Europe would find themselves brought together by happenstance in the middle of the vast American frontier?"

"Life can take some mighty strange turns," Preacher said. "If you'd seen some of the things I've run into in these mountains, you just plumb wouldn't believe 'em."

"I'd like to hear about that, but it'll have to be some other time, I'm afraid."

The mountain man nodded. "Yeah, we don't want to make Knox too suspicious of us. We'd best get back to the wagon and try to catch some shut-eye ourselves."

They turned toward the camp, but then Preacher stopped Bellamy with a light touch on his arm.

"When and if Knox decides to make a move against Eugene and me, you ain't gonna throw in with him, are you?"

"To be honest, almost since the day I joined forces with him and his men, I've been looking for a good chance to get away from them," Bellamy said. "And it's not just you and Mr. Kelleher who'll be in danger. I'm sure he would kill the prisoner out of hand, too, and I can't allow that to happen, especially now that I know who she really is. No, Preacher, you can count on me. When trouble comes, as it inevitably will, I'm going to be on your side."

Chapter 44

The night passed quietly, just as Preacher had expected and hoped. High Cloud and all the warriors he could round up would still come after them, Preacher knew, but with luck it would be another day or two before that happened.

They could use a respite from fighting for their lives, and the more distance they could put between themselves and their pursuers, the better.

It was only a slim chance, but if High Cloud had to chase them too far, the Sioux war chief just might give up, especially if some of his followers began to question the wisdom of going after the white men.

The next morning, Earnshaw prepared breakfast. Eugene Kelleher was still too weak from the blood he'd lost the day before to do much other than ride in the back of the wagon.

Charlotte Courtenay kept her head down and didn't look at any of her captors as they ate. That was probably wise of her, thought Preacher. Up until now, she had managed to keep them from getting a really good look at her face, with the exception of Kelleher.

The less attention they paid to her, the less likely it was that any of them would realize she wasn't a young male warrior. The fact that she had dark eyes, raven black hair, and a slender figure helped her get away with the deception, but it wasn't going to last forever.

Preacher asked himself who she was now, really, Lady Charlotte Courtenay—or Red Dawn Woman? Did she truly intend to abandon her life as a privileged member of European nobility and spend the rest of her days as a Sioux? She had claimed that was what she wanted, but would the day come when she changed her mind?

Preacher didn't know, and he had a feeling that Charlotte probably didn't actually know, either. He was curious about plenty of things and wanted to talk to her at greater length, but he would have to wait for a good chance to do that.

As for Bellamy "Duke" Buckland, that boy was a puzzle, too, although less of one. Preacher had been acquainted with enough Englishmen to know how things worked back there in the old country. Everybody except the oldest son was plumb out of luck when it came to inheriting anything or having much say about their lives. Evidently folks did things the same way in Alpenstone.

Preacher could understand why Bellamy would leave his homeland and come to America to make a fresh start for himself. There was nothing to hold him in Alpenstone. Preacher himself had left home at an even earlier age out of sheer restlessness and a desire to see the world.

That fiddle-footed nature of his had never worn

off, either. As old as he was now, it wasn't likely it ever would!

Preacher was saddling Horse when he noticed Zadicus Knox walking toward the prisoner. He didn't know what Knox had in mind, but he didn't trust the man for a second. He stopped what he was doing and headed in that direction himself.

Knox stopped in front of Charlotte and kicked the bottom of her moccasin-shod left foot. It wasn't a gentle tap, either, but a hard enough kick that it had to sting.

Charlotte jerked her foot back but didn't react in any other way. She kept her head down and didn't look up at Knox.

As Preacher approached, Knox looked around at him and ordered, "Get this filthy redskin varmint up on his feet and throw him in the wagon, if you're still bound and determined to keep him."

"He hasn't had anything to eat," Preacher pointed out.

"I don't aim to waste supplies on a savage animal like that. He can eat again when we make camp tonight if we're all still alive then."

From the wagon bed, Kelleher said, "That don't rightly seem fair. A body's got to eat."

"I didn't see you offerin' to share your breakfast with him, fat boy," snapped Knox. "And I decide what's fair and what ain't. I say load up this Injun unless you want to leave him here with his throat cut."

"I could do that, Zadicus," Earnshaw offered, perking right up at the prospect. "I'd be right happy to cut the little red varmint's throat."

"You may get your chance," Knox told him.

Preacher said, "I'll have to turn him loose from the wagon to get him in the back of it."

Knox just made an impatient gesture to indicate that he should go ahead.

As Preacher knelt beside the wheel and reached behind it to untie the rope binding Charlotte to the spoke, he felt a tiny quiver run through her body. She was tensing her muscles for something, and anything she tried was bound to cause more trouble than Preacher wanted to deal with right now.

"If you're thinkin' about makin' a run for it, that wouldn't be very smart," he whispered. "Just play along for now, blast it. I'll come up with a way to get you out of this."

He was silent for a moment and then added, "It'd sure help, too, if you could keep that fella High Cloud from tryin' to kill all of us. Maybe if we see him in time, you could give him some kinda signal that you're all right, and he'd hold off on attackin'."

Charlotte didn't say anything. He knew she heard him, but she might be too stubborn to take heed of what he was telling her.

When he had untied the rope holding her to the wheel, he saw that Bellamy had joined them. Together, the two men got hold of the prisoner's arms and lifted her to her feet. They half carried, half dragged her to the back of the wagon and lifted her onto the lowered tailgate.

From there, Charlotte scooted forward until the

tailgate could be closed. Preacher was relieved that she had decided to cooperate, at least for now.

A short time later, everyone was ready to ride. Jennings climbed onto the driver's seat, everyone else swung up into their saddles, and the group headed east.

Geoffrey Fitzwarren moved his mount alongside Horse and said to Preacher, "We have to decide what we're going to do about our own goals."

"I figured we were headin' back, since we found out Treadway's dead and we don't have no idea where to start lookin' for your cousin."

"We never reached that decision. Actually, we haven't even discussed the matter except in passing. We were caught up in events, I suppose you could say, and there was really nothing we could do at the time other than go along with whatever Mr. Knox and his friends wanted."

"I don't reckon that's changed," Preacher said.

"We don't have to stay with them," Fitzwarren argued. "We could go out on our own."

"Just the two of us?"

"We still have Mr. Kelleher. That makes three."

"Eugene ain't in any shape to do much except ride in the back of that wagon," Preacher said. "He'd be a little help in a fight, but not much."

"From the stories I've heard about you, you've been all over the Rocky Mountains by yourself."

"I reckon that's true," Preacher allowed with a shrug. "But, no offense, travelin' by myself is a mite easier than traipsin' around the high country with a greenhorn and a wounded man. Also, we've already got the Sioux all stirred up and wantin' to kill us. Most of the time, the only ones out here who I knowed for sure were out for my hair were the Blackfeet."

"Perhaps we could use that prisoner to our advantage," Fitzwarren suggested. "What if we took him back to his village and told his people that we freed him from Knox's party? We could claim, honestly, that Knox wanted to kill him and we prevented that."

If circumstances had been different, a tactic such as the one Fitzwarren described might stand at least a small chance of working, Preacher knew.

The problem was that Fitzwarren wasn't aware of what Knox was planning. Knox had his head set on holding Fitzwarren for ransom. If Fitzwarren tried to desert the group, Knox would go ahead and kill Preacher and Kelleher and the captive. Probably Bellamy, too, if the young man turned on him and tried to help Preacher and his friends.

"It just ain't gonna work, Geoff. We've got too much lined up against us right now. Maybe later, if things work out."

"I don't see how the situation is going to improve the longer we wait," Fitzwarren said, sounding annoyed and impatient now. "That man called Williams may still be out here somewhere, and he could hold the key to finding Charlotte. I'm not ready to give up on locating her. In fact, it's vitally important that I do so—or, if she's no longer alive, that I find solid evidence of her death."

And why was that? Preacher wondered. What was so

all-fired important about Charlotte Courtenay that her cousin was willing to risk so much to find her?

Nothing he had heard from Charlotte or Bellamy about life back in Alpenstone held the answers to those questions.

As Preacher was musing about that, Fitzwarren went on, "I don't like to bring this up, but I have to remind you that I'm the one who funded this expedition, Preacher."

"And I told you I was in charge once we got out here."

Fitzwarren's voice was cold as he said, "I suppose I could explain things to Mr. Knox and see if he and his friends would like to join forces with me and assist in the hunt for Charlotte."

Good Lord, the man had no idea what he was saying! Might as well partner up with a lobo wolf as to strike a deal with Zadicus Knox.

Fitzwarren had no way of knowing that, though.

"You don't want to do that," Preacher warned. "Knox ain't to be trusted."

"Really? He's not the one who wants to back out of an arrangement he agreed to."

Keeping a tight rein on his temper, Preacher said, "Give it a day or two until we see how things are gonna play out with those Sioux."

"There hasn't been any sign of them since yesterday. I believe they've decided to give up their campaign against us. We inflicted so many casualties on them that they don't have any other choice."

Preacher actually hoped that might be case, although he felt in his guts that they were still in danger. Charlotte believed High Cloud would come after them, and she knew him far better than any of them did.

"I realize that it's been less than a day since the last time we clashed with them," continued Fitzwarren, "but every mile we go in this direction may be another mile farther away from the answers I need."

Preacher looked over at the man, his own impatience welling up inside him, and said, "Maybe it's time you tell me just why it's so damned important for you to find your cousin. We've lost four good men already, and if we're gonna go on riskin' our lives, I want to know why."

Fitzwarren's mouth tightened angrily. He might have answered Preacher's question, or he might not have.

They would never know, because at that moment, Bull bellowed from the right flank where he was riding, "Injuns! Injuns!"

Chapter 45

Preacher reined in sharply and turned in the saddle to look in Bull's direction. About two hundred yards that way lay a shallow ridge, and along that ridge a number of mounted figures were riding.

Bull had wheeled his horse and was galloping hell-for-leather toward the wagon, still yelling his head off as he came.

Preacher's instincts warned him and made him jerk his head around to check the situation to the left. A hill lay in that direction, and more riders were charging around the base of it.

He had to give High Cloud credit. The Sioux had struck sooner than Preacher expected and had caught them in the middle of two forces, like the jaws of a bear trap about to snap shut.

Preacher knew without checking that they wouldn't find any good cover behind them. Without even thinking about it consciously, he had studied the terrain as they passed through it. That was just something he did out of long habit. You always took note of places you could fort up and ways you might escape from trouble.

With nothing promising behind them, they had no choice except to go forward.

Knox was up ahead, riding point with Hanley. They had seen the Indians closing in from the sides, too, and Knox had reached the same conclusion as the mountain man. He reined in, turned his horse, stood up in the stirrups, and grabbed his hat to wave it over his head.

"Come on!" he shouted to the others. "Come on, fast as you can!"

Bellamy had been out on the left flank, Preacher recalled. He saw the young man galloping in, riding bent forward in the saddle. He was well out of range of any arrows that might fly from the war party on that side.

The Sioux on that side were coming on fast, though. They would reach the white men ahead of the other warriors now streaming down the ridge to the right.

Jennings whipped up the team and got them charging forward. The wagon careened over the prairie, which was nowhere near as flat as it might look from a distance. The little hillocks and dips made the vehicle rock and bounce heavily on its springs. Kelleher had grabbed hold of the sideboards to brace himself, Preacher saw as the wagon rolled past him.

He hoped Charlotte Courtenay, tied up and helpless as she was, wouldn't get thrown out of the wagon bed by the wild ride, but he couldn't do anything to prevent that.

Instead, he drew his rifle from its sheath and brought it smoothly to his shoulder.

"Let's try to slow 'em down a mite," he said to Geoffrey Fitzwarren, who pulled his rifle from its scabbard as well.

Both men took aim and fired, Preacher first and Fitzwarren a second later. The range was long, but the bullets carried, and the way the Sioux warriors were packed together, a man didn't have to be a crack shot to score a hit. Two ponies went down, breaking the rhythm of the charge for a moment.

As Preacher lowered his rifle, he saw that Bellamy was reining in and turning his horse, even though he was still farther out.

"What the hell are you doin'?" Preacher exclaimed, even though the young man was too far away to hear him.

Bellamy had drawn his rifle, too. He raised it and fired, and one of the warriors in the leading rank of the attacking force pitched off his pony. Bellamy yanked his horse around and kicked it into a run again.

"Brave lad!" Fitzwarren said.

"Yeah, I just hope he ain't thrown his life away."

With no time to reload, Preacher slid his rifle back into its sheath and urged Horse into a gallop. Fitzwarren rode beside him, keeping up as best he could. The big gray stallion steadily pulled ahead of Fitzwarren's mount. Preacher held Horse in a little, not wanting to run off and leave Fitzwarren behind.

The two of them had been arguing just before the Indians showed up, and Preacher still wanted answers to his questions. The only way he could get those answers was by keeping both of them alive.

That might be asking too much with bloodthirsty Sioux closing in from both sides.

Bellamy swept up, angling from the left, to fall in on Preacher's other side. The wagon was a short distance ahead with Jennings lashing at the rumps of the team and yelling at them as he urged them on.

In the back of the vehicle, Eugene Kelleher continued to hang on for dear life. Preacher saw that Kelleher had one leg draped across Charlotte Courtenay's midsection, pressing down with it to hold her in place and keep her from being thrown around.

Earnshaw hazed the spare horses along behind the wagon, but from the way he kept jerking his head back and forth, Preacher figured panic was about to overwhelm the rabbity little man. He would abandon the horses soon.

Knox and Hanley had fallen back a bit to let the wagon get closer to them. Bull loomed up on the far side, getting every bit of speed he could out of his mount. The poor horse labored valiantly under his great weight.

Preacher looked ahead and spotted a dark line making its wavering way across the prairie. Hope leaped up inside him.

That was a wash up ahead, probably dry, although there might be a little water in the bottom of it at this time of year. What mattered was that it might provide them with some cover as they tried to fight off the Sioux war party.

The wash might even be deep enough that they could get the horses down into it, although that was less important than finding shelter for the human members of the party.

Preacher swerved Horse closer to the wagon and called to Jennings, “Keep goin’! There’s a wash up ahead where we can fort up!”

The man jerked his head in a nod to show that he understood and whipped the reins against the horses in the team.

The Indians on the left had closed ranks and were still coming despite the damage Preacher, Fitzwarren, and Bellamy had inflicted. Preacher tried to estimate how many there were, but it was difficult to tell with the way they were bunched up. Ten or twelve, maybe a few more, he guessed.

The warriors on the right who had come down from the ridge had spread out more, he saw when he looked in that direction. He was able to get a better count of them.

Eight warriors racing toward them on swift ponies.

So around twenty in all. Still more than two-to-one odds against the white men. But not overwhelming, the mountain man thought.

The fact that the war party wasn’t any larger made him figure these were all the men High Cloud could find. This was the chief’s last chance for revenge—and to rescue the female warrior he thought of as Red Dawn Woman.

The wash was close now. Preacher could tell it was wide enough the Sioux wouldn’t be able to leap their ponies over it. That would make it harder for the attackers to circle around and come at them from behind. Not impossible, of course, but Preacher would take any edge they could get, no matter how small.

His companions needed time to take cover. He leaned toward Bellamy and said over the pounding hoofbeats of their mounts, "See to the prisoner! Get him into that gully! Gonna be too many bullets and arrows flyin' around to leave him in the wagon!"

Bellamy nodded. The young man's face was grim and intent.

"What are you going to do?" he asked.

"Slow those varmints down!"

Preacher pulled back on Horse's reins, slowing the big stallion. Bellamy and Fitzwarren flashed on ahead.

For the second time during this ill-fated journey, Preacher turned Horse, put the reins in his teeth, drew his Colts from their holsters, and charged directly into the face of the enemy.

Chapter 46

From the corner of his eye, Bellamy saw what Preacher was doing. A large part of him wanted to join the mountain man in what was a magnificent though probably foolish and futile gesture.

Preacher had charged him with protecting Charlotte Courtenay, though, and Bellamy didn't want to let him down. He also wanted to keep Charlotte from harm.

They might not have been friends back in Alpenstone, but she was part of the royal family, after all. Bellamy still had enough of the loyal subject ingrained in him that he didn't want her to be hurt.

Geoffrey Fitzwarren, on the other hand, was also part of the royal family, Bellamy reminded himself—and he didn't give a damn what happened to Fitzwarren other than the fact that right now he was one more gun to fight off the Sioux.

So Bellamy kept going, not reining in until the wash loomed right in front of him. Although its width varied because the sandstone banks were irregular, on average it was around thirty feet from one side to the other and perhaps ten feet deep.

The banks were rough and riven with cracks and humps, but they sloped down gently enough that horses could make it to the bottom. The wagon might even be able to make it.

Bellamy swung down from the saddle and waved Jennings on. He yanked off his hat and slapped his mount on the rump to send it clattering down into the wash.

Fitzwarren dismounted and urged his horse into the wash as well. Knox and Hanley had ridden their mounts down the slope and were already dismounted and on foot, running back to the top of the bank with their rifles.

The wagon team reached the wash. The horses hesitated as the ground dropped out from under their hooves, but Jennings's desperate lashing and yelling kept them moving. A hard, high bounce sent the vehicle into the air as it went over the edge, but the wagon held together as it came slamming down. The wheels stayed on and the axles didn't break.

The impact had to have rattled the teeth of Jennings, Kelleher, and Charlotte Courtenay, though.

The spare horses went down the slope next, boiling into the wash as dust billowed up from their hooves. Earnshaw had conquered his fear enough to stay with them, shouting and waving his hat in the air as he prodded the animals on.

Earnshaw was about to follow the horses into the wash when he cried out and arched his back. An arrow had struck him just above his waist. He twisted in the saddle, reaching for the shaft as he howled in pain, but he had just gotten his fingers on it when another arrow slammed into him, higher this time, between the shoulder blades.

He slid to the side and toppled out of the saddle to crash to the ground. His horse leaped on down into the wash. Earnshaw lay there at the edge, twisted and still.

Bellamy saw that but didn't have time to think about it. He drew both pistols, cocked them, and squeezed off the shots at the Indians rushing in from the right.

Beside him, Geoffrey Fitzwarren did the same, standing there cool and steady. Say what you would about him, the man had nerve, Bellamy thought.

They would all need icy nerves, an abundance of powder and shot, and plenty of good luck if any of them were going to survive the next few minutes.

Preacher waited until he was close enough to be sure of his aim before he began triggering the Colts. Arrows were already flying around him. His keen eyesight and lightning-fast reflexes allowed him to lean slightly to one side or the other several times to avoid being skewered by shafts that came too close for comfort.

He lifted the revolvers and eared the hammers back. The right-hand gun boomed, followed an instant later by the heavy report of the left-hand gun. Back and forth the thunder went, the Colts bucking in Preacher's hands as smoke and flame spewed from the muzzles.

The wind of his passage whipped the powder smoke back around him. It stung his eyes and nose but didn't obscure his vision. He saw several of the warriors topple loose-limbed off their ponies.

One of the mounts flung its head up at just the wrong time and took the bullet meant for its rider. Its front legs folded and the pony went down in a spectacular, flailing sprawl.

The warrior on its back was thrown forward and flew through the air screeching until the sound was cut off when he hit the ground with stunning force.

An instant later, one of the ponies that had been racing right behind stepped on his head, ensuring that the fallen warrior would never get up.

The hammers of Preacher's guns snapped down on empty chambers. He pouched both irons and grabbed the stallion's reins.

"Let's get outta here!" he called. "Come on, Horse!"

In one move, Horse whirled around and leaped into a gallop. Preacher felt the shaft of an arrow bounce off the top of his right shoulder. Another struck Horse's hip, not penetrating but rather goading the stallion on to even greater speed.

Preacher was glad to note that the wagon was no longer in sight, meaning Jennings had gotten it down into the wash. He didn't see the saddle mounts and the rest of the horses, either.

Six men knelt at the edge of the wash, firing rifles toward the Sioux on the other side. Another man lay motionless on the ground not far away, either dead or badly wounded. Preacher couldn't tell who it was, but one more of their number had fallen and appeared to be done for.

Two of the men, having reloaded their rifles, turned in his direction. Preacher recognized Bellamy Buckland and Geoffrey Fitzwarren as they aimed past him at the warriors pursuing him. Smoke spurted from their rifles.

Preacher didn't look back to see if any more of the

Sioux had fallen. Right now it was more important that he reach the wash.

He left the saddle in a running dismount, pulled his hat off, and swatted Horse on the rump with it, prompting the stallion to keep going. The big stallion was more nimble than most horses his size; he had no trouble dancing down the rough slope to the sandy bottom of the wash.

Preacher ran to join Bellamy and Fitzwarren. He could tell now that the dead man was Earnshaw. Several arrows protruded from the body.

Knox, Hanley, Bull, and Jennings moved back and crouched just below the bank's edge as they reloaded. Preacher, Bellamy, and Fitzwarren did likewise a few yards away.

While he was reloading, Preacher glanced toward the wagon, which was stopped at the bottom of the slope with the horses hitched to it shifting around nervously, spooked by the racket and the sharp tang of powder smoke in the air. Jennings had set the brake, though, and it appeared to be holding.

Eugene Kelleher sat up in the wagon bed, holding a pistol in the sausage-like fingers of each pudgy fist. Wounded as he was, he couldn't climb up the bank and join in the defense of the wash, but he was ready to put up a fight if it came down to a last stand.

Which it well might, Preacher knew.

At least, down there where she was, it was more likely Charlotte Courtenay would survive if the war party overwhelmed their position. The fighting would be hand to hand then, and the Sioux would recognize her as a prisoner rather than an enemy to be killed.

Preacher hoped that would be the case if the situation turned dire for the rest of them. He hated the idea of dying when he wasn't completely sure what this whole mess was about, but a fella didn't really get to pick and choose about such things. He would do what he could to survive, and Preacher was a firm believer in the idea that a man's fate was in his own hands, but sometimes that wasn't enough.

That fatalistic thought didn't show on his face or in his voice as he grinned and asked Bellamy and Fitzwarren, "Are you boys all right so far?"

"We're not hurt," replied Bellamy. "How about you?"

"Those fellas are mighty poor shots. They must've fired a hundred arrows at me, and they all missed, although a few of 'em came closer'n I like. That ol' guardian angel was ridin' with me, swattin' 'em away."

"I hope that angel is looking out for all of us," Fitzwarren said coolly. He raised his head high enough to see over the bank, drew a bead with his rifle, and fired. A moment later, Preacher and Bellamy triggered their rounds as well.

Eight warriors remained in the force charging in from that side. Four more angled in from the other direction. All of them were too close now; there was no more time to reload.

"Grab your pistols!" Preacher bellowed. His Colts were empty, so they wouldn't help him, but he drew his knife and tomahawk and braced himself. "Here they come!"

Chapter 47

Some of the warriors leaped from their ponies to cover the last few yards on foot. Others, too caught up in the heat of the attack, stayed mounted and leaped the animals into the wash.

That turned out to be a mistake, as even the sure-footed ponies couldn't keep their balance when their hooves landed on the uneven surface. Screaming, the ponies went down and threw their riders, who tumbled out of control into the wash.

Preacher met the charge of a warrior who screeched wrathfully at him. The man swung a knife that Preacher blocked with his tomahawk. At the same time, Preacher struck with the speed of a big cat, plunging his knife into the Sioux's throat. A quick jerk sent blood spraying out from severed arteries and veins.

A few feet away, Bellamy Buckland fired a pistol at one of the attackers, but the warrior swerved aside at the last instant and the ball ripped past his ear. He tried to bring his tomahawk down in an overhead stroke that would have split Bellamy's head open if the blow landed. Bellamy twisted aside from the swiftly descending weapon, which scraped along his left shoulder and upper arm.

The tomahawk ripped Bellamy's buckskin shirt but didn't do any damage to his flesh. He swung the empty pistol in his hand and crashed it against the Indian's jaw, shattering bone.

The injury was a bad one but not enough to incapacitate the warrior. He tried to open Bellamy's throat with a backhand swipe of the tomahawk.

Bellamy jerked back just in time to avoid it. He struck again with the empty pistol. This time the Indian's knees buckled. Bellamy hit him again and then again, continuing the assault as the warrior slid to the ground.

By the time he got there, his head had been battered into a bloody, misshapen hulk, like a gourd dropped and shattered, and he was no longer breathing.

Preacher met the charge of another warrior, both men blocking and striking and not doing any damage until the point of the knife in the Sioux's hand ripped a furrow in the mountain man's forearm.

A second later, the tomahawk in Preacher's other hand drove down hard against the junction of the Indian's shoulder and neck, cleaving a great wound. The man staggered, slashed feebly at Preacher with the knife, and then fell forward on his face as dark red blood began to pool around his head.

Geoffrey Fitzwarren spun around at the top of the bank and fired both pistols at the warriors who had been unhorsed when their ponies stumbled and fell. One man fell backward with blood welling from a hole in his chest, but the other shot missed. The man at whom it had been aimed caught his balance, yanked a knife from its sheath at his waist, and charged up the slope at Fitzwarren.

A rifle shot cracked and the Indian spun off his feet, then rolled loosely down to the bottom of the wash. Fitzwarren looked over and saw Zadicus Knox lowering his rifle. Smoke curled from its muzzle. Knox grinned and waved, then whirled and swung the empty rifle like a club, driving another warrior off his feet.

Preacher was only vaguely aware of that, because he had his own hands full battling another of the attackers. The Sioux was fast and slippery as an eel, and he managed to rake his knife along Preacher's ribs before the mountain man tripped him up. Preacher struck as the man fell, splitting his forehead with the tomahawk.

Down on the wash's sandy bottom, one of the warriors let out a triumphant yell as he bounded onto the driver's seat of the wagon and raised his knife, intending to bring it down in Eugene Kelleher's back.

Kelleher twisted and rolled and brought up both pistols. The twin boom was deafening. The heavy lead balls slammed into the warrior's torso, and at that range the impact was enough to lift him off his feet and throw him backward.

When he fell, he landed on the team hitched to the vehicle.

The already skittish horses panicked, lunging ahead against their harness. The brake didn't hold. When it gave, the wagon lurched forward, throwing Kelleher on his face. The horses trampled over the body that had fallen between them.

Charlotte Courtenay squirmed across the wagon bed, pressed her back against the sideboards, and pushed with her feet until she slid upward. Her head and shoulders rose above the sideboards, then more of her body until she overbalanced and tumbled out of the wagon. It rolled away from her, leaving her lying there struggling to get up.

Preacher caught sight of that, but he wasn't the only one. Zadicus Knox saw her and must have thought she was trying to escape—which she was. With a snarl on his face, he slid down the bank and started toward her with a knife in his upraised hand, poised to plunge the blade down into her body.

Preacher could have tried to stop Knox with a throw of his knife or tomahawk, but that was chancy and not likely to stop the man in time to keep him from striking at Charlotte.

But Bellamy was closer and also saw what Knox was doing. He took a couple of fast steps and then launched himself in a flying tackle that intercepted Knox and drove him off his feet.

Both men sprawled and rolled on the sandy ground. Knox came up first, saw that it was Bellamy who had stopped him from going after Charlotte, and turned his rage on the young man. He leaped at Bellamy, who barely got a leg up in time to kick Knox in the belly and knock him aside.

Bellamy would have to fight this battle by himself.

Preacher went after the wagon as it jolted along the floor of the wash.

The remaining Sioux were still attacking. Hanley and Jennings were struggling hand to hand with a couple of the warriors.

A few yards away, Bull backhanded one of the Indians and knocked him senseless. Before the man could fall, Bull grabbed him, picked him up, and used him as a battering ram, yelling as he crashed himself and the Sioux into the knot of battling men. White and Indian alike, they went down and scattered like ninepins. Bull tripped and fell with his unconscious burden, crashing down among the men he had just bowled over.

Bellamy scrambled up, knowing that Knox would never forgive him for standing up to him. If anything, Knox would be even more brutal and vicious toward someone he considered a betrayer than he would toward a known enemy. The way he had treated Roscoe all those weeks ago was sufficient proof of that.

Knowing that, Bellamy was ready when Knox bellowed curses and came at him with the knife weaving back and forth. Sunlight glittered on the blade.

Knox thrust the knife, then again, and Bellamy dodged aside both times. After the second thrust, Knox was off-balance enough for Bellamy to step inside and grab his arm. He threw his hip into Knox and heaved as hard as he could.

With a startled yell, Knox came up and around and flipped over Bellamy's hip to slam down on his back.

Bellamy darted back a step to give himself some

room and kicked Knox's wrist. The knife flew out of Knox's hand and landed in the dirt, sliding away.

Bellamy didn't want to give Knox a chance to recover. He tried to stomp Knox in the head, but he wasn't quick enough. Knox got his hands up, grabbed Bellamy's booted foot and stopped it, and then wrenched hard on Bellamy's leg, throwing him to the ground.

Knox rolled onto hands and knees and went after his opponent. Bellamy had landed hard enough to knock most of the breath out of his body. He was struggling to recover when Knox landed on top of him, pinning him to the ground. Knox heaved himself up, dug a knee into Bellamy's midsection, and started slugging at his face.

Bellamy got his arms up and was able to block some of the blows, but enough of them got through to do some damage. Knox's rocklike fists smashed into Bellamy's face and jolted his head back and forth.

In sheer desperation, Bellamy arched his back and bucked up from the ground. He dug his fingers into Knox's thigh and heaved. With a yell, Knox went over on his side.

Bellamy laced his fingers together and swung his clubbed hands, putting as much strength and weight as he could behind the blow as he brought it crashing down above Knox's left ear. That drove the other side of Knox's head against the ground, but it was too sandy here for that to cause much damage. Knox swung an elbow into Bellamy's ribs and knocked him back and away.

Knox rolled onto his side, glared at Bellamy, and, panting for breath, said, "I'm gonna kill you, Duke."

Bellamy didn't waste any of his own breath responding. He just pushed himself to his feet and tried to brace himself before Knox surged up and lunged at him again.

Down the wash, Preacher's long legs carried him swiftly after the wagon. When he was close enough, he leaped, caught hold of the tailgate, and let it drag him along for a moment before he was able to pull himself up far enough to throw a leg over it.

Once he had done that, it was only a matter of seconds before he'd climbed over, scrambled through the wagon bed past Kelleher, and climbed onto the driver's seat.

The reins were still looped around the brake lever. He grabbed them and hauled back, slowing the runaway team. He brought the wagon to a stop and vaulted back into the bed. Kneeling beside Kelleher, he asked, "Are you all right, Eugene?"

"Fine," Kelleher replied. "The girl got out!"

"Yeah, I saw." Preacher looked back along the wash toward the scene of the battle, and what he saw jolted an exclamation out of him. "Good Lord!"

The battle against the Sioux seemed to be over. Bodies, white and red alike, were heaped around. The only struggle still going on was between Bellamy Buckland and Zadicus Knox, who were fighting desperately.

Not far from them, Geoffrey Fitzwarren stood watching the former prisoner as she tried to stand up. Charlotte was still tied hand and foot but finally made it to her feet and began hopping toward the wagon.

She wasn't trying to reach the vehicle, Preacher knew; she had just escaped from it minutes earlier. She was trying to get away from Knox and the others.

Fitzwarren, about twenty feet behind her, unaware of who she actually was, raised a pistol and aimed it at her back.

Chapter 48

Bellamy saw the same thing Preacher did and realized that Fitzwarren was about to gun down Charlotte Courtenay, unaware that she was actually his cousin and not a young Sioux warrior.

That distraction was almost fatal because just then one of Knox's fists hurtled at his face, and if the blow had landed, it would have knocked Bellamy down and probably out. And then Knox would have stomped the life out of him.

As it was, Bellamy jerked his head aside at the last instant. The punch caught him a glancing blow on the side of the head rather than landing with full strength on his jaw. It staggered him anyway, but the near miss caused Knox to leave himself wide-open and off-balance.

Bellamy put everything he had into a straight punch that crashed into the middle of Knox's face.

He felt Knox's nose crunch under the impact. Hot blood spurted over his knuckles. Knox's head rocked back, and with waving arms, he fell.

Bellamy hurdled over him and shouted, "Charlotte, look out!"

At the same moment, from the wagon that had come to a stop about fifty yards away, Preacher called, "Geoff, no!"

Hearing her name called, Charlotte twisted her head to look back toward Bellamy. That caused her to stumble as she landed from one of her hops. She fell just as Fitzwarren ignored Preacher's yell and pressed the trigger on his pistol.

The weapon boomed, but Bellamy saw dirt spurt up from the floor of the wash beyond Charlotte and knew the shot had missed her and plowed into the ground.

Fitzwarren turned toward him, wide-eyed with shock, and echoed in an amazed tone, "Charlotte?"

Bellamy ignored him, went to one knee beside her, and caught hold of her shoulders to turn her over and make sure she wasn't hurt. He paid no attention to Fitzwarren behind him.

But by this time, Preacher had leaped down from the wagon and was running toward them. He saw Fitzwarren drop the empty pistol and pull a knife from his belt. Fitzwarren raised the weapon and stepped toward Bellamy, clearly intent on driving the blade into the young man's back.

"I've come all this way to kill her," Fitzwarren said with a snarl. "You won't stop me now!"

Bellamy heard that shocking threat, and then Charlotte screamed as she looked over his shoulder and saw Fitzwarren closing in with murder in his eyes. Bellamy jerked around and dived at Fitzwarren's legs as the man struck. The would-be killing stroke missed and

Fitzwarren toppled to the ground as Bellamy drove his legs out from under him.

Preacher leaped from the wagon and sprinted toward them. When he reached Charlotte, he bent and scooped her from the ground. She didn't try to fight him as he threw her over his shoulder. She must have realized that she was safer with the mountain man than trying to escape, tied up as securely as she was.

Bellamy hammered punches into Fitzwarren's body and face to subdue him. He had no liking for the man, but even so, he was shocked that Fitzwarren had tried to kill Charlotte in cold blood like that. He didn't know what was going on and he suspected Preacher didn't, either, but they could figure that out later.

Several yards away, Zadicus Knox rolled onto his side, groaned, and began trying to get up. Bull, Hanley, and Jennings were all still alive, too, and were getting their wits about them. Time was running out, and Bellamy knew it. The odds were about to turn against him.

He crashed one more blow into Fitzwarren's face, stunning him, and then scrambled to his feet to run after Preacher, who was carrying Charlotte toward the wagon with a loping stride that covered the ground quickly.

Inside the vehicle, Eugene Kelleher pulled himself to the tailgate and lowered it. He opened his arms and called, "Give her to me, Preacher!"

When he reached the wagon, Preacher practically tossed Charlotte onto Kelleher, who caught her and cushioned her landing. Preacher raced to the front of the wagon and climbed to the driver's seat in a hurry.

Bellamy wasn't far behind him. The young man

grabbed the tailgate and levered himself up and into the bed.

"Let's get out of here!" he called to Preacher as he scrambled forward.

Preacher shouted to the team and slapped their rumps with the reins. "Hang on back there!" he shouted at the horses lunged forward.

Getting the wagon back up one of the banks and out of the wash would be a big job that would probably require hitching extra horses to the vehicle to pull. They didn't have time for that. All they could do was follow the wash in its meandering course across the prairie. They went around the bend, and Fitzwarren, Knox, and the others were lost to sight behind them.

Zadicus Knox was red-faced with fury when Bull took hold of him and lifted him to his feet as if he were nothing more than a child. A few yards away, Geoffrey Fitzwarren was sitting up and shaking his head, trying to recover from the beating Duke Buckland had given him.

Knox got his wits back about him quickly. He looked around, saw that Hanley and Jennings had survived the battle with the Sioux, and dealt with the most immediate threat first.

"Are any of those damn redskins still alive?" he snapped.

"I don't think so, but I'll check, Zadicus," said Hanley.

Jennings helped him, and within moments they were able to report that none of the Sioux warriors had made it through the fight. Once again, no doubt because of the superior firepower their guns gave them, Knox and his men had defeated their enemies.

Some of their enemies, anyway, Knox corrected himself as that thought crossed his mind. Preacher and Duke had gotten away, and the fat man in the wagon. Knox was done with them. They were all dead men as far as he was concerned, even Duke, who would pay the price for defying him.

That left Geoffrey Fitzwarren—and the prisoner Knox had believed was one of the Indians.

Knox found his knife where Buckland had kicked it. He picked it up, then went to offer Fitzwarren a hand. The man took it, and when Fitzwarren was on his feet again, Knox put the knife to his throat and rasped, "What the hell is goin' on here? I was half stunned, but I heard Duke call that Injun by a woman's name, and then you tried to kill him. And her. What is this?"

Fitzwarren had stiffened at the touch of the keen-edged steel to his throat, but he kept his nerves about him and seemed steady enough as he replied, "I assure you, I was as surprised as you are to learn that that savage is actually my cousin Charlotte Courtenay. She's the reason I came out here in the first place."

"You came to find her?"

"I came to kill her," Fitzwarren said. "She's the only thing standing between me and untold wealth and power."

"How in blazes did she come to be pretendin' to be an Injun?"

"I have no earthly idea. It's the last thing I ever would have expected."

"But if she dies, you'll be rich?"

"Indeed," Fitzwarren said.

Knox lowered the knife, then rubbed his chin and frowned in thought.

"If we was to help you get what you're after, you might be inclined to be grateful?" he suggested.

Fitzwarren's face and voice were both as cold and hard as stone as he promised, "If you help me, I'll make it well worth your while, Mr. Knox. You won't regret it, I give you my word on that."

"As long as that redskin—or whoever she really is—dies, you don't care what happens to Preacher and that fat fella?"

"I never did," said Fitzwarren. "They and the other men I hired were a means to an end, that's all."

"And I know it won't matter to you if I kill that no-good Duke Buckland."

"Feel free to do so, my friend."

"Well, then," Knox said as a grin spread across his face, "I reckon you got yourself a deal." He turned to his three remaining men and told them, "Round up our horses, boys. We got some killin' to do."

Chapter 49

Preacher kept the team moving as fast as he could, but the wash's soft, sandy bottom made for slower going than he would have liked. He said over his shoulder, "Eugene, are you all right back there?"

"I'm fine as frog hair, Preacher. All that rollin' around might've made these wounds of mine bleed a little, but they ain't nothin' to worry about."

"How about you, Bellamy?"

"I'm all right," the young man said. "A little winded and shaken up, and I'm sure I'll be sore from those punches Knox landed, but I'm in fighting form, rest assured of that."

"If you've got any pistols, get 'em loaded. We're bound to need 'em. Knox and the rest of that bunch will be comin' after us, unless I miss my guess."

"And Geoffrey?"

The question surprised Preacher a bit because it came from Charlotte Courtenay. Without turning around, he told her, "He was fixin' to kill you."

A tone of wonder crept into the mountain man's

voice as he went on, "Fitzwarren came all this way, went to a heap of time and trouble and expense, risked his life a dozen times to find you, and then he came mighty close to killin' you. Why the devil would he do that?"

"I can think of only one reason," Charlotte replied. "Something terrible must have happened back in our homeland. An illness striking the royal family, perhaps. But something that would result in me becoming the grand duchess and ruling Alpenstone."

Bellamy said, "I'm guessing that he's next in the line of succession."

"I don't know the details because the whole idea always seemed so farfetched, but it's the only thing that makes sense," she said. "As soon as I saw him, I knew who he was, of course, but I assumed he had come on behalf of my parents and wanted to drag me back home whether I wanted to go or not." Her words took on a scornful edge as she added, "Geoffrey always did try to curry favor with his betters any way he could."

"Preacher, I'm going to turn Charlotte loose," Bellamy said. "Surely at this point there's no longer any reason to regard her as a captive."

Preacher grunted as he worked the reins and sent the team around another bend in the wash.

"Reckon the four of us are all caught in the same trap, all right," he agreed. "Miss Courtenay, you promise you ain't gonna try to get away from us again?"

"Of course. If I escaped now, I'd be running right into certain death, wouldn't I?"

"More than likely," Preacher said. "Cut her loose, Bellamy."

The young man did so, carefully wielding his knife to sever the bonds around Charlotte's wrists and ankles. She sat up and massaged her wrists where the rope had chafed them.

"I'm sorry about that," Bellamy told her. "But you have to realize, you had us all fooled. We honestly believed you were a Sioux warrior who wanted to kill us."

"I did, at first," she said. "I didn't know you were from Alpenstone, and I never got a good enough look at Geoffrey to recognize him until later. All I knew was that you were white invaders and High Cloud wanted to drive you from our land. High Cloud and his people spared my life and adopted me, made me one of their own. I fought beside them as a loyal member of the tribe."

Bellamy sighed and shook his head. "You'll have to forgive me. It's just such a . . . a bizarre situation."

"Life can take strange turns," she said as she looked at him. "I mean, you're here, too, and you're from one of the wealthiest and most influential families in Europe."

Kelleher's eyes widened. "Is that true, lad?" he asked.

"I'm afraid so," Bellamy told him with a faint smile. "My family may not be part of the nobility, but they do have quite a lot of money."

"And we're related, you know," Charlotte said. "The two of us."

"We are?" Bellamy asked with genuine surprise.

"Distantly, and partially through marriage."

His smile widened. "You mean I might have been grand duke someday if I'd stayed in Alpenstone?"

"No, I don't see any way that would have happened. Your brother Frederick might have taken the throne if something terrible happened to enough people in the line of succession ahead of him."

"Ah, yes, Frederick." Bellamy couldn't keep a trace of resentment from creeping into his voice. "The first son."

"That's the way things work," Charlotte snapped, "and you've known that your entire life."

"Indeed I have."

The wagon suddenly lurched as Preacher hauled back on the reins and said from the driver's seat, "This is all as fascinatin' as hell, but we got a problem."

The three people in the back of the wagon turned to look past him and saw that fifty yards ahead of them, the wash came to an abrupt end against a sandstone cliff that bulged out, making it impossible to climb. The banks on the sides had closed in while the wagon was fleeing from any pursuit, growing taller and steeper until it would be very difficult for anyone to get to the top of them, too.

Preacher said into the grim silence, "Looks like we got ourselves in a mite of a hole—and there ain't no way out."

"If we go back up the wash, we ought to be able to climb the banks," Bellamy suggested. "We can't take the wagon, but—"

He stopped short and looked at Eugene Kelleher.

"That's right, lad," Kelleher said. "I'm in no shape to go climbin' anything. But if you'll leave me a few pistols, I'll do my best to hold off those varmints who'll be after us. I can sure as blazes slow them down, anyway."

"That ain't gonna work," Preacher said. "For one thing, we ain't gonna abandon you, and for another, we probably don't have time to get outta the wash that way. Chances are, Knox and the others ain't far behind us and might come along while we were tryin' to climb one of those banks. We'd be sittin' ducks for them to pick off without any trouble."

"What do you think we should do?" asked Bellamy.

"Seems to me our only chance is to fort up here. Make them come to us." Preacher nodded toward the end of the wash. "We'll park the wagon up there in front of the bluff, and between it and the overhang, we'll have decent cover. There won't be but one way they can come at us, and that's straight ahead."

Kelleher said, "We have powder and shot here in the wagon, as well as food and water. We can withstand a siege for a good long while, I reckon."

"And maybe we can whittle 'em down a mite while we're doin' that," Preacher said. He lifted the team's reins again. "Come on. Let's get situated and start preparin' for one more fight."

Chapter 50

Preacher manuevered the wagon into position where he wanted it and then unhitched the team. There wasn't room behind the vehicle for the animals in the space between the wagon and the overhanging bluff. He had no choice but to let them go, swatting them on the rumps with his hat and yelling at them to make them trot away along the wash.

They could find the horses and hitch them up again later on—if they survived the inevitable confrontation with Knox, Fitzwarren, and the others.

Preacher's big stallion was somewhere back there, too. He thought about Horse and hoped that if he didn't make it out of this ruckus alive, the stallion would be able to survive on his own. Horse would never allow Knox or any of the other men to ride him, that was for sure. He was a one-man mount.

Thinking about Horse made the mountain man mull over Dog's disappearance. He hadn't seen the big cur since the previous day, during one of those fights with the Sioux war party in the Beartooths. Preacher had expected Dog to show up before now, but there had been no sign of him.

That was worrisome, but Dog had dropped out of sight before and finally reappeared. If he was wounded, he might be staying away on purpose. A wounded dog often sought solitude and would remain alone while its injuries healed.

Of course, it was possible that Dog hadn't survived. He might have crawled off to die after that battle. Over the years, several similar curs had served as Preacher's trail partner, all of them named Dog, all of them devoted and almost supernaturally smart and communicative.

Preacher never questioned that; he supposed some fate sent him those friends and partners. If pressed, he might have speculated that the same spirit lived in all of them, but that was getting too far out there in the tall and uncut for him to be comfortable with, so he just didn't think about it.

While Preacher was tending to the team, Bellamy helped Eugene Kelleher climb out of the wagon. The big man had fresh bloodstains on his clothes where those wounds had opened up, as he'd said. He was pale but determined and insisted he could fight if it came down to that.

"Prop me up against that bluff and put some pistols in my hands," he said. "I'll give those varmints a hot lead welcome if they make it back here."

Having turned the horses loose, Preacher walked around the back of the wagon into their little sanctuary. He said to Bellamy, "Let's make sure every gun we've got is loaded, and we need to have plenty of ammunition within easy reach, too."

Charlotte, who had been watching the preparations, said, "I can shoot, too, you know. I had a fowling piece in my hands almost before I was big enough to walk."

"Is that right?" Preacher said.

Her chin jutted defiantly. "It is, indeed. My great-uncle, the grand duke, taught me to shoot. He said that I have a natural aptitude for it. I'm an excellent shot."

"Well, I wouldn't want to argue with a grand duke," drawled Preacher. He grinned for a second and then grew serious. "But if you go to shootin' at that bunch, you're liable to hit your own cousin."

"Geoffrey?" She made a disgusted sound. "He tried to shoot me just a short time ago, remember?"

"I reckon that's true. After all the weeks I spent with him, it's still a mite hard for me to swallow that he came out here to kill you, not to save you from that fella Treadway. After what happened, though, there ain't no doubt about it."

Charlotte's mouth twisted as if she had just bitten into something sour.

"I wish someone had saved me from Barrett Treadway sooner than they did," she said. "He was an absolutely terrible man. But I was blinded to that fact by what I blithely assumed was love."

"He didn't treat you well?" asked Bellamy.

She shrugged. "He did at first. He was very attentive, very charming. But as time went on, I began seeing more and more of his flaws. He could be a cruel man, both in the cutting remarks he made and in the way he physically treated me."

An angry frown creased Bellamy's forehead. "I'm no great respecter of tradition, but didn't he know that you're a member of the nobility?"

Charlotte let out a humorless laugh. "Of course he knew, but he didn't care. He said that as an American, such things didn't matter to him. I suppose I should have taken that as a warning, but as I said, I was blinded by infatuation."

While the men were loading the weapons, Charlotte went on to explain that Treadway was the one who had come up with the idea of her posing as a male trapper named Charlie Williams.

"The name was entirely false, of course," she said. "There was no Charlie Williams. Although, now that I think about it, there must be dozens of men with that name. Multitudes. But the one traveling with Barrett Treadway was a fictional creation designed to conceal my true identity."

"Why did he want you to do that?" Bellamy asked.

"He claimed it was for my protection, but I suspect he was worried that my family would send someone to retrieve me." Charlotte sighed. "I'll give Barrett credit for one thing: he truly did want to make himself a success on his terms. Traveling to the west and becoming fur trappers was entirely his idea. If he'd simply been seeking wealth, he could have stayed in Alpenstone and married me."

Bellamy looked dubious as he said, "The grand duke

never would have allowed you to marry a commoner, much less an American one."

"You're probably right about that," Charlotte admitted. "At any rate, while Barrett was a truly dreadful man, I suppose he did have a few good qualities. But he never could keep his baser impulses in check, and in the end that brought about his death at the hands of the Sioux." A little shudder ran through her. "I fully expected them to kill me, as well, perhaps after an agonizing bout of torture, but High Cloud interceded on my behalf and declared that I would be taken into the tribe as a slave rather than being killed."

"But you didn't go along with that fate," Bellamy said with a faint smile.

"I should say not! Although I pretended to cooperate at first. I picked up their language very easily. You know I was always very good with languages."

"No, I didn't know that."

"Well, I was. So I did everything they asked of me, but I also let it be known that I wanted to become a warrior. And once I grew accustomed to their ways, I found that I didn't actually mind living among them. There's much to admire about the way they live. But I had no intention of doing so as a slave!"

"This is a mighty interestin' story," said Preacher, "but I hear horses comin'. There ain't anybody else it could be except Knox, Fitzwarren, and the rest of Knox's bunch, whoever's left."

He handed a pair of loaded pistols to Eugene Kelleher, who was sitting on the ground with his back against the bluff, and then gave a pistol to Charlotte.

"See those two rocks yonder, the one sittin' on top of the other?" he asked her as he pointed out the landmark. "A shot from this pistol won't carry no further than that, so if you decide to shoot somebody, make sure and wait until they're on this side o' those rocks."

She nodded in understanding. "I'm more proficient with a rifle, but I can fire a pistol, as well."

Bellamy's rifle was with his horse, as was Preacher's, but they'd had a spare long gun in the wagon. Bellamy had it now, along with the two pistols he normally carried. Preacher's Colts had full wheels, and he had two loaded cylinders to swap out once the ones in the revolvers were empty.

They arranged themselves behind the wagon with Charlotte in the middle, Preacher to her left at the tail-gate, and Bellamy at the front next to the driver's box.

"Nothin' else we can do now but wait," Preacher said.

They didn't have to wait very long. The unhurried hoofbeats stopped on the other side of the nearest bend.

Preacher frowned. He had hoped the enemy would come riding right out into the open so he and his companions would have clear shots at them, but evidently, they were playing things cautiously.

After a moment, a head appeared at the bend, poking out just for a couple of seconds. Preacher thought it belonged to the man called Hanley.

Bellamy started to raise his rifle but Preacher put a hand on the barrel, indicating that he shouldn't try a shot. Sure enough, Hanley vanished almost as soon as they spotted him.

"Would've been a waste of powder and shot," the mountain man said. "Probably wouldn't have made any difference in the long run, but you can't never tell."

More seconds ticked past with maddening slowness.

Then, without stepping into view, Geoffrey Fitzwarren called, "Preacher, I know that you and the others can hear me!"

Preacher couldn't see any point in pretending they weren't here. Hanley would have seen them, just as they had spotted him, and reported the situation to the others.

"Yeah, we're here, Geoff," he responded. "What do you want?"

"You know very well what I want. I came all this way searching for my cousin, and as unlikely and unexpected as her appearance currently is, you have her."

"Yeah, you've been lookin' for her, all right, but you never said nothin' about wantin' to kill her!"

Charlotte looked down into the wagon bed. After everything she had been through, this latest unforeseen development—a betrayal by a member of her own family—must have been hard on her.

Fitzwarren didn't respond immediately, but after a couple of moments, he said, "It's a dreadful shame, and I wish it had never come to this, but it's necessary for the good of our homeland. Alpenstone is in dire straits at the moment. Charlotte, my dear, I regret being the one to have to tell you this, but a terrible fever has swept through the land, and our family was among the hardest hit. Your parents, I'm sad to say, both succumbed."

"I'm sorry, Lady Charlotte," murmured Bellamy.

Her face was pale and drawn, but she shook her head in a curt motion.

"Don't call me that, Mr. Buckland," she said. "I've renounced any titles I might have had, along with my identity as Charlotte Courtenay. I am Red Dawn Woman, a warrior of the Sioux band led by Chief High Cloud."

That still seemed loco to Preacher, but this wasn't the time or place to worry about such things.

When Charlotte didn't respond to his last bit of grim news, Fitzwarren went on, "A number of other members of the royal family have passed on, as well. Alpenstone is currently without a real ruler. Lord Talmadge sits the throne as regent until the next true successor can be located. That successor, of course, is you, my dear. And next in line after you—"

"You don't have to say it!" cried Charlotte, interrupting him. "You're the next in line, you despicable traitor!"

"I am no traitor!" Fitzwarren sounded genuinely offended. "I merely want to serve my homeland. I'm much more suited to ruling Alpenstone than you are, Charlotte, and we both know that."

Her voice choking with emotion, Charlotte said quietly, "That much of what he says is true, at least. I don't want to rule Alpenstone. I never did, and I was relieved to know that the chances of it ever coming about were so slim as to be insignificant. I . . . I can't believe such a tragedy has taken place."

"It's pretty bad, all right," said Bellamy. "What if you told Fitzwarren that you have no intention of ever going back home? He could tell everyone that you're dead, and no one would doubt him or be able to prove otherwise. Then he could assume the throne like he wants."

"I don't think he would believe me." Contempt was obvious in her tone as she added, "Geoffrey was always very thorough, you know."

"I never liked him, what little I had to do with him, which was almost nothing." Bellamy shrugged. "Whatever you think is best, Charlotte. Just don't trust him."

"I could never do that."

Evidently, Fitzwarren was getting tired of waiting. With impatience in his voice, he called, "What's it going to be, Charlotte? Will you come out and surren der to me? If you do, your companions will go free and unharmed, I give you my word on that."

Preacher said, "Now that's a purty lie for damn sure. Knox ain't ever gonna let the rest of us go. He plans on killin' all of us. Shoot, if we're all dead, he'll probably still hold Fitzwarren for ransom like he was plannin' to do all along. That cousin o' yours don't know it, but he's crawled right into a den of rattlesnakes and curled up with 'em. They'll make a nice snack on him, too."

"Geoffrey's ambition always did blind him to reality." Charlotte looked back and forth between Preacher and Bellamy. "So what should we do?"

"Just what we've been figurin' on doin'," said Preacher. "We fight."

"Yes," Bellamy agreed. "We fight." He smiled. "What do we have to lose?"

From behind them, Eugene Kelleher said, "Nobody asked me, but I say we fight, too."

Charlotte's chin came up in the stubborn gesture that had already become familiar to Preacher.

"It appears we have reached a consensus." She lifted her voice and called, "Geoffrey, I have an answer for you!"

His response was swift and eager. "Yes?"

"Go to hell!" shouted Charlotte.

Chapter 51

Silence was the only answer to Charlotte's bold defiance.

Then two rifle barrels poked around the bend and a pair of shots crashed, the reports echoing back from the wash's banks.

At the same time as powder smoke and muzzle flame erupted from the rifle barrels, two figures darted out into the open and dashed toward a cluster of brush and rocks nearer the wagon, where they obviously intended to take cover. Preacher recognized them as Hanley and Jennings.

It didn't surprise him that Zadicus Knox would give two of his men the most dangerous job rather than taking it on himself.

The rifle in Bellamy's hands cracked. Jennings broke stride and stumbled, slowing down as Hanley reached the brush and rocks and threw himself behind them in a headlong dive. Jennings managed to take another couple of steps before he stopped and twisted in agony, revealing the large bloodstain on his side where the ball from Bellamy's rifle had ripped into him.

He pawed helplessly at the wound. His knees buckled

and he dropped limply to the ground. One of his legs spasmed a couple of times. After that, he didn't move again.

Hanley fired his rifle from the spot where he'd taken cover. The ball thudded into the wagon. More shots came from the bend on the other side of the wash. Some of those rounds struck the wagon as well; others whined overhead and hit the bluff, knocking loose dirt and chunks of sandstone that fell around the defenders behind the wagon.

Preacher knew they were pinned down, and by getting Hanley on the other side of the wash, the attackers were able to fire at the wagon from two different angles.

That wasn't going to be enough to roust them out of their shelter. It would take a lucky shot to hit any of them, Preacher knew, and Knox and the others couldn't rely on ricochets doing their work for them. Rifle balls didn't bounce well off the sandstone bluff.

As Bellamy reloaded the rifle, he said over the gunthunder racketing through the wash, "This is a standoff! They can't get to us, but we can't get out of here!"

"Reckon we'll just have to outlast 'em," Preacher said.

Time came to have no meaning as the battle continued and the sun rose higher in the sky until it was directly overhead, beating down into the wash with strength-sapping force. Not much breeze got down here, which meant the heat built up as the day went on.

Without the air moving, the clouds of powder smoke

didn't disperse much, either. The stuff hung in the air, stinging the eyes and blurring vision.

Since Bellamy had the rifle, he did most of the shooting for the defenders, although Preacher triggered a few rounds toward the enemy, too. His Colts had a slightly greater range than the single-shot flintlock pistols.

As far as he could tell, though, none of his efforts did any damage, and the same was true of all the other powder both sides burned.

He had been through sieges like this before and knew that patience was an important asset. Sometimes you just had to wait for the other fella's nerves to break, and then he might do something foolish to try to bring the standoff to an end.

And sometimes fate took a hand and caused things to play out entirely differently.

A shrill, drawn-out cry sounded from the other side of the bend, and as soon as Charlotte Courtenay heard it, she jerked upright and her eyes widened in shock.

"That's High Cloud!" she said. "That's his war cry! I'd know it anywhere."

A flurry of gunshots broke out around the bend, but this time they weren't directed at the defenders behind the wagon.

"High Cloud!" Charlotte cried. She darted out from behind the wagon. "I'm coming!"

Bellamy made a grab for her in an attempt to keep her from leaving cover, but she was too quick for him. His reaching hand missed.

Out in the rocks and brush, Hanley must have seen

Charlotte dashing into the open, and in his eagerness to wing her, he moved enough to expose part of his body as he aimed his rifle.

Before Hanley could squeeze the trigger, Preacher leaped out from behind the wagon and opened up with both Colts. The revolvers crashed and bucked as long tongues of flame licked out from their muzzles.

The range was a little long for handguns, but some of that depended on whose hands they were in. With Preacher wielding them, the Colts were deadly in their accuracy.

The .36 caliber balls smashed into Hanley's body and drove him backward in a jittery dance that caused him to stand up straight. His rifle went off as his finger involuntarily jerked the trigger, but he was already falling and the barrel was pointed upward. The round sailed off harmlessly into the noon-blasted sky. Hanley fell backward over a rock and lay there with his legs still visible, no longer moving.

Charlotte had almost reached the bend, and Bellamy was racing after her, right behind.

"Damn fool kids," Preacher muttered. He glanced over his shoulder at Eugene Kelleher and told him, "I gotta go after 'em."

"Ventilate one o' the varmints for me," urged Kelleher.

Since no more shots were coming toward the wagon, Preacher ran straight toward the bend instead of zigzagging back and forth as he might have done in other circumstances where he was under fire.

Bellamy and Charlotte had vanished around the outcropping of rock that had shielded Fitzwarren, Knox, and Bull. The shooting had stopped. As Preacher rounded the bend at full speed, his keen eyes instantly took in the scene.

Zadicus Knox and High Cloud were locked in a desperate hand-to-hand struggle, each man holding an upraised knife. Each gripped the wrist of the other's knife hand and prevented the blade from falling.

Whoever weakened first and allowed his muscles to buckle would die.

And High Cloud was wounded, with a large, dark stain on the left side of his buckskin shirt. He must have suffered the injury in the earlier battle and had lost quite a bit of blood. That put him at a definite disadvantage in his battle with Knox.

A few yards away, Geoffrey Fitzwarren had drawn the saber he carried and was slashing at Bellamy Buckland with it. Bellamy blocked each stroke of the blade with the barrel of the empty rifle in his hands, but again, one slip, one error, could be fatal if it allowed Fitzwarren's saber to get through.

Charlotte Courtenay stood to one side watching both battles, nervously moving the pistol she held back and forth between the struggles and waiting for an opportunity to pull the trigger. She wasn't likely to get that opportunity, since High Cloud and Bellamy were both in the line of fire and she couldn't risk a shot.

Preacher barely had time to think about Bull and wonder where he was when a huge shape loomed up beside him and crashed into him. Bull's great weight knocked the mountain man off his feet, and when he landed on top, it drove all the air out of Preacher's lungs.

Gasping for breath, Preacher tried to squirm out from under Bull. A huge fist hammered down at him. He jerked his head to the side and avoided the full force of the blow, but it still rocked him and sent his brain whirling.

Momentarily stunned, Preacher couldn't do anything to stop Bull from locking those big, hamlike hands around his throat.

Bull's thick, incredibly strong fingers clamped down and dug into Preacher's neck. Bull was big and strong enough that with the right leverage, he could almost twist a man's head off his shoulders. The back of Preacher's head was pressed against the ground, enabling him to withstand Bull's efforts to break his neck, but he could only tolerate the pressure for a few moments and needed to break loose as quickly as possible.

While Preacher battled for his life against Bull, Bellamy continued blocking the slashes and thrusts from Fitzwarren's saber. His arms were getting tired from having to jerk the heavy rifle back and forth to parry those attacks. His muscles were like lead, and he could tell that his reactions were slowing.

Fitzwarren, on the other hand, seemed as spry and fresh as ever. Of course he did, Bellamy thought bitterly. Fitzwarren was a nobleman, and everyone knew they were better than commoners. Better than rich commoners, and certainly far superior to poor commoners who went off to make new lives for themselves in America.

Fitzwarren lunged without warning, driving the point of his blade straight at Bellamy's throat. At the last instant, Bellamy got the rifle barrel up and flicked the saber aside. The blade's keen edge sliced across the top of his right shoulder and hurt like blazes, but that was better than the saber transfixing his throat.

The missed thrust left Fitzwarren off-balance for a split second and closer to Bellamy than he had been until now. Bellamy shifted the rifle and slammed the butt into Fitzwarren's side. Fitzwarren yelled in pain and tried to whip the saber around in a backhand slash, but Bellamy brought the rifle up and clipped him on the jaw with the stock.

Fitzwarren staggered and fell. Bellamy summoned up the energy to spring after him. He brought his left boot down on the saber to pin it on the ground. Fitzwarren heaved up on it anyway, trying to free it.

The blade snapped.

Fitzwarren screamed in fury and swung the part of the saber he still held. It was razor-sharp and still dangerous, and Bellamy had to jump back to avoid having his legs cut badly. He stumbled, reeling as he caught his balance, and the rifle slipped out of his fingers. Fitzwarren leaped up and came after him, jabbing the jagged end of the broken saber at Bellamy's midsection.

In a desperate move, Bellamy grabbed Fitzwarren's

wrist with both hands and twisted. The two men crashed together and went to the ground again.

Fitzwarren gasped in pain and shock. His grip slid loosely from the saber's hilt. Bellamy pushed himself up enough to see that the broken blade was embedded in Fitzwarren's chest all the way up to the guard. Fitzwarren's eyes were wide with disbelief as he stared down at the weapon's handle.

Then those eyes began to glaze over as death crept in and claimed the heir to the grand duke's throne.

At that same moment, High Cloud's strength finally gave way. His left arm buckled, and the knife in Zadicus Knox's hand flashed down.

High Cloud was able to divert the strike just enough, however, that the blade penetrated his upper chest just below the shoulder instead of his heart, where Knox had aimed it. High Cloud grunted in pain as his knees buckled. He fell, taking the knife with him—which was the best thing he could have done.

Charlotte took a couple of quick steps, circling to the side. She had a clear shot at Knox now. When he looked up at her, he knew that and recognized death staring him in the face. He roared a curse and lunged at her, reached out in hopes of knocking the gun aside.

Before he could do that, Charlotte pulled the trigger. The pistol boomed, and Knox's head jerked back as the ball struck him in the forehead, a couple of inches above his prominent nose. His legs carried him ahead a couple of steps before his nerves and muscles realized most of his brain had been blown out a gaping hole in the back of his head. He was dead when he pitched forward and his face slammed into the ground.

Preacher didn't see any of that. A red haze clouded his vision as he fought to hang on to consciousness. Bull had caught him without much breath in his body when those choking hands closed. He knew he needed to do something, and quickly, to break the big man's hold.

But with that red haze in his eyes and the roaring of his own blood in his ears, he couldn't make his muscles work.

Then Preacher heard another sound besides the roaring—a familiar, deep-throated growl. An instant later, something slammed into Bull, and the terrible hands let go of Preacher's neck and the crushing weight left his body.

With angry snarls and frantic yelling filling his ears, Preacher rolled onto his side and dragged breath back into his air-starved body. As he propped himself on an elbow, he saw a big, shaggy gray shape ripping and tearing at Bull's arms. Bull tried to fend off his attacker, but Dog was relentless.

One of the wildly flailing arms caught the big cur as Dog darted in again. The inadvertent blow landed with enough force to send Dog rolling across the sandy ground.

Preacher had climbed onto hands and knees. Like an uncoiling spring, he leaped and landed on Bull's back. His right arm went around the big man's thick neck. Preacher caught hold of that wrist with his left hand and tightened his grip.

"Let's see how you like it," he said through gritted teeth as he pressed his forearm across Bull's throat like a bar of iron.

The problem was that it was like trying to choke a tree trunk. Slabs of muscle protected Bull's neck. But Preacher was incredibly strong, too, and since he was clinging to Bull's back, Bull couldn't reach him easily.

Bull heaved to his feet. Preacher's feet left the ground and his legs swung back and forth slightly as Bull staggered back and forth. Bull pawed at Preacher's arm but couldn't loosen his hold. The mountain man was locked into a death grip now, and one way or another, only death would loosen it.

The end seemed to take a long time coming, but in reality, it was probably only two or three minutes. Then Bull stopped stumbling back and forth. His hands fell weakly away from Preacher's arms, which he had been unable to pry loose. He swayed for a few more seconds and then fell forward, toppling like a tree.

Preacher managed to maintain his grip. He wasn't going to let go until he was sure Bull was dead, or at least no longer a threat.

The red haze had left Preacher's eyes, but it was still present in his brain when Bellamy Buckland's voice finally broke through it.

"Preacher, you can let go of him. He's dead. It's over."

Preacher blinked a couple of times and drew in a deep breath. He raised his head and looked around. Bellamy stood there a few feet away, holding what Preacher hoped was a reloaded rifle.

Beyond Bellamy, Geoffrey Fitzwarren lay on his back. The handle of the broken saber buried in Fitzwarren's chest told Preacher that the nobleman from Alpenstone would never get up again.

The sound of voices made Preacher turn his head and look the other way. Zadicus Knox was dead on his back, too, with a dark pool of blood forming around his head. The thirsty sand would suck it up after a while.

Not too far from Knox, the Sioux war chief High Cloud sat on the ground while Charlotte Courtenay—the grand duchess of Alpenstone, if you believed what Fitzwarren had said—knelt beside him, dressed in the buckskins of a Sioux warrior, pressing a rag of some sort against a bloody wound in High Cloud's shoulder as they spoke together in low, intimate tones.

"I gave her a piece of my shirt to use as a dressing," Bellamy explained. "The chief doesn't appear to be fatally injured, but he will need some medical attention."

"Looks like he's got himself a nurse already."

Preacher climbed to his feet and looked for Dog. He spotted the big cur standing a few yards away. Dog limped toward him, favoring one leg and with dried blood in several spots on his thick, shaggy fur.

"Looks like you been through the wars, old son," Preacher said as he knelt beside Dog and rubbed both his ears. Dog's tongue lolled from his mouth in a happy grin as he was reunited with his trail partner.

Preacher was grinning pretty big, too. "You've been off recuperatin' after that last battle, haven't you?" he went on. "Well, you showed up just in time, same as you usually do. Ol' Bull might've done for me if you hadn't." Preacher glanced up at Bellamy. "They're all dead?"

The young man nodded. "Yes. As I said a moment ago, it's all over."

Preacher looked at High Cloud and said with a trace of skepticism in his voice, "I hope so."

Chapter 52

As it turned out, High Cloud had no interest in continuing what would have been a one-man campaign against the whites.

Or a two-person campaign, rather, since Charlotte Courtenay left no doubt where her sympathies lay.

High Cloud still looked at Preacher, Bellamy, and Kelleher with hatred in his eyes. He would never forget the warriors they had slain in battle, or forgive them for those deaths.

But since he and Charlotte were the only survivors from the various war parties he had led against those he considered invaders, there was nothing he could do except grudgingly accept their mercy.

While Charlotte patched him up as best she could, she told the others, “He’s been following us on foot ever since the last battle yesterday. He was wounded, but he was determined to catch up. When he finally did, it was Knox and the others he came to first, so they’re the ones he attacked.”

"Would've been just as happy to see us dead, eh?" Preacher said.

Charlotte didn't answer that. Instead, she said, "He did us a favor by breaking up that siege and giving us a chance to take the fight to Knox and his men. And Geoffrey."

She glanced at Bellamy and went on, "I should thank you for killing him, I suppose."

"I was fighting for my own life," he said coolly. "And, to be honest, it was largely an accident that he wound up dying the way he did."

"Well, it's over now," she said as she turned back to High Cloud. "Alpenstone will have to find a new grand duke, or continue with Lord Talmadge ruling as regent until one of the younger members of the royal family grows up."

"You won't go back and take the throne for yourself?" asked Bellamy.

"What do you think?" she replied in a scathing tone. "I wanted to get away from there badly enough that I left with a man like Barrett Treadway. Do you actually believe I'd go back when I can remain here with High Cloud? I'm happy here, and perhaps someday he and I will be married and have a family of our own. I'll consider that a more noble family than the one I came from."

"I've no reason to love them," said Bellamy with a frown, "but I believe you're being too hard on them." He shrugged. "But the decision is yours to make, of course. I certainly have no interest in dragging you back there."

Preacher and Bellamy patched up each other's minor wounds. Then the mountain man rounded up the horses and gave two of them to Charlotte and High Cloud, who insisted that he was in good enough shape to travel. Preacher wasn't sure about that, but as with Charlotte, it was the war chief's decision to make.

Late that afternoon, Preacher sat on horseback next to the wagon while Bellamy climbed to the driver's seat to take the reins. Eugene Kelleher was situated comfortably in the wagon bed again, and this time he had company sitting beside him in the big, shaggy form of Dog, who would ride for a while as his injuries continued to heal.

They all watched as two figures rode into the west without looking back and dwindled in the distance.

Smiling slightly, Bellamy said, "I never would have dreamed that I'd find the things I've found out here."

"There are a million things on the frontier," said Preacher, "and most of 'em will surprise you."

From the back of the wagon, Kelleher asked, "Bellamy, lad, are you going to return to that place you came from?"

"Alpenstone?" Bellamy shook his head. "No, I agree with Charlotte. That's no longer my home." He looked over at Preacher. "There's a lot more to see out here, isn't there?"

"Son, you ain't even scratched the surface yet," the mountain man answered with a grin.

"Then I believe I'll stay for a while and grow up some more. And I can't think of a better way to do that," Bellamy Buckland said, "than by being a Rocky Mountaineer."

TURN THE PAGE
FOR AN EXCITING PREVIEW!

JOHNSTONE COUNTRY.
WHERE VENGEANCE IS GOLDEN.

Shot in the head and left for dead, Smoke Jensen wakes up to find a bounty on his head, a target on his back, and a trigger-happy look-alike pretending to be him . . .

SMOKE JENSEN: WANTED DEAD OR DEADER

Reece Quaid doesn't want to be known as "The Man Who Killed Smoke Jensen." But when the legendary mountain man shows up in the middle of a stagecoach robbery, Quaid has no choice but to shoot him. He didn't even know his victim was the famous Smoke Jensen—until he goes through his pockets and finds his papers. That's when Quaid comes up with a plan. Since he resembles Smoke, he'll simply assume his identity. Rob some banks. Hold up more stagecoaches. And shoot anyone who tries to stop him. Soon the whole world will be asking . . .

Has Smoke Jensen gone bad?

Chapter 1

Smoke Jensen wasn't quite ready to draw his gun, but he was definitely of a mind to punch someone.

That someone happened to be an ugly hombre—wildly askew red hair, a craggy face, and broken, jagged yellow teeth—standing at the bar not far from Smoke who had just said something very ungentlemanly-like to a lady.

The lady's face glowed a bright, embarrassed red. Her eyes darted to the men who sat with her around the rough-hewn table at the stage station. They looked uncomfortable, too. Most of them dropped their gazes to the simple but filling fare spread out on the table. A couple muttered unintelligible comments. If they'd been standing, they would have been scuffing their feet on the hard-packed dirt floor.

But it was evident they weren't going to stand up to the loud, obnoxious man who had just uttered the vulgarities.

Smoke wasn't surprised. They all looked like townies. Men who were well insulated from the dangers of frontier life and unaccustomed to conflicts. He couldn't blame them for that, but still . . . no matter a man's station in life, he ought to stand up for a lady. Always.

So Smoke intervened.

He placed his coffee cup on the scarred bar top, turned to face the ugly patron, and said to the varmint, "Seems to me the lady isn't interested in your advances. If I were you, I'd stop."

The man continued to lean with his back to the bar, his elbows propped up on either side. He chuckled, but that was the only recognition he gave Smoke's words. He kept his eyes on the lady.

Smoke found that rude, too.

Equally as offensive was the man's stench. Not to mention the dirt that clung to the gray pants, tattered brown shirt, and gray vest he wore. There were a few stains that looked to be blood.

Someone else's, more than likely, Smoke assumed.

The hombre opened his mouth to say something—no doubt something crude directed at the lady—but Smoke wasn't about to let that happen.

He decided to shift tactics.

"Friend, I'd be happy to buy you a drink. One for the road. Then you just ride on. Safe travels."

Smoke's eyes darted to the short, balding man behind the bar. Sweat beaded his forehead. It was clear he didn't want trouble in his humble establishment. It was probably a constant fear. They were in the middle of nowhere. The wild, tall uncut of Montana. The man probably saw his share of hard cases ride through.

"The d-drink is on the house," the proprietor said hoarsely.

"See? Can't beat that. I'd take the deal, friend," Smoke encouraged.

Finally, the hombre took his elbows off the bar and turned to face Smoke. He must have recognized something in Smoke's eyes because the fire temporarily dimmed in his. He recovered quickly. Or tried to appear that way, at least.

"You new to this country?" he growled.

Smoke smiled. "Not hardly."

He thought about letting the man know exactly who he was. The name Smoke Jensen carried weight around those parts, even as far from the Sugarloaf as Montana was. But he decided against it. That may only provoke the man more. Being the man who killed Smoke Jensen would make someone awfully famous. Smoke didn't want to pull iron if he could avoid it. The man before him was rude and obnoxious, no doubt about that. That didn't mean he deserved to die, though.

He just needed to learn a good lesson.

The hombre studied Smoke and sneered as if he were a bug he wanted to squash. "Well, since you seem to think we're friends, offering to buy me a drink and all, let me give you some *friendly* advice. Don't go poking your nose where it don't belong. Not around here." He tapped the chipped handle of the iron pouched on his hip. "Could get a man hurt. Maybe even worse." He chuckled.

Smoke sighed.

"What?" the man said.

"I wish you wouldn't have done that."

Smoke's Colt was out, aimed, and cocked almost quicker than the naked eye could comprehend. Everyone in the stage station froze.

A long, heavy moment passed.

Finally, the man gulped, nodded, and slowly backed away. "You best hope we don't meet up along the trail, *friend*."

Smoke smiled. "I'll be ready if we do. Can't say it bothers me much one way or the other."

"If I were you, I'd just leave this well enough alone!" the proprietor said to the redhead.

The ugly man glanced at him but didn't respond. Smoke figured he realized it was best to quit while behind.

And with that Colt pointed squarely at his forehead, the man was clearly behind.

He backed out of the stage station without another word. A minute later, the swift rataplan of hoofbeats resounded loudly through the open door, hurrying across the prairie.

"Mighty glad you were here, mister," the owner said, using a dirty cloth to mop the line of sweat from his wrinkled brow. "That could have turned into trouble mighty easy."

Smoke hoped the barkeep wasn't going to use that same cloth to clean the glasses and mugs, but he didn't voice that concern. Instead, he pouched his iron and turned his focus back to the coffee. It was a bit cooler now but still drinkable.

"My goodness! Thank you, sir," the woman said, rushing up to him.

She had long, silky brown hair, a smooth, unblemished face, and a shapely form. She was probably twenty-five or thereabouts. The blue-and-white gingham dress she wore hugged her curves in a way that could easily capture a man's imagination.

"Don't mention it. I'm just glad everything is fine now." Smoke smiled at her, raised his coffee in a slight toast, and then took a sip.

"You could have been killed!" she said.

Her British accent was heavy. Smoke guessed she hadn't been away from her homeland for very long.

"Did we watch the same ruckus?" one of the men at the table said. He was an old fellow in a dusty brown suit and matching derby hat. White muttonchops framed his face. "That was over before it even got started."

"I ain't never seen anybody draw so fast!" another man at the table said. He was a tall, lanky fellow with a bobbing Adam's apple. His gray suit hung loosely from his frame.

"I have," the old-timer said. "Saw Frank and Jesse James back in Missouri. You talk about fast! Heck, Jesse could pull and plug a man quicker'n anything you've ever seen. I saw him do it, too. Saw it with my own eyes!"

"You ain't never seen Jesse James," the lanky man said, shaking his head. "Sometimes I don't know if you really believe the yarns you tell or if you're just trying to be somebody."

The old man bristled. He mumbled something and

then said loud enough for all to hear, "I seen Jesse James. Sure as shootin'. And I'm telling you, I think this feller is as fast or faster than him!" He got to his feet and walked over to Smoke. "What did you say your name was?"

"Don't think I did," Smoke said with an affable smile. "Just passing through." He took one more long swallow of his coffee, put a coin on the bar, and then tipped his hat to the lady. "Ma'am."

Smoke smiled as he strolled toward the door. He didn't know if the old man had actually ever seen the James boys. He sure had, though. Jesse, at least.

His mind raced back to when he'd been a boy. His pa away at war. His brother Luke gone, too. Young Smoke—Kirby as he'd been known back then—had tried hard to keep that Missouri farm going. But he'd only been one man. Not even a man, really. Just a boy forced to grow up too quickly. And that was a hard-scrabble life, anyway, trying to scratch out crops in those rocky Ozarks.

Then one day Jesse had ridden in with the outfit he'd joined. Smoke had heard the stories. Those raiders were responsible for their fair share of looting and killing. Jesse had been nice to him, though. Even gave him the first pistol Smoke had ever owned.

That was a lifetime ago. Or it felt that way. Smoke wasn't an old man, by any means. But he'd lived a lot in the ensuing years. More than most men do in a whole lifetime.

The group inside the station was still talking about him when Smoke closed the door. He went low, moving quickly, zigzagging to a nearby lean-to where he'd left his horse. He waited. Listened. Scanned the countryside. More than anything, he became one with it, connecting with its patterns. Breathing with it.

Being careful was a habit with him. It had kept him alive this long.

Once satisfied the ugly stranger had truly ridden away, Smoke swung up into the saddle and rode on down the trail. It was going to take him a while to get back to the Sugarloaf. The train he'd sent Pearlie, Cal, and the other hands back on after selling the herd would have been much quicker. But Smoke didn't mind the trip.

He'd chosen it.

He didn't mind the solitude, either.

He had more than enough memories to keep him company.

Chapter 2

There were a lot of things about the old days that Smoke didn't miss.

He'd ridden the vengeance trail. His first wife's murder—and his father's—had demanded he do so.

As he rode along through the beautiful Montana countryside, with the majestic, towering mountains around him, rising into the deep blue sky, his mind continued to drift . . .

Nicole had been beautiful. The first woman he'd ever loved. It had taken a while, there in that little cabin he and Preacher had built in Southwest Colorado. Neither he nor Nicole had jumped at each other the first chance they'd gotten. Smoke chuckled thinking about it. They'd both been shy about such things. Downright nervous, even.

That was back in the days after Preacher had taken him in, teaching him the ways of the mountain man. Then, one day, Preacher just up and rode away, getting one of those wild hairs he was prone to get. That's what he'd said, at least. Smoke knew the truth—he'd wanted to give Smoke and Nicole some privacy. He'd figured that once the two were alone, love would blossom.

That plan of his had worked, too.

Smoke and Nicole couldn't deny the feelings that tend to spring up between a young man and a young woman.

He chuckled as he remembered their first time. They'd both been so clumsy and awkward.

A pang of guilt stabbed at his insides. What would Sally think if she knew he was reminiscing about all this?

The guilt left as quickly as it had come. Sally wasn't particular about such things. Granted, she wouldn't like it much if Smoke was thinking about some living woman in such terms. But she understood that in a way, Smoke and Nicole would always be connected.

She'd borne him a child, after all.

The child that was ripped from him along with Nicole when vicious bounty hunters perpetrated an act of unspeakable evil.

Smoke had answered that horrible challenge. Or rather, his guns had. Every last one of those men had fallen at the barrel of his smoking irons.

They were hardly the last to do so.

Those guns had also roared with flame and death when he'd donned the alias of Buck West, pretending to be an outlaw so he could root out his father's killers.

Emmett Jensen hadn't been a perfect father by any means. He would have admitted as much. He'd left his family for the war. True, it was a cause he believed in.

At first, at least. Smoke supposed like so many he'd grown disillusioned by the war's end.

Years of bloodshed will do that to a man.

Yet Emmett Jensen had still been a man of principle. Nothing would have stripped that from him. So, when men who were supposed to stand on the same principles he did had made off with a shipment of Confederate gold and apparently murdered his other son Luke in the process of committing their villainous act, Emmett had to go after them. Even after Lee's surrender.

Appomattox be damned.

Integrity meant something to the Jensens.

Yet Emmett hadn't been able to finish the job. Smoke, however, had.

As he rode along, he realized he didn't miss the violence of those days. There wasn't a chance to. His days were pretty violent still. While life had periods of relative peace with Sally there on the Sugarloaf, he still found himself involved in more than his fair share of scrapes.

Yet he wasn't a man who relished spilling blood. He took no delight in killing. He just couldn't sit back and watch evil men victimize decent folk. He feared there would come a day when men grew soft and complacent, unable to do what needed to be done in the face of evil, even making excuses for all the wrong being perpetrated on the world.

But Smoke would never abide that way. He couldn't. So, more often than not, it was that sense of justice that fueled his many adventures. In the old days, though, it had been vengeance.

And vengeance is always a heavy load to bear.

No, Smoke didn't miss that at all.

But he did miss how close to nature he used to be. There was something calling to him as of late. Something about the way he'd lived off the land back in those early years, carrying on the traditions Preacher had taught him, living as the mountain men had lived.

"That's what it is," he said aloud.

He turned his head slowly, admiring the wild country.

He'd been feeling nostalgic for that life of solitude, for being out where so few people were. It seemed as if the town of Big Rock was growing by leaps and bounds. Soon, the country would be so full there wouldn't be any wide-open spaces left.

He wouldn't trade his life with Sally for anything. He'd stay on the Sugarloaf until the day he died. Yet even the happiest, most content of men could yearn for those old days every now and again.

That's all this little detour was. Sending half the money from the sale of the herd back with Pearlie, Cal, and the other hands, the rest was tucked safely in a belt that was strapped around his stomach inside his shirt. Now, he had nothing to worry about and plenty of time to enjoy the scenery, take a trip or two down memory lane, and daydream about the future.

Yet something in his gut told him trouble was just over the horizon. He wasn't afraid. But he wanted to be prepared.

Could just be my imagination, he thought. Maybe reflecting on his time as Buck West and that vengeance trail he'd ridden just had him stirred up.

Or maybe it was something more.

His gut told him it was the latter rather than the former.

And Smoke Jensen was a man who'd learned long ago to trust his gut.